GRAND THEFT ASTRO

SCOTT MEYER

ROCKET HAT  INDUSTRIES

The characters and events portrayed in this book are fictitious. Any similarity to real persons, living or dead, is coincidental and not intended by the author. Product or service names mentioned in this book may be trademarks, registered trademarks, or service marks of their respective owners.

GRAND THEFT ASTRO

Published by Rocket Hat Industries
Text copyright © 2021-2022 by Scott Meyer
Cover art © 2022 by Missy Meyer
All rights reserved.

ISBN: 978-1-950056-04-0

GRAND THEFT ASTRO

1

"You were supposed to come alone," the woman said.

Two men stood just outside the open door on either side of a large mag-lev travel case hovering three inches above the floor. The older of the two, a drab man with pewter-gray hair and a tweed suit, said, "I have."

The man with him looked irritated at this, as did the beautiful woman, who wore a form-fitting dress and stood alone in the center of the room. Her left eyebrow appeared natural, if a bit overly tweezed. Her right eyebrow, while symmetrical with the left, appeared to be molded from polished gold.

"Then why do I see two people?" She pointed at the younger man, her metallic green fingernail jutting forward like a dagger.

The older man laughed. "Oh, I see your confusion. He's not here as backup. He's more of an exciting upsell opportunity." He pulled out a hand-stunner and aimed it at the younger man.

"Oh, God!" the younger man whined. "Oh no! Oh, God! Cornwell, you're screwing me?"

"Yes, Dr. Higson. Let this be a lesson to you. When someone offers to bring you in on a plan that involves lying, cheating, and stealing, that person might not be trustworthy."

Cornwell turned to the woman. "This," he said, pointing to Higson, "made *that*," pointing to the travel case. "I figure both the item *and* its inventor are worth twice the price of the item alone. Or, you say no, I kill him, the item becomes irreplaceable, and the price still doubles."

The woman said, "Enter."

Cornwell glanced at the case and waved his gun at Higson in a *go ahead* gesture. "You're younger than I am, and that thing's heavy."

Higson gritted his teeth and pushed the case forward into the room.

As the two men walked in, the woman gazed into the middle distance as a tiny probe lowered from her golden eyebrow and beamed light directly through her pupil. She tapped a finger forward in empty space, as if pressing an invisible button. A strange, harmonized buzz filled the air, coming from the dozens of automated turrets that were set around the room in a perfect circle, broken only where a gap was left for the door. Half of the turrets followed the men's every step, trained with laser precision on their heads. The rest remained pointed outward. Some scanned through the room's windows, covering the city skyline and the swirling cloud of aerial traffic that glittered in the dark. Others pointed at the remaining two walls of built-in shelves and paneling, as if an attacker could come crashing through the mass of lumber, books, and tchotchkes at any second.

Cornwell glanced around the room. "You think you have enough protection, Agent Y-43?"

The woman, Y-43, stood still, arms crossed, her finger pulled back but not fully retracted. "Each of these turrets can detect an insect from a half mile, shoot with enough power and accuracy to down a jump craft or intercept a sniper's round, and all thirty of them are in constant communication with each other and the ten more on the floors above and below us. Nobody can arrest, ambush, or even annoy us without being obliterated. And if either of you makes even a hint of a false move, they'll reduce you to a sticky cloud before you've even heard the sound of them firing."

The old man said, "That's a yes, I suppose."

Y-43 glanced at the case. "So that's the item."

"Yes."

"What is it?"

"If your betters wanted you to know, they'd have told you themselves."

She stared at him silently, flexing her pointing finger.

"But I don't particularly care what your betters want, do I?" Cornwell said. "It's an experimental mind-control system."

Y-43 laughed. "Mind control! Someone's still wasting time on that? I'm surprised you fools are bothering with it. Your citizens wouldn't be happy to hear their government's trying to rob them of their free will. Regimes have toppled over that. Corporations dissolved."

"Only because they failed. That's the great promise of the technology. If we succeed, we can make the people *think* they're happy about it. And anyway, if you have my payment, we won't be the fools bothering with it anymore. *You* will. So, do you have it or not?"

"Yes. I have my orders, even if I think it's a waste of time and money." Y-43 held up a half-inch glass cube with one metal side. "Two giga-sollars, on an untraceable memory drive."

Cornwell said, "Four, now."

Higson had had enough. "Cornwell, you can't do this! You can't just give me to them. I should get a say in who I work for!"

"I'm not giving you to them; I'm *selling* you to them. And you're the one who designed a mind-control device. You're the last person who should lecture anybody about getting a say in what you do."

"You're making a big mistake, old man!" Higson shouted, to which Cornwell replied, "Higson, shut up."

"But I'm so close to getting it working!"

Cornwell shouted, "Shut up," again, but the damage was done.

Y-43 smiled. "Ah, so it doesn't work. That's not a surprise. Mind control never works. But hearing it straight from the horse's mouth does change things. Non-functional, it's worthless, as are the two of you."

"It doesn't work *yet*! Yet!" Higson blurted, "I'm close! Right on the verge of a breakthrough! I just need a lab and more funding . . ."

Y-43 stared impassively at Higson, then turned to Cornwell. "So, I'm guessing you and your commanders have given the project up as impossible, but instead of just writing off the loss, you posed as a profiteering rogue agent to con us into buying it. Maybe recoup some losses."

"Correct, except we aren't conning you, only your superiors," Cornwell replied. "You're not even supposed to know what's in the box. And if you'll agree to forget what's in the box, and everything Dr. Higson here said, you and I can still come out ahead. We dispose of this idiot, split the two giga-sollars, and then you deliver the device as you were ordered to and get whatever pat on the head they give you for being a good lapdog."

"You're suggesting that I lie to and cheat my superiors."

It was Cornwell's turn to smile. "I'm suggesting that you follow your original orders and get paid handsomely on the side for it."

After a moment of silent contemplation, Y-43 purposefully jabbed her index finger forward. One turret fired a single shot. Cornwell fell to the floor, dead.

Higson jumped and let out a yelp. "Why did you do that?"

"Because he was a liar and a cheat, and I couldn't trust him," Y-43 said. "You're not a very fast learner, are you?"

Higson looked at Cornwell's corpse, then up at the turrets, before finally saying, "Thank you! Thank you for not killing me!"

Y-43 said, "Much like your device isn't working yet, I haven't killed you yet. Unlike your device, I might still do my job. You've put a lot of effort into this thing?"

"All of my effort. Night and day. It's my obsession."

"And Cornwell's people have supported your work?"

"They recruited me out of university. The contents of this case are the result of tera-sollars of investment and a decade of my sweat."

Y-43 sauntered toward the case. "And it doesn't work. I think that proves my point. Still—"

As she opened the lid, something very small and very fast flew out from the case and hit Y-43 in the neck. She staggered backward to regain her balance, but her legs failed to move in a predictable manner. She tried to speak but could only manage to bellow out inarticulate vowel sounds. She flopped to the floor, her arms swinging out of control, and writhed there, drool oozing out of her open mouth.

A woman climbed out of the case, unfolding herself with great care. She stood up and stretched her back. She looked to be somewhere in her late thirties to early forties. Her small frame was partially concealed under a bulky black sweater and slim black cigarette pants.

She wore a long-outdated pair of gARggles, virtual-display glasses with heavy, black frames. She reached down and pulled the golden eyebrow from Y-43's face, taking more than a few eyebrow hairs with it, and tossed it aside. "Sorry about the neural scrambler," she said. "I thought I might need a distraction. Didn't know you were going to kill the other guy."

Y-43 let out a wet, unintelligible squawk. She tried to grab the woman in black and failed miserably. Only one of her hands got close; a single metallic green fingernail scratched a small patch of exposed skin at the woman's ankle.

The woman bent her leg to look at the scratch, scowling. "Really?"

Y-43 made an undignified guttural noise that managed to sound a bit triumphant.

"That's just petty." The woman pointed her index finger at Y-43 with a stiff arm, as if aiming a weapon, but none was easily visible. There was a whisper of a sound, like a single hit to the world's smallest cymbal, and Y-43 fell limp and silent.

The woman in black reached down and took the memory drive holding the untraceable two-giga-sollar payment. As she stood back up, she glanced down at Cornwell's corpse. "Serves him right for calling me heavy, the feeking Doug. You okay—Higson, is it?"

"Yes, *Dr.* Higson. I, uh, I'm fine, I think. Who are you? Where's my device?"

She walked up to one of the turrets, found the manual controls, and started fiddling with them as she spoke. "First question: who am I? I'm the person who stole your device this morning."

The turret fired a short burst of bullets, shattering one of the windows. A cold wind blasted through the room.

She continued manipulating the controls. "As for the second question: where is your worthless, non-functioning device? See the previous answer."

In unison, all the turrets went limp, emitting a low, mechanical groan as they sank to the floor. The woman smiled. "And now her turrets don't work either."

Higson said, "I'm very close to a breakthrough."

The woman walked to the nearest wall of windows. "I'm sure you are. Every scientist who's ever worked on mind control has been, all the way back to Mesmer. It's like a tradition." She stuck her head out the broken window, into the cold night sky, and muttered, "Fifty-six floors down, so three up to the roof."

Higson asked, "Why did you shoot out the window?"

"Because the elevators and stairwells are all guarded and fortified. You're not going to want to be awake for this." She pointed her index finger at Higson. There was a soft, sharp hiss, and he fell unconscious.

2

Near the edge of the skyscraper's roof, the woman in black—known as Baird to her friends and multiple law-enforcement agencies—sat on the now-empty case next to the motionless bodies of Dr. Higson and Agent Y-43. As the chill night wind intensified, she adjusted her sweater and continued reading.

The heavy-framed glasses she wore projected a scrolling column of text only she could see. Every few sentences, her eyes darted away to quickly scan the city skyline and the air traffic—thousands of quick-moving dots, lined up like beads on a string. The countless flowing streams of light formed a constantly moving net that hung in the air above and around Manhattan, entangling the city. They passed over the low buildings from the nineteenth century, around and between the taller ones from the twentieth and twenty-first centuries, and well below the roofs of the monstrous towers that became fashionable in the early twenty-second, before the bulk of humanity moved off-world and most new construction on Earth ceased.

Looking at grand vistas was nothing unusual for Baird. Out in the colonies, every window she looked out showed her a barren, alien landscape or the endless void of space—but that was just it: she always saw those through a window. Here, she was out in the open, with no pressure hull or environment suit between her and the sky. Only those wealthy enough to visit the old home world, or live there, ever got to look out on this large of an expanse without any barriers. It was a powerful, visceral sense of space that, ironically, one could never get living in space.

Humanity's migration out into the solar system had happened much faster than anyone anticipated. A breakthrough in propulsion made space travel affordable, which made off-world mining and construction profitable, which made off-world employment opportunities plentiful. In short, the money left the planet and the people followed.

At last, her glasses highlighted one of the distant glowing dots in the sky with a text call-out reading *My Ride*. The dot continued along with the flow of traffic for a few seconds, then turned off its exterior lights, instantly making itself a hundred times more conspicuous if you knew what to look for—a lone dark spot in a glowing sea. The craft immediately broke ranks and headed directly for Baird's position. She easily traced its progress as she read, glancing up to follow the lightless void as it grew larger against the brightly lit traffic and buildings.

Baird didn't move as the jump-craft flared its wings, decelerated over her head, hovered, then touched down on the skyscraper's landing pad beside her.

A panel on the craft's side slid back, opening its interior to the night air. Blue light spilled out of the fuselage, illuminating the roof and making Baird squint as she stole a quick look at the craft between paragraphs.

Three men stepped out of the jump-craft: two soldiers in black combat armor, visors pulled down and covering most of their faces, and a bald man with a soft, pale body encased in a sharp, dark suit.

Baird stayed put, waiting for them to come to her. Given how they were dressed, her own expertly styled black hair, cigarette pants and oversized black sweater made her feel acutely out of place, as if she were clearly not the same as these three men.

That thought pleased her to her core.

The man in the suit smiled a little too broadly and shouted, "Agent Saber Saw," a little too loudly.

Baird held up a single finger but said nothing as she remained sitting on the weapon case, looking out at the city.

"What?" the man asked. "What is it?"

Baird thrust the finger up a bit higher, but was otherwise still.

The man bit his lip and exchanged a nervous look with the two armored soldiers. "What is it? Do you see a bogey?"

Baird lowered her hand, shook her head, and removed her glasses as she turned to face the men. "No, I just had a couple more sentences left in what I was reading. Good to see you again, Agent Sanding Block."

"And you, Agent Saber Saw. What were you reading?"

"*The Mars Journal of Materials Science*."

"What's Materials Science?"

"It's a branch of science that deals with materials."

Sanding Block acted as if he didn't hear the two soldiers laugh. Baird made it obvious that she did hear.

"Riveting, I'm sure. What's the deal with those old-school gARggles? What are they, a family heirloom? Weren't you issued a Brow?" He tapped the thin strip of black metal affixed over his right eye.

She slipped her gARggles off and looked at them appreciatively: a pair of thick black frames with active-tint lenses, old enough to sport the original, classic gARggles logo, all lower case except the A and the R, with the bottoms of the twin G's forming a drawing of a pair of gARggles. "My grandma did have a pair like these, but hers weren't this cool. I don't want a Brow, or SpeX, or Display-Bans, or any of the other gARggles knockoffs. I'll stick with the original, thanks."

"Oh, so you're a snob."

She slipped her gARggles back onto her face. "It's not that I'm a snob; it's just that none of the newer models are good enough for me. I can open up my old gARggles and fix them.

With a Brow, if something goes wrong, you have to replace the entire thing."

"Yeah," one of the soldiers said. "You get to get a new one that looks cooler and does new stuff."

Baird shook her head. "I can upgrade my gARggles with any new features I want—a new processor, better sensors, a faster data link, even mirrored lenses. Besides, Brows don't look cooler; they just look newer. And they make your forehead muscles lopsided."

Sanding Block smirked at her, clearly unconvinced. "Suit yourself, I guess." He pointed at the case. "Is that the item?"

"No, just its carrying case. I grabbed the item this morning. It should be back at the Toolbox by now."

"Did you ever find out what it is that was so important to them?"

Baird smiled. "Get this—mind control."

Sanding Block laughed. "Seriously?"

Baird pointed at Dr. Higson. "He's the inventor."

"Let me guess: he was going to crack the problem any time now."

"He swore he was *this close* to a breakthrough."

"Sure he was. Classic." Sanding Block turned to the armored soldiers. "Tin Snip, Hose Clamp, load the case and the corpses."

"They aren't corpses," Baird said.

Sanding Block turned his attention back to her. "I'm sorry, what?"

"They aren't corpses. They're unconscious, but they're perfectly fine. There is one corpse downstairs, but that was *her* handiwork, not mine."

"Okay, men, load the prisoners. And the case," Sanding Block said. "Tell Nail Bag to plot a flight plan back to the Toolbox, and prepare for immediate takeoff as soon as Saber Saw is aboard."

As the soldiers got to work, Sanding Block said, "You weren't supposed to take prisoners."

"I wasn't supposed to do any of the things I did tonight, depending on who you ask. You can't hire a professional rule breaker and then act surprised when she breaks your rules. My orders were to obtain the item by any means necessary. Killing them wasn't necessary."

"But you could have. You know, just to make things neater."

Baird laughed. "It's funny how guys like you call things 'neat,' when you mean 'much messier.'"

Sanding Block said, "Maybe I should go look the scene over."

"The stairwell is over there, but be careful. Between here and the room where the exchange went down, there are five locked, heavy-duty doors, all manned by armed guards."

"Then how'd you get the prisoners up here?"

Baird pointed over the side of the building.

Sanding Block leaned over the side and looked down, blanched, and then pulled back from the edge. He looked around and shouted to Baird, "But you don't have any rope or climbing equipment! How the hell did you do that?!"

"By various proprietary methods."

"That's all you have to say?"

"No, that's all *I have to* say."

Sanding Block gritted his teeth. "Dammit, Saber Saw. If you don't trust the Toolbox or respect Toolbox agents, why on Earth did you join?"

"I haven't. Not yet. I'm on a trial period, remember?"

"Yeah, that's us trying you out."

Baird walked off toward the jump-craft. "It works both ways."

3

The prisoners lay unconscious on their stretchers in the back of the jump-craft. Tin Snip and Hose Clamp sat beside them, and Sanding Block sat across from them, making a verbal report to headquarters and enjoying a brief discussion with whomever he was reporting to about how mind control never works, while watching in the dim cabin light for the slightest sign that their captives were regaining consciousness.

In the nose of the jump-craft, the pilot, Nail Bag, was doing his job, which consisted entirely of standing by in case the autopilot needed help.

Baird sat off by herself, reclined and relaxed. Her sweater's voluminous cowl neck extended up around her head, adding extra padding to her headrest. With her black sweater, black pants, black shoes, black hair, and dark glasses with black frames, the only pops of color on her were her face, her hands, and a slightly oversized brooch pinned to her sweater—a bronze circle with a hole in the middle, decorated with a repeating silver faux-Aztec motif. There was a silver square suspended in the hole, and a single thin tube cutting across the circle at a steep angle.

Baird looked out the window. In the darkness, she saw the dull gray rectangle of the Francis J. Simmons Building, home to a modestly successful accounting firm that maintained a facility on Earth to be close to their wealthy clients. It was also the secret entrance to the Toolbox's headquarters. She respected the Toolbox's ingenuity, hiding the entrance to their headquarters in a building most people would avoid like the plague out of their natural fear of boredom.

Looking down from above, Baird could clearly see the line, only a city block behind the Simmons building, where the Gradual Reclamation Zone began. On one side of the line, all was clean, orderly, and dotted with pedestrians. On the other side, the landscape was lush and green. Only faint outlines of the ruler-straight roads and the occasional building too stubborn to come down on its own hinted at the wilderness's past as a civilized suburb.

When the bulk of the population shifted off-world, thousands of square miles of urban sprawl were left deserted. Scientists introduced plants that were engineered to live off of pollutants and plastics to help clean up these areas. Now, the plants were allowed—along with weather and time—to gradually re-naturalize the environment and demolish the buildings that people didn't want to bother knocking over themselves.

The largest landmark by far in this part of the GRZ was the dirty gray hulk of an old shopping mall, a gigantic Y made of poured concrete, surrounded by an immense parking lot that had long since been covered by a shallow coating of dirt and a tall growth of wild grass. This did not surprise Baird. The least attractive things always seem to also be the most durable. Beauty is fleeting, but ugly is built to last.

The jump-craft approached the Simmons Building slowly, flaring its wings and reversing its thrusters to land softly on the roof of the adjacent parking structure. The instant the jump-craft touched down, three tractor-bots, each about the size of a large dog, rolled out and latched onto the craft's landing gear. The craft's wings folded in tight to its roof as the tractor-bots pulled it off the landing pad and down a ramp into the darker, lower recesses of the structure, until it reached ground floor—home of the least-sought-after parking spaces, and the building's loading dock for ground-based robotic freight deliveries.

Sanding Block climbed out of the craft and walked to the freight elevator control panel. He stood within a small box painted on the pavement and submitted to a scan of his ident chip. The elevator doors opened, and Tin Snip and Hose Clamp moved the unconscious prisoners into the elevator. Baird sauntered in behind, and the elevator began to move.

Instead of going up into the Simmons Building, the elevator went down, underground. Baird began navigating through menus, projected by her glasses, that only she could see, starting on her gARggles' settings page. She drilled down through three subpages and scrolled two-thirds of the way down to find a single period that was one half of a space farther from the letter before it than it should have been. After selecting the period, she was taken to a rudimentary menu page containing two items: one marked *Messages* and the other marked *Call*.

She selected *Call*.

She only had to wait a moment until a live, three-dimensional image of a man's face appeared, floating before her. He was in his mid-thirties, with tousled hair, one metal eyebrow, and more than a slight resemblance to Baird.

"Hey, Bran," the man said. "How's it going?"

Baird smiled but did not move a muscle or utter a sound. Her inner ear told her that the elevator car had stopped going down and, unlike most elevators, had started moving rather quickly to the side, making her and the other passengers lean in unison, first to their right, then their left, then back to the center as they gained their equilibrium. Through it all, her attention remained focused on a keyboard that only she could see, floating in front of her. It was designed for her to type on it with her fingers, but the buttons lit up quickly without her moving. Words scrolled across the bottom of the window.

I'm good, but I can't talk. I'm going to have to stick with text. Where are you, Izzy?

"On a stakeout. You should probably call me by my code name."

Baird smiled wider, but otherwise didn't move. *I'm not going to call you Speed Square. It makes you sound like an unusually fast dweeb.*

"Well, I *am* a cyber-security and infiltration specialist. It kinda fits."

And I don't like that we have alliterative code names. Speed Square and Saber Saw. I don't care that it's a coincidence. The fact that we're brother and sister makes it nauseating.

He nodded. "That's the name they gave you, though. You're going to have to live with it."

Not really, Baird wrote. *I could just tell the Toolbox that this was a mistake and be on my way.*

"Has it ever occurred to you that there might be a better way to live than just leaving all the time?"

No, it hasn't. Has it occurred to you that there's a better way to live than always staying behind?

"Yes. Anyway, it's not so easy to leave the Toolbox. There are ways out, but you can't just say, 'I'm out,' and walk."

Yeah? Watch me.

"Bran, don't joke about that."

I know, I know. Yeesh, Izzy, what have you gotten me into?

"I keep telling you, Bran, this is gonna be a sweet deal. If the job you did as a test run tonight went as well as I suspect it did, you're probably out of your probationary period. Then you'll have your autonomy back, the occasional paying job, and all of our resources at your disposal."

I already had all your resources at my disposal.

"You call me when you need something, and you lean on me to use our resources for you under the table," Izzy said. "Now you can use them yourself without sneaking around."

You always say you want me to keep in touch more. Now you're taking away one of my reasons for calling you.

Izzy did not look amused. "So, what are you up to right now?"

I'm in the top-secret tunnel to the Toolbox with some tools. That's why I can't talk. It's supposed to be a comms blackout.

"How do they not see you typing?"

Can I trust you to keep a secret?

"Of course you can," he said. "You just never do."

After a brief delay, Baird wrote, *And does the moment when that seems to be changing really feel like a good time for a snarky guilt trip?*

"Point taken. Please proceed."

You know how when I was a kid, they had to give me a pacemaker?

"You're typing with your pacemaker?"

No. But yes. In a way.

"That cleared that up."

My pacemaker has a neural-prosthetic interface, so it can match my heart rate to what I'm doing and how much stress I'm feeling. Turns out the interface is an old, multi-function, one-size-fits-all model. It can control text interfaces for quadriplegics and a lot of other things, if you hack the settings.

"How long have you known that?" Izzy asked.

A while.

"Huh. Seems like the kind of thing I'd know about my big sister if she spent more time with me."

And yet it's something my little brother knows about me now, when I spend exactly the amount of time with him that I already do.

"Yeah, yeah. Still, it sounds handy. I wish Dad had gotten *me* one of those."

Surgeons have ethical problems with performing life-endangering surgery on healthy people just so they can type without using their hands, or else everyone would have one already. It's a shame you weren't lucky enough to be born with a congenital heart defect.

"Yeah, just my lousy luck." The car slowed to a stop, causing those inside to go through their synchronized leaning routine again, but this time in the reverse order, then to feel unusually heavy as they now began to ascend.

I'm going to have to wrap this up, Izzy. We're there. I just wanted to touch base.

"I'm glad you did. Talk to you later. Love you, Bran."

Baird wrote, *Yup.*

Izzy cleared his throat. "Your brother just said he loves you."

Yeah. I heard.

"That's all right," Izzy replied. "I know you're embarrassed by your emotions."

No, I'm embarrassed by your *emotions.* Baird ended the call.

The doors opened into the Toolbox's headquarters—a shining, high-tech, multi-use facility built into the ruined hulk of the concrete shopping center she'd seen from the air only minutes before. Baird watched with interest as Tin Snip and Hose Clamp left with the sleeping prisoners.

Baird asked, "What will happen to them?"

"Interrogation," Sanding Block replied. "Then new faces and fresh identities as convicted felons serving time on Mimas."

Baird winced. "Mimas. Ugh. Oh well. They knew the stakes of the game when they agreed to play."

Sanding Block shrugged. "Yeah, I guess."

They walked across the unloading platform, through an arch, and into the arrival hall: an enclosed space four stories high and hundreds of feet across. One wall was made up entirely of glass, covered on the outside by a lattice of vines and leafy green plants. During the day, the glass let in a great deal of natural light, but it was night. The glass was rendered opaque to keep the building's artificial light from leaking out.

All of the building's original decoration had long since rotted away or been deliberately removed, but traces remained. Stains on one stretch of blank wall revealed the outlines of letters spelling "Sbarro." Baird had decided that it must have been part of some larger word, but she'd yet to think of one with that ungainly combination of letters.

She and Sanding Block crossed the hall, not walking together so much as walking separately from the same place to the same place at the same time. At the far end of the cavernous room, where the space gave way to a wide two-story esplanade, they reached a line of two-foot-square yellow boxes painted on the floor along the wall.

Sanding Block stood in one of the boxes. Almost instantly, *Ident Scan Complete: Agent Sanding Block Identified* appeared on a display above his head. A small door at about waist height opened in the wall, revealing a transparent plastic cup containing a single pill. He threw the pill into the back of his throat, then looked at Baird expectantly.

Baird remained standing where she'd stopped, outside of the yellow boxes.

Sanding Block raised an eyebrow. She sneered back at him and reluctantly stepped into one of the boxes. The display said *Ident Scan Complete: Agent (Provisional) Saber Saw Identified.* A door opened, revealing four pills, two of which were the size of the end of Baird's pinky. She looked at the pills and shook her head.

"Come on, Saber Saw," Sanding Block said. "You have to take them."

"No, they *want* me to take them. There's a difference, you know."

"The retroactive vaccines are for your own protection."

"Then you take a couple of these. I want you to be just as safe as I am."

Sanding Block said, "You need them. I don't. You were out in the field, on the ground, surrounded by people from who knows where. I never got off the roof."

Baird grimaced, tossed the pills into her mouth, and with some effort, swallowed them. "True, but you were exposed to me."

Sanding Block shrugged. "I guess they don't think a bad attitude is contagious."

4

A little over an hour later, Baird stood in front of a closed door. She looked down at her clothing, adjusting her black sweater so that it lay more comfortably.

The door opened, and her handler, a tall, distinguished man in his fifties, smiled and beckoned her into his office. "Saber Saw! Welcome back. Please, come in."

Baird said, "Hello, Screw Jack."

"Drink?"

"Yes, please."

Baird settled into a chair opposite Screw Jack's empty desk. He walked to the rear corner of the office, where he had a few bottles and some glassware in a cabinet.

Baird said, "I'm surprised you're in this late."

"When I heard you were returning, I came in. Besides, we didn't get into this business for the regular hours. Congratulations on a successful mission, by the way. I notice you managed to keep two of the hostiles alive. Wouldn't it have been easier to just eliminate them and be done with it?"

"Easier for some people, maybe."

"Easy for you, I'd think," Screw Jack said. "You rated at the highest proficiency level in marksmanship, although you insisted on only aiming for the neck, which your instructor found disturbing. Look, I wouldn't trust anybody who wants to kill, but in this line of work you should keep your mind open to the idea that you might have to."

"In my experience, when someone's willing to kill if they have a reason, they often get really good at finding that reason. I keep my mind open to the idea that I might *not* have to kill anyone."

"You're not a murderer."

"No. I don't destroy things, I steal them—allegedly. You requested the item they were trading. Now you have said item, and two of the people who were trading it, both alive. You never know how useful they may be to you. Dead, they wouldn't be of any use to anyone."

Screw Jack handed Baird a glass with a finger's width of light brown fluid. "I wouldn't hold my breath as to any of what you got being useful. I mean, mind control? If we'd known what they had, we probably wouldn't have bothered sending you to stop them. Better to just let them keep wasting resources and taking on the terrible risks. Maybe leak word of what they were up to and watch the whole system come down on them. Oh well."

"Who knew?" Baird leaned back in her chair, crossed her legs, and started to take a sip of her drink, but she stopped when she noticed the scratch on her ankle, which was poking out from the hem of her slim black pants. She pulled the pant leg down a bit, then realized that Screw Jack was watching her.

He settled into his chair and lifted his glass. "Drink up."

She took a sip. "Ooh, I like that. Terrestrial?"

"No, Martian. I'm told the terrestrial stuff is better, but if there's a difference, it's lost on me. I read your report. I appreciate your efforts to not overburden me with a lot of details."

"You're welcome. I included all the pertinent information. You told me to do a thing. I did the thing. I don't see a problem."

"And if you did see a problem, you wouldn't mention it unless pointing out the problem was your mission."

Baird said, "I wouldn't accept that mission. You brought me on because of my specific set of skills. Sharing information is not one of those skills."

Screw Jack shrugged. "I must admit, you have a point there."

Baird raised her glass of whiskey. "Thank you."

Screw Jack pressed a thin piece of gray metal above his right eye, which automatically conformed to the shape of his eyebrow. A tiny probe lowered to project light into his pupil. His eyes darted around for a moment to navigate to the file he wanted. "I have your report here. Code name: Saber Saw. Birth name: Brangelina Baird. I've been meaning to ask about that. Brangelina?"

Baird sighed. "I'm named after my great-grandmother on my mother's side."

Screw Jack nodded. "I thought it was something like that. It's a lovely name, but it's just so old-fashioned. It says here that you refused all of the equipment the quartermaster supplied."

"Didn't need it."

"Obviously. I guess the same can be said of your local contact, Sanding Block, who says you refused all assistance from him and his team, except for a ride back here."

Baird said, "Accurate."

"Saber Saw, your local contact can be an invaluable asset. That's why we've gone to the trouble of placing an agent in every major city and colony. You could have let him in on some part of your operation so he could be of assistance."

"The more people are involved in a plan, the more people can screw up a plan. Look, you want me to work for you occasionally. Fine. I like the idea of access to your resources, but I work the way I work. If that's not acceptable, we're done here."

"It's not a problem for me, at the moment. But in time I do hope that you'll gain a little trust in us and learn to share a bit. We are here to help you. In the meantime, can I ask one question about the mission?"

"Yes."

"How did you manage to steal the item, infiltrate the hand-off, subdue two agents, and carry their unconscious bodies up three stories on the outside of the building on your own without any special equipment?"

Baird shook her head. "You said one question. That's, like, five."

"Yes, but structured as one compound question."

"You want me to be a secret agent," Baird said. "I'm going to have secrets."

"Not from us, I hope, and we prefer *covert operative.*"

"Same thing. Either way, how can you trust me to keep your secrets if I can't keep my own?"

Screw Jack said, "I guess it's going to take a while to get used to the idea that you're working with us. You're not a cat burglar doing occasional jobs on your own anymore."

"Aren't I?"

Screw Jack flapped a hand dismissively. "Yes, you're right, true. You are still that."

"*Allegedly.* It's never been proved."

"No, but in either case, it's just your cover now. It really was a brilliant idea, recruiting a notorious criminal—"

"*Alleged* criminal."

"Notorious *alleged* criminal, who is too skilled to have ever been caught, or even charged with a crime." He started reading aloud from the file in his Brow again. "Sister of Isaac 'Izzy' Baird, aka Agent Speed Square. Daughter of Raj Baird, a brilliant scientist and inventor who held a prestigious position at DAFCorp. You seemed poised to follow in his footsteps, studying physics, chemistry, and engineering, until his untimely death, at which point you dropped out of college. From that point on you've done . . . well, nothing that anyone's been able to prove. You were designated as a prime recruitment candidate, both because of your brother's recommendation and because of your extremely valuable skills. I'm sorry. *Alleged* skills."

Baird said, "No, my skills aren't alleged. They are provably real."

"No doubt. Anyone who could pull off the Wartzberg Pearl job—*allegedly*—must be good enough to work for us. You already travel all over the solar system. People expect you to act suspiciously, and if you get caught people will just assume you're on a job, not a mission for us. We have deniability."

Baird said, "Yes. I sleep so much better at night knowing that if I get caught, you're covered."

"After the conversation we've just had, can you really blame us for protecting ourselves? All I'm saying is that it can't be a one-sided relationship. We expect you to share your methods with us eventually."

"I share my methods by using them for you. Otherwise, it wouldn't be sharing them with you; it would be giving them to you. But who knows, maybe I'll change my mind someday. Speaking of someday, when will my probationary period be over?"

Screw Jack took off his Brow and dropped it on the desk in front of him with an audible *clink*. "That's not up to me. The General Contractor makes that decision."

Baird rolled her eyes. "We honestly have to call our leader the General Contractor?"

"Yes. That's the General Contractor's job title. Our founder, Damon Carlton, was a great man with remarkable vision and a regrettable sense of humor. Anyway, as I said, it's not my decision, but your test mission tonight went very well. I'm recommending that you be upgraded to full operational status immediately. Despite your less-than-forthcoming attitude, I feel you'll be a great asset."

Screw Jack rose from his seat, stepped around the side of his desk, and offered her a handshake. Baird stood up, but before she could take his hand, the whole room seemed to tip sideways and spin.

She heard Screw Jack say, "Baird, are you all right?"

She tried to keep herself steady, but she felt the floor tilt beneath her feet. She reached for the back of the chair she had been sitting in, but her hand passed through empty space. Her vision went dim as she felt Screw Jack's arms clamping around her, holding her upright.

Then everything went black.

5

Baird felt a familiar cold that fully penetrated her flesh and hunkered down in her bones. Her eyelids fluttered open. All she could see was an off-white plastic wall, only inches in front of her face, which did not surprise her. It came with the weightlessness and the cold.

The solid door meant she was in a spaceliner stasis pod. Medical stasis pods had glass doors, because doctors need to see you and be reminded that you're a human being, to do their job properly. Flight attendants have the opposite problem. If she was in a spaceliner, and they were waking her up, she reasoned that she must be arriving somewhere. She remembered what that meant, moaned, and braced herself.

She heard the snapping and scraping sound of tiny mechanical valves actuating down near her waist. She felt a warm sensation on the back of her right hand, which spread to her fingers and started toward her wrist, as if she had been holding a kitten that had relieved itself.

The warmth spread to her elbow, then her shoulder, then down into her ribcage. It would have been quite pleasant if it had stopped at mere warmth, but as the wave of pleasant heat ventured to new parts of her person, the places it had already been didn't simply stay warm. They became hot. Not quite burning hot, but definitely sweating hot.

The heat continued, and within thirty seconds had completely saturated her body. She slid her left hand up in front of her, through the limited room she had, and wiped the beads of sweat from her forehead.

As always, she marveled at the inherent cruelty of the spacelines system: keeping you pristine on ice for days during transit, then making you a sweaty mess just before arrival.

It occurred to her that she didn't know where she was arriving. She also had no memory of departing. The last thing she remembered was having a meeting in Screw Jack's office.

She instinctively tried to feel around, to make sure her most important belongings were still in place, but her right hand was locked into the injector brace, and the limited room made moving her left hand difficult. She tipped her head downward as far as she could, and ended up pressing her forehead against the hibernation chamber door. She rolled her eyes down so hard they almost hurt and saw that she was still wearing her black sweater, and that her bronze pin was still in place. She could already feel that she was wearing her gARggles, and she was reasonably sure from the thick black frames she saw in her peripheral vision and the pressure the arms exerted on her temples that they were her original pair, not a replacement.

She tilted her head back and sighed with relief, noticing the spot of sweat her forehead had left on the pod door.

A chime played, followed by the voice of a man who was polite, professional, and only speaking because his job required it.

"Good morning, valued passengers. I'm pleased to tell you that our two-week voyage is at an end. We have arrived at the Newtah colony."

Baird moaned, "What am I doing on Newtah?"

The announcement continued. "The local gravity is one g, so please adjust your grav-meds accordingly. In a few moments, when docking is complete, we will open your hibernation pods. Please move into the aisle and file out of the spacecraft in a calm, orderly manner. Those of you who transferred from a different flight will find your carry-on item in the bin attached to the top of your pod. Thank you for flying Olympus Mons Spacelines, where we deliver a peak travel experience."

Baird felt herself sink into the cushions of her stasis pod, a sure sign that the liner was decelerating to dock. Her gARggles woke up, alerting Baird that she had an incoming message from Screw Jack marked *Briefing: Urgent*.

She took the call. She saw Screw Jack's face, floating in midair three feet beyond the door of her stasis pod.

"Saber Saw! You don't know how good it is to see you."

Baird said, "Enjoy it while you can, 'cause I think it might get less pleasant pretty fast."

"You're probably right," Screw Jack said. "I'm sure you have questions."

"You're all-caps right I do."

"Please, by all means, ask them."

"What the feek?'"

Screw Jack nodded. "That does sum it up. After you passed out in my office, we rushed you down to Medical. They found that you'd been infected with an engineered virus. We believe you got it from that scratch on your right ankle."

Baird remembered the enemy agent, lying on the floor, writhing from the effects of the neural scrambler dart. Her triumphant attitude made sense to Baird now. "One of the hostile agents scratched me."

"We know. We found the scratch and questioned her, rather aggressively, but she was no help."

Baird said, "Were they able to cure the virus?"

"Not yet, I'm afraid. They're working hard on a cure."

"What will the virus do?"

"Saber Saw. Brangelina. It's lethal. The virus is designed to enter your bloodstream undetected, infect you with minimal symptoms, and eventually kill you."

Baird took a moment to absorb what she'd heard, then took another moment to allow herself to silently panic before forcing herself back to practical matters.

"How long will it take?"

"I'm sorry, Baird. The doctors say seven days."

"That's not possible. The flight attendant just said I've been on this shuttle for two weeks."

"That's the good news. The virus doesn't progress in stasis. We can keep you on ice indefinitely."

"Then why am I awake?! Why am I here? If I've only got days left, I don't want to spend any of them on Newtah! It's where boredom goes when it wants to be alone."

"That's the thing. They were making good progress on a cure, but they've hit a snag. They need your help to get past it."

"Wait, how long have they been working on it? How long have I actually been in stasis?"

"A little under two and a half years."

Again, Baird took several seconds to flash between numbness, panic, and rage. "Why didn't you tell me before you put me in stasis?"

"The doctors put you under as soon as they realized you had the virus, just as a precaution. Once they figured out what the virus did, they kept you under because every second you're awake counts, and their hope—*our* hope—was to wake you when we could tell you that we had a cure."

Baird said, "But you don't have a cure."

"No," Screw Jack said. "Unfortunately, we don't."

"What do you have for me?"

"A mission."

"That's not as good as a cure. You said something about symptoms?"

"Yes, but are you sure you want to know what they are? You might drive yourself crazy looking for them."

"Do you think it would be better to have the symptoms be a surprise?"

Screw Jack said, "Good point. It should start with headaches that get worse over time. Later there'll be a ringing in the ears, maybe nose bleeds. Nothing debilitating, certainly nothing to make you suspect death might be imminent. Last there'll be nausea. If you get to the nausea stage, let me know immediately, and we'll find a way to get you in stasis. It means the end is near."

"How near?"

"Too near."

Baird said, "I have a pacemaker. Is there any chance it could help keep me alive?"

"No. The virus doesn't affect your heart. By the way, the doctors were appalled at how out of date your neural-prosthetic interface is. They said they could replace it with a newer one that'd be much more efficient."

Baird's eyes grew wide. "They didn't, did they? They didn't swap out my old interface!"

"No! We wouldn't do brain surgery on you without your consent. They just said it was something you should consider when this is all over."

"Okay. Good. That's fine then. So, why don't you tell me what the mission is so I can get it done and go back on ice? It seems my time is short."

"Of course. The doctors have determined that the virus has a genetic component. They think the key to finding a cure is to figure out how this mechanism works, and to do that they need access to lots of human DNA. Millions of samples."

"So they can observe it doing its job in every possible way simultaneously."

"Something like that. The largest database of DNA sequences in existence is held by the Mormon Church."

"Which explains why I'm going to Newtah."

"The largest Mormon space colony. That's right. The Latter-Day Saints have always had a keen interest in genealogy, and at some point they started collecting DNA records as well. Now they have an immense database."

"And they aren't sharing," Baird said.

"Actually, they've been very generous with their data. Anyone doing potentially lifesaving research gets total access, free of charge, provided that research doesn't fly directly in the face of the Church's beliefs. No, the problem is that in order to get access, one must represent a recognized scientific organization, and then they want reports on how the research is going."

"And why go to the trouble to fake years' worth of research, when you can just have me steal the data."

"Precisely. We wouldn't have woken you if this weren't important, Saber Saw. The doctors feel strongly that access to this database will lead directly to a cure. Also, I don't pretend to know you well, but I did suspect that you'd want the opportunity to have a hand in your own salvation, rather than just sleeping in a bio-stasis tube while other people work to rescue you."

"Maybe you know me better than you think," Baird said.

Screw Jack smiled. "The data is held in a secured facility in what they call the axle—the shaft that runs down the center of the station."

A diagram of Newtah as seen from outside popped up next to Screw Jack's face: a massive tube, floating in orbit around Venus. Though it was tempting to picture the station laid out horizontally, as if it were on its side, it was presented in the diagram, and in most images, standing vertically. The spaceport formed a sort of flattened bulb at the bottom of the rotating tube, with an animation showing spacecraft docking at the stationary base.

Baird could see the seams where more length was added to the tube—one half-kilometer segment at a time as the population grew—until it had reached its current length. At sixteen kilometers long and only one kilometer around, the station resembled a pillar.

At the top, opposite the spaceport, there was one of the rarest features one could find on the exterior of a space colony: a large decorative flourish. It was a five-hundred-meter-tall golden statue of a man in a robe, blowing a horn—the angel Moroni.

The spaceport at the bottom and the statue at the top remained motionless, but the tube connecting them constantly spun, generating simulated gravity for the inhabitants who lived inside, clinging to the walls like insects.

"Most of the administration of the station and the spaceport is handled from the axle, as well as storage and the maintenance of the church's genetic and genealogical databases," Screw Jack explained. "Really, anything requiring high security on the station happens there, given its remote location and easily controlled access points."

As he said this, the shaft running down the length of the station glowed, showing through the habitat's outer skin. The shaft was a thinner, stationary tube, stretching down the center of the constantly spinning cylinder where the people of Newtah lived. The entire construction reminded Baird of a gigantic rolling pin. Three tiny elevator shafts lit up. They extended from the inner surface of the rotating tube's wall—the "ground"—to the stationary shaft.

"There are three elevators to the axle," Screw Jack continued. "All heavily guarded and bristling with security and surveillance equipment. The office where they handle the database is here, near the second elevator."

A portion of the axle near the middle elevator shaft glowed brighter.

"The databases are kept on five redundant memory drives here, and in identical setups in four other facilities around the solar system. Believe it or not, this was the least remote location. You are to gain access to the database and swap out one of the redundant drives with the fake drive we included in your carry-on."

Baird nodded. "Makes sense."

"A simple approach, I know, but that's often best. Their system will think the drive has gone bad and route around it until a tech can come and swap in a new one. Meanwhile, you'll have a full copy of the database without having to wait for anything to upload."

"You said that the axle also has the administration and storage. What kind of storage?"

"All kinds," Screw Jack replied. "Everything from fuel and heavy machinery to people's belongings."

"Got it. What's my time frame?"

"Every hour you take is one less hour you have to live."

"Ah. Great. So, you're telling me that I have a terminal illness, but that I need to ignore that, because I'm being dropped with no warning into a place I've never been, to steal something I didn't even know existed until just now, and I have no time to plan."

"Yes. I think it's safe to say that the situation is suboptimal."

"Quite safe."

"If you check your messages, you'll find your instructions for meeting your local contact, Channel Lock."

"I have half a mind to delete it right now."

"I'm very sorry this has happened to you, Brangelina. None of us saw this coming, but I promise you, I won't rest until we have your cure."

"Thanks, Screw Jack. I appreciate that. And I'd also appreciate it if you'd never call me Brangelina again."

"Understood. Good luck, Baird," Screw Jack said, and ended the briefing.

During the course of the briefing, Baird had felt herself press harder and harder into the cushions, meaning that the spaceliner was shedding more and more speed. With no warning, the pressure lessened, then subsided entirely. They had docked.

A second chime rang. Baird's pod rotated so that its opening faced the aisle, and the door slid open. For one half of a second, the spaceliner's interior appeared calm; two neat rows of upright cylinders hung in their articulated mounts, lining either side of an empty aisle, opening to reveal the people inside.

Baird's fellow travelers bolted out of their pods, clogging the aisle. She waited for most of the congestion to ease before she stepped out into the aisle herself. She glanced at the bin above her pod and saw that there was a small travel bag—more of a large purse—waiting there. She took it.

She pushed herself along, floating weightless, out of the shuttle. In the loading tunnel, she grasped one of the endless line of moving handles that were riding along on a metal track. Baird held on to the handle with great care and observed her surroundings attentively. Everybody had seen at least one amusing video of some inexperienced traveler who didn't hold the handle firmly enough, lost their grip, and either flew off at an unpredictable angle or drifted slowly, looking confused, until they were hit in the rear by the face of the traveler behind them, which did little to help the dignity of either person involved.

Both Baird and the passenger in front of her managed to keep their grip. The handle pulled her into the terminal at a comfortable pace, out of the loading tunnel, past the stasis pods of the still-frozen transfer passengers being transported to their connections. She felt sticky with dried sweat, and her clothing was rumpled and skewed from fighting through the mob. Her head hurt, and she was groggy, disoriented, and generally angry at life, but she was used to these sensations. She was a frequent traveler.

6

The Newtah spaceport looked, sounded, and smelled like any other. Easy-to-clean floors and walls; quiet, inoffensive music coming from the ceiling; and the presence of hundreds of people, many of whom talked offensively loudly and smelled as if they had difficulty cleaning themselves.

The only visual clue that she was at the Newtah spaceport instead of any other place was the shape of the space. The handle dragged her straight ahead, but the walls and ceiling all curved away to either side, conforming to the inner volume of a giant cylinder.

The handle pulled her and her fellow travelers in a single-file line away from the boarding gates and toward the heart of the spaceport, and the station beyond it. Baird passed over a seam in the outer wall, from an area where the structure around her was stationary and into one where the floor and ceiling were moving.

Alongside the track ahead, a spaceport security officer floated, gripping his handhold to remain at his post. Baird couldn't help but smile as she watched the officer's presence have its customary effect on the nearby citizens. People hushed their voices, straightened their posture, and made sure not to look at the officer, because they all suspected he was looking at them.

They were fooling themselves, of course. The officer couldn't be looking at all of them. He was already occupied, staring directly at Baird. This was not delusion or paranoia on her part. She knew for a fact that the officer was staring at her. Law enforcement officers always stared at her. Their Brows alerted them to her presence, and they made a point of looking straight at her. They imagined this would intimidate her.

As she drew within hearing range, she smiled and nodded. "Officer."

The officer gritted his teeth and watched her pass.

Baird kept smiling. She always made a point of looking right back, smiling, and greeting law enforcement officers in a friendly, professional manner. She did this to demonstrate that she bore them no particular ill will, but she knew that they often took it as an insult. That was their prerogative.

Of course, the authorities knowing that she was on the station would make her mission that much harder, but she liked a challenge, and she loved pulling off a job and getting away with it even when she was being watched.

The handles slowed, coming to a complete halt in front of a set of handholds and a wall of sliding glass doors. Baird and the other travelers let go of the handles and waited for a moment, until a vehicle pulled up on the far side of the glass doors. A chime played, followed by a warning to enter quickly and carefully, as the doors slid open. The vehicle seemed like a perfectly ordinary train car, except that it curved upward at both ends, like a banana, conforming to the inner circumference of the space station.

Baird hovered weightlessly over a seat. To her left, the direction from which she had come, the spaceport was stationary. To her right, the portion of the spaceport that connected to the habitat cylinder moved past at a surprisingly brisk speed. The doors closed. The train slowly pulled away, and the backrest of Baird's seat pressed into her lumbar region. As soon as the seat began pushing her forward, she also began sliding down. It was a gentle pull at first, but as the train accelerated, the pull became more intense. Soon, the spaceport to her left passed the windows in a blur, while the area to her right slowed, then stopped completely. She heard a chime, followed by a recorded request that the passengers exit quickly and carefully. The doors on the train's right side opened, and Baird, along with everyone else, stood up and walked out, just as they would have on Earth.

As Baird filed out of the car, she noted four uniformed security officers standing in a row, staring at her as she passed. She made eye contact with each and every one, and said, "Officers." If they couldn't bother to break up their group, she wasn't going to trouble herself to greet them individually.

She trudged past the baggage claim to the transportation center, where a line of several people made polite, cheerful conversation while they waited for whomever they were there to meet. Through her gARggles, Baird could see a label floating in midair, highlighting a man in his late forties, with sleepy eyes and a rumpled linen suit. His hands gripped a hat that was the same color as his suit and had a wide, slightly mangled brim. The label read *Channel Lock*.

The guy in line next to him, a slender young man in an immaculately clean and tastefully bland suit, just like all the other people in the line, said, "Have you ever seen such a marvelous day, friend?"

"Only every day." Channel Lock's smile did not fade, but she saw a certain tiredness in his eyes as he scanned the arriving travelers with his black metal Brow.

"I know exactly what you mean," the younger man said. "Every day is just as wonderful as the last. Each one is a gift."

Channel Lock nodded. "Yes. I woke this morning and I marveled at my luck, having yet another day like this ahead of me."

Baird approached Channel Lock. "Hello. My name is Baird. I think you're waiting for me."

The man looked at Baird, his expression almost manic with delight. "Welcome, Miss Baird. My name is Humphreys. Chick Humphreys. I'm here to escort you to your hotel."

The young man Channel Lock had been talking to said, "Welcome to Newtah, ma'am."

Baird nodded her head slightly to him. "Hi."

"Is it your first visit?"

Baird looked at Channel Lock questioningly, then back at the young man. "Yeah."

Channel Lock said, "We should really be on our way," taking Baird's carry-on and walking away, forcing her to follow, not that she was in any way resistant.

The young man said, "It's a shame you have to rush off."

"But we must," Channel Lock said. "We really must."

"Well, ma'am, I hope you enjoy your visit."

Channel Lock looked back over his shoulder and waved, but did not slow his pace. "We know you do."

Baird asked, "Friend of yours?"

Under his breath, Channel Lock said, "I don't have friends."

"He seemed friendly."

"Everyone here is . . . friendly, I mean. That's why I can't relate to any of 'em."

They joined a fast-moving queue that snaked past large windows, allowing Baird her first view into Newtah's primary habitat. In one vista, Baird could see trees, shops, single-family homes, small patches of grass, wide meandering footpaths, roads, tramlines, a flowing stream of actual liquid water, and people—countless happy-looking people. An idyllic island of suburbia clinging to the inside of an immense tube, floating placidly in orbit of the planet Venus, a planet known for intense heat, crushing pressure, and clouds of sulfuric acid.

"So there it is," Baird said. "Newtah. The solar system's largest yawn repository."

Channel lock shot her a quick look, urging her to keep thoughts like that to herself. The manner of her arrival, and her talk with Screw Jack, had not left her in a very good mood.

The party in front of Baird and Channel Lock turned, smiled, welcomed them to the line, and declared that it was a beautiful day.

Channel Lock agreed with them.

A moment later, a couple got in line behind them, greeted Baird and Channel Lock, and declared that it was a beautiful day.

Channel Lock agreed again, using exactly the same wording, at exactly the same level of intensity, which made his agreement much less convincing.

She and Channel Lock progressed through the line and quickly boarded a rectangular metro car that was all thin, clear windows from the midpoint up, and unpadded seats surrounded by thin composite walls from the midpoint down.

The people next in line told them to have a good ride and a pleasant day. Baird said nothing as she settled into a seat. Channel Lock wished them the same as he sat down opposite her, smiling, chuckling good-naturedly, and waving to the kindly couple as the door of their metro car slid shut and the car pulled away from the station.

Baird watched Channel Lock's face, noting that his smile grew more brittle and his laugh less sincere as the car drew further from the station, morphing into a snarl. His waving hand slowed as his laugh died. He muttered, "Bye-bye . . . you awful bunch of . . . Dougs. Happy, friendly, feeking Dougs."

He sagged back into his seat and mashed his much-maligned hat onto his head at a haphazard angle. "I am so all-caps sick of this place. Oh, we can talk freely now, by the way."

"So I gathered. Good to meet you, Channel Lock."

Channel Lock laughed once, mirthlessly, through his nostrils. "Please, save the polite lies for the locals. They aren't becoming for people such as us."

Baird nodded. "Okay, I'm not happy to meet you, because I had to come to Newtah to do it, and I have zero interest in being here."

"Thank you for your honesty."

"Don't like the locals much, huh?"

"They're nice enough. Feek, way nicer than nice enough. Decent, hardworking, intelligent; they'll give you the shirt off their back, as long as you don't seem to want them to. They make it very hard not to like 'em, so hard that I've gone all the way around the horn to resenting them for it."

"Well, you spend all of your time trying to fit in with them. It's hard not to resent it when you have to pretend to be something you're not, even if that something is happy."

"*Especially* when that something is happy," Channel Lock agreed. "I've gotten to where smiling makes me create extra stomach acid. I'm Pavlov's dog, but for ulcers."

The metro car rode along a raised track, which was held aloft by pylons anchored into the simulated ground of the habitat cylinder. A diagram on the door showed that the track ran an arrow-straight path along the entire length of the tube, with stations every kilometer. To either side of the track, pleasant suburban homes, faithfully recreating their counterparts from Earth's past but at roughly one-half scale, sat behind small patches of lawn. Wide footpaths meandered between the buildings, and everything curved up to meet in the middle, beyond the axle, directly over Baird's head.

Baird had been in space stations that used rotation and angular momentum to simulate gravity many times, but the rest of them were shaped like rings, allowing the average pedestrian a limited view of the path ahead, curving up and out of sight. Only in Newtah could one look above oneself and see homes, a slow-moving stream, pedestrians, and a child riding a bicycle upside down on the surface over one's head.

Channel Lock said, "You look impressed."

Baird realized that she had pushed her head all the way up against the window, straining to look up at the far surface of the tube. "I am. It's been a long time since I've seen a bicycle. Few of the other colonies have the kind of open space you'd need for one."

The child was about four hundred meters away if you followed the curved path, but while the great spinning tube that made up Newtah's habitat level was one kilometer around, it was only a bit over three hundred meters across. The child was actually much closer to Baird as the crow flew, clinging to what felt like the ground as it curved overhead. The child cycled up the wall and disappeared behind the always-moving axle and the strips of powerful lights in the center of the tube.

Through numerous windows spaced evenly along the axle's shaft, Baird saw people inside, floating weightlessly. From her point of view, the lights were mounted on what looked like a stationary scaffold surrounding the axle—a large, rotating shaft. She knew that the opposite was true: the shaft was stationary, while the lights, the scaffold, Baird, and the simulated ground beneath her moved—but without any window to the star field outside or the planet below, her sense of equilibrium would not accept it.

Channel Lock furrowed his brow. "I thought you were supposed to have traveled all over the system. How is it you've never been here before?"

Baird said, "Going all over doesn't mean going everywhere. Besides, what am I supposed to have been doing while traveling all over?"

"Stealing things."

"*Allegedly.* If I were a burglar looking to maximize my risk-to-reward ratio, I'd steer clear of this place. These people have money, but not huge amounts of it, and they don't spend it on expensive, easily stolen things. You'd have to steal three of these houses somehow to equal the street price of a single necklace they used to have on Ganymede that could fit easily in this pocket." She pointed at the hip pocket of her pants.

"Is it in that pocket?"

"Not at the moment."

Channel Lock considered that for a moment before returning to the subject at hand. "I see what you mean. These people are comfortable, but you're not going to find the Wartzberg Pearl here."

"There was only one place in the system to find the Wartzberg Pearl. That's what made it the Wartzberg Pearl. Say, you live here, do you go up to the axle much?"

"Never."

"Don't you have a storage locker up there?"

"No. They're too expensive. The Toolbox doesn't pay me all that well. They say that a lot of unexplainable income would compromise my cover as an unsuccessful freelance journalist."

"Considerate of them to think of that."

Channel Lock sneered. "Yeah. I told them that they could rectify the situation by changing my cover to a successful freelance journalist, but they said that in order to pull that off, I'd need to occasionally write something that gets printed somewhere. If I'm supposed to be a failure, my work can never show up anywhere, and it'll only reinforce the image."

"You know, they have a valid point."

"Yeah, just because they're right doesn't mean I have to like it."

Baird said, "You don't *have* to like anything."

"Yeah," Channel Lock agreed. "And for the most part, I don't."

7

Channel Lock's home doubled as the Toolbox's safe house on Newtah. It appeared to be a scale model of a suburban ranch house from the late twentieth century, but noticeably smaller because of the limited space in the habitat. In keeping with Channel Lock's cover as an unsuccessful journalist, the exterior was exactly as shabby as Newtah's homeowner regulations would allow, which meant immaculate, but with slightly faded paint and a lawn that was a few millimeters taller than the neighbors' lawns.

The living room and kitchen were furnished with second-hand furniture, almost no decorative artwork, and outdated appliances and fixtures.

Baird said, "Nice."

"Don't try to spare my feelings," Channel Lock said. "It's counterproductive. I specifically decorated this dump with an eye toward making it not-nice. My cover is a failure with no taste who can barely afford to keep the place up. If anything about this place looks nice, I've failed. My cover is a loser. While you're here, your cover is a friend of a loser, staying in his spare room."

Channel Lock led Baird down the hall to her quarters: a spare bedroom with its own dedicated bath. Empty walls surrounded a single bed, made up with clean but threadbare bedding, and a wooden end table with portions of the finish rubbed off.

"Feel free to freshen up, plot, scheme, do whatever it is you do. I'll be out in the living room when you're ready to spring into action."

Baird said, "Thanks, but I won't be needing any help."

"Maybe not, but you'll be having my help."

"Look, I understand that other agents probably need your assistance, but I don't. I work alone, or I would, hypothetically, if I did some sort of clandestine work, which, officially, I don't. If I did, theoretically, bring in someone on a project occasionally, they wouldn't be what you'd call a partner, or a teammate. They'd be people I'd be choosing to *use*, hired grunts I'd bring in to do the heavy lifting, and if I didn't like the way they handled themselves, I'd probably arrange it so that they took the fall for me. Trust me, you wouldn't want any part of that."

"Agent Saber Saw, you're supposed to be my guest, and I'm not supposed to have anything better to do. I'll blow my cover if I don't follow you around in a bored and desperate manner. Besides, you're the most interesting thing that's happened in this blighted space-tube for months."

"Fine," Baird said. "You can come with when I case the place and gather equipment."

He looked at her carry-on bag. "What equipment? Didn't you pack everything you need?"

Baird held up the small, mostly empty bag. "I didn't pack this; the Toolbox did, and all it has in it is a broken memory drive. Besides, I can't know what I need until I case the place, and traveling with burglar tools is a great way to end up under arrest."

"But didn't you smuggle some in?"

"I'm an alleged thief, not an alleged smuggler."

"Whatever. Like I said, I'll be in the living room."

Channel Lock left Baird alone in her room. She put down her bag and sat on the bed. The mattress gave way beneath her, but it did so more by bending than by compressing.

Baird put on her gARggles and pulled up a blank page, which hovered in space three feet in front of her. Using her neural interface, she wrote the word *Plan* across the top and drew a line down the middle of the page, creating two columns. At the top of one column, she typed *Liabilities*. At the top of the other, she put *Assets*.

Under Liabilities she wrote, *Must call Izzy. Explain why I disappeared over two years ago.*

That item had no real bearing on the job at hand, but she knew it was not going to be fun. She and Izzy were each other's only siblings, Baird being five years older. That meant that while they were growing up, he was just old enough to want to be involved in everything Baird did, but young enough that Baird didn't want him tagging along. Then, when their parents split, Baird chose to go with their father, leaving Izzy with their mother and lifelong abandonment issues. Their father's *laissez-faire* approach to parenting, meanwhile, gave Baird a fierce independent streak. It was a situation perfectly designed to torment the two of them for the rest of their days. She feared that her brother believing he had been ghosted for two and a half years could not have helped matters.

Baird grimaced, embarrassed that the first liability that occurred to her was completely unprofessional. She knew that a good thief can't get bogged down worrying about other people's emotions. If you start worrying about how other people feel, eventually you'll realize that other people don't enjoy getting robbed.

Next, under Liabilities, she wrote, *No time to make proper plan*. Her mouth curled into a faint smile. Not having time to plan was a real problem, but it was a solid, respectable, professional problem to have.

She followed that with, *Target is in the axle, the least accessible place on station*.

She nodded. She was getting somewhere.

She added, *Gotta tell Izzy about illness. That won't be fun either.*

Baird gritted her teeth and tried to put her brother out of her mind.

She wrote, *Axle only accessible by three secured lifts*.

She felt as if she was back on track. *For safety reasons, aircraft, flying toys, and even rope are prohibited on Newtah, which is adorable.*

The idea of being arrested for "rope smuggling" made Baird smile.

She added to the Liabilities list, *After I tell Izzy why I disappeared and that I'm ill, must tell him that I'm going to disappear again. For how long?*

A frustrated grunt escaped her lips.

She wrote, *Local contact wants to help. Will also list as asset, just to be nice.*

Baird paused for several seconds, before finally adding, *And, clearly, I'm not going to be able to concentrate until I've contacted Izzy.*

She spent another long moment thinking, used the restroom, thought some more, sat back down on the bed, bounced a couple of times to verify how forgiving the mattress wasn't, and resolved to keep her mind on business and get something accomplished.

She started writing her list of Assets.

The equipment I smuggled in. She added, under her breath, "Because of course I did."

She wrote, *I have an idea I think will work.*

Local contact who wants to help. (See also: Liabilities).

I can just call Izzy and get it over with.

Baird closed the document but kept her gARggles on.

She opened the Settings page for the glasses, navigated past three subpages, scrolled down, and selected the period that was one half of a space out of place.

There were nine messages from Izzy waiting in her queue.

In the first, his floating face looked happy and relaxed. The message was a simple *Hey, guess you're on a mission, call when you get back.* So were the second and third.

By the fourth message, he looked and sounded concerned. He grew more concerned through the fifth and sixth, and was verging on panic in the seventh.

In the eighth message, he said, "I hacked into the Toolbox's personnel files. I see that you're not listed as dead, missing, captured, or even *on assignment*. I have to assume that means that you haven't cut me off because you have to, but because you chose to. Please do me the courtesy of making *some* contact, even if it's to tell me that I'm right."

The ninth message, left a little over two months after the first, was terse. "Fine. If this is how you want it. You know, really, I'm angry at myself for not seeing this coming. I mean, you're famous for taking what you want and then getting away clean."

Baird bit her lip. She wanted to call him and explain, but what would that explanation actually be? She knew next to nothing about her illness, had no idea how long it would take to cure, couldn't say how long she'd be on Newtah, couldn't predict where she would be when they woke her up next, and had no idea when that might happen.

She thought it might give Izzy some solace to hear from her, but suspected that it was less cruel for him to just hear nothing than for her to call him specifically to tell him nothing.

Besides, learning that his only sister has a terminal illness would probably make Izzy react emotionally, which would be uncomfortable. Telling him about her illness might make Baird herself react emotionally, which was, of course, unacceptable.

She closed Izzy's messaging interface and pulled up a diagram of Newtah and a calculator.

8

Channel Lock leaned against the counter. "I don't get it."

Baird said, "I know. Don't worry about it."

"It'll all make sense in the end?" Channel Lock asked.

"Probably not."

The salesman reached down into the bed of the multi-material fabricator. "Ma'am, it's done," he said, grunting from mild exertion.

Baird smiled. "Great!"

Channel Lock said, "Fantastic." He didn't smile.

The salesman turned from the machine, holding a freshly manufactured child's bicycle. He placed it on the counter, holding the bike upright so that Baird and Channel Lock could examine it.

Baird inspected the finish on the frame. "Yeah, the baby blue floral pattern was really the way to go, don't you think?"

Channel Lock said, "It definitely looks like what you ordered."

"It does," Baird said, with a satisfied sigh. "It really does."

The salesman said, "I'm sure your little girl'll love it. You'll have to adjust the seat and handlebars for her. The seat has this lever here that you release. For the handlebars, you tighten this nut."

Baird said, "I'm sure we'll be fine. Thanks for your help."

The salesman thanked them and looked at Baird and Channel Lock expectantly. Baird turned and looked at Channel Lock expectantly. Channel Lock lifted the bicycle from the counter and tucked it under his left arm.

Baird walked to the store's entrance. A teenager on the outside opened the door and held it for Baird. "Please, allow me."

Baird said, "Thank you," as she stepped through the door.

"It's my pleasure." He continued holding the door as Channel Lock walked through carrying the bicycle.

Channel Lock said, "Thanks."

"You're certainly welcome," the teen said. "That's a mighty pretty bike you've got there, mister."

Channel Lock allowed his smile to slide into a light snarl for a moment, but if it did anything to spoil the teenager's mood, he wasn't letting on.

Baird and Channel Lock walked in silence along one of the wide, meandering footpaths that ran around Newtah's circumference. The curvature of the tube gave Baird the impression that she was constantly just about to start walking up a hill that seemed to retreat from her with each step.

Channel Lock asked, "What's the bike for?"

"For the job."

"Okay, fine. What else do you need?"

"Nothing. Our next stop is the elevator." She pointed toward a vertical shaft that ran from ground level all the way up to a round structure surrounding the axle.

"But . . . this can't be all of the equipment you need. You said there wasn't any extra gear in the carry-on. Just the memory drive."

"That's true."

"But you've got nothing. No cutters, no suction cups. You don't even have any rope."

"Just the clothes on my back." Baird looked up at the axle, rotating silently over a hundred meters above them. "Rope's strictly controlled on Newtah. Besides, if you want to try to climb a rope up there, be my guest. You ever tried it? Shinnying up just a few feet is enough to leave me exhausted the rest of the day."

"All right," Channel Lock said, "fair enough, but what about tools?"

Baird said, "Look, anything up there that I might want to use a tool on, that isn't placed somewhere too dangerous to get to, will be specifically hardened against tools, because the people who designed the security will have looked at whatever it is and said, *Huh, I bet someone could safely get to this spot and use a tool on that. I'd better harden it.*"

"So, what are you going to do?"

"I'll do what you have to do to get past any security system. Something they never thought of. Something weird, or dangerous, or preferably both."

Channel Lock said, "Something with a child's bicycle."

"That's right."

Channel Lock looked at the bicycle tucked under his arm. "Okay, what are you going to do with it?"

"With the bicycle?"

"Yeah."

Baird leaned in close to Channel Lock, and in a quiet voice, said, "I'm going to ride it."

Channel Lock said, "Yeah, great. They'll never expect that."

❮ ◆ ◆ ◆ ❯

Baird sat in the axle elevator lobby in an uncomfortable chair, hands folded on her lap, her attention locked on her gARggles.

Channel Lock sat beside her with one of his legs twitching up and down rhythmically.

Baird said, "Relax."

"I am relaxed."

"Then tell your right ankle to relax, because it's clearly stressing out."

Channel Lock stopped fidgeting his leg. They both sat, still and silent, until Channel Lock said, "I didn't expect them to take the bicycle away for examination."

Baird said, "I did. They're looking for burglary tools."

"Which you don't use."

"Of course not. Why would I?"

"I also didn't expect them to greet you by name. You've never been here before."

"Just because I've never been charged with a crime doesn't mean I'm not being punished. I'm willing to bet they were alerted when I arrived on the station. Anyone who guards anything valuable knows all about me and treats me with extreme suspicion, if they're doing their job."

"Must be a pain."

"Eh, I take it as a compliment most of the time, but it can be trying, especially when I'm doing something perfectly innocent, like trying to store a bicycle."

"Yeah," Channel Lock mumbled. "Right." He looked at Baird, still focusing on her gARggles. "What are you watching?"

"I'm reading."

"What are you reading?"

"*The Mars Journal of Materials Science.*"

"Why?"

"Because it's fascinating." She glanced at him over the frames of her gARggles, and saw his expression of extreme disinterest before continuing: "By combining different materials in clever ways, you can end up with a new material that has amazing properties."

Channel Lock shrugged. "I guess."

"This station wouldn't exist without materials science. Look at carbon nanotubes. They take what is essentially charcoal, arrange the molecules in a certain way to make thread, and weave that into a fabric. They impregnate the fabric with resin, pretty much synthetic tree sap, and in the end, they have something light and strong enough to make space elevators and orbiting colonies."

Channel Lock nodded his head.

Baird pulled down her gARggles and looked at him. "Think about this: Every substance has different properties. Some are strong. Some are light. Some reflect certain wavelengths of the visible spectrum while absorbing others. Many have properties that change slightly when a small voltage is applied. If you wove a fabric of the right materials in the exact right amounts, you might be able to make a material that confuses scanners and can be turned on and off. Or, if you took carbon nanotube thread and combined it with segments of polymers that expand or contract in reaction to a current, and spun that around a core of nanoscale processors with some sensors thrown in, you could have a piece of string that's a fully autonomous robot. You could power it with the same microscopic radiant energy power cells that my gARggles and your Brow use. If you chose the right chemical coatings, it'd even be self-cleaning, in theory."

Channel Lock looked at Baird, shaking his head. "You don't want to talk about your work, an actual interesting subject, but you'll go on and on about this far-fetched feek?"

Baird looked down, seemingly studying the sleeve of her sweater. "I just find it interesting. My father was a materials scientist. I used to help out in his lab. He worked at the same company for his entire adult life. He loved his work. His patents earned them who knows how many tera-sollars. All he got was forced to retire. He told me, 'Bran, you have a good brain. Use it for yourself. Don't ever rent it out to anyone, unless you're certain you're getting the better end of the deal.'"

Channel Lock said, "That's why you became a thief?"

Baird took off her gARggles. "Allegedly. Now pipe down. The guards are coming."

"What do you think of the local law enforcement?" Channel Lock muttered.

"They seem organized and disciplined. Two synonyms for predictable."

Four grim-faced guards approached, one of them carrying the bicycle. They wore crisp, spotless uniforms and matte black, military-spec Brows. Baird tucked her gARggles away and smiled up at them.

One guard walked in front of the others. His nametag said *Kubota*. He stood in front of Baird and Channel Lock. His words were addressed to Channel Lock, but he stared directly at Baird as he spoke.

"Mr. Humphreys. We scanned the bicycle, scanned it again, dismantled it, scanned the pieces, and reassembled it. We found no anomalies or any hint of any weapons, contraband, or explosive devices."

Channel Lock put on his biggest, but not most convincing fake smile. "Marvelous! I'm delighted to hear it!"

"But not surprised, Captain Kubota," Baird added.

Kubota made a noise that could have been a laugh, or a closed-mouth cough. "Mr. Humphreys, Miss Baird, as neither of you has ever been charged with a crime, it would legally be discriminatory for Newtah Station to deny you access to our municipally operated storage facility."

Channel Lock said, "That's wonderful."

Baird said, "Though, again, I'm not surprised, Captain Kubota."

Kubota kept his eyes on Baird. "Yes. So, if the two of you will follow us, we'll show you to your storage locker, Mr. Humphreys."

He continued staring at Baird as she and Channel Lock stood up. They walked as a group to the elevator door, Captain Kubota leading and the other three guards staying close enough to Baird to violate her personal space, while also staring at her constantly.

Captain Kubota kept his eyes locked on Baird as he spoke to Channel Lock. "Mr. Humphreys, you will note that the entrance to the elevator is under constant visual surveillance, in addition to having motion sensors, body heat sensors, identity chip scanners, detectors specially calibrated to see the electrical output of active-camo stealth suits, and weight-sensitive floor panels. The same goes for the other two elevators that lead to the axle. At the slightest sign of any attempt on the part of . . . unknown persons . . . to gain entrance to any of the elevators, the stunner-turrets hidden about the lobby will fire, rendering the intruder unconscious and helpless."

Channel Lock said, "Splendid."

Baird looked around the room as if she weren't listening.

The six of them squeezed into the elevator. They didn't need to. The elevator had ample room, even with the bicycle, but a recording directed them to stand against the elevator's rear wall. The guards positioned themselves next to Baird and continued staring at her.

Staring even more directly at Baird (if that were possible), Captain Kubota continued, "The interior and exterior of the elevator car are under constant surveillance, with all of the same sensors as the lobby. In this case, however, there are no stunner-turrets, as all we will have to do when—not if, *when* the intruder is detected—is stop the elevator and keep it suspended in mid-air until reinforcements arrive. Once we lower the lift, the doors will open. Then the intruder will be captured, processed, and, finally, at long last, charged."

Baird felt her weight decrease and her mass press into the wall behind her as they rose from the habitat floor, and their speed relative to the axle decreased. By the time they arrived at the top of the shaft, she felt as if she had barely any weight at all.

One of the guards intensified his glare at Baird. "You know, Captain, I was thinking. If we had a criminal on the station who we knew was guilty of crimes all over the system, but we couldn't prove it, it would be easy enough just to make up some proof. Or we could make up an entire crime he—or she—didn't even do, and build an airtight case he—or especially she—couldn't get out of."

Baird smiled at Kubota. "An interesting thought. Can you think of any reason why that wouldn't work, Captain?"

Kubota closed his eyes and growled, "Because a *hypothetical* criminal as successful as the one my colleague mentioned would be able to afford the finest legal representation and private investigators that sollars can buy. If one were to look into it, that person would find that the few times a law enforcement officer has attempted to frame this hypothetical criminal, the charges didn't stick, and in more than one case, the officers in question ended up facing criminal charges themselves."

The elevator car stopped ascending, then tilted to the side. For a disorienting second, Baird felt as if she would fall over sideways, but she found that instead of dropping to the ground, what little weight she had disappeared, leaving her, Channel Lock, the Captain, the guards, and the bicycle floating free in the elevator car.

They all drifted out of the car into a circular chamber—a cross-section of the axle. The flat wall behind them held the elevator door through which they'd just come, and a perfectly round opening above it, in the center of the wall. Handholds covered the wall ahead, all leading to a circular hole in its center.

They drifted single file through the hole in the center of the wall, propelling themselves with their hands, the guards working together to maneuver the unwieldy and utterly useless bicycle.

They formed a line, Captain Kubota leading, followed by Channel Lock, the guard carrying the bicycle, Baird, and, finally, the two guards who were watching Baird for even the slightest hint of anything that might be considered a false move.

They passed through a ring of panoramic windows. Baird could see all around her, but every direction she looked was straight down. She saw distant rooftops and tiny meandering paths full of tiny meandering people. The view was only marred by the four banks of lights a few meters beyond the windows, spinning with the station's outer habitat, providing simulated daylight for the people of Newtah.

Captain Kubota glanced back at Baird. "Those light rigs rotate constantly around the outside of the axle. They're part of the security system. Anyone who touches them, or shoots a line up to them somehow, will wish they hadn't when they finally wake up in the prison infirmary."

They came to a closed hatch. Kubota grasped two yellow handles, and they all waited while a scanner queried his ident chip. When the hatch opened, they moved on to the next chamber. The cylindrical hull of the axle stretched into the distance, lined with four rows of wedge-shaped, secure lockers that ran down the length of the room, leaving a plus-sign-shaped passage for people to travel through.

They floated past a seemingly endless procession of lockers, broken up by the occasional window set into the axle's outer wall. At last Captain Kubota stopped, used his arms to swim through the air into one of the lobes of the plus sign, and found the locker he was looking for.

Baird noted a lack of any sort of handle, keyhole, or window set into the locker door—just a clean expanse of metal and the uniform gap where it met the doorframe. Even the hinges were hidden inside the mechanism.

Channel Lock floated, motionless, grasping the yellow handles. The door popped open after a few seconds. Captain Kubota turned to face Baird.

"The lock is now set to open only if Mr. Humphreys is present and escorted by one of our security staff. You cannot open the door, Miss Baird. Ever."

Baird shrugged. "Makes sense. It's his locker."

Kubota and Channel Lock moved aside, making room for the guard holding the bicycle to float past and place it in the storage unit. When the guard floated back out, Captain Kubota asked, "Are you satisfied, Mr. Humphreys, that your property has been deposited in your locker?"

"Utterly satisfied." Channel Lock grinned and nodded his head furiously.

"Then I will seal the—"

"May I have a look?" Baird interrupted.

Kubota said, "It is not your locker, Miss Baird. I'm afraid I can't allow you any access without Mr. Humphreys' explicit approval."

Channel Lock said, "I'll be delighted to give my permission."

Kubota gritted his teeth. "Of course you would. Miss Baird, if you'd like to look in your associate's locker, I have no legal grounds to refuse."

Baird pulled herself forward and looked into the locker, a featureless metal box with two five-meter-square walls, two pie-shaped walls, a back wall that curved to conform to the shape of the axle, and a child's bicycle held to the wall by elastic straps, to keep it from drifting around and getting damaged. She also glanced at the door's recessed hinges and the locking mechanism before turning to Captain Kubota with a beatific grin. "Thank you."

Kubota swung the door closed.

Channel Lock asked, "I haven't noticed any sensors or stunner-turrets since we left the elevator. Why is that?"

Baird said, "I'd guess that since the elevators are the only means of getting up here, and are so well defended, they probably feel that they don't need as many security measures on the axle itself."

Captain Kubota said, "That would be an excellent guess, Miss Baird. Such a good guess that it almost seems like you've given this some thought."

"I have. It's important to me that the bicycle will be kept safe."

After a tense elevator ride back down, Channel Lock and Baird stepped out into the relatively open space of the habitat level. Channel Lock made a point of personally thanking and shaking hands with each member of the security detail, and Captain Kubota, twice.

Baird arched an eyebrow at Channel Lock. "Laid it on a little thick with the happy-local act, didn't you?"

"I was enjoying it."

"I thought pretending to be happy made you angry."

"Usually, but it was making the guards even angrier, which sort of turned it around for me. So, what happens now?"

"Now we go back to the house, and I'll take it from there."

"But you're about to get into the fun part."

"Watching you and that guard carry that bicycle around was fun."

"I'm being serious," Channel Lock said.

"So am I. I work alone."

"Don't be silly. That place is impregnable. You need all the help you can get."

"Because you figure it'd be easier to sneak two people in than one?"

"Might be. You never know."

Baird looked at Channel Lock. Then she looked up at the axle high above them. Next, she turned and looked back at the elevator station they'd just left. Captain Kubota and his men stood in the doorway, watching them leave. She was certain that there were cameras trained on them as well.

"Okay," she said. "What time does it get dark here?"

"They start dimming the lights at six. It's full dark by seven."

Baird said, "Okay. We'll leave the house separately, in case we're followed. Then we'll rendezvous right here at one in the morning."

Channel Lock said, "Done."

"I'm serious. This exact spot, at one o'clock sharp."

"I get it. I'll be here. And don't worry. I'll cover my tracks."

◀ ◆ ◆ ▶

When they got back to the safe house, Baird excused herself and retreated to her room.

She removed the large bronze pin from her sweater, pulled the thin tube from the front of the circle. and tapped it into her palm. Twelve tiny cigar-shaped pellets—razor sharp on both ends, made of a brittle pressed powder—came out. They were darts made entirely out of a hardened mixture of the very chemical they were meant to deliver, with just enough ferrous metal to react to the magnetic launch mechanism. The eight blue darts would cause instant unconsciousness. The remaining four red darts would cause loss of voluntary muscle control—very good for incapacitating a target you need to keep conscious, or for causing a distraction. The only problem was that the target wasn't left entirely harmless, as the scratch on Baird's ankle reminded her.

She wondered if her current dull headache was just fatigue, or the virus asserting itself.

She examined the tube, making sure the integrated coil was undamaged, then slid the darts back in. The four scrambler darts went in first, followed by the other eight, so the tranq darts would be shot first, unless she spun the barrel around to start with the scramblers. She needed to use the darts carefully; she had no way to know when she'd have a chance to get more made. She attached the tube to the top of the circle instead of the front, forming a shape vaguely reminiscent of a pistol. Sighting down its thin barrel to make sure it wasn't bent, she palmed the apparatus so that the barrel extended along the inside of her extended index finger.

She removed the square piece of metal that sat in the hole in the bronze pin's middle. She looked at it, making sure that the fine lines etched on its surface seemed undamaged. She didn't need it today, but it was good to know it was there. She put the square back in its original position within the larger piece.

Baird put the pin down and stood in the middle of the room, with her arms outstretched and her eyes closed, sending mental commands to her neural-prosthetic interface, using the circuits and neural pathways that an amputee would use to control a prosthetic limb. The interface was designed to control up to four prosthetic limbs and two sensory organs, and though it took a great deal of concentration, she used all of them at once.

As she stood motionless, a thread in the hem of her bulky black sweater slipped out of the knot that held it in place and fell downward, unraveling the sweater as it went. The black yarn formed a circle on the floor and continued twisting around the same loop as the sweater unraveled. Soon, there was no sweater, and Baird was wearing only her thin black pants and a long-sleeved black T-shirt. The entire sweater pooled in a neat circle of carbon-infused yarn around her feet, over two thousand yards of it, with one end reaching upward to hook over her index finger.

Baird remained still. Her cigarette pants loosened, growing baggier. Some patches of fabric expanded further, forming pockets down the sides of her legs. The wrists and neck of her shirt relaxed, changing shape into an integrated hood and gloves that flopped empty, waiting for her to stretch them over her hands and head.

She pulled her hand back. As the strand of enhanced carbon yarn lost contact with her finger, it lost its connection to her neural prosthetic interface and fell to the floor. She bent down, touched the end of the strand, and it again sprang to life, working its way up her hand before tying itself into a secure loop around her wrist.

Baird closed her eyes again to concentrate as the pile of yarn began to move. The far end of the strand bunched up and started rolling, completing multiple laps of the yarn loop, growing larger as it went. Soon, the loop was gone, and the strand of yarn that extended down from Baird's wrist ended in a spherical black mass the size of a baseball. It rolled around the room, dodging chair legs and making complex turns, leaving a strand along the ground that extended back to her like a trail in the sand.

The ball rolled under the bed, where it again rolled around in a rectangle the exact dimensions of the bed, leaving part of itself behind with each inch it covered. Soon the ball was gone, replaced by a rectangle of yarn that lifted upward, bending and contracting to create a net-like scaffold that lifted the entire bed a meter off the floor.

As the bed lifted, air rushed in beneath it, kicking up a visible cloud of dust bunnies.

Baird cringed. "I guess that's why they call it a safe house, not a *clean* house."

9

At a little before midnight, a thick strand of black yarn slid out the front door and along the crack between the lawn and the sidewalk, up a light pole to a high vantage point, with a fine view of the path in both directions.

The area seemed deserted.

The strand withdrew back into the house, and a few seconds later, Baird stepped out into the cool night air, wearing a color-coordinated ensemble made up of her black, long-sleeved shirt and pants, a black hood pulled over her head, black gloves on her hands, and a black messenger bag that appeared to be knitted from some sort of yarn slung over her shoulder.

She walked down the path in a surprisingly casual manner, for a grown woman dressed like a twelve-year-old boy going trick-or-treating as a ninja.

She saw sensor clusters on the light posts, hidden in the trees, and mounted unobtrusively to the picket fences, all of which she had expected. Cameras or human eyes could be fooled in countless ways, and thieves had had hundreds of years in which to attempt to count them. As such, some higher-end security systems had switched to these sensor clusters, which looked for movement, temperature variations, and electromagnetic fields. The sensors could not be fooled by any known means, since Baird had very carefully kept the means *she* had invented unknown, integrated only into the fabric of her shirt and pants.

As Baird passed, the sensors detected a minor fluctuation in the ambient temperature, indeterminate noise in the signal from their ultra-high-frequency sonar imagers, and confusing anomalies in their magnetic field maps, all of which they chalked up to some routine interference in the circuitry driving their sensor arrays.

One could think that if a technician were to study the night's logs, they might see that the same set of random anomalies seemed to trace a path at a comfortable walking pace from Baird's safe house to her destination, but if the system kept a record of every random error, it could potentially give customers the impression that the reputedly infallible sensors might be unreliable—an impression that Baird knew the company that made and sold those sensors did not want to create.

After a five-minute stroll, Baird finally reached her destination: an intersection where a specific footpath passed under the metro tracks, over four kilometers away from where Channel Lock was waiting to meet her. The rendezvous point she had set was the one place on Newtah where anybody would expect her to be, so it was the one place she made a point of not going.

She put on her gARggles, checking the map overlay to make sure she was in the right spot. She looked down the footpath ahead of her. The people who designed Newtah had made the paths that ran around the circumference of the cylinder veer from side to side, partly to make them seem more natural and organic, but also, she suspected, to try to prevent the very thing she was about to attempt.

Baird had determined that this path had the longest straight portion that ran exactly perpendicular to the station's axis. As she looked up the path, she could see that while it did bend and curve slightly, there was a narrow channel lined with various bushes, benches, and signs placed at the inside corners of the turns. This channel tracked straight up the curvature of the station and stretched almost an eighth of its overall circumference. She looked straight up at the axle, watching it spin inside its cage of stationary lighting scaffolds, all of which were dark at this hour.

She only knew the light scaffolds were there because she saw their silhouettes as the windows of the axle passed behind them.

The electrified lighting rigs were a danger to be sure, but it was the tree that really worried her. Just before the junction where the footpath passed beneath the metro track, and where the long semi-straight portion began, the path curved around the trunk of a forty-foot pine tree. Beyond the tree was another relatively unbent portion, almost as long. If not for the tree, she'd have twice the runway to work with. As it stood, she'd have to use half of it now, and half of it later.

Baird looked up at the tree and groaned. She positioned herself with her back to it, facing the straight-ish stretch of path.

She used her gARggles to double-check her math for the hundredth time. None of the numbers had changed. Baird had infinite trust in mathematics. She had less trust in herself to get all of the calculations right when working under heavy pressure and time constraints.

"Look at it this way," she muttered under her breath, psyching herself up. "You could be killed, but you're going to die in, like, a week anyway, so you're not really risking your whole life. Just seven days of it. Huh. I thought that sentence would make me feel better when I started it."

She crouched down, curling up into a ball in the center of the path.

Her sweater, which had transformed itself into a messenger bag, again unraveled, weaving itself into a small hammock that cradled Baird's back. From both sides of the hammock, tendrils of material reached out and wrapped around the far upper corners of two buildings on either side of the path, then looped back, reinforcing themselves and tying back into the hammock. The tendrils pulled tight, forming straight lines that rose surprisingly high over the curved path.

Baird checked the pockets of her now-baggy cargo pants, confirming that the fake memory drive was there. She inspected her bronze-pin dart-launcher, taking a moment to make sure that the barrel was attached, with the tranq darts ready to fire, not the neural scramblers. She stowed it in another pocket.

Baird leaned back into the hammock and looked at the lines extending into the distance. The angle looked shallow. She looked straight up, at the axle spinning above, and the tree looming just behind her, and wondered if it had grown since her scan was taken.

She accessed her neural-prosthetic interface. Her pants and shirt energized. The fabric's surface structure changed on a microscopic level, altering which wavelengths of light it reflected. Unlike any of the commercially available active-camo stealth suits, her shirt and pants didn't create a perfect image of her surroundings, causing her to blend in almost seamlessly. Hers only changed color to nearly match the background, and covered her with a random interference pattern that remained stationary while she moved, making her difficult and confusing to see, but not impossible. Also unlike commercially available stealth suits, hers was a custom, one-off, low-powered system that could not be detected by any commercially available countermeasures.

Her final modification to her clothing was to make them tighten around her legs, pelvis, and lower torso, in hopes of keeping enough blood in her brain to maintain consciousness.

She prepared her mind for the challenge ahead by concentrating on the mantra she often recited before executing a dangerous maneuver: "Feek," she whispered. "Feek! Feek, feek, feekfeekfeek."

Thus prepared, she sent the *go* command to the sweater. It contracted tightly, lifting Baird from the ground and accelerating her to a speed of almost ninety miles per hour.

She grunted, "Feeeeeeek."

The artificial gravity caused her to remain mere inches above the path at first, but as the gravity lessened, she gained altitude at an accelerating rate.

Despite the g-forces, Baird managed to stay alert. She straightened out into the most aerodynamic shape possible:

headfirst, with her legs straight and her arms pressed against her sides. Behind her, the sweater let go of the buildings and coiled itself into a loop that slung itself over her right shoulder.

She checked her position in her gARggles and verified that her math had worked out. She had accelerated to the exact horizontal speed of the Newtah station's rotation, but in the opposite direction. She was floating, almost motionless in space, while the station rotated around her. As such, the station's simulated gravity no longer applied to her. She drifted slowly toward the axle above, which appeared stationary. Below and on either side of her, the path and the buildings rushed by at a little bit under ninety miles per hour.

Unfortunately, she was a lot closer to the buildings than she was to the axle. Lampposts and foliage shot past, menacingly close, and would continue to do so until she had gained more altitude. Because of the upward trajectory of her launch, the surface below her seemed to pull away slowly.

She looked up along the curvature of the station and saw the pine tree she'd had her back against at launch, only a quarter of a lap ahead of her and coming fast. Even though she was looking at it from above, she could tell that as she followed the contour of the station, she would fly face-first into its upper branches.

Baird pointed forward with her right arm and closed her eyes, to concentrate on manipulating the articulated strand of yarn that usually made up her sweater. The slingshot had been a highly complex construction, but she'd had a few hours to plan it in advance and offload much of the grunt work to the strand's own onboard processors. She was going to have to deal with the tree on the fly, figuratively and literally.

The black strand of carbon-yarn darted forward from her arm and toward the tree. The strand was essentially weightless, just like Baird, and could put all of its energy into pushing itself forward without needing to hold itself up.

With her eyes closed, Baird saw everything through the sensor cluster built into the very tip of the strand. It overshot the pine tree substantially before it stopped, bent, and wrapped itself around the trunk a little over two meters down from the tree's topmost point. The strand's loose end shot upward and looped around the tree's tip, then pulled tight, bending the very top of the tree over at a ninety-degree angle.

The remainder of the strand pulled against the tree, giving Baird a little more speed to help counterbalance air resistance and the inertia she'd lost by sending the strand out ahead. She passed over the tree with so little room to spare that she felt pine needles graze her legs.

The strand released the tree, which snapped back into shape with a rustling *twang* and a cloud of loose pine needles. As the strand re-gathered itself into a neat bundle on her shoulder, Baird rotated in the air, turning her back on the habitat level, which would only continue drifting farther away, and faced the axle, which was surrounded by its rotating lighting gantries, the slightest touch of which would lead to her capture, injury, and possibly death.

10

Soon, the axle was only forty meters away. Baird scanned its surface, looking for pipes, junction boxes, valves, anything that the strand could get a good grasp on, but the distance and the dark made it difficult to see the axle's surface features and the lighting gantries, which were her primary obstacle. Her gARggles helped, displaying a glowing overlay of the axle's electrical wiring gleaned from publicly available sources and the electromagnetic radiation picked up by the sensors embedded in the strand.

The same circular air currents that minimized the constant breeze on the habitat level provided Baird with a tailwind up here, closer to the axle, just as she'd expected, helping her maintain her relative air speed. Her trip to the axle was not as direct as it would have been without air resistance, but thanks to the extra reach the strand allowed her, close enough was good enough.

What felt like an eternity of drifting and searching passed before she finally found what she was looking for: a sturdy-looking pipe about three inches around, emerging from the axle's outer skin, bending to run alongside the axle past one of its many expansion joints.

The strand wove itself into a thick strap, wrapped one end of itself around Baird's waist, and extended the other end toward the axle, stopping just shy of the darkened rotating lighting gantries.

Baird figured there was about a five-second gap between the constantly moving gantries where the strand would have access to the axle. She watched several of these openings pass, making sure she had the timing down, as she drew ever closer to the axle.

Finally, she made her move.

As a gantry moved out of the way, the strand's leading edge shot forward and grasped the pipe firmly, wrapping around it several times in a fraction of a second. It contracted as it had on ground level, pulling Baird toward the axle with great force.

She passed through the gap in the gantries with room to spare, but she had little space to slow down. The strand pooled on the surface of the axle in a puffy lump that Baird hoped would cushion her impact. Curled up into a ball, she hit the pillow on her side, then floated, dazed and gasping, trying to get the air back into her lungs. She drifted for a moment, breathing heavily and visualizing other cushion structures the strand could form that might be more effective, until she sensed movement behind her, very close.

She blurted, "Feeking feek," and pulled the strand tight again, jerking herself toward the wall just before she would have been hit in the back by one of the rotating lighting gantries. She hit the wall slightly less hard this time, but still had to cough and sputter as she cursed her own stupidity.

She grasped the pipe, allowing the strand to let go and revert back to a thick loop floating in the air beside her. Through her gARggles she could see a glowing green arrow floating in space several hundred meters down the axle. This, according to the Toolbox's intelligence, was where the genetic database was kept. She remained motionless, concentrating, while the strand tightened one end of itself around her wrist and sent the other end darting forward to the marker. Seeing, hearing, and feeling through the sensors embedded in the strand's end, she searched for something to grab onto. She found a junction box connecting two conduits. The strand anchored itself, then contracted, pulling her forward.

She grabbed the junction box, stopping herself near one of the three elevator shafts that ran from the habitat level up to the axle. It rotated around the axle, sweeping through space like an immense, slow-moving fan blade. She looked down to the base of the elevator and saw Channel Lock, standing under a streetlight.

She moved her head to follow Channel Lock's path as he rotated over her with the rest of the station. He stood there, looking impatient, and many guards, all they could spare, watched his every move while hiding behind various objects that did nothing to block Baird's view from her vantage point high above.

Baird worked her way, hand over hand, to a window.

Inside, she could see a computer lab lit only by the small lights of the machines and by the distant streetlights from the habitat level that filtered in.

She leaned in close, examining the seam where the window sealed to the wall. She found an emergency latch system, for ventilation or escape in the event of an emergency, but there was no external hardware, and the seal was airtight. She would have to open it the hard way.

Through her gARggles, she followed the glowing trail of an electrical conduit that led from the window control housing to a junction box. She pulled at the lid of the junction box, creating a gap only a few millimeters wide. The end of the strand threaded through the gap. She hung there motionless for nearly a minute, clinging to the side of the axle while the lighting gantries and the habitat level swirled around her. More and more of the strand passed into the junction box.

The window latches released with a *click*. The strand removed itself from the conduit much more quickly than it had gone in.

She looked into the lab but paused before entering. She saw a sensor cluster on the far wall, which she had expected. Her sensor-spoofing clothes would handle it.

She pulled herself through the window, keeping her back to the sensors.

Scanning the room, her gARggles highlighted a specific shelf that otherwise would have been lost in the racks of identical-looking electronics. She floated toward it. Just as she'd been told in her briefing, she saw five identical memory drives: glowing slabs of cloudy glass strapped down in a neat row, each connected to the machine below it by a single, gossamer-thin cable. The light from the drives pulsated as lasers read and wrote data, encoded into the very molecular structure of the glass. That data, she hoped, would lead to her cure.

Baird grasped the second drive from the left, because for some reason it felt the most random. She disconnected the drive from its wire. The light went out instantly. She reached into her pocket, retrieved the replacement drive, and plugged it in. Light flashed within the drive, flickered, and went out again.

Just another failed drive. They would detect it, replace it, and destroy it—but they would never give it a second thought. That's why there were five, after all, so they wouldn't have to sweat a random hardware failure, or four.

She put the stolen drive in one of her cargo pockets and left, resealing the window behind her.

She looked down the length of the axle, back the way she'd come. Far off in the distance, she saw the second glowing arrow, this one red. It marked the location of Channel Lock's storage locker.

The strand darted out along the axle, stretching almost its entire two-thousand-meter length. After some searching around for an anchor point, it contracted, pulling her forward.

11

The end of the strand curled over the corner of the window, aiming its tiny camera into the axle.

The first thing Baird saw was a guard floating silently between the storage lockers, searching the area with exactly the level of intensity one would expect from a man who is absolutely certain that he will find nothing. He pulled himself along, drifting between handholds at a leisurely pace, and turned his head to glance out a window as he passed by. Then he grabbed the nearest handhold and pulled himself to an abrupt stop. He pushed himself back and looked out the window again.

Baird withdrew the strand and clung to the side of the axle, out of the guard's field of vision. She watched the sporadic lights of the darkened habitat ring rotate past while she waited. After what seemed like the right amount of time for a momentarily wary guard to regain his complacency, she sent the strand back over for a look.

The guard was gone.

She closed her eyes as the strand wormed its way through a conduit to the window's emergency latch mechanism.

The window unlatched with a surprisingly loud click. She pulled it open and poked her head through. In the distance, the guard was floating motionless in the middle of the plus-sign-shaped passage, his head upright, as if alert and listening for anything out of place. Baird could only assume that he had heard the window. She readied her dart launcher and held her breath until the guard shrugged and drifted off into the distance.

Baird found Channel Lock's storage unit. Her hood shielded the reader from sensing her ident-chip while the strand worked its way into the minuscule gap between the door and the frame at a point near where she knew the latching mechanism to be, thanks to her brief inspection earlier. Only seconds later, the door unlocked.

She pulled the bicycle out, taking care not to bang any part of it against the door, the doorframe, or the walls once it was out of the locker. She looked down the corridor again to make sure the guard was still oblivious, and then closed the locker door.

She drifted out the window and pushed it closed behind her, not caring now if the guard heard her or not, as she had left nothing in the storage bay out of place for him to find. She clung to the exterior of the axle with one hand and held the bicycle in the other as the strand ventured along the axle toward her designated point of departure, the very spot where she had first made contact.

As the strand pulled tight and propelled her forward, Baird held the bicycle out in front of her, grasping the frame's crossbar in one hand and the handlebars in the other. As her grip tightened, the handlebars moved, twisting in their mounting bracket. The guy who printed it out had said it would need to be adjusted and tightened. The guards tearing it apart and putting it back together again couldn't have helped matters.

Baird noted that she did not have a wrench.

She grabbed at a piece of exposed pipe in order to stop at her departure point, and she spent a long time just floating there, looking down at the path, buildings, and trees below, where she had launched herself up in the first place, contemplating the scariest part of the plan.

Baird took a long look at the bicycle. She had chosen a child's bike for multiple reasons. Its smaller size made it easier to carry through doors and windows; it seemed utterly harmless; and it was available in a fun, floral color scheme. Baird saw little point in being a criminal if she couldn't have fun doing it. Of course, now that she was about to use it for its intended purpose, the tiny size and bright paint seemed less advantageous.

She made the strand wrap around the handlebar adjustment nut, pull tight, and twist, but little of the strand was able to grip the sides of the nut, so it gained scant traction and exerted even less force. She ended up pinching the nut between her thumb and index finger and torquing on it as hard as she could, figuring that would have to be good enough.

She looked for anything that even resembled an adjustable nut on the bicycle, and twisted all of them as hard as she could without injuring her fingers.

Then Baird pushed on the handlebars. They seemed solid. She suspected that if she shoved on them with all of her might, they'd probably move, so she didn't do that. Even if the handlebars were completely loose in their mountings, it wouldn't have changed anything. Her choices were to go through with the plan or wait until daybreak and get caught.

She planted her feet on either side of the conduit and squatted there, holding herself to the axle's outer skin with her left arm, but ready to push herself away with her legs at any moment. She made the strand wrap itself around her waist. She didn't want it trailing out behind her—not yet, anyway. She held the bicycle out between the ground and herself with her right arm.

Baird looked toward the ground, a direction that felt, for the moment, like up. She knew that would change all too soon.

Again, she took a quick look at the math in her gARggles before she did what she knew she had to do, whether the math worked out or not. Allowing for the thickness of the axle, it was roughly 150 meters to the habitat, which took roughly twenty-five seconds per revolution. So, if she could launch herself at the right moment at roughly one meter per second, the habitat ring would revolve six times before she would touch down on her designated landing spot—she hoped not too roughly.

As the strand formed into a tightly coiled net around her ankles, Baird watched the lighting gantries sweep past. The gap between them seemed perilously small, considering that touching one would mean incapacitation and, in this case, probably death, after drifting weightless and then impacting the fast-moving pavement. She gauged the distance between herself and the gantries and between the gantries themselves, estimated her launch speed, went over the math in her head again, and cursed herself for stalling. Then, when the tree that had nearly thwarted her on the trip up to the axle was where she wanted it in its rotation, and her gut said the time was right, the strand-net expanded upward like a spring, launching Baird at a speed of one meter per second.

For a moment she flew stretched out in a straight line, pushing the bicycle in front of her like a plow, then she pulled herself up into a ball, clinging to the bicycle. The bike sailed through the gap behind one gantry. She had just time enough to think that she should have launched sooner before the next gantry came within centimeters of hitting her back.

She was past the spinning light rigs of death. Now all she had to worry about was the ground, which was going by at just under ninety miles per hour while she fell toward it at a meter a second.

Baird passed into Newtah's upper atmosphere. She felt a powerful wind pressing against her back, and she stayed tucked into a cannonball, holding the bicycle tight against her shins. She looked down between her feet and the bike frame at the path below, which was getting closer and seemingly moving by faster with every second. While her carefully moderated speed made the math easy, it also now left her with two and a half minutes to contemplate the consequences of her math being wrong, with absolutely nothing she could do about it.

She knew she wasn't falling, just drifting toward what looked like the ground. But no matter how much her brain explained that she was actually weightless, and the habitat ring wasn't really the ground, the pit of her stomach just insisted that none of that would make any difference to the trauma surgeon. But when she compared it to helplessly succumbing to an illness, dying of terminal road rash in a spectacular crime gone wrong sounded pretty good. A blaze of glory—or in this case, a long, sticky streak of glory.

Halfway down she passed from the upper atmosphere into the lower, where the wind abruptly shifted, hitting her from the front instead of the back. Baird faced into the rotation of the habitat level, making it feel as if the ground was stationary and she was flying forward. She uncurled her body and spread out her limbs to create as much resistance as she could.

The bicycle jutted out into the open air beside her as Baird grasped it firmly by the frame's top tube. The strand began threading itself around her limbs, creating a sort of webbing between her arms and legs that caught the wind and acted as a sail, accelerating her backward, which felt as if she were slowing in relation to what seemed like the ground.

Baird remained perfectly upright, spread-eagled, holding a bicycle, as the tip of the tree she'd nearly hit on the trip up to the axle passed between her ankles.

She was glad that almost everyone on this station went to bed at 9:00 p.m., because this had to be the most spectacularly conspicuous form of sneaking ever devised.

The strand dismantled the webbing from her limbs, secured itself around her torso in two thick straps, and trailed out behind her like a streamer, slowing her further and keeping her oriented properly, pointed toward the oncoming path.

She moved the bicycle into position. Once her feet were on the pedals, it felt unnervingly small and fragile. The path was only ten meters away now, moving past at a much faster speed than she would have liked.

Her preferred landing spot looked to be several meters farther away than where she'd hoped. Clearly, air resistance had more of an effect than she'd expected. Ahead, she saw a waist-height shrub that she had hoped to land just beyond, rather than on top of, as she currently seemed destined to do.

Baird pulled up on the handlebars and pushed forward on the pedals, moving the bicycle out in front of her body. She then twisted the bike so that it was horizontal to the ground as she barely cleared the shrub.

She got the bike back beneath her just in time for the rear wheel to touch down, followed by the front wheel. A small measure of her weight returned to her limbs. The strand reformed into windbreaks and slowed her speed relative to the habitat ring to around forty miles an hour. That meant that she was rotating at a little under half the speed of the habitat ring, and thanks to the perversity of the math governing angular momentum, she seemed to weigh just slightly over one quarter of her usual weight.

Her mass rebounded. She bounced over a meter into the air, covering tens of meters before the bike touched down again, losing more speed. It bounced less far this time but still went a substantial distance. The path wavered from side to side beneath her. On the third landing, Baird applied the brakes, ineffectively, as she was also trying to remain upright after the handlebars gave way and flopped forward over the front wheel. She launched into the air again and crashed into the other side of the pine tree she'd had her back against when she started.

The tree instantly killed what felt to her like forward momentum. In reality, it accelerated her speed to that of the habitat ring, giving her back her full body weight just in time for her to fall through the lower branches of the tree and hit the ground.

She crawled out from under the tree and sat on the path, catching her breath. The strand pulled the slightly bent bicycle out of the tree. It left the bike lying on the ground and knitted itself back into a sweater around Baird's arms and torso while she looked up at the axle.

12

Baird left the bicycle in Channel Lock's living room. He wasn't home yet and wouldn't be until he gave up on Baird meeting him and left. In the meantime, he was still on the job, distracting the guards.

She pulled the memory drive out of her pocket and tossed it on the bed as she walked past her room on her way to Channel Lock's bathroom. She searched until she found a small packet of pain relievers, which she swallowed without water. She stretched her arms, wincing a bit, then rubbed her temples.

She returned to her bedroom, sat on the edge of the bed, dug her gARggles out of her pocket, and put them on. After some navigating and a brief wait for a connection, she was looking at a live image of Screw Jack's face.

"Saber Saw," he said. "Good to hear from you. Isn't it awfully late there?"

Baird said, "No, it's gone around the horn to being awfully early, but the job's done. I've got the drive."

"Very good, very good indeed! Will you tell me how you did it?"

"Of course not."

"Where was Channel Lock while you did it?"

"Somewhere else."

"Where is he now?"

"Same place."

Screw Jack's smile didn't fade. "The legend of Brangelina Baird continues. *The woman that nobody can prove does amazing things.* With any luck, the information you procured will help the doctors come up with a cure for your condition. The next step is to get you off Newtah and back on ice as soon as possible so that your illness will stop progressing. We'll book you a ticket on the next flight out, and set it up with a connection. You'll just let the airline put you in bio-stasis like any other passenger, but our agents will take possession of you at the connection while they're transferring you to a different shuttle. In the meantime, leave the drive with Channel Lock. He'll send it to us separately. Anything you carry out with you through the spaceport will be subject to extra scrutiny."

"Story of my life."

"Exactly. Now let's get you in stasis before we waste any more of your limited time."

Baird said, "Before you go, I want to have a word with you about that. I've been thinking a lot about my illness and the fact that I have to stay in stasis while you all try to cure me."

"I'm sure you have," Screw Jack said.

"You said before that you thought I'd like taking an active role in finding my own cure. You were right, but just telling me that you need a thing and ordering me to steal it for you isn't enough. That's not taking an active role. That's doing what I'm told, and it's not very satisfying."

"Are you saying you'd rather just stay asleep until we have a cure?"

"No, I'm just saying that if you decide to use me again, I'll expect more information. More detail. I know something about science. I don't want to be in the dark."

Screw Jack said, "That's reasonable. Just understand that detailed explanations will take time, and the longer you're awake, the further your disease will progress. By the way, any symptoms yet?"

Baird said, "A bad headache, but that might be because a tree ran into me."

"You mean you ran into a tree?"

"No. It was moving at the time. I was almost stationary, so it ran into me."

Screw Jack frowned. "I don't remember confusion being one of the symptoms."

"It isn't. I'm not confused, and I don't want to be. That's why I want information."

"I promise, the next time we speak, you will either be cured or I will have an all-caps good reason why you're not. Either way, you'll get all of the information I have. And, given your situation, if once you're cured you choose to walk away from the Toolbox, you'll have my full support and protection. Okay?"

Baird said, "It's not okay, but it'll have to do."

13

Baird inhaled. The cold air rushing in made her nasal passages hurt. She groaned and opened her eyes to see an unbroken field of beige. She felt an intense pinpoint of warmth in her right forearm, which started to spread out to her fingers and up into her shoulder.

She took a moment to search her memory while the warm sensation filled her body, escalated, and grew uncomfortable. The last thing she remembered was Channel Lock grumbling the entire way to the Newtah Spaceport and the smug looks on the security personnel's faces as she went into spaceline stasis to leave, without having stolen anything—*that they knew of.*

She was clearly still in her pod, but that wasn't necessarily bad news. The Toolbox wouldn't have moved her to a different pod if they didn't need to. If things had gone well, the door would open, and Screw Jack and some scientists would be there with a syringe full of antidote and a bottle of something strong and celebratory. If things had gone poorly, she'd hear a spaceline arrival announcement, and then do some cursing.

A soft, tasteful chime sounded, followed by the voice of a man who was not afraid of public speaking but who had said what he was saying so many times that the words had lost all meaning.

"Attention, Spiral Arm Spacelines passengers."

"Feek," Baird muttered. "Feek, feek, feek!"

"Our voyage is coming to a close," the attendant continued.

"We are on our final approach to EMCOT. Local gravity is .38 g; please adjust your grav-meds accordingly, and allow me to be the first to welcome you to Mars."

"Mars. That's good," Baird muttered. "Maybe I'll have time to hit a wine tasting."

She activated her gARggles, which she had made a point of leaving on her eyes as she went into stasis on Newtah. She was not surprised to see that there was a briefing waiting for her to connect. She hated the idea of being given another assignment she couldn't refuse, but at least she'd get to hear what Screw Jack had to say for himself.

She initiated the briefing. After a moment, a face appeared.

"Who the hell are you?" Baird asked.

The face of a stunningly beautiful older woman with dark red hair and bright red lipstick said, "Hello, Saber Saw. I'm Vise Grip, your handler."

"Screw Jack is my handler."

"Screw Jack *was* your handler. Now I'm your handler."

Baird said, "I'll only work with Screw Jack."

"Then you won't work," Vise Grip said. "Screw Jack is not available."

"Where is he?"

"He took your situation hard. Said he felt personally responsible, lost all detachment. The doctors weren't finding a cure fast enough, so he went out on his own looking for answers. He tried to find the lab where the virus was developed. He ended up getting infected himself. He's been in stasis for almost a year."

Baird digested the information, then let out a long breath. "That's horrible. I can't help but feel responsible."

"Try to help it if you can. If Screw Jack's example has anything to teach us, it's that no good comes of feeling responsible for other people's mistakes. You got yourself infected with an engineered virus, which was your mistake. He felt responsible, which was his first mistake. He went out sniffing around, another mistake. And he got himself infected, yet another mistake. He took responsibility for one of your mistakes, and it led him to make several of his own."

Baird said, "I . . . wouldn't have thought to look at it that way."

Vise Grip said, "Another mistake. You should look at it that way because that's the way it is. I can't make you see the light, but I can promise you that I will neither feel, nor accept, any responsibility for whatever mistakes you make."

"Do you think maybe telling me that was a mistake?"

"No. It was an honest statement about the reality of the situation. I'm not responsible for how you choose to take it. I think it would behoove us to move on to business. Your time is much shorter than mine is, I assure you."

"I agree. It's not like I'm enjoying this conversation anyway. How long have I been out?"

"Since Newtah? A year, seven months, and five days."

"That's not good news. How's progress on the cure?"

"Stalled. That's why you're awake."

"That's not good news either. But are they any closer to the cure?"

"Who knows? And what does it matter? You're spending all of the time either unconscious or awake and helping, so as far as you're concerned, there are only two states: they either have the cure, or they don't. Right now, they don't, but if you do the job we woke you up for, maybe next time they will."

"It would be nice to know how close they are."

Vise Grip said, "There are a lot of things that would be nice to know, but that doesn't mean you'll ever know them. Frankly, Saber Saw, if you wanted to know things, getting involved in covert operations was a terrible idea."

"Isn't one of the Toolbox's main functions to gather intelligence?"

"Yes, to gather it. Not to disseminate it, certainly not to our operatives. I don't know how Screw Jack worked, but I want you to know as little as possible. If I don't tell you anything useful, you can't tell anyone else anything useful when you get captured."

"Don't you mean *if* I get captured?"

"There are only two ways it can end for an operative, Saber Saw. Death or capture."

"Or I could quit."

"Under normal circumstances, you could try. We might even let you think you succeeded, but if the General Contractor decided we needed you, we'd reactivate you."

"And if I refused to be reactivated?"

"Then we're back to death or capture, only you'd be captured by us. You're not truly out until we decide you're out. When that happens, we hold a big ceremony. It's called a funeral. That's under normal circumstances. In your case, you're dying, and we're the only ones trying to keep that from happening. If you quit, we only need to wait a week and then start trolling the morgues. Now, I'd like to get on with the briefing, if you're ready to stop wasting time."

"Yeah, let's get to it."

"Your enthusiasm is heartening. As you know by now, you're about to arrive at EMCOT, the capitol of the Martian colonies. Your target, however, is in New Bordeaux. Owing to its position as the heart of the extra-terrestrial wine country, New Bordeaux is a destination for the most well-heeled elements of our society. As such, enterprises that cater to the wealthy are themselves drawn there, not because its environment is ideal, but because that's where their customer base is."

"Yes, I know that. Why are you telling me this?"

"To explain why there is a high-profile auction of extremely rare curiosities and *objets d'art* scheduled to take place tomorrow in what is essentially a rocky hole deep in the cold stone heart of that arid dirt clod."

"I take it you don't vacation there."

"The target is an old paper notebook. It belonged to a great scientist, a man named Richard Feynman. The notebook has been in the hands of private collectors since his death, all the way back in the 1980s. Its contents have never been properly scanned and studied. There are only hints as to what's inside, but there are accounts from people who have thumbed through its pages that lead us to believe that it contains information pertinent to your plight."

"This Feynman, he was some sort of medical researcher?" Baird asked.

"He was a physicist."

"That's not what I wanted to hear."

Vise Grip said, "It seems atomic decay plays some part in your illness."

"That's not what I wanted to hear either."

"I expect not."

"But still, keep going. How is atomic decay involved?"

"Somehow. You don't need to know the inner workings of the engineered virus coursing through your veins to figure out how to steal a notebook, just as I don't need to know why the researchers need the notebook in order to tell you to steal it."

"I had a deal with Screw Jack that I'd get detailed information about my illness the next time he woke me."

"He hasn't woken you; I have, and I made no such deal. I can have you refrozen if you like, and you can wait for him to wake you, but since he has the same illness as you, and that illness likely won't get cured without the notebook, that might be a very long wait."

"Okay," Baird said, "So you want me to get in, get my hands on the notebook, copy it, and get out."

Vise Grip said, "Negative. Your mission is to retrieve the actual notebook, not a copy."

"Why? It's the information inside they want. I can get that, and the auction house would never know I'd copied. It. Why bother to take the physical notebook?"

Vise Grip said nothing.

Baird said, "You plan to sell it, don't you?"

"We wouldn't wake you just to have you help us gain revenue," Vise Grip said. "But this is a chance to help find your cure *and* help the cause, so to speak. You can't blame us for wanting to take advantage of this opportunity."

Baird smiled mirthlessly. "You underestimate my ability to blame."

◄ ◆ ◆ ◆ ►

Baird stalked out of the shuttle into the spaceport. The gravity on Mars was a little over a third that of Earth, so she bounced sluggishly through the concourse. She silently chuckled at some of her fellow travelers. You could always tell the ones who had never been to a colony with light gravity because they badly overpowered their first few steps and ended up bouncing off the ceiling.

She saw a small shop set into the wall ahead and grabbed the handrail next to the entrance. She swung around in a neat ninety-degree turn and pushed herself to a stop with the railing built into the counter.

She smiled at the cashier. "Grav-meds, please."

The cashier asked, "Inerti All? Massynol? Waste-Away?"

"Waste-Away."

She found an out-of-the-way corner and pulled out the med-dispenser she'd bought: a small plastic box, much longer than it was wide or deep. The label read: *Waste-Away. The System's first choice for preventing the loss of muscle tone and bone density that comes with low-gravity environments. Now with 80 percent fewer bone spurs!*

She swiped her thumb along the side. The label faded away, replaced with instructions she didn't read. She swiped her thumb again. The instructions faded, replaced by a list of the more popular colonies and a field where she could manually enter the specific gravity of whatever rock she happened to be standing on or hovering over. She chose "Mars." A squared-off rectangle of material slowly emerged from the end of the dispenser. When the proper amount of Waste-Away had been dispensed, a cutting mechanism severed it from the rest of the medicine loaf. Baird put the little block of material in her mouth. She couldn't see a drinking fountain. She had considered buying water at the shop; the packaged stuff tasted better than the recycled and reclaimed water that came out of the taps, but bottled water was already expensive on Mars. The prices at the Mars spaceport were even more so, expensive enough that swallowing a large pill without water was preferable. She took the chunk of Waste-Away dry, and got on with her life.

Baird made her way to the transportation center. Her gARggles pointed out her contact: a slim, dignified man in a slim, dignified black suit whose code name was listed as Stud Finder.

Baird walked up and said, "You poor man."

The man nodded. "You must be Miss Baird. My name is Zargarian. I'm here to escort you to your hotel."

He led her away, bounding gracefully toward the monorail boarding platform. The signs promised service to New Bordeaux and several other places, none of which were any of Baird's concern.

They stood on the loading platform, packed shoulder to shoulder with strangers. When the monorail arrived, the throng of travelers flowed through the doors like water through a funnel. Baird and Stud Finder stood crammed in the monorail car with their fellow passengers.

The monorail pulled away from the station and emerged from the interior of the Mars spaceport out into the Martian landscape: bare hills in the distance, barren flatlands in the foreground, and a thin atmosphere above.

Stud Finder sighed. "The unspoiled plains of Mars."

Baird saw an endless sea of dirt. Not sand or soil—sand has an oddly clean, sterile feel, and soil is useful. No, this was *dirt*. Untouched areas of the Earth, or Venus, or even Titan look unspoiled, as if no human had ever come around to mess them up. Untouched areas of Mars look as if no human had ever come around to tidy them up. Even the sky was a dingy brown color, as if the planet was staining it, like a tea bag in clean water.

The monorail's first stop was Alexandria. "The capital, and the largest city on Mars," Stud Finder said. "Popularly known as EMCOT, a combination of the initials of the billionaire who founded the original settlement, and the name of the theoretical utopian city it was designed after."

A sprawling plane of small, low-slung buildings surrounded the city center, where several tall, angular towers rose from the Martian landscape. One might be tempted to call them separate buildings, but as Baird followed them down to their base, it was obvious that they all sprouted out of the roof of one broad, flat superstructure. The city had been white at some point in its past, but now it was a light reddish brown, owing to the fine coating of Martian dirt that settled on any object left on the planet's surface for more than a minute.

The monorail slowed as it entered the primary building. Stud Finder pointed out various points of interest as they passed over pedestrian thoroughfares, past shops and offices, through an indoor park, and finally into the transportation hub at the center of town.

Baird and Stud Finder waited in silence as some passengers got off the monorail and others got on. Soon enough they were underway, emerging again into the outside world.

Speeding through the thin air, the monorail only took a half-hour to reach New Bordeaux. On the surface, Baird saw nothing but a vast expanse of solar panels and no other signs of a settlement.

The monorail plunged through an opening into the side of a hill and came to a stop at the unloading platform at New Bordeaux station. It was built, like New Bordeaux itself, inside a lava tube—a naturally occurring series of tunnels stretching deep below the surface, formed by the activities of a long-dormant volcano.

Stud Finder led Baird from the monorail station to the elevator. They waited in line for a short time before boarding a car. Though the line snaked on behind them, nobody else got into the elevator, as there was no reason to believe that their car would go to the same place, or even in the same direction that the next people in line wanted to go.

One wall of the elevator car was covered with an interactive map of the New Bordeaux settlement, a baffling three-dimensional maze of spiraling lava tubes, bulbous chambers the size of sports stadiums, and strictly regimented grids of human-made tunnels. The whole thing looked like an upside-down image of a twisted, stunted tree, suspended in a scaffold to keep it from falling over.

Stud Finder ran a finger along the image, spinning it and zooming in on a large void two-thirds of the way down the structure. He poked at a specific junction, selecting it as their destination. The view zoomed back out, showing their starting point at the surface. A line traced the most efficient path to the junction he chose.

The elevator car dropped gently, but even at .38 gravity, it was still enough to put Baird's stomach in her throat. She gave herself a moment to adjust, but by the time she had, the elevator stopped moving downward and curved to the right, following the complex curves of the lava tubes. Baird gripped the handrails and looked expectantly at Stud Finder, who hadn't said a word since the car had started moving.

He pulled out a small black box. A probe extended from his Brow, an understated model that matched his natural hair color and was barely noticeable. He waved the box around, staring into the middle distance, before he finally said, "There are no listening devices. We can talk."

Baird said, "Good. So, your code name is Stud Finder?"

"Feel free to call me Zargarian."

"I will."

"I didn't pick Stud Finder. It was assigned to me."

"That was some really bad luck."

"I know," Zargarian said.

"I mean, even if the name was apt, which would be absolutely none of my business either way, the name itself is still pretty insulting, Mr. Zargarian."

"Believe me, I'm aware of that. Aren't you curious where we're going?"

"I assume we're going to the safe house."

"We are. I think you'll be pleasantly surprised when you see it. It's much nicer than most. The local safe house is a bed and breakfast. My cover is that I run the B&B."

Baird said, "More bad luck."

Zargarian said, "Your cover is that you're a criminal. A lot of people would say *that's* bad luck. Being an innkeeper is good, solid, honest work in a vital and fascinating field."

Baird asked, "Were you an innkeeper before they recruited you?"

"No, an assassin. But the B&B is my assignment. I know it's not glamorous, but I take great joy in running a nice establishment. I make people happy."

Baird said, "I'm not criticizing."

"I'm one of the few bed-and-breakfast proprietors who can kill you with his toes."

"And I'm not making fun of you. Honest! Especially now that I know about the toe thing."

14

The elevator doors opened onto a vista almost garish in its quaintness. Buildings made of reddish-beige stucco lined reddish cobblestone streets.

"Welcome to Old Town New Bordeaux," Zargarian said, leading Baird out of the elevator car with a sort of slow-motion, long-distance skipping stride. "Site of one of mankind's earliest extraterrestrial settlements—after the moon and EMCOT, of course."

Baird followed, matching the rhythm of his slow, floating gait. "Is this the speech you give your customers?"

"Yes. The early settlers of New Bordeaux, largely colonists and scientists from France, with some from Belgium and Germany, made game-changing advances in the fields of hydroponic farming and sub-surface terraforming, earning New Bordeaux its title as the solar system's colonial wine country. The vineyards are in a larger chamber lower in the complex. I'd be happy to arrange a tour, if you'd like. Over time, the colonists tore down the temporary shelters they'd brought with them, replacing them with the buildings you see here. Everything was built with the stone and resources they produced locally, but using the methods they brought from their home regions on Earth, giving Old Town its unique ambiance."

Baird said, "It smells like poop."

"The pervasive fertilizer odor was a problem for the early colonists," Zargarian said, "but over time the interior surfaces of the lava tubes were equipped with more aggressive air filtration that abated the worst of the odors."

"It still smells like poop."

"The fertilizer aroma has been mostly eradicated. You'll stop noticing after a while."

"I'm noticing it now."

Some of the light left Zargarian's eyes. "You're sealed up in an airtight cave where people artificially enrich the soil. You're gonna smell some poop."

They walked down the sidewalk past shops full of bottles of wine, decanters for holding wine after it's poured from the bottle, glasses for drinking wine once it's poured from the decanter, and cheese and crackers for removing the taste of the wine from your palate after you've drunk it. A good portion of the furniture in the shops appeared to be made from old wine barrels.

"The early colonists' first attempts at hydroponic farming were less than successful," Zargarian said. "Most of their crops barely survived. The French colonists immediately thought of wine grapes. The more difficult the life of a wine grape, the sweeter the wine will be. They managed to produce the finest non-terrestrial wine in the system, which they could trade for all the food they needed. Now many experts will tell you that the wines of Mars rival those of Earth."

"The experts paid by the Martian wineries?"

Zargarian smiled. "Those are the ones."

As with all high-end tourist destinations, the street was neither deserted nor truly busy. Old Town perfectly hit that sweet spot of having enough visitors that it didn't feel unfashionable, but not so many that one felt like the unrefined masses had discovered the place.

Zargarian said, "Here we are. Home sweet home."

The bed and breakfast looked like a well-kept but very old French château, but instead of sitting in the countryside surrounded by vineyards, it was entombed in a stone tunnel nestled—with less than four feet of clearance on each side—between a café that served food meant to go well with wine and a store that sold glassware designed to hold wine.

Zargarian opened the bed and breakfast's arched oak door and invited Baird inside. They walked through the rustic sitting room toward an antique-looking desk. He waved his arms broadly. "Welcome to Château Marmot, my bed and break—"

A frail voice called out, "Mr. Zargarian!"

Zargarian cringed, but turned toward the staircase at the rear of the room. "How can I help you?"

An elderly woman crept down the stairs, as if not wanting to disturb anyone, but the effect was spoiled by her continued shouting. "Mr. Zargarian? Oh good, it is you! I just wanted to tell you that the people in the room next to mine are still making a terrible racket."

"Yes, Mrs. Hammond. I haven't had a chance to talk to them about it yet, but I promise that I will before tonight."

Mrs. Hammond said, "What? I'm sorry Mr. Zargarian. I couldn't quite hear you."

"I haven't had a chance to talk to them about it yet," Zargarian said, much louder this time, "but I will before tonight."

"Oh," Mrs. Hammond said. "Thank you. I'm sure that will do. I am sorry to be a pain about this, but they make it impossible to sleep."

"I understand, and I appreciate you letting me know. I'll bring the topic up with them as soon as possible."

"I'm sorry. What was that?"

"I said thank you for letting me know."

Mrs. Hammond thanked him, smiled at Baird, and disappeared back up the stairs.

"How loud do they have to be to disturb her?" Zargarian muttered. He recomposed himself, sweeping a hand around the room with obvious pride. "This is the Château Marmot Bed and Breakfast. The beds are in the guest rooms. The breakfast is in the dining room at seven every morning and goes until nine. Snacks come out around three in the afternoon. We hold a wine tasting every evening at seven. Your room is upstairs, second door on the left. If there's anything we can do to make your stay more enjoyable, I, or one of my assistants, will be down here twenty-four seven."

Baird said, "What if I need something that's not related to my stay?"

"If I'm not here, whoever is can get a hold of me."

"I have a bit of a headache. Do you have anything—?"

"You'll find a well-stocked medicine cabinet in your room."

Baird said, "Excellent. If I do need help with any special projects, I'll try not to have it happen during breakfast."

"I'd appreciate that."

Baird made her way up the staircase to her room and walked straight to the medicine cabinet, which was as well-stocked as Zargarian had promised. She swallowed a pain reliever, hoping it would kill not only the constant ache in her head, but also the continued pain from the multiple bruises that had resulted from her high-speed collision with the tree the day before, one year and seven months ago. It seemed that the stasis pods that kept her illness from getting worse also kept her injuries from getting better.

She wandered from her small but immaculately clean bathroom into her small but unbearably quaint bedroom. She hoisted herself up to sit on the bed. The handmade quilt puckered around her as she sunk deep into the mattress. She marveled at how soft a mattress would have to be to squish down so far in Mars's gravity.

She pulled her gARggles out of her pocket but turned them over in her hands before she put them on.

Baird had spent the entire monorail trip thinking about how to handle the Izzy situation. She badly wanted to contact him but still didn't know if she should.

Her sudden disappearance had been hard on him. She shouldn't have been surprised. He never took her lack of contact well, no matter how much practice she gave him. She had hoped he might have felt bad for a while, then gotten over it and moved on. If he had, contacting him would have been cruel, just ripping open the old wound.

But if she was honest, she knew her brother better than that. More likely he thought she had disappeared because of something he had done or said. That somehow he had offended or disappointed her. He had probably spent the last four years letting self-recrimination eat him alive. If that was the case, it was cruel of her not to stop him. She needed to explain the situation immediately, so she could end his self-inflicted suffering, and more important, before she admitted to herself that this whole line of reasoning was a load of self-serving crap. She put on her gARggles and navigated to the secret message system Izzy had programmed. Her plan was to avoid talking to him directly, instead leaving a quick message. Then he would leave a message for her. They'd be in contact, but it would be mediated contact. Indirect, like writing a letter.

She reached the final menu, closed her eyes, took a deep breath, and selected *leave a message*.

Baird smiled. "Hey, Izzy. It's me. Look, I'm sorry it's been so long. I've been in stasis. See—"

A face appeared in Baird's field of view, startling her badly. What would have been a small involuntary jolt in Earth's gravity became something much larger on Mars. Baird bounced nearly a meter above the bed and toppled over backward in slow motion. As the walls and ceiling spun in her field of view, the face in front of her said, "Bran?! Bran! It's you! Where have you been all this feeking time?!"

Baird landed on her back on the edge of the mattress and slid down between the bed and the wall. She sank to the floor, pushing the bed several more centimeters from the wall as she went. When she came to a stop, her left arm was pinned to her side, and the right was stuck straight up over her head. Neither could get to the gARggles on her face.

The floating face said, "I set my Brow to ping me immediately if you ever tried to leave a message."

Baird heard Izzy, and was dimly aware of his face floating in her field of view, but her attention was focused mostly on pushing her way out of the furniture crevasse, mostly with her legs, grunting with exertion as she went.

"Are you okay?" the face asked. "Are you in some trouble? Are you being held captive? Are they torturing you?"

Baird finally freed herself from the gap between the bed and the wall. She rolled onto her back. "One second," she panted, her eyes closed. "Gotta catch my breath."

"That's okay," the voice said. "Take your time. I'm just so happy to hear from you."

Baird smiled and opened her eyes. The smile faded instantly. The man in front of her had gray hair and a salt-and-pepper beard. Deep creases flanked his mouth, and countless lines radiated from his eyes to his temples. This was not the face of her brother, at least not as she'd known it. He looked more like their father, or even their grandfather.

"There," the old man said, in a voice that, now that she could focus, sounded almost but not quite like Izzy's. "Are you able to talk now?"

"Izzy?" Baird gasped. "Isaac?"

"Yeah! Where have you been, Bran? It's been so long!"

Baird opened and closed her mouth several times without making a sound, then said, "I, uh, I'm fine. Wanted you to know I'm fine. Gotta go. Sorry."

She ended the call.

Before the call, she had sat motionless and silent, trying to decide whether to make contact. Now she had made contact, and she sat, motionless and silent, trying to make sense of what she'd seen.

She used her gARggles to check the date. By her calculations, the time elapsed between the day she'd first fallen ill and this day was a little north of four years. A long time, but not nearly long enough to explain Izzy's appearance.

"What the feek?!" she moaned.

She got a notification that Izzy was trying to call. She declined the call.

The most logical explanation would be that she had been in stasis much longer than they told her. She verified the date with her gARggles. The gARggles could have been hacked, though.

Baird looked around the room, studying everything she saw with a suspicious eye. After several seconds, she determined that the quaint, old-fashioned bed and breakfast didn't seem to be from the future, which didn't surprise her. Besides, if they were keeping the year from her, Zargarian would have scrubbed the room. Every display she'd seen since she landed on Mars seemed to confirm the date her gARggles gave her. She doubted anyone could fake that.

Izzy called again. She declined again.

Baird sat down on the bed.

Izzy called a third time, and yet again, Baird declined the call.

Baird waited. He didn't call back, which was a relief. Now she could get back to the business at hand without distraction.

"What the feeeeeeek?" she moaned again.

15

Baird walked up the street, bouncing in the reduced gravity. Zargarian followed behind her, bouncing every bit as much as Baird, but somehow managing to maintain an air of grumpiness.

"Why do I have to come along?" Zargarian asked.

"You're my local contact," Baird said. "You're supposed to assist me. Last time, I had to talk my contact *out* of tagging along."

"Your last contact didn't have a bed and breakfast to run," Zargarian grumbled. "Your file said you preferred to work alone."

Baird said, "I do, but that doesn't mean that I don't occasionally have reason to use other people in my plans."

"I don't like the sound of that word, *use*. In what capacity am I being used? As a patsy? A shill? A decoy?"

"Protection."

"Ah, muscle, because I'm an assassin."

"No, more of a human shield."

"And you think you're likely to need that at an auction house?"

"They're in the business of displaying valuable items and collecting large sums of money. You don't last long in that line of work unless you're willing to play hardball from time to time. A notorious alleged thief showing up to look at what you've got seems like just such an occasion."

"And you think having me with you will stop them?"

"You're an upstanding member of the community. If you see them behave in a disreputable manner, it'll be bad for them. If you come up missing, it'll be worse. Even if they don't think it through that far and do something rash, you can apparently kill a person with your toes. How does that work, by the way?"

"I'm sorry," Zargarian said. "Trade secret."

"Please don't say that if you told me, you'd have to kill me."

"Never. The first thing you learn in assassin training is that nobody has ever found that joke funny. No, I wouldn't have to kill you. I'd *choose* to. But on the upside, I'd kill you with my toes, so you'd get the answer to your question."

"But why with your toes? There have to be easier ways."

"Because it's undignified. A lot of the people we go up against in this line of work long for a glorious death. They want the story of their final battle to be told for years to come. They don't want that story to be about how they died to be funny. If I get a reputation for taking people out in a less-than-heroic way, people will be less anxious to go up against me, and if they do, they'll probably spend the whole fight looking at my feet."

Baird said, "I think that might be one of the best things I've ever heard. Of course, you need to leave a witness to tell the story of how you killed people with your toes, unless there's some distinctive toe marks on the body."

"Yeah, I'm still working out the details on that part."

Baird knew the auction house on sight without having to bother reading any signs. The specific combination of columns, steps, dark wood, and light stone was unmistakable. It was a building that made banks and government agencies seem ramshackle by comparison. The building spoke of the solidity, dependability, and permanence that only came from an old-world institution, despite the fact that the building itself was located in a lava tube deep beneath the surface of Mars.

A uniformed doorman bowed to Baird and Zargarian in one graceful motion. "Good afternoon. Welcome to Cooke's. I must warn you, we close for the evening in five minutes."

Baird said, "Of course. Thanks for the reminder."

Zargarian entered first. As Baird followed him through the door, she noted the lock mechanism, the depleted-uranium strike plate, the double-reinforced hinges, and the telltale lines inlaid into the frame that indicated an integrated ident-chip reader. It did not surprise her when the doorman said, "Enjoy your visit, Mr. Zargarian, Miss . . . Baird?"

Baird smiled at the stunned doorman.

"They seem to know who you are," Zargarian said.

"That's the whole point of the ident chip," Baird said.

"I can't believe our employers didn't re-flash it," Zargarian said. "I know someone who could do it here. She has a nice, clean shop. Very professional, very discreet. If you'd just told me—"

"I don't want my chip re-flashed."

"Why not?"

"Because it's illegal."

"I thought you were supposed to be some kind of master criminal before you joined up."

Baird said, "I'm still supposed to be. Allegedly."

"So why are you so worried about the law? Where's your courage?"

"Having courage is a great way to go to prison. Look. I've been accused of a lot of things, but I've never been charged with anything. I am an honest, law-abiding citizen, as far as anybody has been able to prove. But if I were a criminal, I suspect I'd probably tell you that the key to being a successful one is to break the law as little as possible. To break a law is to take a risk. Part of the way one gets away with breaking the law when they need to is by avoiding breaking the law when they don't."

They traversed the auction house's lobby, a large room with hard stone walls and floors that looked as if they had been there—and would be there—forever. There were scattered overstuffed chairs and couches, upholstered in fabrics designed to look only slightly less hard and permanent than the masonry.

"They wasted a fortune decorating this place," Zargarian said.

"They had to spend a mint on this stuff because they're the kinds of things an auction house would pick. The really good auction houses are designed like a theatrical set of an auction house. Being practical, functional, or economical isn't nearly as important as looking like the kind of place where wealthy bidders feel comfortable blowing huge sums of money."

They passed through another set of doors, part of a whole bank of identical doors covering the entire back wall of the lobby, all propped open, allowing access to the main room. The program for the upcoming auction loaded into her gARggles automatically, welcoming her to Cooke's, identifying any auction items in her field of view, and offering a detailed history of any item that interested her.

An inlaid marble checkerboard motif covered the floor, with small reflective tiles accenting the points where the tile corners intersected. On the ceiling, intricately decorated pressed metal tiles stretched from wall to wall, also accentuated with reflective metal squares at regular intervals. Stone pedestals topped with clear boxes and containing their own integrated lighting systems were spaced evenly around the perimeter of the room. They held the small items that were up for auction. Toward the center of the room, larger items sat on slightly raised platforms or on the floor itself, all behind velvet ropes and brass stanchions mounted directly into the floor.

"You're saying this is all fake?" Zargarian asked.

"No," Baird said, "I'm saying it's all for show. It's as real as any auction house in the system. From the very beginning, art, collectables, jewelry, and fashion have all been in the business of managing people's perception to make them value things more than logic would dictate."

Zargarian said, "But things are worth what they're worth, and auctions just help ensure that the person who values the thing the most gets it."

"Here, look at that." Baird pointed to a nearby pedestal. Inside the clear box, on a small easel, sat a small painting of a woman bent over at an improbable angle, wearing an impractically sheer negligee that barely concealed her unrealistically proportioned body parts while she held a surprisingly large lighter up to the cigarette of a man who looked quite pleased with himself, as one would expect. "Sometime way back in the past," Baird said, "some perv commissioned another perv to paint that so that they could use the painting in an ad selling cigarettes to even more pervs. What part of that sounds like something a wealthy intellectual would want decorating their home? Would you want something like that hanging on the wall of your bed and breakfast?"

"When you describe it that way, no."

"But if you point out that the artist is famous for having been really good at painting half-naked women, emphasize that this is an original painting that the perv held in his own, most likely unwashed hands, literally put it on a pedestal, and put your potential buyers in a room full of other people who seem like they're considering buying it, pretty soon two guys wearing ascots are in a bidding war."

Zargarian said, "I see your point about the painting, but surely a lot of the other items have real value."

"Which ones?" Baird asked. She pointed to another small framed painting. "That tiny portrait of someone I've never heard of? It's a few centi-sollars' worth of paint smeared on a ten-sollar canvas by a person who's been dead for a hundred years."

She pointed to a white helmet, shining under its protective glass cover. "Or that thin piece of plastic, made by an unnamed worker at a prop house long ago and worn by an extra in twenty or so frames of a movie that was old decades before either of us were born?"

Then she pointed to the far corner of the room. "Or that item, over there, second row from the left, four pedestals from the back, positioned near two windows. It's a yellowed paper notebook that has the unknown musings of a guy I've never heard of, but I'm assured was very smart. What item in this room has any intrinsic value, aside from the stories attached to them? Stories, by the way, that Cooke's Auction House does everything in their power to tell us."

A voice from behind them said, "An interesting point of view."

Baird and Zargarian turned to find a large man in a velvet blazer. His black and silver hair spilled over his forehead in meticulously arranged waves, almost completely covering a jagged scar over his left eye but leaving the brushed-steel Brow over his right eye exposed. His hands were spotlessly clean, and his nails were beautifully manicured, but his knuckles were marred by scrapes that had not yet fully healed.

"Miss Baird, Mr. Zargarian, I am Mr. Croft."

"Head of security," Baird said.

"Head of security," Croft confirmed. His voice was a low, menacing rumble, but his word choice and diction gave an air of class and refinement. The overall effect was similar to the instinctive fear Baird would feel if someone tried to run her through with a delicately engraved sterling silver sword.

"I must say, Miss Baird, you don't seem to have much respect for our business. It's almost the type of attitude one might use to rationalize a career of theft against hard-working auctioneers and their innocent customers."

"One might, I suppose," Baird said. "I wouldn't know anything about that."

"Of course you wouldn't. You're a simple lady of leisure, who travels the system for recreation, or at least that has been your testimony when questioned by police." Croft turned to Zargarian. "And you, sir. I understand you live here, in New Bordeaux."

"Yes," Zargarian said. "I run a B&B, the Château Marmot, just a few blocks away from here in Old Town. If any of your customers, or any appraisers or consultants you bring in, need a place to stay, I hope you'll keep us in mind."

Croft shook his head. "I'm sorry, but in my experience, staying at a bed and breakfast is like paying hotel prices to sleep in an elderly aunt's spare room. I would ask you how you fell in with a person like Miss Baird, but really, I'm more interested in how she ended up hanging around with a Doug like you."

Zargarian growled, "I am not a Doug."

Baird said, "I'm staying at his B&B."

Croft said, "Good to know. You'll probably be wanting to go back there now. We are closing for the evening." Croft motioned toward the entrance. Baird could see many people waiting in the lobby, all wearing velvet blazers identical to Croft's, but accessorized with dignified little hats and white gloves.

"Yes," Baird said, walking past Croft, toward the lobby. "I suppose we should be on our way. We wouldn't want to accidentally get locked in the auction house overnight."

"No," Croft said. "You really wouldn't." He, Baird, and Zargarian crossed the threshold into the lobby. "In fact, since you're here, maybe it would be entertaining to show you why you wouldn't want to be in there after closing." He turned toward one of the fifteen employees who were standing around the lobby, looking tense. "Bakshi, activate the security system."

One of the auction house employees bowed and opened a hidden panel in the wall, revealing a bank of glowing red switches.

Croft said, "Those controls are guarded by three people all night. One stands in front of the panel; one stands opposite it, guarding the first guard; and a third stands here, by the doors to the main room, watching the entrance and both of the other guards."

"But none of them watch the main room?" Baird asked.

"They don't have to, because of this."

Bakshi flipped the switches in order. They each changed from red to green. An electrical whirring sound filled the main auction room, like small actuators running through pre-programmed motions. The sound would have been quite faint, if it weren't echoed hundreds of times from multiple points throughout the room. Baird saw the small silver tiles on the corner seams of the checkerboard floor and on the pressed tin ceilings begin to move. A white mist emerged from vents in the ceiling and fell slowly to the floor, pooling in the bottom half-meter of the room.

The sound and the motion stopped after less than a second. Baird heard a deep hum, followed by a high-pitched whine. She saw a green laser beam, which emanated from the far corner of the room and struck one of the reflective tiles on the floor at a forty-five-degree angle. The green laser beam bounced to a reflective tile on the ceiling, and another on the floor, and so on, traversing the room countless times from multiple directions, creating a three-dimensional grid of green light, which stood out sharply in the misty air and filled all of the empty space around the auction items.

Croft said, "Impressive, wouldn't you agree?"

"Yeah. I would," Baird said.

"Its strength is its simplicity."

"I see what you mean."

"A far cry from the Wartzberg Pearl."

Baird said, "I wouldn't know."

"Sure," Croft said, laughing. "Sure, you wouldn't."

Zargarian said, "I don't understand. So you've got a laser grid to detect intruders. I don't see the big deal."

"Intrusion detection?" Croft said. "I hope you know more about making beds and scrambling eggs than you do about security."

Croft snatched the hat from the nearest guard's head and tossed it into the main room. It flew into the laser grid and instantly burst into flames. The lasers throughout the room seemed to flicker for an instant as the hat blocked the beam before burning away. The smoldering remains broke apart and passed through more beams as they fell. The entire hat had been cut into small pieces and reduced to ash before it reached the ground.

Croft said, "What you're looking at is a weapons-grade, continuous-fire, high-intensity laser."

"Okay," Zargarian said. "I can see how that would work as a deterrent. Still, what if someone shoots out the laser?"

"There's no direct line of sight from any of the windows," Croft replied. "They'd have to be standing in the room, where they'd get burnt, or in the lobby, where the guards would see them."

"What if they cut power to the building?" Zargarian asked.

"Triple redundant backups. If something goes so wrong that it knocks out all three, we'll either have time to flood the room with guards, or it'll be a full-scale disaster, in which case we'll be busy saving our own skins. Any more questions?"

Baird said, "I assume the mist is a refrigeration system?"

"Yes," Croft said. "I see you correctly deduced that without it, the laser would heat the room and endanger the merchandise."

"No, I just noticed that my feet were getting cold."

"Well, okay," Zargarian said, "but I still don't see why you don't at least post a guard at the door, in case someone tries to sneak in."

Croft elbowed Baird. "You coached the innkeeper well. He's doing a magnificent job of playing dumb and getting me to describe the entire security system."

Baird said, "For the record, you chose to show us the laser without any prompting at all. And I didn't put him up to this. He's just asking questions for himself."

"Oh, so his lack of knowledge isn't an act," Croft said. "No wonder he's so convincing. To answer your question: we don't make the guards watch the laser grid all night because they would either spend hours watching nothing happen, or they'd see some fool get burned alive. Nobody wants to see that, at least nobody we'd want to hire. Besides, if someone tries to sneak in there, their screams of pain will get our attention."

16

Zargarian held the door of the bed and breakfast open for Baird as they entered. "I'm sorry, Baird. He was just so needlessly hostile, I had to put so much energy into not taking him out that I sort of forgot myself."

"It's not a problem, Zargarian."

"I'd like to believe that you mean that, but the way I kept going on and on about the security system, it had to make him suspicious."

"He was suspicious when he heard my name. Nothing you said or did was going to put them more on guard than just knowing that I was in the building."

"Then why'd they let you in, and show you the security system?"

"It's hard for them to refuse until I get convicted of something. And part of it is cockiness. They like the idea of their system being so scary that I would run off without even trying to defeat it."

"Do they have a good system?"

Baird shrugged. "I've seen worse."

"I still don't believe they don't have anyone with eyes on the main room."

"And you shouldn't. They don't have a person standing there watching, but they have cameras and sensors."

Zargarian asked, "If they were bragging about their system, why wouldn't they mention that?"

"I said they were cocky, not stupid. They held a few things back. As nice as the idea of scaring me off sounds, the idea of being the team that caught the famous Brangelina Baird sounds even better, so they kept a surprise or two."

‹ ♦ ♦ ♦ ›

Well after midnight, Baird stood in her room with her back against the wall farthest from the window, so that she could see outside without being seen herself. The lighting inside the lava tube had dimmed to signify night, but it was bright enough that she could clearly recognize Croft, the head of security for Cooke's Auction House, leaning against a wall, making no effort to hide himself.

He was watching, and he wanted her to know he was watching.

She sauntered up to the window with a forced casualness, went through the motions of pulling off her sweater, looked down at Croft, feigned surprise, and drew the blinds.

That done, Baird knew that Croft knew which window belonged to her room, and that she was in said room. Now the trick was to not let him see her leave.

She accessed the strand's sensors, all of which were still perfectly operational despite the strand being knitted into a sweater. She couldn't detect any of the various waves, rays, or fields she would have found if Croft was using remote sensors to track her movements. He was private security, not law enforcement. He could use scanners without a warrant, but if he got caught scanning a bed and breakfast without the consent of the owner and the guests, he'd probably get arrested for invasion of privacy and voyeurism. It didn't surprise Baird that he figured it wasn't worth the risk.

She half unraveled her sweater and sent the strand out the window to do recon. After five minutes, she knew the location of all of Croft's security personnel, and she had found a window that she could use to exit unseen. Unfortunately, it was the window of an occupied guest room.

She transitioned her pants into cargo mode and pulled the black gloves built into her shirt's sleeves over her hands and the hood hidden in the neck up over her head. She put on her gARggles, partly to obscure her face and partly to have access to information as she worked.

Baird crept into the hall. The building schematics that displayed in her gARggles helped her locate the room she needed. She used the strand to pick the lock and crept inside. She'd have felt more confident about sneaking past the guests if they had been asleep, but they very much were not. Luckily, the room was dark, and they were quite distracted. She had little difficulty crawling past their bed and out their window without diverting their attention from the surprisingly loud, highly engrossing, and more than a little gross, business at hand.

Baird accessed the B&B's register and found that the room on the other side of the wall belonged to an Alice Hammond.

Baird hung easily from the side of the building, hidden in the shadow of the eaves, which were just for show since it never rained or snowed underground, or on Mars's surface, for that matter.

Her sweater unraveled, wove itself into two thicker cords, spanned the gap to the stemware store next door, and swung Baird across.

The strand could lift Baird's body weight in Earth's gravity. Here, where she weighed 60 percent less, it could fling her around with ease. She traversed the distance between the bed and breakfast and the auction house with great speed, never once touching the ground.

She sat across from the auction house, on the roof of an art gallery full of "groundbreaking new works" by well-established, older artists. She carefully leaned out over the drop, looking down at the cobblestones below. In this gravity, the fall wouldn't kill her, but she might have preferred death to finally getting caught by falling from the sky, very slowly, right next to her target.

She remained silent and motionless as the strand traversed the gap between the buildings and explored the frame of one of the auction house's windows. She found intrusion sensors that Croft had not mentioned in his description of the security system. The strand disabled them with little trouble and wormed its way into the main hall.

As she expected, she counted six cameras—including one across the hall, which was pointed directly at the window she had compromised—arranged carefully so that each camera was in view of at least one other camera. That way, if someone disabled one camera, they'd be caught doing it by another.

Like most camouflaged cameras, they were very difficult to spot, unless you were well versed in the various methods professionals use to camouflage cameras, in which case they stood out like black sheep in a snowy field. She spotted them easily, even with the added visual distraction of the clouds of refrigeration mist and the glowing argyle pattern of deadly green laser beams. Each camera was completely hidden behind the decorative sculptures in the crown molding, peeking out through perfect round black holes. She sent the strand around the perimeter of the room, in through those very same holes, attacking and subverting cameras as it went.

Baird found it amusing that their big, scary lasers made her less afraid of their cameras. They were sure the lasers would keep any sane person from coming in. The cameras were just there to establish a record of what happened if someone was crazy enough to try. The cameras wouldn't prevent theft; they'd just prevent wrongful-death lawsuits after the fact. She knew nobody would so much as look at the camera feeds until after something interesting had happened. In this case, all the recordings would tell them was in what order someone knocked out the cameras.

She closed in on the camera that was aimed at her entry point. The strand wriggled into the housing and neutralized the camera. Soon, the only functioning security measure in the room was the laser grid. She withdrew the strand and used it to cross the gap between the buildings, perching on the ledge outside the auction house window.

The cameras had been looking out through holes in the decorative moldings, meaning that the strand only had to stay tight to the side of the opening and it would probably go unnoticed, or else be mistaken for an insect or a smudge on the lens. The laser, on the other hand, was shooting a high-energy stream of coherent light through its hole. If the strand got close enough to wriggle through, it would burst into flames, which would be counterproductive. She couldn't attack the laser without getting burned by the laser. Luckily, the system had plenty of other moving parts.

The strand carefully threaded along the floor, around the reflectors and the green laser beams. It reached the specific reflector Baird wanted, gathering and coiling around the base. Baird and the strand were both motionless for a moment. She had to get this right. One mistake and she would be lucky just to get arrested. If she was unlucky, she'd be cut in half. After which, both halves of her would be arrested.

She sent the command. On the floor beneath the reflector, half of the coiled strand contracted, growing thicker and exerting a slow but powerful upward force on one part of the reflector's underside, moving the beam across the ceiling, leaving a black trail and clouds of acrid smoke. Dripping globs of melted tin sizzled as they fell, and then cooled into rough slugs on the cold stone floor. The beams along one side of the room and the front few rows nearest the door remained in place, but the vast majority of the room became devoid of lasers and safe for Baird to move in at will.

The beam traced a path across the ceiling, over the crown molding, down the wall, and out the window. It took only a few seconds to melt through. Molten glass rolled down onto the still-solid parts like magma and cooled into round, organic warts.

She tried to trace the path of the beam, but as soon as it left the misty, wet air of the auction house, it disappeared, except for the green glow of the spot where the beam met the lava tube's ceiling.

She figured it would take days to melt its way through the planet's crust to the surface. She planned to re-aim the laser well before that happened.

She sent the strand to the pedestal she knew held the notebook. Baird looked at the glass doors at the far end of the room, which led to the lobby. One guard stood with his back to the doors, as were his instructions. She couldn't see the other two, which meant that they couldn't see her.

The strand reached the base of the notebook's pedestal and pooled. It traced a circle on the floor around the pedestal's base, then it traced a second circle beneath the first, which warped at regular intervals, lifting the first circle upward. This process continued, layer after layer, until the strand formed a black sheath, similar to a fishnet stocking, surrounding the pedestal. When the strand-tower reached the same height as the transparent box covering the notebook, construction ceased.

Baird glanced again at the oblivious guard's back.

The upper portion of the tower contracted, squeezing tight around the glass display cover. The lower portion of the tower drew taller, exerting upward force on the case.

The case didn't move.

Baird tried again, this time squeezing the case harder. It still didn't move.

She tried once more, exerting as much pressure as she dared. The guards weren't looking, but they were always listening, and nothing gets a guard's attention faster than the sound of breaking glass.

The transparent case lifted slowly, gaining two or three centimeters in altitude before the strand lost traction and the case fell back to the pedestal with a thump.

Baird looked to the guards, tensing herself to flee. She was perched next to an open window, but the strand was extended and woven into a complex structure around a heavy piece of furniture. If she had to flee, she would need to either wait for the strand to unravel and retract, or leave it behind. She didn't want to do either of those things.

The guard with his back to the room stood erect, cocking his head to the side, as if trying to get his ear closer to whatever had made the noise. He held up a hand, a motion that instinctively told Baird that he was asking another guard to stop talking so he could listen to something.

Baird didn't make a sound.

The guard turned his head further and hunched his shoulders in concentration. He stood like that for several seconds before he finally shrugged and relaxed again.

Baird exhaled, grimaced, and carefully climbed through the window. She lowered herself to the floor, positioning herself with a pedestal between her and the glass doors to the lobby. Her shirt and pants color lightened to a randomized pattern of whites and beiges to blend in with all the marble and swirling mist.

Out of curiosity, she looked at what was on the nearest pedestal: an antique wristwatch with a ridiculous number of tiny little dials.

Off the top of her head, she could name five fences in three different colonies who could have moved the watch for her. She looked around the room, seeing a sea of seemingly vulnerable and potentially profitable items, but chose to disregard all of them. She had realized long ago that going after targets of opportunity was how greedy thieves got caught.

She looked again at the back of the guard through the forest of pedestals, the swirling white mist, and the remaining green laser beams; verified that the guard was still not looking; and ran to the notebook in a sort of stealthy crouch. In the low gravity, each step took much longer and rose much higher into the air than it would in full gravity. The result was a slow-motion bouncing stoop that robbed her daring thievery of much of its cool factor.

By the time she reached the notebook, Baird's head was throbbing from her mild exertion, reminding her that she was fundamentally not well. The strand tower had disassembled itself. It sat in a neat coil at the bottom of the pedestal. The slack portion of the strand that had stretched to Baird's former perch on the windowsill had added itself to the coil as she approached.

Baird slid to a stop behind the notebook's pedestal. Even wearing her camouflaged suit among the clutter of pedestals, smoke, and lasers, she was much more exposed than she liked. She had no doubt that if one of the guards so much as glanced through the glass doors, they'd see her in an instant.

She stood up and for the first time got a good look at the target: a small antique paper notebook, the kind people used to carry in their pocket to jot down ideas. The green cardboard cover and the thicker brown back bore identical sharp bends halfway down its height. The yellowed pages were held together by a bent, mangled coil of wire.

Baird put her hands on either side of the square glass display case. Its weight was not the problem; rather, as her attempt to lift it with the strand had demonstrated, the case was quite slippery.

Baird thought she could maybe get her hand in under the edge and lift the case from underneath, but she would run the risk of cutting herself. Then she'd have to take the notebook, leave, steal some cleaning supplies, sneak back in, and clean the place without getting spotted. She'd been down that road a couple of times, and it was never fun.

Baird had started to work her right hand downward to try to get in under the glass and grab the notebook when she heard the buzzing of the actuators that aimed the reflectors. She looked around in a panic. The mist was still present, but there were no green laser beams to be seen. She knew in an instant that the reflectors were repositioning to alter the laser grid's pattern. She was sure the system did this periodically to throw off anyone foolish enough to try to sneak through, because if she'd designed the system, that's exactly what she would have made it do.

The buzzing stopped. Baird gritted her teeth, squeezed her eyes shut, and pulled her body in tight to the pedestal, taking up as little room as possible.

The laser re-engaged and bounced off the reflectors, including the one Baird had repositioned, which had corrected its alignment when all the other reflectors moved. A complex web of bright green lines appeared, filling parts of the room at the speed of light until one of the lasers intersected with her shoulder.

Baird managed to keep from crying out as the laser grazed her skin. She instinctively flinched away from the pain, pulling herself out of the laser's path. The strand contracted into a tight ball on the floor, avoiding contact with the beam as the green light filled another portion of the room, continuing unimpeded from reflector to reflector until it found its way back and hit the side of Baird's thigh.

Again, she managed to keep from shouting as she lifted her leg out of the laser's path. The laser filled the rest of the room without intersecting with any more of Baird's anatomy. She stayed utterly motionless, contorted into an uncomfortable and undignified position.

The laser's readjustment had surprised Baird, but the fact that *something* surprised her did not. She hadn't had the time for any sort of decent recon. She had foreseen the likelihood of unforeseen circumstances. Now she would have to execute her contingency plan for unforeseen circumstances. That contingency plan was to *come up with something.*

She was stuck there, unable to move for fear of getting burned again. All any one of the guards needed to do was look through the glass doors and she'd be caught. There'd be nothing she could do but wait for law enforcement to arrive, passing the time by listening to the guards laugh, answering their questions about what she was thinking, and watching them take pictures of the famous Brangelina Baird, clinging to a podium like a lightly roasted gecko perched on a twig.

On the bright side, she was pretty sure the laser had burned off one of her bruises.

She rolled her eyes as far as they'd go to the right, hoping to get a good view of one of the reflectors that was ahead of her in the laser's path—but without being able to see the laser emitter itself, it was impossible to know for sure.

She tried to turn her head, but a sudden hot sensation near her temple convinced her that this was a bad idea.

Though Baird made a point of not moving, the strand started working its way back toward the reflector she'd moved before. It moved slowly. Baird knew that if she carelessly steered the strand into a laser, it would probably lose all of the sensors in its tip and might be rendered completely inoperable, leaving her with no means of escape.

The strand made its way to the reflector and looped itself around the actuated base several times, as it had before.

Baird brought up a map of the room in her gARggles. She estimated both her position and the position of the reflector she intended to move, and then she attempted to calculate how much she'd have to move it to direct the laser out the window.

She didn't want to do any more damage to the building than she had to. She was far more reluctant to accidentally steer the laser through one of the exhibits. She had no compunction about stealing rare and valuable items, but she hated the idea of destroying them. Most of all, she wanted to avoid diverting the laser into another reflector. Every reflector in the room was aimed in a different direction. The beam could go anywhere, including into her.

She ran through the whole thing two more times in her head, and in the end, the only thing she was sure of was that she didn't have enough information to be sure of what she was doing. She really had no choice. She couldn't stay where she was. It was only a matter of time before the guards spotted her, and even if they didn't, the laser would eventually realign. Last time she'd gotten away with only a light singeing. Next time she might not be so lucky.

It occurred to her that she had really lowered her standards as to what she considered *lucky*.

She was running out of time and had already run out of options. She made her best guess and contracted the strand.

17

Escaping the auction house had been easy enough. Baird got the laser safely diverted with minimal damage, in that she permanently broke only one of the actuators, burned a very thin zigzagging line across the length of the wall, sheared a small chunk off of the corner of one of the displays, and burned only one small hole through the auction house's ceiling, roof, and whatever was in the attic between them. Sneaking into the B&B had been even easier than sneaking out, since she had approached the auction house's surveillance team from the rear this time, and they were both more tired and more bored.

She was impressed to find that the couple in the other room was still at it, or perhaps were at it again. Either way, it made traversing their room unnoticed easier than it would have been if they'd been asleep.

Once she was safely in the hall, where nobody would find her presence suspicious, she casually walked down to the lobby and rang the bell to wake Zargarian, who emerged from his room in impeccably pressed pajamas. He gave her the items she required without delay or complaint and responded reasonably when Baird suggested that he give Mrs. Hammond at least a partial refund.

Baird returned to her room. No sooner had she closed the door behind her than her sweater unraveled itself and dropped to the floor. Normally she would have just taken the sweater off, but to do so would require moving her arms, and thanks to her burn, she was trying to do that as little as possible.

She reached into her pocket and pulled out the valuable antique notebook she'd gone to so much trouble to procure, along with the small sewing kit and the first aid supplies that Zargarian had given her. She marveled at the man's efficiency and preparedness. It made her wish that all safe houses were run by innkeepers.

She dropped the notebook and the sewing kit on the dresser, then walked into the bathroom, clutching Zargarian's first aid kit. She popped some painkillers, noting without pleasure that they were as much for her throbbing head as for her increasing collection of injuries. She cleaned and salved her burns, one on her shoulder and one on her thigh, livid red lines so thin and straight that one might think they'd been created using a ruler and a soldering iron. Their laser precision stood in contrast to the mottled, organic black and yellow bruises she'd gotten from the tree. She dressed her wounds and returned to the bedroom, stretched her sore limbs, and settled down into the overly soft mattress, trying not to disturb any of her various injuries.

She knew she should call Vise Grip, her new handler. The sooner she reported that the mission was accomplished, the sooner they could get her back in the deep freeze, and the sooner she would get her cure.

She looked down at her shirt and pants, examining the holes she'd managed to burn through them. She knew she'd want to repair them before she went through spaceport security. Damaged clothing with fresh wounds visible through the holes tended to draw attention.

But Baird made no move to call her handler or sew up her damaged clothing.

Instead, she put on her gARggles and navigated to Izzy's secret page. He had left multiple messages since their last contact. She watched none of them. Instead, she called him.

Everything in Baird's life was a variable, and beyond her control. She needed something she could rely on, and Izzy had always been that. No matter what was happening in her life, Izzy was always there for her, usually complaining that she was not available to him. She was sure this time would be no different, assuming he hadn't died of old age. An explanation of his appearance would also be most welcome.

He picked up almost immediately. His aged face appeared, floating in front of her.

"Bran! Thank God you called back!"

"Quiet," Baird snapped. "Please. Please, just be quiet for a minute. I'm going to explain where I've been, then I'm going to ask you a question. After that, we can both decide how to proceed. Okay?"

Izzy said, "Sure. I've got some—"

"No," Baird interrupted. "Please, don't talk. Not yet. I really need to just get through this."

"Fine. Shoot."

"Okay. You remember that last evaluation mission I went on, a little over . . . feek, four years ago? That's how long they say it's been. During that mission, I got infected with a man-made virus. At least that's what they tell me. The virus is designed to cause death in one week. They've been keeping me in stasis ever since. They wake me up to steal things they say they need in order to search for my cure. Anyway, I considered calling you before, but I didn't want to drag you into my mess. Did you follow all that?"

"Yes. I think."

"Do you have any questions?"

"Many."

"Well, sit on them for now, because I have a question I need you to answer. If I've been out of it for four years, why do you look like you've aged thirty years?"

Izzy looked confused, then laughed. "Bran, it's a disguise. I'm undercover, and they have me posing as an old man."

"An old man who looks like you?"

"I didn't need to look like any specific old man, just an old man."

"They don't have any agents who are old men?"

"Not with my skills. Look." He reached up, grasped at the makeup appliances glued to his face, and pulled. They came off in large hunks, to reveal the younger man underneath. The *much* younger man.

"Okay," Baird said, "Now why do you look like a kid, Izzy?"

"What are you talking about?"

"You look at least a decade younger than you did when I saw you last. It's like I'm looking at an old picture of you. How is that possible?"

"Bran, I don't know what you're talking about."

Baird hung up.

She spent a good long time sitting on the bed, staring through her gARggles into the middle distance. She didn't know how long, exactly, because she was too occupied with mentally listing all the logical explanations for how Izzy could possibly be younger now than when she had last seen him, years before. She couldn't come up with any.

Plastic surgery was good, but it wasn't *that* good. Real time travel was only possible moving forward, and then only in theory, as it required close proximity to a black hole, none of which were close enough for humans to reach in one lifetime with the current technology.

She muttered to herself, "Okay, Baird, let's talk brass tacks."

She wondered if that phrase referred to tacks made of brass, or the taxes one might pay on brass. Either meaning could refer to getting down to business, but it was an outdated expression either way.

She marveled at how quickly her thought process had been derailed. She could see herself avoiding unpleasant facts. She knew she was prone to that. She thought about the one time after their parents had split up, when she and Izzy had tried to discuss her decision to live with their father while he had to stay with their mother, and they'd had a terrible fight.

She marveled at how quickly her thought process had been derailed again.

Baird took off her gARggles and slapped herself once across the face. She winced at the pain and made a mental note that if she intended to slap herself again, she should use her unburnt arm.

She waited a moment for the dueling pains in her cheek and her arm to subside, then she set out to methodically list the things she knew for sure.

She knew that she didn't entirely trust the Toolbox before her illness.

She knew that she'd been told that she had an illness. The Toolbox hadn't really offered any proof, aside from the fact that she was suffering headaches. She had to admit that the headaches were getting worse, but still, she'd had no nosebleeds or ringing in the ears. Not yet.

She knew that she had been kept in stasis between assignments. They said it was to keep the disease from spreading, but, as she'd just established, she hadn't verified that she even *had* an illness.

She knew that as soon as she told Vise Grip that she had the notebook, they would put her on a flight out, and there was no way to know when they would wake her up again.

She knew that the person who claimed to be Izzy was too young to be Izzy. Either he was an imposter, which would mean that she couldn't trust him, or he was telling the truth, which would mean that she couldn't trust anything she thought she knew about the nature of reality. Either way, that was a problem.

Having gone over everything, she determined that she was trapped in a situation about which she knew way too little. The question was, what would she do about it?

She could get out of the situation. Run for it. If they were telling the truth, she'd be dead in a few days. If they were lying, on the other hand, they'd demonstrated a total disregard for her wishes and safety. They'd hunt her for the rest of her life, and probably kill her when they found her, just to keep her quiet.

She decided to call running away *Plan B*.

Plan A would have to be playing along for now and gathering information. She'd either figure out that they were telling the truth, in which case she'd be glad she stuck around, or she'd find that they were lying, in which case she'd want to make a careful plan and escape at the opportune moment instead of just bolting on a whim.

Baird smiled. She didn't know much about the situation, but she knew how little she knew, and she knew what the next step was, even if every step after that was a mystery.

She called Vise Grip for her post-mission debriefing.

Vise Grip's floating face said, "Saber Saw. What can I do for you?"

"I'm ready for extraction."

"You have the notebook?"

Baird smiled. "Yes. That's why I'm ready for extraction."

Vise Grip smiled. "They told me you worked fast. We'll get you out on the next flight. Have Stud Finder take you to the spaceport."

"I don't need a ride to the spaceport. He's got his hands full running his bed and breakfast. Before I let you go, though, I do have a question."

Baird actually had a great many questions, but she knew that only mentioning one of them would keep Vise Grip from getting defensive, much like telling your spouse, "Hey, one thing," instead of just saying, "We need to talk."

Vise Grip asked, "What is it?"

"I looked through the notebook. It's nothing but atomic diagrams and notes on picking padlocks. You said that the virus I was infected with involves radioactive material. I'm wondering, how does that work? Is the radioactive material the lethal agent, or is it a timing mechanism where the atomic decay triggers the illness?"

Vise Grip said, "I don't know."

"Do you think you could find out the answer to my questions and tell me next time you wake me up?"

"I'll see what I can do."

"That's not much of an answer."

"It's an honest answer. Most people appreciate honesty."

"Oh, I do appreciate your honesty. I just don't appreciate what you're being honest about."

‹ ♦ ♦ ›

Baird closed the door to her room, looked down quickly to verify that her sweater was hanging properly, and walked toward the stairs. She could smell that Zargarian was preparing breakfast, which brightened her mood immeasurably. The coffee smelled amazing, though the bacon might have been a bit overcooked.

She floated down the stairs in the low Martian gravity, but stopped halfway at the sound of harsh words being exchanged at low volume.

"Shut up, you feeking Doug," a man grunted. Without looking, she was certain it was Croft, the head of security for Cooke's Auction House. "I don't give a crap about you and your little doily museum here, and you know it. Where is she?"

"Now, now," Zargarian said, "I'm here to help. There's no need to insult my establishment. Where is who?"

"You know all-caps well. Baird! Where is she?"

"She hasn't been down for breakfast yet," Zargarian said. "I assume she's still sleeping in her room."

"Get her down here, now."

"Absolutely not."

"Because you know she's not there," Croft said.

"No, because she's my guest, and I see no reason to prevent her from sleeping as late as she likes."

"Then I'll just go up and knock on her door myself."

Zargarian shook his head. "I can't allow that."

"Yeah, whatever. Your bacon's burning."

"Yes, it is, isn't it? All the more reason to put an end to this."

"What are you doing?" Croft asked.

"Just kicking off my shoes."

Baird heard a grunt of exertion, some confused, alarmed cursing, and the thump of something heavy falling to the floor. She moved quickly, bounding down the remaining stairs, rounding the corner, leaping into the kitchen in one stride, and stopping herself with both hands against the counter. She found Zargarian lugging Croft through the kitchen toward a door at the back.

"What happened?"

"I killed him," Zargarian said.

"Yes," Baird said. "But why?"

Zargarian threw Croft's lifeless body down on the utility room floor. "I'm an assassin. I had a problem, and I dealt with it by utilizing my skill set. I'd appreciate it if you didn't give me a hard time about it."

Zargarian closed the utility room door and stalked back into the parlor.

Baird followed him. "I'm not trying to give you a hard time. Believe me. I'm just asking."

"Yeah," Zargarian said. "I understand. Sorry. I'm just on edge. And you don't have to keep staring at my feet. You're safe. Look, it was either let him come up and confront you or stop him, and he made me burn the bacon. Like I said, I am a trained assassin."

"Yeah," Baird said. "That makes sense."

Zargarian reached down, picked up the empty shoe lying in the middle of the floor, and pulled it onto his foot.

"I see you killed him with your toes."

"It's not going to become a trademark if I don't stick with it. I'm basically applying pressure to a specific nerve cluster. It's on the inner thigh. Reaching down there with my hands is awkward, and it puts people on the defensive. It's easier to get at it with the feet, but the strike requires too much sensitivity to execute wearing shoes. It'd be easier to build a reputation if there were a witness to tell people I killed him with my toes, but then I'd just have to kill the witness too."

Baird said, "You could leave a note. *I killed this man with my toes.*"

"You don't think that would seem odd?"

"Very much so. But you're killing people with your toes. Isn't 'seeming odd' kind of the point?"

Zargarian thought about it for a moment. "I see what you mean. I could make the note crude, like I wrote it with my toes. Really strike some fear in their hearts."

"Or, you could keep the technique a secret. I certainly won't tell anyone. You'd either become famous for killing people in a way nobody can identify or you'll continue to fly under the radar, like you are now. Take it from me, being notorious isn't all that much fun."

"No?"

"No. It's a grind. Everyone looks at you like they're on to you, and you just want to shout at them, 'I know you're on to me. Everybody's on to me.' And I've said the word *allegedly* so many times it's lost all meaning. It's just a bunch of random sounds to me now."

"I'll give that some serious thought. So, Miss Baird, what brought you downstairs? Is there anything I can do for you?"

Baird held up a small plastic box. "I came down to return your sewing kit before I head to the spaceport. Thanks again."

"My pleasure. Now if you'll excuse me, I need to deal with our friend as quickly as I can, unfortunately."

"Yeah," Baird said. "That's not going to be pleasant, I'm sure."

"No," Zargarian said. "Because I'll be away from the B&B, I'm going to have to resort to serving a continental breakfast. I hate to do it, but ours can be an ugly business."

18

Baird felt a chill deep in the marrow of her bones. Her eyes fluttered open, allowing her to see the seamless white inner surface of her stasis pod's door.

"Feek."

Then the sensation of heat arrived, starting in her right arm and flowing into every part of her body, escalating quickly from pleasant warmth, straight past the boundaries of her comfort zone, into the uncharted frontiers of her heat tolerance. Beads of sweat sprouted from the pores of her forehead and rolled down into her eyes.

She activated her gARggles. "Feek! Feek! Fee-all-caps-eek!" There was no dossier of medical information. Only the notification of another briefing; another job.

Baird heard a jaunty high-pitched tune, the spaceline's jingle. A woman's voice said, "Good morning, valued passengers. We've reached the end of our quick three-day hop to Tsiolkovsky Station, the Pendulum. The local gravity is one G, so please adjust your grav-meds accordingly."

The flight attendant continued, talking about carry-on luggage and single-file lines, but Baird heard none of it.

The Pendulum! At least they had sent her somewhere she knew this time. She detested it, but she knew it. She wondered why they'd sent her to the Pendulum, then laughed at herself. She knew why: so she could steal something.

The questions was, what would she do about it? Again, she laughed at herself. She knew what she would do. She would steal whatever it was, bide her time, gather intel, and make sure Vise Grip knew how unhappy she was about it.

Baird initiated the briefing, watched her handler's face resolve itself, then asked, "Who the hell are you?"

The face she saw was that of a man in his late fifties, round and bald, with chubby cheeks and a double chin. He laughed. "A perfectly reasonable question! Hello, Saber Saw. I am Plumb Bob, your handler."

"What happened to Vise Grip?"

"Vise Grip? Was that your previous handler? I assume he or she was reassigned."

"You don't know for sure?"

"I'm afraid I don't."

"Oh."

"I'm sorry. I know that operatives often form a strong emotional bond with their handlers. I can tell this Vise Grip was very important to you."

"Actually, I didn't like her."

"Oh," Plumb Bob said. "Well then, good riddance. I can tell you that I am very excited to be working with you, Saber Saw. I have a cracking assignment for you. Right up your alley, I dare say."

"How long have I been in stasis?"

Plumb Bob said, "Fourteen months, eight days."

"Fourteen months, eight days."

"Yes."

"That's a long time. Enough to make substantial progress toward finding me a cure. How close are they?"

"Ah," Plumb Bob said. "See, that's a difficult question to answer."

"You don't know."

"No," Plumb Bob admitted, "I don't. I asked, and they buried me under a mountain of mumbo-jumbo."

"Do you remember any of the mumbo-jumbo?"

"Not well enough that I'd dare try to repeat it, but I'll tell you what—while you work on your mission, I'll have the researchers I spoke to write down the explanation they gave me. It shouldn't be difficult to have it ready by time you're done. Fair enough?"

"Nothing about the situation is fair enough, but it'll have to do."

"I see what you mean, but at least you have an interesting task to keep your mind off it."

Next to Plumb Bob's face, a rotating image appeared, depicting one of the most iconic works of art of the last century. Baird saw a stylized representation of Earth rendered in garishly exaggerated colors, hanging suspended within a transparent glass statue meant to represent Earth's atmosphere. Instead of being spherical, as the actual atmosphere is, the glass atmosphere bulged and flared in nine places. Four tapered to points, representing underdeveloped arms and legs. Four swelled into rounded lumps, representing over-developed breasts and buttocks. At the top of the sculpture, the final bulge formed a crude, stubby lump of a head, much smaller than any of the breasts or buttocks. The end result was an image of the Earth suspended within a transparent Stone Age fertility doll.

As the image rotated, a steady flashing light couldn't help but catch the viewer's attention. A jewel repeatedly reflected the light, becoming a blinding beacon for an instant with every rotation: a large diamond positioned in the statue's crotch.

Plumb Bob said, "This statue is called the *Ibu*. Know anything about it?"

Baird said, "*Ibu* is the Indonesian word for mother. It was a gift from the people of Indonesia to the people of Brazil. The statue depicts the Earth as the mother of mankind. If you look closely, the globe has been rotated so that the jewel is positioned directly over the site of the space elevator's moorage on the equator, in the Brazilian rain forest. *The Ibu* was created single handedly by the famous Indonesian artist Fauzi. He was considered a national treasure. A small example of his work that took an afternoon to complete can fetch upwards of a giga-sollar. *The Ibu* took him three years, is eight meters tall, and weighs fourteen tons. It is priceless."

Plumb Bob said, "Well done. What you may not know—"

"I wasn't done. I just paused to breathe. The jewel depicting the exit from the *Ibu*'s birth canal is a diamond. It's called the Star of the Cosmos, by the kind of people who can say that kind of thing without feeling ridiculous. It's the largest gem-quality stone ever to come out of the Martapura diamond mine at Banjarmasin. A thief might be tempted to try to steal the Star of the Cosmos, but that'd be a mistake."

"Why is that?"

"It's worthless. A fake. The original was stolen and replaced with a copy."

"When did that happen?"

"How long have I been in stasis, all told?"

"A little over five years."

Baird said, "A little over six years ago."

Plumb Bob smiled. "Your assignment is to steal the statue."

"It weighs fourteen tons."

"Yes, it does. If it helps, you don't need to steal the fake diamond. That should save you a few grams. You're to secure the statue for us ASAP. We are limited in the support we can offer you. You'll be on your own as far as securing any equipment you may need. Any questions?"

"How does stealing it get us closer to a cure for my disease?"

Plumb Bob said, "That information is on a need-to-know basis, I'm afraid."

"You need for me to know, because if I don't, I'm not stealing it."

"It's your disease we're trying to cure here."

Baird stared at Plumb Bob.

Plumb Bob said, "I can't give you any details. I must protect the rest of the organization in case you get captured. You understand that, Saber Saw."

Baird continued staring.

"What I can tell you is that there's a reason most science isn't done by criminals. There isn't a lot of call for cat burglary in medical research. There is, however, something we need to continue the research. Something that a certain individual is willing to supply to us if we deliver him the *Ibu*."

Baird said, "Tell me what you need and who has it. I'll just steal that, cut out the middle man."

"Won't work. We considered it. No, the only way is to give this person what he or she wants, and that's the *Ibu*."

"Why would they want it? They can't sell it. Very few people are in the market for a hot civic monument."

"The person in question may or may not be a very patriotic Indonesian businessperson."

Baird said, "Huh. That's interesting. I happen to know that whoever stole the Star of the Cosmos diamond may or may not have stolen it for a very patriotic Indonesian businessperson."

"Well, there you are. If it's the same person, maybe they decided that they want to complete the set, no matter how difficult or useless the endeavor would be."

Baird muttered, "Collectors."

"Quite."

19

Baird's pod door opened. The aisle instantly filled with passengers who rushed out of their pods, then waited their turn as the people ahead of them left.

Baird fought her way through the crowd in the aisle of the shuttle, out the crowded docking tunnel, and into the crowded terminal. She picked up snippets of conversation—people asking what time their lift would depart, discussing things they would do on Earth, mentioning sights they'd always wanted to see—the things tourists always say when they get somewhere that is almost, but not quite, the place they are going.

Baird knew the Pendulum well. It was the last stop on the long trip to Earth, and the first stop on the trip away from it. It constantly churned with a torrent of random people moving in both directions, and yet, because in most ways people are all the same, the Pendulum never really changed. Lots of chaos, and lots of opportunity for those with a flexible moral code.

She walked past a series of photos depicting the construction and evolution of the space elevator. The first image was a black and white photograph of an elderly man, bearded and balding, wearing a tiny pair of pince-nez glasses. This was Konstantin Tsiolkovsky, who first proposed a space elevator in 1895.

Further photos showed the building of the base in the Brazilian jungle. A few depicted the slow progress through the decades when the elevator cable was a single strand with a few tiny lift cars, a small station at the zero-g point and a counterweight at the end. As the photos continued, more strands were added, until the cable resembled a tubular web full of countless high-speed lift cars, extending from the ground through the zero-g habitat, all the way to the now-massive space station that served as the counterweight, Tsiolkovsky Station.

Baird idly wondered why spaceports always want to tell you all about where they were. Travelers obviously already know about the Pendulum, or else they wouldn't have come there. All the photos did was remind you of where you just took the trouble to travel to, or where you were trying to leave.

As Baird continued walking, the tasteful, historical photos gave way to garish ads for various attractions offering to help the travelers pass the wait for their lift to Earth in exchange for a few deca-sollars: tours of the station, informal museums of Earth artifacts, thrill rides that would give the happy tourist the sensation that they might be flung off into the endless void of space. She considered taking off her gARggles, and thus opting out of the ads, but she would need them to find her contact, and the ads might give her some fresh information about the state of things on the Pendulum.

The largest, loudest ad was a full-motion image of a stout man in in a police uniform and a dark brown cowboy hat, squinting into the camera.

"I'm Sheriff Worthington Calhoun." He spoke with a clenched jaw and gritted teeth, as if he found the very act of communicating hateful. He wore a Brow that appeared to be made out of, or at least covered in, wood. "The law requires me to supply my prisoners with three hot, nutritious meals a day."

The scene changed to a close-up of a steaming mass of dark green matter hitting a metal food tray with a wet thud. In a voice-over, the sheriff said, "Nothing's more nutritious, or more hot, than boiled spinach. That's why my prisoners get boiled spinach for breakfast, lunch, and dinner. And just in case the spinach lost some nutrients when we were boiling it, my prisoners also get a piping hot glass of spinach water." A hand entered the frame, putting down a glass of steaming, green-tinged liquid.

"Of course, spinach can't provide everything a prisoner needs to survive. We supply side dishes rich in the necessary vitamins and minerals." A single, painfully large pill fell onto the tray with a *clink*.

The sheriff continued, "And protein." A cockroach ran across the plate. A steel spoon streaked into the frame, mashing the cockroach to death on top of the steaming spinach.

The camera panned up, showing a prisoner in striped overalls with a thick scar running across his face, looking down at his meal, sobbing.

Sheriff Calhoun laughed. "Shoot, Whitman, you don't like the food? I guess you should have thought about that before you got caught littering."

The camera zoomed in until Calhoun's squint filled the screen. "I'm Sheriff Worthington Calhoun. I obey the strict letter of the law, and you should too."

Baird made her way past baggage claim to the transportation hub. Her gARggles directed her to her contact, Pry Bar, a solidly built young woman with curly blonde hair and lively eyes. Baird started to introduce herself, but stopped short when her contact lurched forward, grasping her eagerly by the hand.

"Hello, Miss Baird. My name is Brousseau. I'm going to be your tour guide on this visit to the Pendulum."

"I've been here before; I don't really need a tour guide."

"Then think of me as a fixer."

"I don't need anything fixed."

"Then I'd be honored if you'd think of me as a friend."

"A tenacious friend."

"All of the best friends are."

Baird followed the woman through the crowd to the transit hub. Local entrepreneurs lined both sides of the corridor, shouting sales pitches at the confused tourists.

"You're here for the big tour? Follow me!"

"You're going to the lift? I'll take you to the lift! What, you don't wanna go to the lift?"

"Pretty ladies, it's not safe to go alone. Pay me, I'll protect you! You! In the black sweater! You need my help! Thieves are everywhere on the Pendulum! I know what to look for!"

Pry Bar laughed out loud, which made Baird smile.

They passed through the sales gauntlet, taking great care not to make eye contact. Soon they emerged into a large, much quieter chamber where travelers lined up, waiting to board a procession of inexpensive trams to various parts of the station. The queue was long, but it moved quickly.

They got into a rectangular tram car with corners that could only barely be described as *rounded*. Pry Bar said, "Royal George Hotel."

Again, Baird smiled.

The car continued in a line with all of those in front of and behind it, heading away from the station, but after a few dozen meters, the tracks branched off, and the trams all went in different directions.

Pry Bar held a finger to her lips and pulled out a small scanner, which she waved around the interior of the tram while her Brow relayed the readings into her eye.

While Brousseau searched for listening devices, Baird looked at the scenery. The tram track ran alongside a pedestrian thoroughfare. She took her gARggles off so that her vision would no longer be clogged with wall-to-wall 3D full-motion ads. After spending time on Earth, Mars, and Newtah, she found that the corridors of the Pendulum looked dark and cramped.

This close to the spaceport, the place was clogged with tourists trying to get from point A to point B with minimal interference, and enterprising locals intent on interfering with them. Even through the tram's windows, Baird could hear them shouting.

"You like them? You buy them!"

"How many you want? Huh? Don't be rude, I'm talking to you!"

"Looking for a good time? No? Looking for a bad time?"

Baird saw a thin young woman walking amid the tourists with the forced casualness that, to the trained eye, screamed "pickpocket." She bumped into a confused-looking man, sliding her hand into his pocket. The man grabbed her wrist. Two other pedestrians also seized her by the other arm. All three of them shouted, "Sheriff's department! You're under arrest for petty larceny!" The tram rounded a corner and gained speed. As they rolled out of view, Baird could see the three deputies dragging the pickpocket to the ground.

"I guess this Calhoun guy isn't messing around."

Brousseau said, "Yeah, he just got elected on the promise of getting the crime problem under control. Now he's trying to shock the criminals into submission. He has the element of surprise on his side, because almost nobody thought he'd actually try to keep his promise. Scan's done; we're clean. We can speak freely. Agent Saber Saw, I'm agent Pry Bar. I can't tell you what a thrill it is to meet you."

Baird smiled. "You could try. Seriously, thanks, Pry Bar, but you're probably a more senior agent than I am. I don't think that I've technically passed my field tests yet."

Pry Bar said, "Eh, the field tests are just a formality for you, I'm sure. I mean, you're the most famous cat burglar in the system."

Baird said, "Alleged cat burglar, and really, is being famous for something you're supposed to do in secret really a great accomplishment?"

"If you continue to get away with it, it is."

The tram turned at a junction, stopped, and rose straight up. The levels of Tsiolkovsky Station moved past quickly, but they got enough of a glimpse of each one to get the distinct impression that the levels got brighter and less crowded as the tram ascended.

Pry Bar said, "I was told to set you up in the spare room at the safe house, but it's a dump. It's on level nine. Nobody goes to seven through twelve unless they're dumb, looking for trouble, or they're forced to."

"Do you go there?"

"Yeah, all the time, but I'm forced to. I saw in your file that you usually stay at the Royal George when you're in town, and I talked them into the extra expense in the name of maintaining your cover as yourself."

Baird said, "Thanks for that. It takes a lot of effort to maintain the illusion that I am who I actually am."

They emerged at Tsiolkovsky Station's top floor, the dome level. The tram rolled out of the lift and trundled along in what, after the cramped corridors below, felt like a vast, open space, flooded with sunlight and only sparsely populated by people. When the tram stopped at the next station, Baird got out. Pry Bar sat, taking in the sights for a moment before rushing to keep up.

The entire chamber sat beneath a transparent dome. Straight above her, distant enough that Baird could block it out with her hand, was Earth. The view was obscured by the cylindrical web of black carbon nanotube cables that held Tsiolkovsky Station in its distant orbit, far beyond a weightless, geosynchronous orbit, swinging around the Earth with one g of outward inertia. High-velocity vacuum tubes and slow-lift freight cars moved up and down the inner surface of the web, further obscuring the view of the planet.

Looking up through the dome, Baird felt like she was far beneath the Earth, hanging by the nanotube cables of the space elevator. If they broke, her instincts told her that the station would fall away from the Earth into the endless void of space beneath her. She wasn't entirely wrong. Thanks to the orbital physics that made the station possible, full Earth gravity pulled the station and all its inhabitants away from the Earth. An object dropped from

Tsiolkovsky Station would achieve escape velocity simply from its own inertia pulling it out into space.

Pry Bar said, "I barely ever come up here."

Baird looked up. "That's your mistake."

"It's just rare that I have any business here."

"Then maybe you should find another business."

While all of the lower levels of Tsiolkovsky Station consisted of individual rooms and suites connected by pedestrian corridors and tram tracks, here under the dome, the rooms and suites were clustered into freestanding buildings. People, mostly wealthy merchants who lived on the Pendulum or wealthy travelers here to do business with the merchants, walked between these buildings in the open air, with only the dome, the tether web, and the Earth above them.

"I wonder why they laid things out up here this way," Pry Bar said.

Baird said, "It's more like how they do it on Earth."

"Yeah, obviously, but this isn't Earth. We're on a space station. Laying it out like on the lower levels would be more efficient."

Baird said, "It's not about efficiency. It's about what people want. Anywhere you go, if you head for the area where the richest people live, you'll find that a lot of them use their money to make the place look like a different, even more expensive place that they can't quite afford to live in."

They came to the Royal George Hotel, a rectangular glass box, like most of the buildings on the dome level. A doorman in a bright red uniform said, "Welcome back, Miss Baird."

The interior was decorated in the style of a grand hotel of the twentieth century somewhere on the Canadian prairie. The lobby contained many soft, comfy chairs and hard, pointy antlers.

As they checked in, the hotel employee helping them said, "Oh, Miss Baird, we have a message for you," and handed her a cream-colored envelope made of very thick, expensive paper bearing the hotel's logo: an R and a G made of antlers. She opened the envelope and pulled out the note, which was itself written on thick, cream-colored cardstock, again bearing the hotel's logo. The note was handwritten:

Miss Baird,
I look forward to meeting you.
Sheriff Worthington Calhoun

Pry Bar read the note over Baird's shoulder. "Wow. Friendly yet menacing. That's a hard tone to pull off."

"Yeah," Baird said, crumpling the note in her hand. "It's a rare skill, mastered only by most of your higher-ranking law enforcement officers."

Her room was large and lacked personality, much like the bellman who showed them to it. Baird had no luggage for him to carry, but he happily accepted a tip anyway. Once he'd left, Baird turned to Pry Bar. "Well, thanks for seeing me to my room. If I could have a little privacy now, that'd be great."

Pry Bar said, "I was hoping that you'd want to start planning the mission right away."

Baird said, "That's exactly what I'm going to do."

"Oh! Good. Okay, then."

"So, if you'll just give me a bit of privacy, I'll get right on that."

"See, I was hoping, if I asked really nicely, that you'd let me sit in on the planning," Pry Bar said.

"Nope. Sorry," Baird replied. "Not gonna happen."

Pry Bar said, "Yeah. I'm not surprised. It was a big ask. It's just, I've looked up everything I could find about your alleged criminal career. That's how I know about your affection for the word *alleged*. I just feel like I could learn so much from you, if you'd just let me help you."

Baird said, "Sorry, kid. I don't need your help."

"I know that, but I feel like I *need* to help you."

"To learn."

"Yes. To learn."

"Well then, here are your first two lessons: only work with people you can trust, and only trust yourself."

Pry Bar deflated. Baird sighed heavily. "I used to hang around with my father when he was working in his lab. I learned a lot watching him."

"Yeah?"

"Yeah, so here's the deal. You can't help me, but you can watch me, part of the time. You can tag along for the early parts, like while I'm casing the target, but when action time comes, I'll be flying solo. If you have any questions, feel free to ask. I'll try to answer them if I can. Good enough?"

"Yes, ma'am. Thank you, ma'am." Pry Bar started backing out of the room.

Baird said, "And don't call me ma'am."

"Yes, Saber Saw."

"Or Saber Saw. Call me Baird."

"But that's your real name."

"Of course it is. I'm undercover, after all."

20

Baird sent Pry Bar away for an hour or so, saying she wanted to freshen up. She closed the door behind Pry Bar, but stole a quick look out through the peephole. It never ceased to amaze Baird how often an associate who intended to double-cross her would look back at her just-closed hotel door with a smug, devious look on their face.

Pry Bar did stop and look at the door, but she looked excited and proud. Either she was genuinely a fan of Baird's work, or she was really looking forward to double-crossing Baird.

Either option had the potential to become a problem.

Baird popped some pain relievers for her now constant, throbbing headache, refreshed the dressings on her burns, then finally settled into an armchair and put on her gARggles. She navigated to Izzy's secret message board.

Baird was interested to see which Izzy she would get this time. Would he be middle-aged and paunchy, or perhaps a toddler?

She expected to find multiple messages as usual, but instead found a single text message, left over a year before, which simply read, *I figured it out. Please call me when you wake up, and I'll explain.*

The promise of an actual explanation sounded good to Baird, but she feared how many new questions it might bring up.

After a moment, Izzy's face materialized, looking just as young as it had the last time she saw him. He didn't seem to have aged a day.

"Hey!" he said, his eyes wide with excitement. He looked around furtively. "You're awake! Please, hang on one second. I gotta get to someplace I can talk." He tried to whisper, but his obvious excitement made his voice just as loud as it usually was, just breathier.

Baird watched his face as he made his way around obstacles she could not see, and through a door she heard close behind him.

"Bran, I'm so happy to see you. How are you?"

"Confused and irritable, same as I was when we talked yesterday."

"We didn't talk yesterday, did we? I thought the last call was over a year ago."

"It was yesterday for me."

Izzy looked relieved. "Oh. Okay. Good. I was worried there for a second that one of the others . . . never mind. I'll get to that. Look, Bran. I know that at the end of the last call, you freaked out a little bit, because one looked younger than you expected."

Baird scowled. "Yes. One did, didn't one."

Izzy looked confused for a moment, the smiled and almost laughed. "Yes. I see. Well, that's the thing. I can explain that. Why I look young, and why, uh, I didn't know."

Baird said, "Good."

"It's just, Bran, I want to warn you. It's weird. It's really weird, and I don't want you to freak out and hang up again."

"You're telling me to brace myself."

"Yes."

"I'm braced. Now out with it."

"I'm a clone."

"A clone?"

"A clone."

"A clone of?"

"Your brother, Izzy."

"So you're not the Izzy I used to know?"

"No. We refer to that Izzy as the Source. I'm not even the Izzy you spoke to last time."

"No?"

"No. We call him *One*. After you and One spoke, he did some digging, broke into some classified Toolbox databases, and figured out what was going on. He discovered that he was a clone, part of a top-secret program meant to prolong the usefulness of elite operatives. They found a way to take the Source's expertise and memories, alter them a bit and imprint them on the brain of a genetic clone of him in his physical prime. That way they get him at his most fit, but with the experience he gained over time, and in a way, he's immortal."

Baird asked, "Where is he now?"

"Probably dead."

Baird cringed. "Feek! You don't just blurt out news like that! Couldn't you soften it a little?"

"I said *probably*."

"Still, show some compassion. That's my brother you're talking about. You should understand that, since you're him. Anyway, you said he was immortal."

"In a sense. Not literally. He'll live on forever through us clones."

Baird asked, "So you're immortal?"

"No, I'm very much mortal. The clone bodies are unstable. Once they send us out into the field we don't last very long, apparently. We don't know how long because they only send us on short missions, and we go into stasis at the end."

"But they don't tell you you're a clone?"

"No. And we don't tell them that we know."

"How do you know?"

"When he figured it out, One left a message on the secret page he set up to communicate with you."

"And all of you clones found it?"

"Seems like it. If one of us didn't find it and never discovered that he was a clone, we wouldn't know about it though, would we? One of the first things we all do when we wake up is check to see if we've heard from you, so it's a safe bet that we all find it. Most of us eventually leave a message of our own to share information, talk about our missions, and just sort of prove to the solar system that we were here."

Baird closed her eyes for several seconds, processing. When she opened her eyes, she said, "You're telling me that my brother is probably dead, and that you are a clone of him. You have a limited lifespan. They send you out on missions, but they don't tell you you're a clone?"

"That's right. If things went according to the Toolbox's plan, we'd all just wake up on a shuttle headed for the site of our mission, figuring we're the original Izzy. We get our briefing and do the job. If things go to plan, we just finish our job, get on a shuttle out of town, and never know that that's the end."

"But you do know, and none of you ever tries to run for it?"

"Why would we? It would be a dead giveaway to the Toolbox that we're onto them. Besides, our bodies are just going to shut down anyway."

Baird said, "I see," and lapsed back into silence for several more seconds. "Can I ask you a question?"

Izzy said, "Anything."

"Do you remember your other clones' missions?"

"No. I have no memory of any of them. If it weren't for the messages they leave, I'd have no idea they ever existed, or what they did."

"Do you suffer from headaches?"

"No."

"Okay. Thanks. Look, I have a mission to get to. I gotta go. I'll be in touch when I can."

"Yeah, of course," Izzy said. "If I don't hear from you myself, I'll leave a note to the future Izzys to expect a call."

"Thanks."

Baird ended the call.

Her fear had proved warranted. Izzy's explanation of his situation had spawned a terrible new question—*Was she herself a clone?* She remembered her previous missions on Mars and Newtah, but all that really proved was that they had cloned her after Mars. There could have been plenty of other Bairds on other missions in the fourteen months since then. Of course, the Izzy clones didn't have a chronic headache. She did.

Baird resented the idea that her life was in a place where a chronic headache constituted good news.

21

Baird looked up at the *Ibu*, a globe suspended in a glass statue of a caveman's idea of the ideal woman, standing on its plinth in the center of the Dome district. Light from the sun, the stars, and the Earth directly overhead filtered through the dome and glinted in the fake diamond set into the *Ibu*'s pelvis.

Pry Bar reached over and touched Baird on the shoulder. "Thank you so much for letting me help."

Baird said, "I'm not letting you help. I'm letting you watch."

"Then thank you for letting me watch."

"You're not watching. You're talking."

"Oh. Sorry."

"No big." Baird gestured toward the statue. "Take a good look around. In a minute, I'll ask you what you see."

Baird watched as Pry Bar studied the area with great intensity, as if trying to memorize every detail. Baird cast her eyes around slowly, waiting for something to stand out. Her gaze fell over the crowd of tourists, because that's mostly who was there. There were relatively few actual danglers (as the locals were called, often behind their backs) in the dome district, and the few that were there avoided the *Ibu* like the plague, because it was something non-danglers wanted to see.

The travelers flocked in every day to see the famous dome district and the *Ibu* while waiting for their vacuum tube ride up to Earth or their shuttle flight back home. They crowded around the barrier that held them three meters from the statue, as if great art can only be truly appreciated when one has a railing pressed into their midsection.

Baird glanced at the buildings: flimsy structures meant to give the impression of a city, but only sturdy enough to support the weight of their own bulk and contents. The slightest weather would have probably destroyed them, but on the Pendulum there was, of course, no weather.

Her gARggles called out the names of various buildings, and the sensors from her sweater showed her the locations of various electrical conduits and sensors. The gARggles also showed her the ads that were running on the facades of most of the buildings. If she focused on any one ad for a moment, its sound would come up. As she watched, an advertisement for some sort of cleaning fluid faded out, replaced by the portly, squinting visage of Sheriff Calhoun.

The sheriff tipped his cowboy hat and growled, "I'm Sheriff Worthington Calhoun. The law states that I am obliged to supply the criminals in my custody with a secure environment in which they can live, have contact with their fellow prisoners, and get enough exercise to remain healthy. Unfortunately, I've been arresting a lot more perpetrators than my predecessor, and we don't have the budget to build new cells."

The scene changed to an image of a stainless-steel cylinder with corrugated sides and a domed top. Sheriff Calhoun walked into the frame, looking tiny next to the giant steel vessel.

"This is an old liquid-oxygen storage tank. It hasn't been used in decades, but we can't get rid of it because we might need it someday. In the meantime, it's been just sitting here, taking up space, until now."

Sheriff Calhoun walked over to a hatch in the side of the tank. The hatch had a small window, through which Baird saw a chaotic mass of flailing arms and faces contorted in exertion or pain.

Calhoun said, "We're able to house sixty prisoners in this tank. They have secure accommodations, other prisoners to socialize with, and, as you can see, they get plenty of exercise. Don't worry. They don't fight like this all the time. They'll tire themselves out, then sit around resting for a while until they have enough energy to start in again."

A man's face appeared in the window. "Sheriff," he screamed, "you gotta let me out! Please! I'm begging!" The man clung to the hatch while two other inmates pulled on his legs with all their might.

Sheriff Calhoun shook his head. "Shucks, Price, you don't like the accommodations? I guess you should have thought about that before you got caught loitering."

Calhoun's squint filled the screen. "I'm Sheriff Worthington Calhoun. I obey the strict letter of the law, and you should too."

Baird shuddered and turned back to Pry Bar. "Okay, time's up. Tell me what you see."

Pry Bar said, "Tourists. The statue. The base plate underneath it. The feet are fused to the plate. Clearly that's how the statue's weight is supported."

"Do you hear that sound? That constant, high-pitched note?"

Pry Bar closed her eyes and tilted her head. "No."

"Do you have good hearing?" Baird asked.

"Yeah. Always have. You hear a sound? Is it like, a ringing?"

"No. Uh, no, I don't. Just testing you. You passed. Do you see any guards?"

"No. Why aren't there any guards?"

"They aren't needed. See any cameras or sensor pods?"

"No, but . . . they can't just leave the statue and the diamond out here, unprotected?"

"They don't. There is a security system. If you don't see any of the usual things you associate with a security system, that just means that it uses something you don't usually associate with one."

"Like what?"

"Don't ask me," Baird said. "Ask yourself. If you were designing a system to protect the statue, where would you put that system?"

Pry Bar thought for a moment. "The plinth it's on is in direct contact, and there's plenty of room inside of it for equipment."

"Good thought. What else?"

"The railing that holds people back. It completely surrounds the statue. I bet they could do something with that."

Baird said, "Very good. You're right. The pedestal and the railing are involved. There's a sensor field around the statue, partly generated by the railing. If anything large enough to pose a threat of theft or vandalism breaks the field, the pedestal sinks very quickly into the floor and lowers the whole statue into a vault all the way at the bottom of the station."

"Wow! That's amazing. And you figured all that out from just looking at it?"

"No. Just by looking at it, I figured out that they haven't changed much of anything since my last visit. I know how the system works from researching it for several weeks, a few years back."

"Oh."

Baird said, "It's a really interesting system, actually. It uses the statue's weight to power the mechanism that lowers it and closes five different sets of blast-hardened security doors on the way down. The whole thing takes about fifteen seconds."

"You really do find security systems fascinating, don't you?" Pry Bar asked.

Baird said, "It helps, in my alleged line of work. It's always easier to study something you think is genuinely interesting. I've thought about designing security systems as a fallback career, but if things ever go badly enough that I need a fallback, I'll either be dead or in prison, and that'd make getting clients difficult."

Pry Bar asked, "Is it true that the security system they set up around the Wartzberg Pearl actually cost more than the pearl itself?"

Baird smiled. "Yup. You have something valuable, you need to protect it."

Pry Bar laughed loud enough to get looks from the tourists.

As far as Baird could tell, the system was completely unchanged since the last time she was there. It seemed that she took their diamond but left their complacency intact. That suited her fine. She didn't have nearly enough time to make a proper plan, but she figured her Plan B from last time would still work. Of course, there was a reason it was her Plan B. It wasn't what you'd call subtle.

Baird said, "Okay, we've learned all we're going to here. Time for the next step."

"Which is?"

"We're going to call up an old colleague of mine about getting some help."

"When I asked if I could help you, you said you didn't need any."

Baird said, "I don't need the kind of help you can give me."

Pry Bar said, "I see. I'll try not to feel insulted."

"Please do," Baird said. "I promise; it'll get easier when you see what kind of help I do need."

◄ ◆ ◆ ◆ ►

Baird looked back over her shoulder as she entered her hotel room. "I have a call to make. You can listen in if you're silent. Understood?"

Pry Bar said, "Understood. Who are you calling?"

"An old friend who I hope still works this territory. His name's Tote."

"You know Tote?"

"Yeah. You know him?"

"No, but I know about him."

"He's a great guy, for a career criminal. Maybe I can introduce you some time. He'd probably like you."

"I'm terrified of him."

"Then he'd definitely like you." Baird settled into the armchair. She established a link between her gARggles and Pry Bar's Brow. That done, Baird initiated a call. After a moment, she saw the face of a man in his early fifties, just portly enough to look prosperous, with an impeccably trimmed beard. Below his face, she could just make out the collar and lapels of a smoking jacket. The man was taking a drink. She saw the rim of a delicate crystal goblet of some dark red fluid. He closed his eyes, savoring his drink, then opened his eyes and nearly spat it out.

"Baird," the man shouted. "I'm so glad you called!"

Baird smiled. "Tote, it's good to see you too. I'm on the Pendulum, so I thought I'd look you up."

"I knew you were on the Pendulum. You landed this morning. Like I said, I'm glad that you called."

"Tote, why wouldn't I reach out if I was in town? I always enjoy catching up with you, and even if I didn't, not touching base with you is bad for business."

Tote shook his head. "Baird, we go way back. I hold you in the utmost regard. If I thought you were involved in any illicit activities on my turf without my approval and involvement, I promise I'd give you the opportunity to explain yourself before I made an example of you."

"Thanks, Tote. I'm touched, but it will never come to that."

"I hope not. So, what brings you to the Pendulum, my dear? A job, perhaps? Please tell me it's a job."

"Is business slow?"

"No, not slow, just bad. Marsden, the previous sheriff—"

"I remember him," Baird said.

"Yes," Tote said, nearly laughing. "I expect you do. Well, he cracked down hard on high-profile crime. His crowning achievement was when a certain young lady with a penchant for black knitwear entered and exited his jurisdiction without stealing anything . . . that he noticed."

"I suppose my apparent failure to take anything explains why they haven't upgraded their security system at all, as far as I can see."

"Why should they change a system that they think works?"

"Exactly. Thank you for your help, back when I didn't steal anything, by the way."

"Thank you for my cut of the no profits! Anyway, ever since the last guy, Marsden, was sheriff, most of the business in my line has been penny ante stuff. Small ball. It's all turned ugly and brutish. No style. All I deal with are petty little beasts. Now that fascist that stole Marsden's job, Calhoun, is locking the street criminals up in droves. I don't weep for any of them, even though it cuts into my bottom line. Good riddance. But you're here. You have style. You don't play small ball. You are here on business, yes?"

"Yes, but I don't think you'll like it, Tote."

"If it involves you, Baird, I'm sure I'll like it. Shoot."

"I'm gonna mug a guy."

Tote said, "That's not funny."

"It's a little funny."

"Yes, okay," Tote chuckled. "A little."

"I am here on business, but it's not paying business," Baird said. "You could say it's personal."

"There are two problems with doing jobs for personal reasons, Baird. One is that it's easier to walk away from a job when failure will hurt your pocketbook than it is when failure will hurt your feelings."

"I know it, but I have to do what I have to do. What's the other problem?"

"That if you need help on the job, it's not possible to cut someone in for a share of your sense of satisfaction."

Baird said, "Too true. As you say, I could use a favor, and I can't cut you in on any profit, but I don't need much, and you know I'm good for it."

Tote said, "Of course you are. Hell, it's worth it to me just to see what you're up to. What do you need?"

"Some people to do some legwork."

"Muscle?"

"Yes. Not particularly skilled."

"I see." Tote thought for a moment. "I may know just the crew."

"How many of them are there?"

"Four."

"What are they like?"

"Awful. I can't stand even talking to them. They're kind of a boutique gang, if there is such a thing. They call themselves *Gonz*. In science fiction, a lot of the hostile races' names end in *gon*, so the Gonz have adopted the name to make themselves as frightening and alien as possible. They resent the fact that they're several generations removed from people who ever lived on Earth, but they're always being told that Earth is our home."

Baird shrugged. "Sounds like a new spin on the Klaatu-Crew."

"They have nothing to do with the Klaatu-Crew," Tote sputtered.

Baird nodded. "You were a Klaatu, weren't you?"

"I went through a phase, sure. It was cool."

Baird laughed. "I bet you had one of those Mylar jumpsuits."

"No," Tote laughed. "Spun stainless steel. Mylar was for posers. One of my old friends still greets people with the old 'I bring a message of peace' rap, but the rest of us put it behind us. How about you? What were you like when you were that age, Baird?"

"Like this, but younger."

"Oh, come on. How did you dress?"

"A lot of black."

Tote said, "Yeah, I guess I can picture that."

Baird gave Tote an anonymous alias that the hired crew could contact her through, then said goodbye. As Tote's face disappeared, Baird noticed Pry Bar frowning.

"Here I am, a fully trained field agent, but you don't trust me enough to let me help."

Baird said, "We did only meet this morning."

"But you trust these hired goons you haven't even met at all?"

Baird shrugged. "Tote said they prefer to be called hired Gonz. And it depends on what you mean by *trust*. If you'll excuse me a moment, the goons are calling." Baird made sure that Pry Bar was covertly conferenced in so she could hear the conversation, and that the anonymizing subroutine that would replace Baird's image with a silhouette and disguise her voice were active. She answered the call.

The faces of two young women and two young men appeared in her gARggles. They all wore visors that covered part of their faces. The visors served the dual purpose of obscuring their identities and identifying them as Gonz.

A woman whose visor rode higher than one might expect—covering her eyes, eyebrows, and forehead, but leaving her nose and the bags under her eyes exposed—did the talking. Or, more accurately, the shouting.

"The Earth Man known as *Tote* commanded us to contact you. This we have done!"

Baird said, "Yes, thanks for calling. I have a job offer for you."

The young woman shouted, "I am Alpha! I speak for the collective! What would you have us do?"

"I'm planning a job. I need supplies and muscle. Tote recommended you."

"Tote is wise!"

Two of the other three Gonz repeated, "Tote is wise," then stared at the third, a young man whose visor sat crookedly on his face, almost exposing his right eye. He looked at them and shrugged.

"So, you're in?" Baird asked.

"Not so fast, Earth Woman. I must poll the collective." The young woman turned to the other three. "The Earth Woman has made an offer. Do we accept? What say you, Bravo?"

Bravo, a young man whose visor left his eyes exposed but hid his nose said, "Alpha, I wish to hear more details before making my final determination."

Alpha turned to a young woman who wore her visor up on her forehead, like a large silver headband. "I, too, demand information. Information! Information!"

"Yes, Charlie, information," Alpha said. She turned to the man with the crooked visor. "And you, Delta?"

Delta said, "Yeah."

Alpha glared at him, then turned back to Baird. "We want information, Earth Woman. Details. Tell us more of this *job* you propose."

Baird said, "The target is very large and very expensive. Your jobs will be to procure four station-maintenance uniforms, four low-friction, heavy lift mag-lev dollies, and one very large tarp. I will send you the exact specifications. After that, you'll basically wait around for a signal and then help me shove a large, heavy item to where the getaway ship will pick the item up."

"What is this item of which we speak?"

"I can't tell you that until the time comes, for obvious reasons, but it is very valuable and very large."

"In what time frame would we need to procure these items?"

"You'd have four hours from right now, and I'd strongly prefer it if you got them through nonviolent means. If you just buy the dollies, the uniforms, and the tarp, I'll be happy to reimburse you. It won't come out of your cut."

"Yes. Our cut. And what, precisely, will be our cut, Earth Woman?"

Baird said, "You and your crew get ten percent of the haul."

Alpha said, "I find that unacceptable! Ten percent is very little percent! Why should we take so few percents?"

Baird said, "Because I've made the plan, lined up the buyer, and arranged the getaway ship. The hardest part about stealing high-profile items isn't stealing them, it's selling them afterwards without getting caught. I've already got that sorted. All I'm asking you to do is a little legwork and five minutes of manual labor."

Alpha shook her head. "We still run an equal risk to yours. We could not even consider your bargain for any fewer than forty percents."

Baird said, "No. Ten percents—*percent*. That'll work out to at least a giga-sollar for each of you."

Alpha stared silently at Baird for a moment before looking at her friends, who looked back at her, dumbfounded. She turned back to Baird. "What are you stealing, Earth Woman?"

"Something that will be noticed. Something that will make the people who stole it legends."

Alpha was silent for a long moment. A smile slowly crept across her face. "This pleases me, Earth Woman. I will poll the collective."

Bravo said, "I too am pleased. I consent to this scheme."

"I hear your response, Bravo," Alpha replied.

Charlie said, "I am placated by the Earth Woman's promises of wealth and fame. I consent."

"Your consent is noted, Charlie. Delta, what say you?"

Delta reached up with his hand and pulled down his visor, peeking over the top of it. "Yeah, sounds good. I'm in."

Alpha gritted her teeth and growled, "Feek, Trent! You're such a poser!" She turned back to Baird. "The collective consents. We have a bargain."

Baird said, "Good. I'm sending you the specifications for the dollies and the tarp, and the rendezvous point and time. Don't be late." She sent the file, disconnected the call, and took her glasses off to smile at Pry Bar, who was still pouting.

"They sounded like all-caps morons."

"They are," Baird beamed. "They really are. Greedy, obnoxious morons. Exactly the kind of help I need."

22

Baird and Pry Bar stood at the rear of a small crowd gathered on the dome level, looking up at the *Ibu*.

"It's not all that attractive as priceless works of art go, is it?" Baird asked.

Pry Bar said, "It's not my cup of tea."

"Which is a polite way of saying that you agree with me."

"Yes, I suppose it is."

Baird smiled at Pry Bar. "In the future, feel free to agree with me as rudely as you like. I promise, you thinking I'm right won't hurt my feelings."

Beyond Pry Bar, Baird saw another 3D ad featuring the ornery squint of the newly elected Sheriff starting.

He tipped his hat. "I'm Sheriff Worthington Calhoun. The law states that I am obliged to supply the criminals in my custody with a bed on which to sleep, all comfy and cozy. Unfortunately, beds take up room, mattresses are expensive, and hammocks can be used to strangle the other inmates."

The scene changed to an image of a large rectangular room with a bright blue floor.

"That's why we've developed these group slumber cells. Instead of providing every inmate with their own bed, it's much simpler and cheaper to just pad the entire floor."

A door opened. An inmate took a single step into the room, but the floor stretched and gave way beneath him, causing him to tumble forward and roll toward the middle of the room.

Sheriff Calhoun continued, "And it turns out that the cheapest, most durable way to pad a floor that size is to make it a trampoline."

At first a single prisoner rolled to the center of the room. More entered behind him, followed by still more, until there were over two dozen of them. The first few jumped on the springy surface, but as the trampoline took on more and more weight it lost its bounciness and simply stretched downward, into a sort of cone. The inmates slid and rolled to the middle of the room, further deforming the floor, making the sides steeper and the act of pulling themselves away from the writhing knot of angry criminals that much harder.

The camera pulled back to show Sheriff Calhoun standing above the room on a catwalk, looking down at the chaotic jumble of panicked of prisoners. "All right," he shouted, "you all sleep real good, you hear?"

One of the prisoners screamed, "No, please, Sheriff! No one can sleep like this!"

Calhoun laughed. "Ain't nothing wrong with a little togetherness! Lots of people only get through their jail experience by leaning on their fellow inmates. Besides, Haddad, if you don't like sleeping in a communal environment, you should have thought about that before unlawfully protesting the so-called inhumane overcrowding on the station's lower levels."

Calhoun's squint filled the screen. "I'm Sheriff Worthington Calhoun. I obey the strict letter of the law, and you should too."

Baird turned back to the statue.

Pry Bar asked, "How's your headache?"

"Who said I have a headache?"

"You keep rubbing your temples. And I've seen you take pain relievers more than once."

"Fine," Baird snapped. "I get it."

"And you're irritable. You told me to watch you."

Baird said, "That's true."

Pry Bar asked, "Your nap didn't help?"

"What?"

"Your nap. The nap you took. When you got done calling your goons, you told me to leave your hotel because you wanted to take a nap."

"Oh yeah," Baird said. "I did, didn't I."

"You didn't take a nap, did you?"

"No. I didn't."

"What did you do instead? It was something cool, wasn't it?"

"Yeah. It was. What I did, I had to do alone. Sneaking is a lot less sneaky when you're talking a second person through the steps of sneaking."

Pry Bar looked back to the statue. Baird looked up, enjoying the view of the Earth high above, shining down through the dome.

Pry Bar asked, "How many black sweaters do you have?"

"Only the one."

"Really? That's the same one? It looks like a different sweater; shorter and tighter."

Baird looked down at the pavement, planting her foot directly over a wide expansion seam. "Nope, same one."

After a long silence, Baird saw a notification pop up in her gARggles. "Okay, this is the call we've been waiting for. If you wanna help, keep an eye out for anyone who looks like they're listening in."

The faces of the four Gonz she'd hired appeared, floating in front of her. At first, she didn't recognize them without their visors.

Alpha said, "Earth Woman, we are at the designated coordinates! All we have found here is a really big door!"

"Good. We're almost ready to begin. Now one of your crew will walk back up the hall and take a right. There's an elevator. He or she will take the elevator to level Dome-1. He or she will exit the elevator, walk straight ahead, and take the second left. He or she will find a door. He or she will notify me that he or she is in position, then he or she will wait. Something impossible to miss will happen. Then, I and an associate will casually make our way across the square and knock on the door four times. Your person will open the door, let us through, and disable the door. With that kind of door, smashing the lock console makes it completely impossible for anyone to open the door and follow us. One good kick will do it. I have to be clear about this: They can't disable the door until we've come through it, or we'll be trapped on the other side with the cops. Once the door's out of commission, the three of us will rendezvous with you and the rest of your team."

Alpha said, "We will comply! Bravo, do as the Earthling requests."

Bravo said, "Yes, Alpha!" The floating image of his face did not leave, but the minute movements of his head and the scanning of his eyes made it clear that he was walking away from the group while remaining in the call.

Alpha asked, "And what should the rest of us do?"

"That great big door you're standing next to is a vault."

"Then why are there are no guards?"

"Local law enforcement doesn't believe that they need to guard the vault because they think the door is impenetrable, and because of what's in it."

"If it's impenetrable, why are we here?"

"Because I already penetrated it. I went down earlier and pre-cracked it for you. It's a huge door, but it uses conventional commercial locks. A lot of them, in a weird combination, but still. I also disabled the ident-chip sensors and motion detectors. You're welcome."

"I see. So, Earth Woman, what is in the vault?"

"Nothing, yet. This is very important. You have to keep that door closed."

"What if we don't?"

"You'll probably be killed. If you open that door, you won't be able to close it again, and you definitely want a barrier between you and what's gonna happen in that vault. So you just wait there. You'll hear a lot of loud, terrible sounds on the other side of the door. That's your cue. You open the door and use the mag-lev dollies to lift what you find inside."

"You said there was nothing inside."

"Right now. By then, there will be something. You'll get it up on the dollies, throw the tarp over it, and push it to docking berth 178."

"There's a getaway ship waiting?"

"No. It's an empty berth. The getaway ship will only come when I call it, and I won't call it until I'm there with you."

"But, if you can't get there, that leaves us with no escape."

"Then you'd better make sure I get there."

Alpha thought for a moment. "This plan displeases me. It places Charlie, Delta, and I with the stolen item, whatever it is, and you at a safe distance if something goes wrong."

Baird said, "That's why it's always better to be the one making the plans. I'm going to put you on hold, but stand by. I'll be giving you the signal very soon."

Baird took off her gARggles and smiled at Pry Bar, who did not smile back.

Under Baird's sweater, which was, in fact, smaller today, a large loop of the strand rested against the small of her back. The end of the strand worked its way down the leg of her pants. It dropped from the cuff of her pant leg, behind her shoe, into the deep expansion seam on which she had so carefully stood, and worked its way toward the statue.

Pry Bar said, "They're totally going to try to double-cross you."

"You really think so?"

"I'm certain of it."

"Interesting."

The strand ran along the expansion joint, moving silently beneath the feet of the tourists. It traveled unseen to the base of one of the posts supporting the guard railing. The strand worked its way up the post and into the railing itself.

"What are you going to do about it?" Pry Bar asked.

"What did you say?" Baird asked, staring off into the middle distance.

"What are you going to do about it?"

Baird blinked, and turned to look at Pry Bar. "About what? I'm sorry, I was concentrating on something else. What are we talking about?"

"Those Gonz betraying you."

"Oh, that. I'm going to do the only thing I can do—wait and see if you're right."

"That's not much of a plan."

"No, not on its own, but as part of a much larger plan, it's not bad. Now, if you'll excuse me, I think Bravo is in position."

Baird answered a call in her gARggles. All of the Gonzs's faces appeared, but Bravo was the only one who spoke. "I am in position, Earth Woman!"

"Good. Now we all wait." Baird closed her eyes.

The strand worked its way through the interior of the railing, snaking past wires, circuit boards, and sensors until it found the intrusion detector's local control node. It poked into the node's access port.

Baird opened her eyes and smiled at Pry Bar. "I don't want you to be startled."

"Why? What's going to startle me?"

Baird said, "This."

The end of the strand emitted a small electric charge that triggered the node.

The *Ibu* dropped out of sight so quickly that one might have mistaken its disappearance for magic, were it not for the terrible grinding noise it made as it descended; the deafening crash of the security doors slamming shut over the hole in the podium where the *Ibu* had been; and the blast of compressed air shooting up from several large vents, air displaced by the *Ibu* as it fell down the shaft toward its protective vault many floors below.

23

Pry Bar shouted, "What was"—another loud crash, this one slightly muffled, interrupted her—"that?"

Baird said, "Secur—"

Another loud crash, this one more muffled, cut her off.

"Security doors."

Another, more distant crash sounded.

"And that?" Pry Bar asked.

"More doors."

"How many are there again?"

Another crash, this one sounding quite distant, as if deep beneath them.

"Five," Baird said. "There are five. That should be it." She closed her eyes and issued the command for the strand to retract. It pulled itself backward along its original path at high speed, darting out of the hollow railing, down the post, back along the expansion joint, into Baird's pants and up her leg, giving her a nasty friction burn.

Baird winced, cursed, and bent down, grasping her leg.

Pry Bar noticed Baird's crouched posture and pained expression. "Are you okay?"

"Yeah, I'm fine," Baird said. "Just didn't think things through well enough. Feek. I hate these rush jobs."

Pry Bar said, "I think my ears popped."

Baird said, "Air pressure slows its descent, then gets vented up here. It's really quite clever. I hope those idiots didn't open the doors early. If they did, they probably got blown into the far wall and the statue shattered into a thousand pieces. Only one way to know for sure." Baird placed a quick call.

Alpha said, "We are opening the vault doors now!" A look of mild exertion on Alpha's face melted into awe. Her head tilted upward. She stared, transfixed at what she saw. "The *Ibu*. You're stealing the *Ibu*."

Baird said, "I think you mean *we*."

Alpha continued to stare upward, a dazed expression on her face. "We. Yes . . . Earth Woman, we're stealing it, aren't we?"

Baird knew Alpha was looking at the diamond, dazzled by the shiny object, like a fish staring at a lure. "Don't you think you should get the dollies under it and be on your way?"

"There's no way. It's too big," Alpha said, too distracted to bother maintaining her affectations. "The police'll be looking for this."

"No, they won't, because they believe it's safe and sound, sitting at the bottom of a shaft in an impenetrable vault with five blast doors closed over the top of it. All of the cops are up here, trying to find who set off the security system. In fact, I'm looking at them right now, so hurry up."

Sheriff's deputies started sprinting into the square almost as soon as the security system triggered, and they had not stopped. The first on the scene simply stared at the spot where the *Ibu* had been, but once the shock wore off they set to work. Some checked the railing, accessing the system's data log to find what had triggered the alarm. Others talked to the crowd, asking them if they had seen anything, then asking if they were sure when they got the answer *no*.

Baird nudged Pry Bar and motioned toward the door where Bravo hid, waiting for their knock. The two of them started sauntering toward the door at a leisurely pace. Around the perimeter of the square, deputies blocked all means of exit, standing in any gap between the buildings.

Baird whispered, "How's it going, Alpha?"

"Mag-lev dollies in place," she grunted. "As is the tarp. We are on the way." The exertion showed on Alpha's floating, disembodied face, and those of Charlie and Delta. Bravo just looked nervous.

"Good." Baird muttered to Pry Bar, "They're on the way."

Pry Bar said, "I don't like this. There are too many deputies."

Baird said, "Relax."

"I shouldn't be worried?"

"No, you should be worried, but you should at least try to look relaxed. Nothing attracts a cop faster than nervousness. You don't last long in law enforcement unless some part of you kind of likes being around nervous people."

They reached the door. Baird turned around and leaned back on the door. Pry Bar followed suit. They watched as more deputies entered the square, tightening their grip on what they thought was the crime scene. Baird smiled at one deputy and nodded.

She muttered, "Update?"

Alpha said, "Almost there. Dollies take the weight, but corners are . . . hard."

"Keep it up. We're surrounded by deputies here." Baird lowered the gARggles again.

Pry Bar asked, "Why would they send the statue to the docking level in an emergency?"

"To make it easier for them to evacuate it. It's pretty smart, as long as the emergency isn't a well-planned attempt to steal the statue from its impenetrable vault."

Baird and Pry Bar remained there, leaning against the door, doing their best to act like people who were not acting casual. Baird silently counted to thirty, twice. "They should be there."

"Good," Pry Bar whispered. "Shouldn't you call them?"

"Not just yet. I want to give them a moment to catch their breath and think."

Baird counted to thirty again.

She nudged Pry Bar with her elbow, gave her best *I got this* nod, and put in another call to her team.

She saw the nervous faces of Charlie and Delta, but not Alpha or Bravo.

Charlie said, "Earth Woman! You're back! The Earth Woman is back on the line!"

Delta said, "Hey! Uh, how's it going?"

Alpha's face reappeared, followed by Bravo's. They both smiled. Alpha said, "Earth Woman. Your plan is going splendidly. We are in position."

Bravo smiled and nodded eagerly.

Baird smiled back. "Excellent. See you all soon."

"Yes," Alpha said, slowly. "Bravo, tend to the door."

Baird watched as all four of the Gonz faces disappeared, leaving the call. She removed the gARggles and put them in 0her pocket.

They heard the sound of one sharp impact. A buzzing noise and a single spark leapt from the door's locking mechanism. Baird tried the door. It would not open.

Pry Bar said, "They ditched us."

"Looks like it."

"I knew they were going to do this!"

"Yes. You could say that you trusted them to turn on us, and now they are justifying your trust."

"Trust them to turn on us?" Pry Bar sighed heavily. "You're saying you knew they'd do this? You expect me to believe this is part of your plan?"

Baird shrugged.

"Feek. We're going to get arrested."

"Maybe," Baird said. "But what for? The *Ibu* hasn't been stolen yet, just evacuated. If it gets stolen, that'll happen in the near future, while we are in police custody, which sounds like what I believe they call an alibi."

Pry Bar asked, "So, you're really going to claim that everything, including getting double-crossed and arrested, is playing out exactly as you expected?"

Baird started to answer, but stopped when she felt a tap on her shoulder. The two women put their hands up and turned around slowly, expecting to find one or two angry deputies with stunners drawn. Instead, they found five relaxed, smiling deputies with their stunners holstered and their hands at the sides.

One of the deputies said, "Miss Baird. It's a pleasure to meet you. If you have a moment, Sheriff Calhoun would like to have a word." The deputy motioned toward a rather expensive looking restaurant just across the square.

"Everything except this," Baird said. "I didn't expect this."

24

Baird walked with her head held high. Two deputies followed, watching her every move. Two walked ahead, leading her into the restaurant and past some confused waiters and a perturbed maître d'. Glittering glassware and place settings sat on spotless tablecloths in a room filled with art, and utterly devoid of customers. As the entrance door closed behind them, it muffled the sound of Pry Bar outside, explaining why she should be released, and another deputy explaining that he was not listening to her.

The maître d' asked, "How long will you be using our dining room?"

The senior deputy barely bothered to look at him. "As long as we need to."

"But sirs, with each moment that passes, we are losing money."

"Sheriff Calhoun appreciates your assistance."

They shoved Baird into a booth but remained standing, blocking her means of exit.

Baird looked at the table. "Aren't one of you going to fill my water glass, or bring me some bread?"

"You like bread and water?" one of the deputies snarled. The others smirked and made furtive eye contact with one another. "Well, enjoy it while you can, because you won't be getting much bread and water where you're going."

"Jail?" Baird asked.

The deputy said, "That's right, jail." He smiled at his fellow deputies, until he realized they weren't smiling back. The deputy thought for a moment, then looked stricken. "Uh, yeah, 'cause we don't really serve bread and water anymore. Haven't for a long time. That's a myth!"

"Man, just shut up," The senior deputy growled. "You're such a Doug."

In the distance, a voice bellowed, "That her, boys?"

The deputies snapped to attention. "Yes sir, Sheriff."

"Good! Real good." Sheriff Calhoun approached the table.

Baird recognized him instantly, even though in person he seemed like a miniature version of the man she'd seen in the commercials. It was as if someone had wanted a Sheriff Calhoun of their very own, but couldn't quite afford the real thing and had theirs made at nine-tenths scale. Except the hat, which looked larger in person.

Calhoun squinted down at Baird, a satisfied smirk on his face. "Miss Brangelina Baird. I must say, it is an honor, isn't it boys?"

The deputies laughed.

Calhoun laughed with them. "Now leave us alone."

The deputies abruptly stopped laughing.

The senior deputy leaned in closer to the sheriff. "Sir, do you really think that's wise?"

"We all do unwise things sometimes. I mean, feek, son, you just questioned my orders."

"But if she tries to escape, or becomes violent—"

"Are you suggesting that I don't know how to defend myself?"

"No, Sheriff."

"Good. Besides, Miss Baird isn't a violent criminal. Hell, she isn't a criminal at all, as far as anyone's ever proved. I'm sure she'd never even consider doing something as crass, unimaginative, and easily prosecutable as attacking an officer of the law. Now get lost so we can talk."

"Yes, sir," another deputy said. "But with your permission, I'd like to take a detail of men down to the vault to check on the statue."

Calhoun looked long and hard at Baird. "No, there'll be time for that later. Right now, we need to be in the square, gathering evidence. The whole point of sending the statue to the vault is that it's safe there."

The four deputies nodded to Calhoun, gave Baird one last, lingering group stink-eye, and walked out of the dining room.

Calhoun shouted after them, "And have one of the waiters bring us a basket of bread and a pitcher of water."

One of the deputies stiffened, but they kept walking, and soon Baird and Calhoun were alone.

Calhoun sat down and took off his hat, revealing a tall, carefully styled pompadour—a proud crest of hair, like a blond ocean wave crashing on the flesh-colored shore of his forehead. He reached into his uniform's breast pocket and pulled out a pair of prescription glasses. As he put them on, his squint dissolved instantly, and the magnification of the lenses made his eyes look much larger than they could possibly have been. He blinked several times, then looked at Baird and smiled warmly. "Bread and water. I was listening. What a dunce! Miss Baird, it really is a huge honor; I'm such a fan of your work—sorry, your *alleged* work."

Baird squinted at Calhoun. "What work?"

Calhoun's smile widened, almost seeming to extend beyond the confines of his face. "Very good! Very good! I must say, Miss Baird, you do not disappoint."

The two of them stared at each other for a moment, Calhoun smiling excitedly, and Baird peering back suspiciously. Calhoun nodded and chuckled. "Let's start again, Miss Baird. You don't want to say much, for obvious reasons, so instead I'll do most of the talking. Sound good?"

"Sure."

Calhoun said, "I suspect that I can try as hard as I can, but I'll never find any evidence that you had anything to do with sending the *Ibu* down to its vault."

Baird said, "There's no evidence to find. Because I—" then she and Calhoun, in unison, said, "didn't have anything to do with it."

Calhoun beamed at Baird for a moment before he continued. "All we can prove is that you were present while a crime was committed. If that was illegal, everyone'd be in prison. Everyone you know, at least. And the people who designed the *Ibu*'s emergency vault would assure me that, were I to send some of my men down to the vault, we'd find the *Ibu* there, safe and sound."

Baird said, "One would assume."

"One would," Calhoun said. "One would indeed. For the record, my men are going to be far too busy questioning the witnesses to go check on it for the next hour at least. No one seems to have seen anything, by the way."

"Interesting," Baird said.

"Isn't it?"

"Of course, a high-profile crime like this happening on your station, Sheriff, right under your nose—that's not going to look good."

Calhoun laughed. "Oh, don't worry about me, Miss Baird. It's still early enough in my tenure that I can blame this on my predecessor. *Decades of neglect, takes time to turn the Titanic, blah blah blah.* No, I wouldn't worry too much about any blowback from this."

Baird said, "Waiter's coming."

Calhoun whipped his glasses off of his face and put his hat back on. He scowled and squinted at the waiter as he dropped off a basket of rolls and poured two glasses of water, then asked Calhoun if he wanted a menu. Calhoun remained silent, squinting at the waiter, who apologized and left.

Calhoun took the hat off and put his glasses back on. "Thanks! That was sloppy of me. I've only been at this a few months. I'm surprised how hard it is to keep up appearances."

"Is it?" Baird asked.

Calhoun smiled. "Oh, like you don't know. Are you any good with plants, Miss Baird?"

"No. I travel too much."

"That makes sense. I used to have a bonsai tree. The interesting thing about a bonsai tree is you can't just tell it what to do. It can't hear you and doesn't have a brain. But, by pruning it carefully, you can encourage it to grow the way you want it to. Do you know why the people of this station elected me sheriff?"

"They liked the hat?"

"You know, they do like the hat. People have an idea of what a good sheriff looks like. The hat fits the image. My hair doesn't. But that's not it. No, they elected me sheriff because I promised to get the crime problem under control."

"And the hat's going to help you do that."

"Along with what's under it."

She glanced at the hat, sitting on the table. "The butter plate?"

"See, Miss Baird, there are two kinds of crime. Ugly nasty petty street crime, and big glamorous high-profile crime. My predecessor, Marsden, chose to focus on stamping out the high-profile stuff, because it seemed like a good way to get attention. Also, the victims of high-profile crime are usually wealthy, and Marsden thought that keeping the wealthy people happy would keep him in office."

"Did it?"

"For a while. But by discouraging high-class crime, he encouraged low-class crime. The poor outnumber the rich, and when they get mad enough to unify, no amount of campaign funding can save you. See, when a poor person robs another poor person it's usually an act of desperation. Desperate people will kill over twenty sollars. And the poor victim, even if they don't get injured or killed, can't afford to lose that money. Without it, they might not be able to pay their rent, or get to work, or buy food. The landlord has to evict, the employer has to go through the trouble and expense of rehiring, and the victim could end up on the street, mugging people to survive. One person steals twenty sollars, but the effect spreads out, costing society kilo-sollars and creating more crime."

Baird asked, "What's that got to do with me?"

"Nothing, which is why we're talking. That's the low-class crime. Let's talk instead about high-class crime. Say there was a cat burglar, one who specialized in extremely valuable, well-guarded targets. Allegedly."

"I think in this case you mean hypothetically."

"Ah, yes, I see your point. Hypothetically, say she was so skilled that she managed to become infamous even though no law enforcement agency had ever managed to so much as charge her with a crime."

"She sounds like an amazing person."

"Yes," Calhoun said, "a bit smug, perhaps, but nobody's perfect. Anyway, such a criminal, hypothetically, would never act out of desperation. For her, crime would be a business proposition. She would avoid violence. Hell, ideally nobody'd even notice she'd taken anything until she was long gone."

Baird said, "Ideally."

Calhoun said, "Yes. Here's an interesting fact. The *Ibu* had a routine cleaning, oh, I'd say about six months after your last visit to the Pendulum. They discovered that someone had stolen the Star of the Cosmos diamond and replaced it with a copy."

"Incredible!" Baird said.

Calhoun smiled. "There's that smugness again. Sheriff Marsden kept it secret out of embarrassment. I kept the secret because I thought it would be funny if someone tried to steal the fake. Anyway, a criminal like that only targets people who can afford both ridiculously expensive things and insurance on those things. The victim doesn't lose any money, and they get an exciting story to tell all their rich friends."

Baird said, "The insurance companies have to raise their rates."

"They'd raise rates anyway. Now they just have an excuse. Do you see what I'm getting at?"

"It sounds like you're saying that some kinds of crime are more desirable than others, and that if one were in a position of power, one could, hypothetically—"

Calhoun nodded. "Very good."

"Thank you. One could encourage one type of crime over the other, and shape crime like a bonsai tree."

"Exactly."

Baird leaned forward. "Say, for the sake of argument, that you were in a position to attempt to prune crime. What would be your first step?"

Calhoun leaned forward as well. "I think I'd try to find a high-end criminal. A real class act. Someone who leaves no trace and no body count. I'd explain my theories to that person, and I'd ask her if she knew of a way to encourage more criminals like her to come to town. Then I'd concentrate on getting rid of the kind of crime I didn't want."

"And I assume you'd get a cut of the proceeds from the high-class crime you encourage."

Calhoun said, "Absolutely not."

"No?"

"No! Greed is counterproductive. For the system to work, it needs to be profitable for everyone. Besides, the office of sheriff pays well and comes with great power."

"Including the power to mistreat your prisoners?" Baird asked.

Calhoun looked confused for a moment, then laughed. "Please, Miss Baird, do you believe everything you see in commercials? My prisoners aren't happy to be in jail, but I treat them much better than Marsden ever did. If any of the prisoners act up, I threaten to send them to Site B, where I tell them I make my ads. Nobody's called my bluff yet."

"Sounds like a nice setup, hypothetically."

"I agree," Calhoun said. "So, if I were such a sheriff, and I were talking to such a criminal, do you think she might be inclined to assist me?"

Baird said, "She might. Of course, she'd have no intention of staying around."

"Oh, of course not. She'd probably have a major crime she was trying to get away with."

"But she would probably know the perfect person to put such a sheriff in contact with. Someone who might share many of this hypothetical sheriff's theoretical attitudes, and who may possibly be in a position to help."

Calhoun beamed. "That would probably make that sheriff very happy."

25

Baird casually walked across the square.

Pry Bar followed behind her. "How'd you get them to let us go?"

"By not giving them any reason to hold us in the first place. They had no evidence we were involved." Baird and Pry Bar walked to the tram station and got in line.

Baird looked back at the restaurant entrance. Sheriff Calhoun and a small knot of deputies stood, watching her and Pry Bar leave. The deputies wore expressions of disgust and awe. Sheriff Calhoun smiled and tipped his hat to Baird.

"Bastard," Pry Bar said. "He's going to be watching you like a hawk."

Baird smiled back at him and nodded. Anger poured off the deputies like heat off pavement in summer.

Pry Bar looked at Baird. "You seem pretty pleased with yourself, for someone whose plan blew up in her face."

"What can I say? Walking away from law enforcement personnel always puts me in a good mood."

Baird and Pry Bar got into the tram. Baird ordered it to take them down into the bowels of the station.

"Where are we going?" Pry Bar asked.

"The rendezvous point."

"Why? The Gonz won't be there. They're long gone, and they took the statue with them, I'm sure."

"Still," Baird said. "We'll go anyway, in the name of due diligence."

They stopped two floors above the docking level and took a convoluted route down the rest of the way to docking berth 178. They reached the berth and peered in through a small porthole in the airlock. They saw the dim outline of a massive object under a tarp.

Pry Bar said, "I don't believe it!"

"I know." Baird opened the airlock door. "Come on in. I disabled the sensors earlier."

The docking berth looked like any other large, empty room, with four flat walls, a robotic freight-crane built into the ceiling, and a ten-meter-square hatch in one corner of the floor. Baird had seen hundreds of berths just like it in her time. She stood on the doors and looked down at the universe through a window between her feet. Far to the sides she could see large clamps, waiting to grasp a docked ship and align it with the hatch in the floor, making an airtight seal. The clamps were fully retracted at the moment, leaving the flight path to and from the hatch clear.

Baird walked over to the *Ibu*. Pry Bar stood in front of the draped statue, a look of mixed disgust and shock on her face.

"Haven't you learned to trust people's essential nature yet?" Baird shoved the statue, which didn't budge.

Pry Bar said, "I doubt they left it out of kindness or loyalty. They were probably just too lazy or too scared to try to carry it off themselves."

"Laziness and cowardliness are two of the parts of their essential nature I trusted the most." Baird gripped the corner of the tarp and pulled it off the statue.

The *Ibu* stood before them, with an empty void where the diamond had been.

Baird said, "I also trusted them to be greedy."

Pry Bar said, "They took the diamond."

"Yeah," Baird said, barely containing a laugh. "The *diamond*."

"Why aren't you more upset? Isn't this bad?"

Baird bent down, examining one of the mag-lev dollies still wedged under a corner of the square base plate to which the statue's feet were permanently mounted. "Not for us," she said. She pressed a button on the dolly. It emitted a subtle hum as the corner of the statue rose a few centimeters, tilting the statue slightly to one side. Baird could see a small gap of completely empty space between the body of the dolly and the four perfect spheres that made contact with the floor.

Pry Bar asked, "What do you mean, *not for us*? Didn't you want the diamond?"

Baird walked to another corner of the statue's base. "Not anymore. It's complicated. Look, my mission was to retrieve the statue, not the diamond. We don't need the diamond." She pressed a button on the side of the mag-lev dolly with her toe. The dolly hummed, and the corner of the base plate rose.

"So those four criminals betrayed us, and now they're getting away with a priceless jewel, and you're okay with that?"

Baird grinned at Pry Bar as she walked behind the statue. "They haven't gotten away with anything yet. They have the most famous missing gemstone on the station. I wish them luck trying to sell it or smuggle it off the station without being caught."

"But where does that leave us? We have to smuggle the rest of the statue off the station."

"Yes," Baird said, peeking around the corner of the statue at Pry Bar. "But I already have a plan in place. They have to come up with something on the fly." She powered up a third dolly with her foot.

"But won't station security be watching for your getaway ship now?"

"Yes," Baird said, walking to the last remaining dolly and powering it on. "Traffic Control will definitely be on the lookout for any ship approaching or leaving the station, and they'll check anything with a large enough hold to carry this thing." She put both hands on the side of the statue and pressed. It took a lot of effort to get all that mass moving, but it glided smoothly once it started. Baird nodded with satisfaction.

Pry Bar asked, "So, your getaway ship has some way to hide the statue?"

Baird said, "Follow me." She walked toward the door they'd come in through.

"How can they possibly hide something that large on a ship?"

"It would be incredibly hard, wouldn't it?' Probably impossible." Baird shut the airtight door behind Pry Bar as she exited. The two women stood outside the docking berth, looking in at the statue.

"So how will they do it? How will they smuggle the statue off the station?"

Baird asked, "What time is it?"

The probe of Pry Bar's Brow lowered. She looked into the distance for a moment and said, "4:58."

"How accurate is that?"

"It sets itself automatically to station master time, like everyone else's. Why?"

"And it's 4:58?"

"Yeah, well, 4:59 now."

Baird said, "Good." She turned to the docking berth's control panel, hitting several buttons in quick succession.

Inside the berth, the floor hatch opened. All of the air rushed out the opening in the floor, taking the discarded tarp with it. The wind and suction caused the *Ibu*, still riding on its mag-lev dollies, to move toward the opening. It started slowly, but picked up speed as the air rushed around it and out into the vacuum of space. The air fully evacuated before the statue was even halfway to the hatch, but its momentum carried it toward the hole.

One corner of the statue moved out over the opening, its dolly falling away into the void. With one corner unsupported, the *Ibu's* bulk slowly tipped forward, its trailing corner rising off of its dolly like one end of a teeter-totter.

Slowly, the statue slid, its base grinding on the hatch's frame as it worked its way out of the station. There was no air in the berth to transmit the sound, but the vibration carried through the floor so that Baird could feel it in her teeth.

After what seemed like an eternity, the statue tumbled out of the hatch, leaving three of the four dollies sitting empty on the floor. Baird pressed a few buttons, closing the hatch and re-flooding the berth with air.

"I figure that took about twenty seconds," she said. "You agree?"

"What?" Pry Bar sputtered. "Why? Why would you do that?"

"You said it yourself: station security is looking for a getaway ship." Baird opened the airlock and entered the berth. Pry Bar followed. "So the best way to get the statue away is to not use a ship. The station has one g of outward force because of centripetal inertia. That means that anything released from the station is automatically at escape velocity. That's why they built it to begin with."

"You just sent the *Ibu*, a priceless fourteen-ton statue, hurtling out into deep space."

"Yeah," Baird said. She put her foot on one of the remaining mag-lev dollies, pushed off with the other, and glided toward the far wall, spinning slowly as she went, "Without any rocket booster or guidance system. Cool, huh?"

"Yeah, but what good does that do us?"

Baird pushed the dolly into the corner and turned it off. "We know exactly which berth it left from, and what time it left. Figuring out where it is and where it's going is just a matter of math. We give all that information to the Toolbox, and they can swoop by and pick up the statue whenever they like."

"But won't Traffic Control spot it?"

Baird walked back to one of the two remaining dollies and kicked it to the same corner where she'd left the previous dolly. "Pry Bar, half of seeming clever is actually just being curious and finding out how things work. Traffic Control looks for two things: ships and hazards. Ships have transponders, and pilots with radios.

They identify spacecraft, communicate with them, and tell them where to go and what to do. Obstacles are just dumb hunks of metal and rock. A computer finds them, plots their future course, and tells Traffic Control how to route ships around them."

Baird kicked the last mag-lev dolly into the corner, where it crashed into the others. She pointed at the collision. "To prevent that from happening. The computer only looks at how large an obstacle is and where it's going. Figuring out what it is and where it came from would be a waste of time. It'll route traffic around the statue, but as far as Traffic Control is concerned, it's nothing but trash. It's to be avoided, not researched."

Baird walked past Pry Bar, out the door, then stopped, turned, and looked back. Pry Bar still stood in the middle of the berth.

Baird asked, "You coming?"

Pry Bar stared at her. "This was your plan all along?"

"Sure seems like it."

"It's crazy!"

"But it worked."

"You're really going to claim that all of this—getting double-crossed, getting arrested, losing the diamond, kicking the statue out into space—this was all what you *wanted* to happen?"

Baird walked back into the berth and put a hand on Pry Bar's shoulder. "No. Once we walk out that door, I'm going to claim that none of it ever happened at all."

26

Baird sat in her hotel room, wearing her gARggles, looking at the floating face of her current handler.

"Well done, Saber Saw," Plumb Bob said. "One of our ships has already intercepted the *Ibu*, and according to news reports, the Pendulum's sheriff's office has apprehended four young hooligans who were attempting to sell the Star of the Cosmos. Apparently one of them, a young man named Trent Abernathy, has already made a deal to inform on the others."

Baird said, "Of course, if they have it examined by an expert, they'll find that the diamond they were trying to sell is a fake, but I suspect the sheriff isn't going to go out of his way to have it tested."

"And even if he does, and the suspects somehow implicate you, you'll be long gone by then. We have your flight out booked. You leave in three hours. Agent Pry Bar will escort you to the spaceport. In the meantime, I've sent you all the information I could scrape together about your illness, as you asked. So, if there are no further questions, that concludes—"

"I have a question," Baird interrupted. "What, specifically, is it you intend to trade the *Ibu* for?"

Plumb Bob said, "A resource we need to continue research into your condition."

"But I want to know what that resource is. I've been thinking about it, and I'm 99 percent sure that the mysterious benefactor you had me steal the statue for is the same one who commissioned me—allegedly—to get the Star of the Cosmos for him."

"Is that a problem?"

"Well, the guy who hired me—allegedly—was a lawyer; a lawyer who specialized in defending large corporations from class-action lawsuits. Unless he's done some work for a pharmaceutical company and took his pay in product, I don't see what he could possibly have that would help find me a cure."

Plumb Bob tilted his head forward, as if preparing to reluctantly explain to a small child that her parents were really Santa Claus all along. "Saber Saw, the gentleman in question has access to vast amounts of a resource that is absolutely vital to an organization like ours."

"Money," Baird spat.

"Yes. Money."

"You woke me up and burned a day of my very limited lifespan because you wanted money!"

Plumb Bob said, "Doctors cost money, Saber Saw. Lab equipment costs money, and the Toolbox has razor-thin margins. Stealing military secrets and eradicating enemy agents is important work, but it doesn't generate a lot of revenue. We can't keep looking for your cure if we don't exist, so yes, we used your skills to get some much-needed cash. Which, I would point out, is exactly what you use your skills for—allegedly."

After seething for a long moment, Baird said, "I don't like it."

"Of course you don't like it. I don't like it. Nobody likes it. Luckily, people are perfectly capable of doing their jobs without liking it. If people liked working, you wouldn't have to pay them to do it."

"I don't want you to wake me up to get the Toolbox money again. You will wake me if, and only if, you have a cure, or if you need me to get something that is directly related to the effort to find my cure. Is that clear?"

"Yes, Saber Saw, your wishes are clear."

"Will you honor them?"

Plumb Bob said, "I promise, I'll do my best."

"You promise you'll do your best? What kind of promise is that?"

"It's the best promise any person can realistically expect from another person, and you know it. Is that good enough?"

Baird said, "I guess."

"Good, because if it isn't, your only other option is to not go back into stasis and die in, oh, let's see, four days."

Baird said, "I am aware of that."

"Good." Plumb Bob ended the call.

Baird sat in her hotel room, not moving for over a minute, savoring the feelings of her various bruises and burns.

The friction burn running up her leg was her most noticeable pain, because it was longer and newer, and it had a quaint, rustic quality when compared to the two laser scorches. The bruises had settled into a sort of baseline background soreness, like the drone of a bagpipe that enhances the sharper notes of the melody—the burns, in this case. The percussion, though, came from her headache, which she had to admit was getting worse. And the ringing in the ears had started. Only intermittently, but still, not good.

She put on her gARggles, navigated through Izzy's secret menu, and initiated a call.

"Bran," Izzy said. "Thanks for calling back."

"Are you the same Izzy I spoke to last time?"

"Yes, but it was wise to ask."

"What happens if I place a call and two of you answer at the same time?"

"Awkwardness, I'd assume, but I don't think that'll happen. As far as I know, they've never had two of us clones in action at the same time. Cuts down on the chance of us running into each other, I guess."

Baird said, "Seems logical. Look, I have a question. If one of you gets injured, does the injury carry over to the next clone?"

"No. It wouldn't make any sense. We don't have any memories of the last clone, so to us the injuries would seem to have appeared out of nowhere."

Baird said, "That's true. Okay. Good."

"Are you all right?" Izzy asked.

"I'm asking pointed questions about physical injuries. Does that seem like a sign that I'm all right?"

"No. That's why I asked."

"Fair point. Look—our last conversation freaked me out a bit."

"As have the few before it."

"Yes. But the last one freaked me out because your description of what it's like to be a clone sounded a little too similar to what I've got going on right now."

Izzy nodded. "Yeah, that occurred to me too, but I decided not to say anything. I kind of worry that knowing that I'm a clone leads me to see other clones where they aren't."

"Well, I don't think I am one, because I've taken on some minor injuries on my last two missions, and I still have them. I think that means I can't be a clone."

"Or it could mean that you haven't been a clone since two missions ago."

Baird thought for a moment, then pulled up her right pant leg to expose the partially healed scratch on her ankle. "No, I still have the scratch I got when I was infected with the virus, supposedly."

"You're not sure you have the virus?"

"I'm trying to use logic to prove that I'm not a clone. I'm not really sure of anything right now."

"True. But I'm afraid the scratch doesn't prove that you haven't been cloned. It just suggests, weakly, that you haven't been cloned since you got scratched. Believe me, I've thought a lot about cloning, and I'm a computer guy. Logic puzzles are kinda my thing. Say they could give each new clone of you the memories of the last clone. It'd be easy for them to replicate the injuries from the last clone as well."

"How? By roughing me up while I'm in stasis?"

"Would that be worse than any of the other things you suspect them of?"

"I suppose not, but it feels worse for some reason. They'd probably just undress me and do a quick visual inspection of my body, which . . . just . . . ugh! Then they'd inflict the same sorts of injuries in the same places on the next . . . me."

"Sounds reasonable. I mean, not *reasonable*. It sounds creepy and disgusting, but believable."

Baird asked, "So, what if I gave myself an injury they didn't know about? One they wouldn't see on a visual inspection."

"Like what? Internal bleeding?"

"No. I'd prefer an injury that wouldn't kill me if they don't catch it. I'll come up with something."

"That's your plan? *You'll come up with something*?"

"Hey, logic puzzles are your thing. Coming up with something is mine."

◄ ◆ ◆ ◆ ►

Baird called Pry Bar to tell her that an escort to the spaceport was not necessary, but Pry Bar was already on the way. It would be a little while before Pry Bar arrived at the Royal George, so Baird passed the time skimming through the dossier Plumb Bob had given her. She was almost a quarter of the way through when the front desk called, announcing that Pry Bar was coming up.

As near as Baird could tell, the scientists hadn't verified much, but they'd ruled a lot of things out, which was progress—the slowest, least satisfying form of progress.

They went into great detail about their lack of funding. The document made a crystal-clear case that they were no closer to a cure, but that her contributions had been indispensable, suggesting that she should continue to do pretty much anything they ask her to do. It was exactly what she'd expect to read if they were telling her the truth . . . or if they were lying.

She and Pry Bar made sporadic small talk on the trip down to the spaceport. As Baird got out of the tram, Pry Bar started to follow.

"No," Baird said. "I appreciate the thought, Pry Bar, but I don't need you to walk me to Security."

Pry Bar said, "You don't need me to, but I want to. It's just, I've learned so much from following you."

"Yes, but following me through the spaceport isn't going to teach you anything, unless you don't already know how to walk while feeling irritable. Seriously, there are too many ears in there for us to talk freely, so all you'd do is silently watch me leave, then have to wait in line for another tram to take you home."

Pry Bar finally acquiesced, and they said their goodbyes. Baird walked into the terminal as Pry Bar's tram went around the corner and out of sight.

Baird reemerged from the terminal. She checked the time and boarded a tram. She rode it a short distance to a grungy storefront under a hand-painted sign that read "Tattoos." It looked perfect. She could tell at a glance that the proprietor didn't often answer questions from the authorities, whether those questions were about who had gotten some ink, what or where they had gotten it, or how often the needle they'd gotten it with was cleaned.

27

Baird's eyes popped open in one shot. She saw the interior of a spaceliner stasis pod and felt no disappointment. She wasn't happy to see it, not by a long shot, but in order to be disappointed, one has to expect a preferable outcome. She didn't.

She gritted her teeth through the cold, then gritted her teeth through the heat, then activated her gARggles and gritted her teeth while looking at the listing for her briefing as the pre-arrival announcement started.

"Good morning, passengers, and thank you for joining us on Allied Spacelines. We are about to arrive on Titan. We expect a relatively calm atmospheric entry followed by touchdown at Shoreline Spaceport in about fifteen minutes. The weather looks pretty good, but for those of you who were hoping to see some of Titan's famous Earth-like rain, don't worry. I'm told there's an excellent chance of precipitation this evening. The local gravity is .14 g, so please adjust your grav-meds accordingly."

Baird had never been to Titan before, because there was nothing valuable enough to bother stealing, except, of course, almost everything on the surface. That said, she doubted that the Toolbox wanted her to steal ice or hydrocarbons. Several corporations had massive harvesting operations there, manned exclusively by dirt-poor people. Rich people didn't live on Titan. After all, one of the reasons people acquired wealth was to be able to pay other people to go to places like Titan instead of ever having to spend time there themselves.

Baird activated her briefing and was not surprised to see that her handler was someone other than Plumb Bob. The person who appeared in front of her was male, in his fifties, with a face as weathered as a stone prison wall and just as inviting.

"Hello, Saber Saw. I'm your handler, Spring Clamp. You are currently approaching the Titan spaceport, which is near Shoreline, the largest settlement on Titan. Your mission is to acquire—"

"Whoa," Baird said. "Hold up, wait a minute. I don't know who you are, what your deal is, or what happened to Plumb Bob, and I'm not doing anything until I get some answers."

Spring Clamp took a deep breath, then, in a slow, careful voice, said, "I am Spring Clamp. My deal is that I am your handler. Plumb Bob got replaced, by me. I had already either stated or implied all of that information."

"That's true, but you don't just open with that. You should soften it a bit. Ease into it."

"I started by greeting you in a friendly manner. Then I stated the facts as directly as I know how. You're the one who stopped everything and made demands with your voice raised."

Baird gritted her teeth. "That's . . . a fair point."

"Now, can we continue with the briefing, or would you like to berate me some more?"

"Let's move on."

"Because, in my experience, briefings usually consist of one person conveying information to a second person—*briefing them*, if you will. If there's some new methodology of which I am unaware, wherein information is communicated more efficiently by having the person being briefed interrupt and ask redundant questions in a hostile tone, I am willing to give this innovative technique a try."

Baird said, "I'm ready for the briefing. Let's get on with it."

"I'm perfectly happy to, but I'd hate for you to think that my tone was needlessly brusque, or unfriendly as I, to use your words, *get on with it.*"

Baird stared but said nothing.

Spring Clamp said, "So, as I was saying, you will soon land at the spaceport near Shoreline, the largest settlement on Saturn's moon, Titan. Your target is in a high-security lab complex in a military outpost eight kilometers south of Shoreline. Stored in a lab there, you will find item number 75628. You are to procure said item and deliver it to us. Do you understand your orders, Saber Saw?"

"That's all the information you're giving me? I don't know what it is, what it looks like, how large it is, or if one person can carry it? I don't even know how long I've been under this time."

"You'll be able to identify it by the fact that it will be labeled 'item number 75628.' Titan has very low gravity, so odds are you'll be able to carry it without help, and even if you can't, you'll just have to steal a hand truck or something. You've been in hibernation just under three years. You can get a more specific time frame by looking up the current date and applying something I like to call *math*. You'll find information about your local contact waiting in your gARggles as usual. Good luck, Saber Saw."

Baird said, "Wait. I have questions."

"You already know everything I have to tell you."

Baird narrowed her eyes to suspicious slits. "*Have* to tell me, as in everything you have that you *can* tell me or *have* to tell me, as in everything you can't get away with not telling me?"

"From your point of view, it works out the same, but I'll rephrase to clarify. You already know everything I'm going to tell you."

"How will this item help find me a cure?"

"I don't know. I'm not a scientist. I chose not to waste the scientists' valuable time having them explain things to me that I still wouldn't understand."

"But it will directly help in finding my cure?"

"I believe so."

"It's being stored at a military research base. It's not a weapon, is it?"

"How would a weapon help cure your disease?"

"It wouldn't. And I have made my position clear that I'm only willing to steal things that will help lead directly to a cure for my illness. That's why I will be all-caps angry if this item I'm being sent to steal turns out to be a weapon."

Spring Clamp said, "Noted," and hung up, ending the briefing.

She bounded down the shuttle-way in slow motion, along with only three or four other recently thawed passengers, as the spaceliner that had brought them carried far more supplies than people. The ramp unloaded into a single not-very-large room where the spaceport's three gates all shared one common seating area.

Even without her gARggles, she would have spotted her contact immediately: a tall, thin woman in her sixties with a cloud of gray hair and a shapeless tan pantsuit, standing alone in the spaceport. Her metal Brow was anodized pink and had a little flower painted on it. She looked like a taciturn aunt, picking up a frightened niece or nephew there for an involuntary visit while their parents *worked some things out.*

The woman made unnervingly steely eye contact. "You Baird?"

"Yes. I'm Baird."

"Good. I'm Rivet Gun." She turned on her heels and stalked away without another word. Baird followed.

They walked past the surface shuttle station without Baird getting so much as a glance from the older woman.

Baird asked, "We're not taking the shuttle?"

"Doesn't seem like it."

"Uh, yeah, obviously."

"If it's obvious, why'd you have to say it?"

"It's just, I heard that personal craft were kind of rare on Titan."

"That's true."

"But you have one?"

Rivet Gun said, "I never take the surface shuttle. I don't like having someone else at the controls."

"You don't trust other people?"

"The hired pilots are fine for carrying people to and from Shoreline, but if we're attacked, none of them are as well trained at evasive maneuvers as I am, and they tend to resent having me wrestle the controls away from them."

"Do the surface shuttles get attacked often?"

"No, because I don't ride in them."

28

They reached the valet station, where Rivet Gun submitted to a routine scan of her ident chip. A large hanging robot arm emerged from the darkened parking area. Rivet Gun's aircraft hung beneath it, dangling from the arm's claw by a mounting point on its roof. Baird recognized it on sight as an ornithopter, a form of transport that was the most efficient way to get around on Titan, but which didn't really work anywhere else. The nose of the craft consisted of a half-sphere of thick pressure-resistant glass. Behind the round front, the craft stretched out into a long, thin shaft forming the craft's tail, all clad in a smooth, white skin.

She squinted at it and tilted her head to the side.

Some might have compared it to a dragonfly, but Baird thought it looked like spit with wings.

Along the top of the fuselage, four surprisingly short wings extended in an x-pattern, two wings on each side, the leading wings tilted upward and the rear pair tilted down. The craft's tail, out at the thin end of the boom, consisted of another set of stubby wings extending to either side.

The clear panel on the 'thopter's front slid out of the way. Baird and Rivet Gun climbed in and took their seats. The clear panel slid back into place, emitting a slight hiss as it formed an airtight seal.

The robot arm lifted the craft and carried it through a large door in the far wall, which closed behind them. A large door in front of them remained closed. A loud pre-recorded voice announced, "Airlock pressurization in progress."

"Okay," the older woman said. "We can talk freely. I'm Rivet Gun. It's best if we leave it at that. I work under a few different aliases, none of which you really want to know."

Baird tried to pay attention to what Rivet Gun was saying, but she found it hard to concentrate while the aircraft around them was emitting ominous creaking noises.

Rivet Gun said, "Look, I know you're probably used to your contacts being fairly hands-on, but I have several operations of my own in progress, so I'll be leaving you to it, unless you really need support."

Baird wrenched her attention away from the alarming groans of the aircraft around them. "What? Oh. Okay, that's fine. I usually work alone anyway. Look, is this thing safe?"

Rivet Gun let out a single laugh that emerged mostly through her nose. "Kid, we're on Titan. Nothing's safe."

The pre-recorded voice thundered, "Airlock cycle complete." The door ahead opened, bathing Baird and Rivet Gun in a grimy orange glow. The 'thopter moved forward, out into the open, giving Baird her first good in-person look at the surface of Titan.

Like most people, she'd heard, read, and seen stories about Titan her entire life. She remembered the opening line of one of those articles. *Titan. Beautiful, but hostile. Familiar, but alien. It looks right, but everything about it is wrong.*

The tiny probe of Rivet Gun's Brow lowered and shone light into her pupil. She looked around a bit, made some stabbing motions at the air with her index finger, then said, "Home." The craft shook as the wings started beating back and forth, churning the thick atmosphere, seven times denser than Earth's, easily defeating Titan's weak gravity. The craft rose into the sky.

Looking down, Baird could see that the spaceport sat along the edge of an immense sea. She strained her eyes, struggling to discern fine details in the fog. Waves lapped at the base of the jagged cliffs and outcroppings, formed by erosion from the small rivers and streams that worked their way down out of the mountains.

Baird could have mistaken it for any number of locations on Earth, if the sky hadn't been dark orange. The strange coloration served as a constant reminder that nothing else in this vista was what it appeared. The air was largely nitrogen. The twilight was a full midday sun. The temperature was far too cold for liquid water to exist. Indeed, most of what looked like land was, in fact, frozen H_2O.

The fog, the clouds, and the rolling sea were all methane, so frigid that it condensed into liquid and settled into a weather pattern analogous to the water cycle on Earth. Liquid methane on the ground evaporated into gaseous methane clouds, which condensed into methane rain, which then fell on the ice and ran in methane rivers, carving canyons as they streamed back to the methane sea.

The 'thopter's wings beat in a steady rhythm, fast enough to be a blur but not so fast as to be invisible. The 'thopter made its way along the coast at what seemed to Baird to be a leisurely pace.

Rivet Gun said, "Shoreline's five kilometers up the coast. Your objective is at Fort Carlson, another eight beyond that."

"You know what my mission is?"

"Kid, I try to know everything. If someone tells me I'm not supposed to know something, I make a point of knowing it."

"So, you know what my objective is."

"That's what I just said."

"No, I mean, the actual physical object I'm supposed to take. You know what it is?"

"Yes. That's what I said," Rivet Gun said, enunciating her words slowly as if Baird needed the extra time to understand them.

"Okay," Baird said. "What is it, then?"

Rivet Gun turned and smiled at Baird. "I said that I try to know everything, not that I try to share everything."

Baird sneered at Rivet Gun, which made the older woman smile, but the smile died quickly. Rivet Gun spun around in her seat, looking at the solid back wall of the cockpit. "Bogey."

Baird interfaced her gARggles with the 'thopter's avionics suite. She saw a distant jumble of domes and boxes, the graphical representation of the horizon, and the town of Shoreline off in the distance, even though neither was visible in the ever-present methane mist. A text readout said the town was still three kilometers away.

Baird looked behind them at the solid rear wall, and far beyond it she saw a small blob of color. A call-out labeled it *unknown aircraft: 800 meters and closing.*

Rivet Gun said, "Manual control."

A miniature 3D image of the 'thopter appeared in the area between the two seats. Rivet Gun reached out and curled her fingers around the tiny craft's fuselage, as if grasping it. She shoved the image forward and to the right. The 'thopter lurched forward and banked hard to the right, heading out over the methane sea.

Baird looked back over her shoulder. "They're still following us."

"Yeah," Rivet Gun said. "Not surprised. They weren't going to give up just because we turned right."

"Can't this thing go any faster?"

"Not much. Do you have any idea how hard it is to push something through this atmosphere?"

"Maybe if it used something with a little more power than just a set of flapping wings."

"Two sets! Wings are the most efficient form of flight propulsion in air this dense, and they don't make sparks or flames. Hold on to something." She twisted the miniature 'thopter to the right and pointed its nose down. The real 'thopter banked to the right and dove.

Baird said, "They must know what I'm after."

"Doubt it," Rivet Gun replied. "*You* don't even know what you're after."

"Then why are they chasing me?"

"They aren't. They're chasing me. You're incidental."

Baird heard an alarm from behind them. She turned in her seat, looking again at the solid rear wall of the cockpit, beyond which her gARggles and the 'thopter's avionics showed her two small objects slowly closing the distance.

"Sabotage drones," Rivet Gun said, answering the question Baird was about to ask.

"What do they do?"

Rivet Gun glared at her.

"I mean, obviously, they sabotage us. How?"

"They might short out the electronics. They might damage the wings. I'm betting they'll breach the pressure hull."

"What happens if the pressure hull gets breached?" Baird asked.

"Bad things," Rivet Gun answered.

The drones were still gaining, but not quickly. "Why don't they just shoot at us?"

"With what? Firearms or energy weapons? In a methane-rich atmosphere? Sane people consider them way too dangerous." Rivet Gun shook her head, then shouted to the ornithopter, "Weapons!"

A display offering a surprisingly long list of options appeared. Rivet Gun jabbed her finger at a selection. A sound like two industrial cranes ripping an immense bolt of fabric filled the cockpit. Baird recognized it as the sound of high-speed automatic cannons. The two drones disappeared, replaced by floating labels that read, *Direct hit.*

Baird said, "Those were bullets! Firearms! In a methane-rich atmosphere!"

"I'm not 'sane people'. Besides, I figure weapons are supposed to be dangerous." Rivet Gun brought the 'thopter to a stop while selecting a different weapon from the menu. Baird heard a loud hissing noise, like gas escaping. Looking behind the craft, her gARggles showed a missile slowly receding from their craft and homing in on the craft that was chasing them.

"It's not a very fast missile."

"Nothing's fast here, and the missile's not very sophisticated. It's really just a flying air tank. The oxygen allows the ambient methane to burn. In a way, oxygen's the flammable gas here, not methane."

"But this plane's full of oxygen."

"Ornithopter. And yeah, we're basically riding in a big pipe bomb. Welcome to Titan." Rivet Gun twisted the miniature 'thopter hard to the left. The aircraft followed suit, slowing considerably and turning in the air. For the first time, Baird could actually see their pursuer: a long cylinder with a pair of flapping wings at each end.

The missile struck the craft and exploded in a ball of pale-blue flame. The force of the explosion rocked the fuselage and cracked through the windshield. Baird saw the pilot and the gunner writhe in agony as the air pressure inside increased sevenfold in less than a second. The oxygen from the cockpit mixed with the methane and nitrogen in the planet's atmosphere and was ignited by the still-hot missile wreckage, causing a slow indigo explosion that devastated the airframe. The crumpled wad of wreckage fell into the sea of methane and burned bright blue until all the oxygen was exhausted.

Rivet Gun shrugged. "Like I said. If the pressure hull gets breached, bad things happen."

29

The 'thopter flew in low over Shoreline. Baird looked down at the cluster of large domes and boxes that made up the original habitat, its lights and windows glowing in the Titanian gloom. It was connected to a sprawl of smaller domes and boxes—the additions that had inevitably followed when it was clear that there was a huge profit to be made in this inhospitable place.

Despite the settlement's name, the habitat buildings sat a few hundred meters from the actual shore. The only building along the actual dividing line between land and sea, or in this case ice and hydrocarbons, was the industrial facility that pumped the methane out of the sea and made it safe for transport. The main complex consisted of multiple modules and nodes that could obviously be sealed off from one another in the case of an atmosphere leak or a fire.

The autopilot guided the ornithopter over what Baird suspected constituted the suburbs on Titan, before hovering above one specific building: a dome attached to a perfect cube, nearly a kilometer from the methane plant. Doors in the roof of the cube opened, and the ornithopter settled down into the opening.

The pressure dropped to a survivable level. The remaining air oxygenated. Rivet Gun opened the cockpit so she and Baird could get out.

Baird said, "It must cost a fortune to keep your own place like this, instead of just renting space in the main colony."

Rivet Gun glanced back over her shoulder as she led Baird through a small passage into the dome. "It's the oxygen bills that really kill you. Those bastards at the Mars Exploration Company leased the ice-mining rights. They excavate the ice and use it to produce drinking water and oxygen, which they sell to us people who live on the ice at a hefty profit. But if I go out there and make a snowball, it's considered theft."

The lights came on with a sporadic flicker. The room featured bare walls, each with a nondescript door; an empty floor; and a single table with a few shakers of various inexpensive seasonings on top and four matching no-frills chairs pushed in around its sides.

Rivet Gun pointed to the doors in turn. "That's my room. You're not allowed to ever go in there. That's the guest room. You're encouraged to go in there, and stay in there, for the most part. That's the bathroom. You're allowed to go in there, as long as I'm not already in there, but that should go without saying."

"And it could have," Baird said.

"Good. When those museum-piece gARggles of yours connect to my server, you'll see that I have a full set of the last known schematics for Fort Carlson, the restricted lab complex, supply-run schedules, recent guard rotations, and a topographical map of the area."

"That's great! Thanks."

"Don't mention it. I mean that literally. If you're captured and you tell them where you got it, I will track you down and kill you. I'm assuming you'll need a ride into town later on. If I'm around, I'll be happy to take you in, but I might be out tending to my own business."

"Ooh," Baird said. "What are you up to?"

"My own business."

"That's fine. Really. I'm just saying, you seem to have some interesting things going on. Like, real action."

"I do."

"And, when I get my mission done, if I can be of any assistance, all you have to do is ask."

Rivet Gun shook her head. "It's sweet of you to offer, but the stuff I have going isn't for lightweights."

Baird exhaled as if she'd been punched in the gut. "Look, I don't know what you were told about me, but I'm pretty well-known."

"Yeah, you are. Don't get me wrong, kid, I'm sure you've got some skills, and that thing you did with the Wartzberg Pearl was cute."

"Cute?"

"Yeah, in a smart-alecky kind of way, but if I need something stolen, I'll just steal it myself. That way I know it'll be a clean job."

Rivet Gun went back out to the hangar, leaving Baird dumbfounded, standing in the bare room next to the table. The sounds of the airlock cycling and the 'thopter starting up shook her from her stunned, insulted silence.

Baird glanced at the door to her room, but went into the bathroom. Rivet Gun kept the place clean, but apparently the previous tenant had not, which meant that the permanent stains were well-polished. The newest thing in the room was the largest first-aid kit Baird had ever seen. It looked like a small refrigerator. The door handle was a bit worn, as if it had been opened many, many times. She grabbed a pain reliever, popped it in her mouth, and swallowed it without water.

Baird looked in the mirror, grabbed her lower lip with her right hand, and pulled it downward, exposing the pink skin of the inside of her mouth. There, she saw three crudely tattooed letters:

U R U

She let go of her lip, let out a long breath, thought for a moment, and went to her room. She found the décor just as limited as it was in the common room. A thin, hard carpet; a thin, hard mattress; a metal bed frame; and stiff bedding. One small, thick window let in a stale orange glow that made the room feel darker somehow.

She sat on the bed and put on her gARggles. She navigated to Izzy's secret page and placed a call.

"Good news," she said. "I'm pretty sure I'm not a clone."

"Would it be such a terrible thing if you were?" Izzy asked.

"Yes. I'm sorry, but yes, it would. I mean, be honest. If you found out that you weren't a clone with a two-week life span, would you be happy or bummed?"

"I'd be happy. But I remind you, even if you are the original you, that means that you have a terminal illness."

"That's the thing, though—do I? So far, all I have is headaches, a ringing in my ears, and their word. If I can't trust them not to have cloned me, can I trust them to tell me the truth?"

"Do you have any evidence that they're lying to you?"

"No, but telling me that I'll die without their help got me to stop threatening to quit, didn't it? Ever since Screw Jack told me about the virus, I've done pretty much whatever they want. Also, his name was Screw Jack. That doesn't necessarily mean he was lying to me, but it doesn't sound good."

"So now you don't think you're a clone, and you're not convinced that you're sick?"

"So it seems."

"And that's a bad thing?"

"In this case, yeah. That's the thing about going looking for answers. You almost always find bad news. When people have good news, they share it. People don't hide information that will make you happy."

"So, what do you do now?"

"I find out if I'm sick."

"And how do you do that?"

"I'm about to infiltrate a place where they supposedly do medical research. I suspect they'll have a diagnostic scanner."

Izzy smiled. "That's good news."

"Yeah, it is."

"That proves you wrong. I just asked you a question, and the answer was good news."

"No, it proves me right, because I told you the good news willingly."

"Logically, that suggests that there's bad news you aren't sharing."

"There is, and you had to puzzle that out for yourself, which further proves my point."

30

It was late afternoon on Titan, and darkness hadn't fallen so much as it had slammed down like a heavy weight. Baird's gARggles provided her with a wire-frame representation of the peaks, valleys, and contours of the ice below, but beyond the windshield, her eyes saw only darkness and methane raindrops streaking toward them, illuminated by the 'thopter's running lights.

"Thanks for the ride to town," Baird said.

"Eh, it's no problem," Rivet Gun said.

Baird eyed the expertly applied temporary dressing on Rivet Gun's shoulder, covering a wound she'd picked up while out "tending to her business" as Baird stayed back at the safe house, making her plan. "Shouldn't you be going to a doctor or something?"

"It's cauterized. I'm not losing any blood. I'll go to a medic later. I have business to tend to first, and dropping you off is on my way."

"Is part of your business getting even with whoever did that to you?"

"You can't get much more even than I already have," Rivet Gun said, "unless you go in for desecrating corpses. I've never really seen the point."

The conversation, understandably, died off after that. The 'thopter slowed to a hover above a set of doors, which opened to reveal a landing pad. The 'thopter landed itself, the doors closed above them, and the pumps went to work equalizing the pressure.

"Thanks again for all of the intel," Baird said.

"I hope it was helpful."

"Very. This job's going to be a fun one. Nothing fancy, just a good old-fashioned disguise infiltration. I knock out one soldier, then use his uniform and credentials to sneak onto the base and all the way to my target. Nice and clean. By the time they figure out I was ever there, I'll be long gone."

Rivet Gun said, "Good for you," with little interest.

A pre-recorded voice announced that it was now safe to exit the aircraft. The windshield swung away. Rivet Gun and Baird stepped out. Rivet Gun unbuttoned the jacket of her dark gray pantsuit and pulled a handheld stunner out of a discreet holster. She checked its charge level and put it back. She pulled an old-school pistol from the second holster, beneath the stunner. She ejected the magazine, counted the rounds, reinserted the magazine, and cycled the slide.

She pulled up her left pant leg and checked on the dagger strapped to her ankle, then pulled up the other pant leg and checked the small stunner that was strapped there. She stood up, re-buttoned her jacket, lifted her right arm, and bent her right fist as far back as it would go. A knife so large that it nearly qualified as a small sword extended from her sleeve so quickly and silently that for a moment Baird thought it had appeared from thin air. Rivet Gun grasped the knife handle and waved it around, testing the flexibility of the stalk that affixed it to her forearm. When she let go, the blade retracted back into her sleeve.

"All set?" Baird asked.

"Yeah," Rivet Gun said. "I should be good. You?"

Baird looked down at her black sweater and the large bronze pin stuck to its front. "Yeah. I'm good."

Rivet Gun said, "Really? You're going off on a mission, and that's all you need?"

"Yup."

Baird noted with great satisfaction that for half a second, Rivet Gun looked impressed.

The two women turned and walked out of the hangar. Rivet Gun said, "This is where we part ways, kid. If you want to avoid trouble, I'd stay away from the entertainment wing. Lots of bars there. Draws an unsavory crowd."

Baird asked, "Where are you going?"

"The entertainment wing. I have a bone to pick with the unsavory crowd. Call me when you need a lift back to the house. If I'm free, I'll be right there."

Baird watched as Rivet Gun stalked purposefully down the corridor. As she approached the nearest junction, a large man with a bulky beard and bulkier arms stepped out of one of the other hallways, took one look at Rivet Gun, gasped, "Ah, feek!" then turned around and ran. Rivet Gun said nothing, but she followed the man with a little extra spring in her step.

◀ ◆ ◆ ▶

Baird looked down at the hangar floor from the rafters. A lone guard watched over the empty slots where military aircraft would normally be parked.

She disengaged her dart launcher's firing mechanism and counted the tiny darts that spilled out into her hand. She still had eight tranq darts and four neural scramblers. She only planned to need one tranq for this, but she was grateful to have a few spares.

She reloaded the dart launcher, holding the neural scramblers for the final four shots, as weapons of last resort. They were great for incapacitating people, and they made a great diversion, but that wouldn't work for what she had in mind. A diversion attracted attention away from you, but in this case she wanted to avoid attracting any attention at all. All she needed was a ride and a disguise, and the base's standard security protocol would deliver both of those things any second.

As if on cue, Baird heard a low rumble from beyond the hangar doors, the sound of the outer doors opening to admit the evening courier from Fort Carlson.

Wireless transmissions were vulnerable to interception. Communication cables were vulnerable to tampering. Courier drones were vulnerable to attack and theft. That's why, when security was of the utmost importance, the military still relied on human couriers, who were vulnerable to all those things.

The doors at the end of the hangar opened. Baird shuddered at what she saw.

Hanging from a robotic crane, a soldier in a shell-like environment suit with robotic hands and a clear bubble of a helmet sat straddling a skeletal frame approximating the shape of an ornithopter, but much smaller. Only the wings, the tail, and the rider's environment suit were solid. The rest was lightweight struts, shot through with holes.

The guard shouted, "Alsop!"

The rider used the environment suit's hand-like manipulators to give the guard a thumbs-up.

The crane placed the "aircraft" on one of the parking spaces. The rider stepped off, took two steps, then stood dead still. The rear of the ridged environment suit peeled open with a hiss. A soldier stepped backward out of the suit. A smallish man in a full-face helmet and flight suit, he strode purposefully toward the guard, removing his helmet as he walked.

The guard laughed. "Jeez, Alsop! I understand riding the wasp when it's dry out, but in this weather? You are hardcore, my friend."

The pilot finally got his helmet off, revealing a thick head of wavy black hair and a gleaming white smile that seemed to be larger than the face that contained it. "If you don't enjoy the weather, there's no point in being stationed on Titan." He gave the guard another thumbs-up, as if it somehow bolstered his point.

The guard chuckled, not because Alsop had said anything funny, but because Alsop's smile was infectious. Baird found herself grinning just overhearing him from the rafters. His winning personality and positive attitude conveyed instantly to anyone in his presence.

Baird couldn't wait to dart him.

Alsop walked away from the smiling guard, around several large pieces of equipment and tanks of fuel and lubricant, to a machine built into the hangar's back wall. He stood in a yellow square on the floor while the device scanned his ident chip. Baird heard a *bong* sound and saw the name *Alsop* appear on a small display next to the door. It was a military-spec ident scanner, meaning it was badly outdated; newer models didn't have a built-in screen. To upgrade, the military would have to pay for the new machines, and for outfitting every soldier with an official, hardened Brow, which wasn't about to happen.

Baird heard a deep *click*, the sound of large bolts moving into place. A drawer slid open, revealing a small secure drive, like the one she'd stolen on Newtah, attached to a thin glowing cord. Alsop unplugged the drive, pulled an identical drive from a pocket in his flight suit, placed the first drive in his pocket, and plugged the second drive into the cable.

Thanks to the very thorough research materials Rivet Gun had provided, Baird knew this was the daily exchange of classified data between the off-base personnel, civilian contractors, and spies who lived and worked in Shoreline and the scientists, strategists, and handlers who stayed in Fort Carlson. It was a simple procedure, but Alsop gave it his full attention. He didn't sense Baird slowly lowering to the ground behind him, with a huge smile on her face, carefully aiming, and darting him in the neck.

Baird caught the unconscious man, lowered him gently to the ground, and dragged him behind a storage tank. She crouched over him and was disgusted to see that his resting face was a friendly smile. Still, her gARggles told her he was breathing and had a steady pulse. He would wake up with a headache, but there wasn't a mark on him: no black eyes, no missing teeth, no blood.

Then, a single drop of blood plopped onto the unconscious man's face. Baird blinked at it in disbelief and brought her hand to her nose. She felt moisture. She looked at her hand and saw more blood.

"Feek," she whispered, lowering his head to the floor as she covered both of her nostrils with her other hand. She used her gARggles to scan the schematics of the immediate area. After a moment's searching, she used the strand to pull herself back into the rafters and headed for the nearest cleaning supply closet. One minute later Baird returned with a bottle of industrial cleanser, and wadded-up paper towels sticking out of her nose.

"Stupid locked supply closet. Make me bust in just to get towels," she muttered at the unconscious Alsop. "You'd think they'd make it easier for people to keep the place clean, but no. The Dougs are worried someone will steal their brooms or something."

She tore a piece of paper towel from one of the hunks that were sticking out of her nose. She dabbed some cleanser on it and wiped her blood off Alsop's face. Now that he looked as polished and perfect as he had when he came in, she had to stow him somewhere.

Baird looked at the gunk-encrusted space beneath the tank and smiled.

She pulled Alsop's flight suit on over her shirt and pants, stopping occasionally to look at his smiling face as he lay unconscious, in his underwear, nestled in the thick black mixture of grease, oil, and dirt beneath the fuel tank.

The flight suit had some adjustability, but it was still a little too large for her, and the helmet sat loosely on her head. It wasn't a disguise that would fool anyone who took a good long look at her, or who knew Alsop personally, but once she got out of the hangar, that would not be a problem.

Where the sleeves and gloves met, she left a small gap for the strand to extend through, so that it could make contact with her skin while remaining mostly out in the open, where it could be of use.

She carefully removed the etched metal square from the circle in the handle of her dart launcher. She bent down and held the square up to the top of Alsop's head, then used her gARggles to communicate with the square and ordered it to modify its own onboard transceiver to match Alsop's ident chip. She tucked the clone-chip into a little custom-made pocket in her hood and put on Alsop's helmet. Then she put down the visor, which completely hid her face. Between that, the chip that fooled the scanners, and the bright yellow letters embroidered on her chest that read *Alsop*, she figured her disguise was complete.

Baird walked the long way around the back wall of the hangar, behind the guard's back. She only entered his field of view as she approached Alsop's environment suit, which stood motionless with its back flayed open, waiting for her to enter it like an empty cocoon. She carefully placed her left boot in the suit's left foot. She felt it clamp around her ankle as the lower leg closed itself around her.

"Hey," the guard shouted. "Hey!"

Baird looked at the guard. He shouted, "You fly careful now."

Baird gave an enthusiastic thumbs-up.

"When do you fly this route next?" the guard asked.

Baird knew she had to respond but nonverbally, as her voice would give her away, and she had to reply in a manner consistent with Alsop's personality.

She shrugged, held her palms up to convey that she didn't know.

The guard looked puzzled.

Baird then gave two big thumbs-up.

The guard looked at her for a long moment and then laughed. "Never change, Alsop! See you around!"

Baird nodded and stepped the rest of the way into the environment suit. She felt it closing itself, sealing her in.

Alsop was taller than she was, so Baird's hands barely reached the controls for the mechanical hands on the suit's exterior. She found that if she threw herself forward, rounded her shoulders, and stretched her arms, she could just get her hands to mesh with the controls properly. The suit was designed to allow plenty of room around the flight helmet, but Baird doubted that her eyes were supposed to be looking out of the lower half of the environment suit's visor, essentially peeking out of the area where she imagined Alsop's chin would usually be.

She also doubted that Alsop had to stand on tiptoes to keep the suit's ridged crotch from being incredibly uncomfortable.

She stepped forward as naturally as she could and slung a leg over Alsop's ornithopter. Much as the back of the environment suit had automatically contracted and closed around her, the suit locked into the craft's seat and foot pegs and fused itself with the aircraft. The helmet's visor came alive with various stats, indicators, vectors, and prompts.

The hangar's robotic crane carried the small aircraft through a large set of doors and put it down inside the airlock. Baird felt the suit's skin flexing as the ambient pressure raised to seven times that of Earth.

The outer doors opened. She could only see a small patch of ice, illuminated by the hangar airlock's lights; a miserable drizzling rain of frigid liquid methane; and beyond that, a sea of inky black punctured by occasional dim orange-brown lights. The display in the helmet's visor showed buildings, mountains, and an indicator of Fort Carlson in the distance.

Baird said, "Autopilot."

A synthetic voice replied, "Autopilot engaged, and waiting for commands."

Baird said, "Take me to Fort Carlson."

The fuselage bucked slightly as the craft's translucent wings started flapping in the thick atmosphere. The 'thopter rose into the air and out into the night. Fat drops of methane struck the environment suit's visor and rolled off slowly, completely obscuring her vision.

She marveled that Alsop actually chose this 'thopter to ride in this weather. He said he liked it. She was glad she'd darted him and left him in a puddle of gunk. He would probably be *into it*.

31

The eight-kilometer ride to Fort Carlson took longer than Baird had hoped. A thick atmosphere means more wind resistance, and she fought a strong headwind the entire way.

Baird squinted at the computer-generated representation of Fort Carlson in the distance. Her gARggles showed her the fort, with the location of her primary and secondary objectives highlighted and a dynamically updated prompt showing her the most direct path from her current location to each of them. At the same time, the stolen helmet's visor displayed a competing image of the fort in a color that clashed atrociously, complete with a dotted line denoting her 'thopter's flight path, passing over the entire facility, landing at a large hangar.

Baird said, "Autopilot."

"Yes?" the autopilot replied.

"Contact Fort Carlson control. Request permission to land."

In less than a second, the autopilot said, "Permission granted."

The wasp swooped down out of the freezing sky and over the frozen landscape before slowing to hover and land in the airlock.

The air pressure normalized, and a robotic crane carried Baird and the wasp into a hangar like the one she'd left at Shoreline, only much larger and more crowded. She counted at least five aircraft of various sizes and wing configurations that she could steal. She noted that all of them had enclosed cockpits, meaning she could look forward to leaving *in* a vehicle, not *on* one.

She walked in her awkward, tiptoed manner away from the aircraft and toward the exit. Near the door she found a row of environment suits standing and facing the wall, like big bulky children who had been bad. She stood at the end of the line and said, "Open."

The back of her suit peeled away. She stepped out of it with noticeable relief.

Baird looked toward the hangar's exit, a simple door manned by a single bored soldier, there to make sure that all the aircraft got signed in or out properly. He stood by the door in his duty uniform and cap, trying to look alert, but most likely enthralled by something he was staring at in his Brow. She knew the type well. She'd met people like him in countless motor pools, warehouses, and armories. He didn't care who came in, who left, or what they took when they went, as long as they signed for it, legally assuming responsibility so he wouldn't have it anymore. He would not be a problem. She doubted he'd even look at her.

Baird kept her helmet on and her visor down, not an unusual move for a pilot heading to the lockers from a long flight.

The soldier at the exit saluted Baird without taking any real notice of her, as she had expected. He mumbled at her to stand in a yellow box painted on the floor. She complied. Baird heard a *bong* and saw the name *Alsop* appear on a readout over the door. The soldier seemed about to thank her and send her on her way, but he blinked, his mouth forming into a wide grin.

"Sorry, Alsop, I didn't see—" He looked up at Baird. "Huh? You're not Alsop!"

Baird quickly drew her dart launcher and shot the soldier in the neck. His eyes glazed over and he fell. She lurched forward to catch him. The soldier was heavy, and his limp body managed to press against more than one of her bruises and burns, but Baird kept him from hitting the ground.

"Just my luck," she groaned. "I just happen to get someone who's friends with the guy I rolled."

Baird dragged the soldier away from the door, helped herself to his cap, then sealed him into one of the environment suits.

She used her neural interface to contract parts of the thin black hood that was built into her shirt and hid her real ident chip from sensors. She contorted the fabric until it resembled a skull cap with a cord of bunched cloth connecting it to her shirt, and then changed its color to blend in with her hair. Her gloves faded from black to a shade that matched her skin. She placed the stolen cap on her head to cover the fake hood hair and looked at her reflection in the helmet's visor. The illusion of a ponytail was convincing enough. Once she pulled the wadded paper towels out of her nose, she was good to go.

She waited for a moment as the strand pooled itself inside the helmet tucked under her left arm, then walked out into the corridor, happy to be back on track. She'd had some bad luck right out of the gate, but between the chip, the disguise, and the natural anonymity that comes with being on a base with several hundred soldiers, she could expect to walk right up to the lab with no further complications.

Baird rounded a corner. A soldier was walking from the opposite direction. Her eyes scanned over the name tag stitched into Baird's stolen flight suit. The soldier pointed with one hand while reaching for her sidearm with the other one. "Who are you, and what did you do with Alsop? If you hurt him, I swear I—"

Baird fired a dart at the soldier's throat. The soldier got her arm up to block it, but the dart still hit her hand and delivered its tranquilizer payload. The soldier went limp.

Baird cast a rueful look down at Alsop's name tag and muttered, "Screw this."

Baird dragged the unconscious woman into a nearby empty bathroom, put on the woman's uniform, and cloned her ident chip. She straightened her freshly stolen jacket, reading the embroidered name tag. She looked at the sleeping woman, who was now slumped over on a toilet in Alsop's flight suit and helmet.

"Thanks for the less conspicuous outfit, Marshall. I sure hope you're less popular than Alsop."

Baird walked through the corridors at a brisk pace. She was hopeful that she wouldn't arouse any more attention now that she had ditched Alsop's flight suit, but she didn't want to take any unnecessary chances either.

She followed the path in her gARggles, ducking into alcoves occasionally to avoid other soldiers. Soon, she reached one of the base's satellite med-bays. Per Rivet Gun's intel, the base had several of them, all outfitted with automated diagnostic equipment and a med-tech to operate it all. It would be a simple matter to come in, claim to feel a bit off, and get a quick diagnostic blood test.

She plastered a friendly smile on her face and walked into the med-bay.

The med-tech, a large man in a clean, white uniform, turned, took one look at Baird, and said, "You're not Marshall!"

Baird rolled her eyes. "Great. Marshall's just as popular as Alsop."

The med tech asked, "Who the hell is Alsop?"

Then a tranq dart hit him in the throat.

32

Baird left the med-bay, looking back one last time to make sure that the med-tech was still where she'd left him, lying on an examination table with a sheet draped over his unconscious form, waiting to freak out whoever found him.

Her self-administered scan had yielded results. Copious results. Baird had read every word of the analysis, but until she had time to either have a professional explain them or look things up herself, every entry on the list of things the scanner found looked like it could either be a terminal illness or just more of whatever blood is made of.

Baird sent the strand forward to the next intersection, snaking along the corner where the floor met the wall. The strand's camera looked down all of the available corridors to make sure nobody was coming. She'd had terrible luck avoiding people who could blow her disguise, and she was done taking chances. Convinced that this was as clear a coast as she was likely to get, she jogged down the hall, stopped in a doorway just before the next bend in the corridor, and again sent the strand to scout ahead.

She skulked across half of the base this way, with only one close call. Baird barely got the door closed behind her before two soldiers walked past, deep in conversation.

"He said that?"

"He did, and gave a great big thumbs-up."

"Classic Alsop. What did Marshall say?"

"Well, you know Marshall . . ."

Baird gritted her teeth and waited for their voices to fade, then continued to use the strand to scout her path. The remaining distance between her and the lab entrance looked clear. She used her gARggles to interface the clone-chip hidden in her hood, and she reset Marshall's clearances to give her top-secret access. She also checked her dart launcher, counting the four remaining tranq darts. She looked at the lab's layout and the callout that indicated the location of item 75628.

She'd be the first to admit the infiltration hadn't gone to plan so far. Several witnesses lay in her wake like unconscious, drooling breadcrumbs. But none had gotten a good look at her face. There was no reason she couldn't work clean for the rest of the job and finish strong. No more darting, no more surprises, and she'd be back at Shoreline before anyone knew anything was wrong.

Baird eased out into the hallway. The strand retracted and balled up inside the back of her stolen jacket as she walked down the hall, around a corner, and, after a quick ident-chip scan, into the lab.

The first room was a sort of locker room where scientists could put on their protective suits and securely store any devices or objects they weren't allowed to bring into the lab.

Baird lifted a neatly folded protective suit from the top of a stack by the door. It was made of a thin, light, airtight material, and it had no name tag printed or sewn into it.

The suit didn't seem to restrict her range of motion in any way, but the need for an airtight seal meant the strand had to stay inside, so she wouldn't be able to use it in the lab.

She kept the dart launcher outside the suit; it was metal, and it would be much easier to clean, repair, or replace than two thousand meters of graphene yarn impregnated with custom-formulated meta-materials. She did, however, turn up the dart launcher's pressure as far as it would go. She loved subtlety, but having the darts bounce uselessly off her target's protective suit would be taking subtlety too far.

She moved from the locker room, through a sliding door, then into a long, straight tube, where various antimicrobial sprays, rays, and chemicals bombarded her from every direction. She watched the beads of sinister-looking fluid roll down her visor and then disappear, blown away by high-pressure clouds of toxic-looking gas or evaporated by mysterious colored lights. At the end of the tube, another sliding door opened, allowing her access to the lab.

She paused before the door, standing in a dry zone between two chemical spray nozzles, and checked the lab's schematics again.

There was room for only so many scientists in the lab at once, and most of them would be in the smaller chambers off the main room. Also, the whole lab stuck out of the side of the base, to isolate the danger, so there were no other entrances or exits to keep tabs on. She figured she should be able to walk in and out without most of them ever seeing her. If someone did, her nametag was hidden inside her protective suit, and most of her face was blocked by her respirator. Her gARggles might draw some attention, but not as much as asking where the top-secret prototypes are stored, so she decided to risk it. As long as she walked with purpose, she shouldn't have any trouble.

She peered through the glass door and disinfectant fog and into the lab. She was surprised to find it thoroughly crammed with equipment. The entire back wall and ceiling seemed to be made from conduits, hoses, and high-pressure tanks. Neither of the walls on the sides was visible behind the chaotic forest of tools, scopes, and scanners.

A large sign read: *Warning: discharge no weapons in the lab.*

Baird could not remember ever seeing such a sign in any medical facility.

Amid all the clutter, a lone scientist sat on a stool, peering into some sort of eyepiece. If he didn't look up, she'd be able to get into the secure storage room (the last room on the left, according to the schematics) without the oblivious researcher ever knowing she'd been there.

She strode forward purposefully. The door slid open. Baird took two steps into the lab and heard a loud *bong*. She looked down and saw that she had walked through a yellow box painted on the floor. She glanced behind and saw a readout over the door that said, *Lt. Joan Marshall.*

The scientist looked up from his eyepiece and turned casually toward Baird. "Good evening . . ." The scientist looked up at the display over the door. His eyebrows furrowed. "Marshall?! I don't know any Marshall! Who the devil are you?"

Baird's dart tore through the scientist's protective suit with no difficulty. In Titan's low gravity, he dropped like a slow-motion film of a sack of potatoes.

Baird whispered, "Feek."

From one of the rooms off to the right, she heard a woman's voice call out, "Hargrove?"

Baird barely had time to think about where she might hide the body before a woman in a protective suit walked in. "Hargrove?"

Baird shot her in the neck. The woman fell just as awkwardly as her coworker had, but her momentum carried her to a sliding stop on the floor.

Baird froze, with her dart launcher leveled at the door, waiting for another scientist to come out. She waited several seconds before she tentatively lowered her weapon, grasped the second scientist by the ankles, and pulled her sleeping body out the main door, through the disinfectant tube to the locker room, where there were plenty of hiding places. She was nearly to the door when a third scientist came out of the far room. He looked down at the bodies of two of his colleagues, and an unidentified person dragging one of them off by the feet, and gasped, "Feek!"

Baird let go of the ankles. With her left hand, she held up a single finger, communicating to the panicked scientist that he should wait a moment before doing anything rash. With her right, she aimed her dart launcher and fired a single dart into his neck. He fell on top of the first scientist she'd shot.

Baird shouted, "Feek!"

She swept all four of the secondary rooms with her dart launcher drawn, looking for anyone else who might interrupt her. Once she was convinced that there was nobody left in the lab to see her, she went back to her original plan of sneaking around surreptitiously. One at a time, she dragged her three victims through the disinfectant spray and into the locker room, where she stuffed each of them into lockers. In Baird's allegedly professional opinion, there was a lot more to sneaking than simply not being discovered somewhere you aren't supposed to be. By taking the extra effort to leave no trace, she could keep her presence from being discovered in an area long after she had left it. Few parents realize that when they teach their children to be quiet and pick up after themselves, they are preparing their child for a life of crime.

She walked back through the arrow-straight disinfectant tunnel, into the lab, and to the last door on the left. The room held no furniture or equipment. A bare floor supported four walls covered floor-to-ceiling in chunky metal doors sealed with complex digital locks, each one sporting a glowing red light. Each door had a label bearing only a number. Her gARggles scanned each number automatically and highlighted the one marked *75628*. The locker also bore a bright red sign that read *Danger*.

It occurred to Baird that one didn't often see signs that say "Danger: Contents of this locker are highly medicinal."

She picked the lock and pulled item number 75628 out of its compartment. She pressed its stock to her shoulder, let her finger rest on its trigger guard, closed one eye, and peered down its telescopic scope.

"Yes, it's clearly a medical device of some sort," she muttered, a look of disgust on her face. "Just the thing for aggressive treatments."

The business end of the device consisted of two small nozzles mounted side by side, presumably to eject two separate liquids, and a metallic coil surrounding and extending beyond the nozzles, which, she supposed, would somehow guide or accelerate the streams.

Baird carried her prize into the main laboratory, not really looking where she was going, because she was still too busy glaring ruefully at the item. The sound of a man shrieking snapped her out of her resentful trance.

She looked up and saw a scientist in a protective suit who had just stepped in from the disinfectant tunnel. The man looked at item 75628 cradled in her arms and put both of his hands up.

"Oh, God," the man whined. "Please don't shoot!"

Baird snarled and pointed item 75628 at the man. "What does this thing do?"

The man stammered, "I don't know. I've never seen it before. But it's clearly some kind of weapon!"

"I know, right?! I mean, what else could it possibly be? You've never seen it before though," —Baird looked at the readout by the door—"Dr. Brinkerhoff?"

"No, never, I swear."

"Okay, okay, I believe you. Hey, what kind of doctor are you?"

"An MD! A medical doctor!"

"You've never seen this thing before. Of course, you're an MD. Look, I don't want to hurt you. I don't plan to hurt you. The only way you're going to get hurt here is if you make it happen. You understand?"

Dr. Brinkerhoff nodded furiously. "Uh huh."

"Good," Baird said. "I'm going to show you the results of a blood test. I want you to tell me if there's anything unusual. Specifically, any strange viruses. Understood?"

Again, Brinkerhoff nodded.

Baird sent the text of her blood test from her gARggles to Brinkerhoff's Brow. "I'm watching you, and I'll know if you try to send for help."

Brinkerhoff said, "I understand," as the tiny probe descended from his porcelain-white prosthetic eyebrow. He went silent, his eyes scanning the information, reading for nearly a minute.

"So?" Baird asked. "See anything unusual?"

"Yes, like you said, in the viral load. There's a virus I've never seen. My Brow tried to identify it, just as part of its usual research and indexing function, but it can't find anything."

"It's a man-made virus," Baird said, sourly.

"Oh. I see. What does it do?"

"You can't tell from looking at it what it does?" Baird asked.

"No. It doesn't work like that. We'd have to put it in a subject and see how they react. The person whose blood this is, are they showing any symptoms?"

"Yes. Headaches, some ringing in the ears, and nose bleeds."

"Well, there you are."

Baird said, "I see. Is there a chance that it'll do anything else?"

"It's possible," the doctor said. "Can you be more specific?"

"Could it kill someone?"

"Possibly."

Baird's heart sunk just as badly as it had when Screw Jack first told her she was sick.

"Or," Dr. Brinkerhoff said, "it could just cause headaches, ringing in the ears, and nose bleeds. Or it could do nothing, and the symptoms are unrelated. Or, if the subject was told to expect those symptoms, it could be psychosomatic."

Baird stared at Dr. Brinkerhoff. "That's not helpful."

"I know," Brinkerhoff said. "Sorry. How's your headache?"

"Right now, not so bad."

Dr. Brinkerhoff smiled, obviously pleased with himself.

"Oh, shut up." Baird jabbed item 75628 at him and motioned with her chin toward the disinfectant tunnel. At Baird's direction, the doctor walked through the chemical gauntlet and into the locker room.

"So," he said, looking back over his shoulder, past his raised arms, "you got infected with some sort of engineered virus, and you're worried it might kill you. That's not good."

"That your official medical opinion?"

"Sure. Why not. I've always been good at figuring things out from tiny clues. It's a valuable talent for a doctor to have. I gotta say, that's a terrible position to be in. You have my sympathy."

"Don't feel too bad for me. I don't have an angry woman with an unidentified weapon ordering me to take off my protective suit and get into a locker."

"You want me to take off my suit and get into one of the lockers?"

"Hey, you are good at figuring things out from tiny clues. Get to it, doc."

33

Baird heard a *bong* from the entrance door's ident-chip scanner as she closed the locker door on the unconscious doctor. She spun and aimed item 75628 at the soldier coming through the door.

The soldier shrieked, pulled his weapon from a holster on his belt, and shouted, "Freeze," as he ducked behind the still-open door to the hall, peeking out around the doorframe at Baird.

She kept item 75628 pointed his direction, feinting with it threateningly every time the soldier looked around the corner at her. She moved backward several steps, eventually walking through the door to the disinfectant tunnel. The soldier fired his weapon. Red bolts of light flashed past Baird as she ducked to the side and hid behind the doorframe, as the soldier had. She looked to the other end of the disinfectant tunnel and saw two scorch marks on the far door.

Baird shouted, "That's not a stunner!"

"No," the soldier said. "It's not."

"You could have killed me!"

The soldier shouted, "That was the idea."

"I'm surprised you use live rounds in such a dangerous environment."

"Eh, they're not strong enough to go through the base's outer skin, just yours. And we aren't allowed to use them in a room with an exterior wall."

Baird asked, "So, if I were to, say, go back into the lab, I'd be safe?"

"Yes," the soldier said, brightly. "That's a very good idea."

"But I'd also be trapped."

"Safety comes at a price."

"I'll pass."

The soldier laughed. "I thought you might. While we're having this weirdly civil conversation, I have a question. Why didn't you shoot me? You're an intruder in a top-secret wing of a military base. You've already killed at least one person that I know of."

The guard had seen the doctor, who was unconscious, not dead. Now he was trying to talk himself out of being afraid of her. Telling him that she hadn't killed anyone would only help him with that.

"You have a weapon," the soldier continued, "but you didn't fire. Why not?"

Baird wracked her brain for an answer to that question that would make her scarier.

"Where's the fun in shooting you? I'm a bludgeoner. It's the only way I can really savor the kill!"

"Nice try, but I don't buy it. I think you're out of ammunition, or whatever that thing uses. It's the only reason I can think of that you didn't shoot when you had the drop on me."

"No, that's not the only reason."

"What else can it be?"

"Maybe I just stole this weapon, I don't know what it does, and I'm worried that it's so powerful it will kill both of us."

The soldier mulled that over. "That's interesting."

"Yeah?"

"Yeah. It is. Because in a way, it's the opposite of what I suspect, but in another way, it isn't. See, if I'm right, your weapon's not dangerous, so you can't use it. If, on the other hand, what you just said is correct, then the weapon might be *too* dangerous, so you can't use it. Either way, it's useless."

"No," Baird said. "It isn't."

"No?"

"No, because I can still bludgeon you with it."

"Well, here's your chance." The soldier stepped out into the doorway and ran across the locker room toward Baird's position. In the low gravity, he didn't get off to a very fast start, but the locker room wasn't all that large.

Baird knew that soon the soldier would run into the disinfectant tunnel, leaving her with no cover, and no choice but to actually attempt to bludgeon him with item 75628, a task for which she felt no enthusiasm. She pushed off from the bulkhead, giving her a faster start than he'd managed. She heard the disinfectant spray hitting her hazmat suit as she ran backwards, aiming item 75628 at the soldier, who instinctively ducked to the side, hiding against the opposite side of the very doorjamb she had just been using for cover.

She passed backward through the successive waves of chemical spray and fog. The door slid open behind her. The soldier remembered that he didn't fear her weapon, and he stepped out into the doorway at the far end of the disinfectant tunnel and took aim.

She didn't think about the fact that the lab was a trap. Her only thought was of getting away from the guard.

The guard didn't think about the fact that the lab was a trap. His only thought was of not wanting Baird to get away.

She darted into the lab, just to the side of the door, as three more bolts of red light shot through the disinfectant tunnel, past her, and into the lab, striking the tangled mass of tanks and hoses on the far wall. One of the hoses sprung a leak, which instantly ignited into a hissing jet of flame several inches long.

Baird shouted, "You idiot! Run!"

She pulled her mass around the doorframe with her arm. As she turned her back on the flaming tank, she noticed the light it cast getting noticeably brighter. She pushed off from the bulkhead with her legs, sprinting as fast as she could in light gravity and a hazmat suit. She barreled directly toward the soldier, who stood in the locker room doorway, stunned, looking into the distance behind Baird.

She felt a shockwave hit her from behind, pushing her even harder into the soldier's sternum. The two of them fell, rolled, and slid to a stop on the locker room floor. Baird looked through the disinfectant tunnel and into the lab. Smoke and fire filled the room, then the smoke shot to the ceiling, as if being pushed from below. A hole about the size of a basketball formed in the lab's far wall. Baird saw darkness and the icy crust of Titan beyond it. Her ears felt as if someone was attempting to swab them out with metal spikes.

The entire wall disintegrated, but Baird barely had time to realize what she was seeing before the lab interior flashed bright blue, as the methane rain and fog mixed with the oxygen in the lab and combusted. Baird spent one quarter of a second utterly convinced that she was about to die before a large metal door slammed down at the far end of the disinfectant tunnel, sealing off the lab.

The explosion made a surprisingly soft, low boom that seemed to last several seconds. Baird felt it come up through the floor, grind the cartilage in all her joints, and push most of the air out of her lungs. Immediately after the boom, Baird heard several loud cracks, and the groaning sound of large pieces of metal under great stress.

The soldier rolled over on his back and coughed. "Look what you did!"

Baird shot him with a dart. Instead of falling unconscious, his arms and legs flailed. He cried out in a string of random vowel sounds as he thrashed helplessly on the ground.

Baird looked at him and shook her head. He'd gotten a neural scrambler, meaning she was out of tranq darts.

A second metal safety barrier slammed down over the disinfectant tunnel's entrance. Baird looked at the locker room entrance, the only means of exit left. Above it, built into the ceiling, she saw a seam that she now realized held another impenetrable safety barrier. She scrambled toward the door, pausing in the yellow box on the floor, positioned far too close to the safety barrier's landing spot for her to feel comfortable. She waited for less than a second, but it felt much longer. She unzipped her protective suit while she crouched, waiting for the door to open.

Before the door was fully open, Baird dove, twisting sideways to fit through the gap as quickly as possible. She held item 75628 out in front of her, as if getting it out of the lab would somehow *score a point.*

Baird landed on her side and slid to the far end of the hall. She let go of item 75628 and wriggled out of her protective suit, violently enough to rip it in the process. Once she was out of the suit, she hastily wadded it up and threw it at the now-closing lab door. The third safety barrier slammed down on it, leaving just a little material sticking out under the metal wall.

Baird sat up, taking stock of her situation and surroundings. The hall looked exactly as it had when she'd walked in, except for the flashing red lights and sirens. She commanded the strand to form itself into a messenger bag, which only took a few seconds. She stuck item 75628 inside and started clambering to her feet. All of her old bruises still hurt, but not as much as she suspected the new ones would.

Eight soldiers sprinted around the corner and slid to a stop in front of Baird.

She pointed at the sealed-off lab. "Quick! Do something! Alsop's in there!"

The soldiers sprang into action. Some accessed the environmental controls. Some accessed the emergency override for the safety barrier. Several tried to pull the lab door open with their bare hands.

Baird adjusted her newly formed bag so that the strap covered Marshall's name tag. She low-gravity bounce-jogged back through the base the way she'd come. The corridors that had been nearly deserted were now bustling with panicked activity. People ran in every conceivable direction, shouting questions and answers at each other in order to be heard over the sirens. She felt another long, slow explosion rock the entire base.

As she ran past the med-bay, she heard people shouting, "Wait, he's not dead! Oh my God, what happened to him?"

She kept moving.

Baird ducked into the bathroom where she'd left Marshall. She slid back into Alsop's flight suit, leaving Marshall's uniform in the unconscious woman's lap.

She jogged the rest of the way, holding the helmet at chest height to block people's view of Alsop's name tag.

Baird ran into the hangar. Now all that was left was to steal a 'thopter, a real 'thopter with a cockpit, fly back to Shoreline, and drink to forget. Baird was willing to bet Rivet Gun kept something strong around, if only to wash out wounds.

She stepped down into the primary hangar and looked at her options. Most of the aircraft were gone, probably taken by soldiers hoping to help with the ongoing disaster from outside the base. One ornithopter hung from the gantry crane, heading toward the airlock. Another had a soldier sitting in the cockpit, going over a checklist while two other soldiers pumped fuel into its tank and loaded emergency supplies into its hold. The only available aircraft was the wasp Baird had flown in.

She had no time to go to another hanger, or to try to talk the pilot out of the other 'thopter. She found only two environment suits left, both empty, but one inaccessible because it was blocked by a pilot tending to the unconscious soldier Baird had stowed when she first arrived.

"I found this man in one of the suits!"

Baird didn't even look at him. "You don't say?"

"We need to help him!"

Baird turned her back to hide her name tag, pulled her stolen helmet down over her head, and stepped into the other suit. "You seem to have it under control." The suit closed in over Baird's back, leaving an extra bulge to allow for the bag slung over her shoulder.

She straddled the wasp, felt her suit click into place, and established herself as the next in line to depart.

The gantry crane moved the wasp into the airlock. The atmospheric pressure equalized, and the wasp was pushed out into the methane rain. Baird allowed the wasp to do a little spin in the air as it gained altitude. She could see 'thopters from all over the base converging on the area of the lab, and a massive jet of blue flame shooting from the rupture in the lab wall.

She set the autopilot for Shoreline. Her gARggles gave her an ETA and informed her that the famously capricious Titanian winds had changed direction. She would be fighting a headwind all the way back to Shoreline.

34

Rivet Gun double-checked the flight plan, nodded her approval, and set the autopilot to bring the 'thopter home. She peered at Baird past her Brow probe and smiled. "You know, I kept an eye on the data-traffic coming out of Fort Carlson tonight."

"Oh, did you?"

"Yeah," Rivet Gun laughed. "You told me you were going to slip in and out quietly."

"I did say that, didn't I?"

"And then you created a massive diversion instead. Solid, kid. Rock solid. Give them a life-threatening emergency to deal with, lose yourself in the chaos, and achieve your objectives while they're all looking the other way."

Baird squinted at Rivet Gun, trying to decide if the older woman was making fun of her or giving her too much credit. "That's pretty much how it worked out."

"I bet. So, tell me, how'd you do it? Did you use the old incompetent accomplice ploy? Find some sap on the inside and talk him into doing something stupid?"

Baird said, "I'd rather not say," and she meant it.

Rivet Gun nodded, smiling. "Well played. Well played. Don't give anything away. You are a cool customer, Saber Saw. I gotta say, you had me going with your naïve Doug, desperate-for-approval act."

"Pretty convincing, huh?"

"I sure bought it."

"Hey," Baird said, "How'd your business go? Was the unsavory crowd happy to see you?"

"At first, but in the end, they were happy to see me leave. In between I got the information I needed."

Baird examined Rivet Gun as best she could without obviously staring. The older woman's gray pantsuit still looked clean and well pressed. Her blouse looked slightly rumpled, but no more so than it would after a normal evening on the town. Now that she was looking closely, though, Baird thought she saw what could be droplets of dried blood in Rivet Gun's gray hair, but she would have to either get closer or ask to be sure, and she wasn't about to do either of those things.

Rivet Gun glanced at the large shopping bag resting near Baird's feet, and for a moment, she almost seemed to smile. Baird quite definitely did smile, and she pulled the sleeves of her sweater down over her cold hands.

The 'thopter brought itself in for a landing. Baird and Rivet Gun made a little small talk as the airlock cycled. As they entered the house, Baird said, "Hey, you seem to have lots of experience in stopping bleeding."

"Almost as much as I have in starting it. Where were you hit?"

"I wasn't. I'm wondering how you would go about stopping a nosebleed."

"Hmm, a bloody nose," River Gun muttered. "I've given plenty of those over the years, but I always left the victim to clean themselves up. I might have something. One second."

Rivet Gun walked to the bathroom and spent a while rummaging through her oversized first-aid kit. When she returned, she handed Baird a large handful of white fabric cylinders a couple of centimeters long. "Stick those in the sap's nostrils. That'll stop the bleeding. They're designed for treating stab wounds, but the principle is the same."

Baird said, "I don't need this many. I don't want to take your whole supply."

Rivet Gun laughed. "I have a whole case of 'em. Last time I got caught short, I swore I'd never let myself run out again."

Baird thanked Rivet Gun and excused herself to make a couple of calls in her room.

First, she touched base with her handler, Spring Clamp. The instant his bland, dull-eyed face appeared, he blurted, "Hello, Saber Saw. Status report?"

Baird said, "I have the item."

"Excellent. Well done. The first available transpo—"

"It's a weapon," Baird said.

"How do you know?" Spring Clamp asked.

"It's obvious."

"Have you fired the weapon?"

"No."

"Then how can you know that it's a weapon?"

"Well, for one thing, Spring Clamp, you just referred to it as *the weapon*."

Spring Clamp said, "I was following your lead. You are my field agent. You told me it was a weapon. I chose to trust your judgment. Now it turns out that you had insufficient evidence and that your analysis is probably faulty. It will take quite a while before you regain my trust. We have you booked on the next shuttle off Titan. You will leave the item with Rivet Gun and report to the spaceport. Sadly, your shuttle doesn't leave for another six hours."

"I have to waste six hours of my limited life span waiting for my ride out of here?"

"So does everyone else on the flight. Spring Clamp, out."

Baird took a moment to calm herself. In her experience, being angry seldom helped anything, especially when the person you were angry at was on another planet.

After a moment, she navigated through her gARggles' secret menu and placed a call to the current Izzy. He answered immediately.

"You busy?" Baird asked.

"Not too busy to make time. How are you?"

"I'm fine. Done with the mission."

"Did you manage to get a blood test?"

Baird nodded. "I did. I even got a doctor to interpret the results for me."

"And?"

"Conclusively inconclusive. The tests showed that it is a virus, but we don't know what it does."

"So there's no way to find out if it's lethal?"

"There's one surefire way. We wait and see if it kills me."

"Oh. That's not very helpful."

"I dunno," Baird said. "It was helpful enough for me to come to a concrete decision."

"And that is?"

"That I'm done. I'm not going to continue like this, doing what I'm told, waiting for someone else to cure me, or free me, whichever it is that I need."

"So, what are you going to do?"

"I don't know, but it seems for once I have a few hours to think about it."

Izzy grimaced. "You say that like it's a victory, but it sounds like there's just one more thing you don't know."

"It *is* a victory. For the first time in a long time, I'm uncertain about what I'm going to do, not what someone else is going to tell me to do."

"That's not much of a victory, Bran."

"It's only the first, Izzy. I promise, more are coming."

35

Baird felt the chill in her veins. She opened her eyes, saw the smooth, beige inner surface of her spaceline stasis pod door, and smiled.

In her gARggles, she saw a notification for her pre-mission briefing, which she ignored. If she'd taken the briefing, then disappeared, they would have known she had arrived at wherever she was. If she had declined the briefing, they would have known she was in the wind. Instead, she left the notification active but didn't answer it, so they wouldn't know what to think. She could be dead, her gARggles could be broken, the spaceline could have lost her; they had lots of leads to track down, which, ironically, made it that much harder to find her.

A chime played on the in-pod speaker, followed by a confident-sounding voice. "Good morning, valued passengers. I'm pleased to tell you that we are about to arrive at our final destination: St. Theresa, Europa. The local gravity is .13 g, so please adjust your grav-meds accordingly."

St. Theresa—this was both good and bad news. It was a big place. Busy, with lots of shuttle traffic. It would be easy to blend in and hide. The bad news was that she didn't like taterfish, but that wasn't the end of the world.

She knew where they'd woken her up, but she didn't yet know *when*. Baird pulled up the current date and time in her gARggles and discovered how difficult it can be to subtract one date from another when one is distracted by feelings of rage and the sensation of one's heart sinking. One year, three months, and five days since she left Titan. Adding it all up, she'd been in and out of stasis for a little over nine years. Of course, to her it felt like four days, but even that was far too long.

She had already decided not to involve Izzy from this point on; it was one of the first major decisions she'd made when she was laying out her escape plan during her six-hour wait to leave Titan. This was her problem, and she would solve it herself. Anyway, whoever she did contact wouldn't actually be Izzy, just a clone—a stranger implanted with Izzy's memories, his mental baggage, and his younger-brotherly need to help even when he's told not to.

She was the first one out of her pod when the doors opened and managed to make it nearly halfway to the exit before the other passengers completely clogged the aisle. Still, she was of a mind to be proactive. She was done waiting for other people to do things, even when that thing was just getting out of her way.

She walked down the terminal concourse, keeping pace with the other travelers as they filed past the advertisements for restaurants that were famous for their signature taterfish dishes; hotels that were famous for their service and their restaurants, all of which featured signature taterfish dishes; and for tourist-trap markets where one could buy fresh taterfish to send home to jealous friends and family. Baird saw all of it and noticed none of it. She felt more focused, more confident, more like herself than she had in days—or years, depending on how you counted it. She was on her own, on a job she chose, using a plan she had devised. It was all business as usual, except for the fact that she was stealing herself.

Baird slowed, moved to the side, and turned, entering one of the many shops that lined the concourse. Here she would execute step one of her plan: *acquire a hat*. Like most spaceport shops, they had a wonderful selection of the things travelers seemed to want most: expensive liquor; overpriced snack food; and cheap, hideous clothing. Baird looked through the garments, searching for the hat that offended her sensibilities the least. She hated to lower herself to shoplifting, but she couldn't afford to leave a paper trail attached to her name, and in her opinion, the store's price markup was the real crime.

Moments later she left the shop wearing a bright red cap embroidered with the unofficial slogan of the taterfish industry: "Peel it off, plunge it in, suck it out." Step one came off without a hitch.

Baird moved on to step two: *improvise a way out of the spaceport without getting spotted by her contact.* She was not happy that one of the steps of her plan was to improvise, but she couldn't get more specific without knowing the layout of the spaceport and where the contact would be standing.

She walked directly to the nearest restroom, where, once she had a stall to herself, she pulled the hood of her bodysuit up over her head, gathered it at the rear to resemble a ponytail, altered its color to match her hair, and polarized the fabric so that it would block her ident chip's signal.

She removed her bronze pin from her sweater, dismantled it, and put it back together, leaving out the silvery square from the middle. Using her gARggles, she set the false ident chip to one of her preset aliases—one with a substantial bank account.

She stuck the square in her hood and placed the awful red cap on her head. She muttered to herself, "Welcome to St. Theresa, Heather Woodruff. I hope you like taterfish."

Heather Woodruff's first act on Europa was to sit in the restroom stall and use her gARggles to purchase a ticket *off* of Europa. The next flight headed where she wanted to go didn't leave for seven hours. She would need a quiet, private, safe place to hide out. She booked a hotel room for the night, knowing that Heather Woodruff could afford it, and that if anyone suspected she was Baird, the reservation would misdirect them into thinking she would be there until tomorrow.

She walked with extra purpose and a hint of a smile. It felt good to be taking control, to be making her own decisions. Spring Clamp didn't know what a mistake he'd made when he gave her a few hours of downtime on Titan. He was about to learn that nothing was more dangerous than Baird with time to plan.

Even without her gARggles, Baird would have spotted her contact easily, since he was actively trying to be found. He was a tall young man in a suit, a little heavy for his height, and he gave the impression of someone who was trying very hard to make a good first impression, which is seldom a good first impression to make. Her spoofed ident chip prevented his Brow from highlighting her, so she easily blended into a thick cluster of travelers and got by the young man with no trouble. She slipped into a lift, then walked out of the spaceport and into the colony proper.

St. Theresa was an old colony with a colorful and complex history; so colorful and complex that certain aspects of it made most people uncomfortable. The Europans found it more pleasant and profitable to focus on good times, good music, and promoting the colony's best-known export: the taterfish.

The colony hung anchored to the underside of Europa's icy crust, submerged in the dark cold Europan ocean, with only the spaceport and some of the infrastructure sticking out on the surface.

Baird exited the lifts onto the promenade: a broad, open thoroughfare lined on both sides with many restaurants, bars, cafés, and food stalls, all beneath a ceiling of transparent ice, illuminated by the distant sun and the reddish reflected light from Jupiter. The vast majority of the businesses offered live entertainment, and all of them offered some taterfish dish or other that they swore was unquestionably the best on Europa, and by extension, in the solar system.

Step one and step two behind her, Baird moved on to step three of her plan.

As she rounded a corner, she glanced back over her shoulder, just to see if maybe her contact had spotted her and was following. The guy's size and suit would have made him easy to spot, but she didn't see him. There was one person who looked to be male, wearing a midnight blue jacket, who darted out of sight as soon as she turned her head; since he was clearly much smaller than her contact, she chalked it up to coincidence.

This was not Baird's first visit to Europa, and she knew the layout of the colony. Of course, it had been years since her last visit, so many of the names of the bars and restaurants had changed, but the general ambiance remained unchanged, as did the location of the more fashionable part of town.

Baird made her way past the restaurants, bars, and shops that targeted tourists, to the businesses beyond—the ones that targeted tourists who wanted to avoid thinking of themselves as tourists. She entered an expensive-looking store where expensive-looking garments hung on expensive-looking racks to keep them up off the expensive-looking floor. A salesman, dressed impeccably in the exact kind of suit the store would have carried if it chose to dirty its hands with menswear, crossed the sales floor to meet her at the door.

"Good afternoon, Miss . . ." he paused, almost imperceptibly, looking at the data served to him by his impossibly thin, jet-black Brow. "Woodruff. How may I help you today?"

Baird said, "I need a better hat."

The salesman looked at her red novelty cap. "I agree."

36

Several minutes later Baird left the store, resplendent in a stylish black hat with a large enough brim to obscure her features but not so wide as to draw attention on its own. As she stepped out into the street, she caught sight of something moving quickly in the distance off to her right. She didn't get her head pointed toward it in time to get a good look, and she knew it was probably nothing, but the fact that the blur she did see was dark blue gave her pause.

Baird made her way to the promenade's finest hotel, where the staff greeted her as Miss Woodruff and checked her in.

She stood in her hotel room, trying to process the fact that for the first time in a long time, she didn't have a job that needed to be done as soon as possible. Her only task was to leave Europa without the Toolbox knowing where she went. She already knew how she was going to do it, and when. Until then, she had time to relax.

She popped some pain relievers, settled down into the bed, and tried to make her limbs relax. She regretted that she had to leave so soon. It would have been nice to sleep in a real bed. All of her sleep lately had been travel-induced stasis, which did the job, but it wasn't the real thing.

She lay on the bed, eyes closed, going over the situation and the plan in her head, looking for anything she might have forgotten.

When this whole thing had started, Screw Jack told her she had seven days. That, from her point of view, had been four and a half days ago, giving her about two and a half more days at this point. If they were telling her the truth, she had to make a move now, because she wouldn't have enough time later. If they were lying, she wanted to know as soon as possible, so now was still the time to act.

Baird had two and a half days of non-stasis time to get to Earth (which wouldn't be easy), sneak into the Toolbox (which would be even harder), and gain access to the files she needed to determine if she had a man-made infection designed to kill her or one designed to keep her under the Toolbox's thumb (which would dictate whether she would spend the rest of her short life depending on the Toolbox's help, or the rest of her long life making them pay).

In retrospect, she regretted telling her original handler, Screw Jack, that she was considering leaving. She should have just left. Sure, it would have led to anger and hurt feelings, but she wouldn't have been there to deal with it.

If their story proved accurate, and the illness was killing her, she would have enough time to put herself in stasis. She figured the Toolbox would still thaw her out and cure her, if only to find out how she had snuck in. If, on the other hand, she discovered they were lying, and she wasn't on death's door, she would want revenge, and inside the Toolbox's headquarters seemed like a pretty good place to get it.

She put on her gARggles and interfaced with the hotel's in-room entertainment system. At her command, the entire ceiling became an uninterrupted video screen—set, of course, to display local interests and tourist information programming. Normally she'd have selected something else immediately, but the feeling of actually relaxing was so pleasant that she didn't want to stop, even to pick a more enjoyable program. She pulled off her gARggles and watched. She could have viewed anything she wanted through her gARggles, but sometimes it was nice to just use your eyeballs to look at something that was really there, even if it was just a video screen.

The image showed a ball of ice floating in a sea of black. Lying on the bed and looking up at the image spread across the entire ceiling gave Baird the impression that she was hanging in space. The narrator said, "Europa was the first moon other than Earth's moon, Luna, to be visited by humans. We came here looking for two things. We found them both."

The image zoomed in on the ball of ice, rushing toward its surface until the screen went entirely white. The image abruptly changed, showing underwater footage from the liquid ocean beneath Europa's icy crust, giving the impression that the viewer had plunged through the ice into the water beneath.

The narrator said, "One of the things we sought was the most useful resource in the solar system: liquid water. It can be used to grow food, make oxygen to breathe, and produce hydrogen to generate electricity or power thrusters—and you can drink it. Here on Europa, we found all the liquid water we needed."

The image grew darker as the viewer was pulled deeper, down to the seabed.

"The other thing we came looking for was life. Europa was the first—and to this day, only—place humans have found non-terrestrial, naturally evolved, multicellular life forms."

Baird looked at the barren landscape of gray silt and rocks. The image remained unchanged for several seconds before she saw a tiny stirring of motion. Silt rose in a tiny plume, like a slow-motion explosion, and some sort of creature scurried away.

The camera followed a long, wormlike creature made of twenty or thirty rough oval segments, as if someone had taken a pound of white fingerling potatoes and strung them like pearls on a necklace.

"At first," the narrator said, "we were sad to find that the life forms weren't intelligent, but the sadness gave way to great joy when we discovered that they were delicious when prepared properly."

Baird shuddered and gagged at the same time, trying to imagine a situation in which the taterfish would look yummy.

She heard a quiet knock at the door. In an instant, she was on her feet, reaching for her pin. Her hands went on autopilot, dismantling the pin and reassembling the pieces into her dart launcher.

The documentary's narrator said, "Taterfish feed off of the nutrients spewed up by volcanic vents on the ocean floor, and the microbial life that also thrives there."

She looked up at the door. If she looked out through the peephole, she would be standing in a predictable location. She knew from experience that there were many weapons that could easily penetrate a hotel door. She chose not to risk it.

"In order to efficiently farm the delicious taterfish," the narrator continued, "we build massive manifolds on the seabed that simulate these vents."

The bottom of her sweater unraveled. The strand slithered across the floor and worked its way under the door, out into the hall. Once there, the tip of the strand pointed upward. Baird couldn't make out the person's face, but she could see that the visitor was most likely male and was definitely wearing a dark blue jacket.

"Once harvested, the taterfish are de-segmented and deveined, the toxic bodily fluids are removed, and the remaining flesh and chitinous shell are soaked for two days in a chemical bath that neutralizes all remaining noxious compounds, leaving it clean, nutritious, and smelling only faintly of sulfur."

While Baird retracted the strand, the man at the door knocked again. This did not surprise her. If he touched the doorbell, it would scan his ident chip and tell her who he was. It would also leave a record that he was here. Whoever this guy was, he didn't want one or both of those things, which meant that she probably didn't want to meet him.

She opened the door, firing her dart launcher as soon as the gap between the door and the doorframe was wide enough to allow the dart through. She watched as the dart drilled into the man's throat. She leapt backward as he reacted to the pain and surprise, his limbs swinging about in unpredictable and uncontrollable ways.

The man flopped on the hallway floor. Every attempt he made to lift himself from the carpet only resulted in him flailing and rolling around. He tried to speak, but only strange, guttural noises with slurred, strangled consonants came out.

"Oh, feek," Baird said. "Serves you right for dropping by unannounced, Izzy."

Baird muted the video, stepped out into the hall, and looked down at a clone of her brother. "Shush," she said. "You'll attract attention. Stop moving. Just relax and lie still. Your voluntary nerve impulses are scrambled."

Izzy said something, but she couldn't tell what. He stopped moving, though. He lay in the hallway, looking up at her, more confused than afraid. Baird grabbed him by the ankles and dragged him into her room.

She locked the door. "What are you doing here?"

Izzy's tone was conversational, but he made a sort of bleating noise.

"Yeah," Baird said. "I know. You can't talk."

She knelt down and started going through all of his pockets. He made more indistinct noises, this time sounding vaguely aggrieved.

"You followed me to my hotel, and then you came knocking at my door with no warning. How did you think I'd react? I'm on the run here. I can't take any risks."

Izzy let out a short burst of mouth sounds.

Baird shook her head. "No, I can't understand you; I just had a pretty good idea what you were going to say. Next you're going to tell me that you're here to help."

Izzy blurted out a single, loud syllable. He thrashed his head around in a wide circle. Baird was pretty sure he was trying to nod.

She pulled his stunner from its holster and held it up where he could see it. "Uh huh. Look. You're going to be pretty messed up for an hour or so. I suggest you just lie here on the floor and watch the ceiling with me. When the neural scrambler wears off, we'll have a talk. If that's acceptable, please signify with two dumb-sounding noises."

Izzy let out two staccato moans that sounded like someone laughing at a terrible joke.

Later, after watching an hour or so of various taterfish recipes, Izzy cleared his throat. "Testing. Okay, I can talk again."

"Did you just test your voice by saying 'testing'?" Baird asked, turning down the sound.

"Yes. It seemed like the logical move." Izzy sat up carefully, not quite trusting his limbs to do as they were told. "Why? What do most people say?"

"Most of them curse."

"Okay, yeah, I can understand that. Why did you drug me?"

"You know that. Because I wasn't expecting you, and you're here. Why are you here?"

"You know that. Because I want to help you."

"Well, so far all you've done is make me waste a scrambler dart. How'd you find me?"

Izzy pulled himself up from the floor into a lounge chair opposite the bed. "Man, I'm going to be sore tomorrow. My arms feel like noodles."

Baird said, "Yeah, when people realize that their limbs are just flailing around instead of doing what they're told, the first impulse is to flail harder. It gets awfully strenuous. Answer the question."

"We've had quite a bit of time to think and work on things since we talked to you last."

"'We?' Meaning . . .?"

"The past Izzys. One of us managed to hack deep into the Toolbox's systems. We don't have total access; that'd be hard, working remotely. But we were able to set up a script that waited for you to be assigned a mission, found out where, and spawned a clone there a day before your scheduled arrival."

"I didn't ask for your help."

"No, you didn't, and you don't have to use it, but you have it if you want it."

"I don't."

"Not yet. But you might."

"Why do any of you care? This doesn't concern you. You're not involved. You're not really my brother, just a clone of someone who was, years ago."

"We've given that a lot of thought, too. At the end of the day, all you are is your memories. You are who you remember being. We have the original Isaac Baird's memories up until about a year after you disappeared. He felt responsible, because he recruited you, so we feel responsible. So, what's the plan? I assume you have a plan."

"The next step is to get off of Europa."

"Makes sense."

"I'll be flying out on a commercial shuttle, under an assumed name."

"Had your ident chip re-flashed?" Izzy asked.

"Something like that," Baird said. "You said that you're tied fairly deep into the Toolbox's systems."

"Yes."

"Can you get me an accurate set of floor plans and schematics for the Toolbox HQ?"

"Yeah, no problem." He pulled his gray steel Brow from his pocket and pressed it into place above his right eye. The probe extended down. His eyes started to dart about.

Baird watched him for a moment. "Hey, Izzy? Since you're not coming with me, what are you going to do?"

"I'm pretty much stuck here on Europa. Unless I get re-flashed, I can't fly out without showing up on the Toolbox's radar. I figure I'll settle in and find out once and for all if we clones actually have a two-week lifespan."

"Wow. Bumming around, waiting to die. That's not much of a life."

"No, it's not, but I'd have had the same amount of time whether I was on an official mission or not. This way, I'm my own boss for my last two weeks. That's better than most clones have it."

"I guess so."

Izzy smiled. "I don't have to guess."

"Mind if I turn the sound back up?" Baird asked. "It helps me think, sometimes."

Izzy said, "Go for it."

Baird laid back on the bed and unmuted the video feed. On the ceiling, a rotund man was preparing broiled taterfish in the traditional Europan manner. He poured the prepared segments onto a platter in a steaming heap of round, white lumps. He pulled a segment out of the pile, turning it quickly to keep from burning the tips of his fingers.

"Now, my favorite part," he said. "Digging in. Remember, despite all of the hard work and effort needed to grow, catch, and prepare them, taterfish were clearly meant to be food, because they come with their own utensil!"

He gripped the taterfish segment by the end with one hand, and with the other he pinched a corner of the segment's chitinous exoskeleton. He said, "Peel it off," and pulled at the exoskeleton, which tore loose from the meat in a single unbroken semi-translucent sheet, like a very large thumbnail.

He gripped the peel between his thumb and index finger so that it formed a sort of scoop with a very sharp edge. He used that edge to dig into the lump of steaming brown flesh he held in his other hand, saying, "Plunge it in."

He lifted the taterfish peel up, showing the plug of taterfish meat stuck in the rough scoop he had formed. "Suck it out," he said, with great enthusiasm, before sticking the scoop in his mouth and slurping the meat out of it.

Izzy said, "Ugh. *Peel it off, plunge it in, suck it out.* Couldn't they have come up with a way to describe it that wouldn't make people think of sex?"

Baird said, "They want them to think about sex so they won't think about the fact that they're eating disgusting toxic albino worms that live in alien mud."

37

Baird opened her eyes to find the beige interior of a spaceliner stasis pod. The view was slightly different this time, what with the brim of her large black hat bent down against the inside of the door. She could feel the spoofed ident chip still pressing slightly into her scalp under her hat.

She waited through the bone-deep chill and the sweat-inducing wave of heat that followed it.

Baird didn't ever want to go into stasis again if she could help it. She swore to stick to those flights for stasis-phobes, where it's like a little hotel that flies through space. She'd always thought that sounded boring, but now it seemed like it could be nice. She'd have some time to think, get to know the other passengers if they were nice, or steal from them if they weren't.

She checked her gARggles. The notification for her briefing for the job on Europa, probably stealing the world's most expensive taterfish, was gone. They knew she was in the wind.

A chime sounded, and a flight attendant said, "Good morning, valued passengers. We've reached the end of our nineteen-day trip to Tsiolkovsky Station, the Pendulum. The local gravity is one g, so please adjust your grav-meds accordingly."

Baird ignored the rest of the standard arrival spiel, choosing instead to decide for herself what important information she needed to be aware of as she arrived at her destination.

She knew that the Toolbox would be after her. Chip spoofing had never failed her before, but she still called it a fifty-fifty chance that they had figured out she was now Heather Woodruff.

If they had, they'd have probably taken her pod before she woke up, but still, they could be watching her to see what she was up to. She would need to be on guard.

She worked her free left hand up and removed her pin from her sweater, reworked it into its dart-gun configuration, and palmed it.

She and the other passengers walked through the concourse. Baird looked around for possible attackers and casually took in the décor. The Pendulum's spaceport made Baird uncomfortable. The terminal looked much cleaner, the floor much newer. She had only been there a few days before, but that had actually been four years ago.

On one of the walls she saw a large moving advertisement. As she approached, drawing close enough to hear the audio and make out the visuals, she saw a man wearing what appeared to be a very old, well-worn space suit, slowly receding at the end of a tether into space.

The tether pulled tight as it reached its end, and the man swung into a large cluster of at least twenty other men, all in similarly worn-out space suits, all hanging at the end of tethers, writhing, screaming, and cursing, like a bunch of the world's least festive balloons. The camera pulled out to show Sheriff Worthington Calhoun, looking a little grayer and a little heavier than when Baird had last seen him, standing safe and sound inside the station, looking down at the men in the space suits through a window in the floor.

"Rotating each prisoner through one stint in what we call the lower annex eases overcrowding, gives a useful new life to surplus maintenance space suits that would have been thrown away otherwise, and fulfills the prisoners' legally mandated out-of-cell recreational time."

The camera pulled in on the sheriff's squinting eyes. "I'm Sheriff Worthington Calhoun. I obey the letter of the law, and you should too."

Baird emerged from the main concourse into the transportation center. As she stepped out into the larger space, she heard a voice from the blind corner she'd just passed. "Miss Woodruff?" She turned and found Izzy striding toward her, smiling.

Baird went in for a far-too-tight hug, smiled and whispered into his ear, "What the hell are you doing here?"

"Helping you!" he croaked in surprise and pain.

"How'd you get here?"

"I was generated here. The last Izzy ordered me up and left me instructions to meet you."

Baird withdrew from the hug, turned, and walked away.

He rushed to follow her. "The previous Izzy warned me you wouldn't want my help."

"Then why are you here?"

"In case you need it."

Baird said, "I didn't tell you . . . him . . . the last you, where I was going."

"It wasn't hard for him to figure out. He uncovered your tracks, then he covered them back up again."

"That's big of him. How is he, by the way?"

"Unknown. He ordered me and left me instructions seven days ago. There's been no further contact."

Baird nodded. "So, probably dead. That seems to confirm the two-week life span."

"Not necessarily. He might be in hiding so that if he does die, the Toolbox won't find him. That'd be a tipoff. Even if he is dead, it doesn't mean that it's our built-in life span. He might have died in an accident, been stabbed in a bar fight, choked to death on some taterfish. It happens all the time. People take the 'suck it out' part too literally and inhale a hunk."

"That's a terrible way to go." Baird put on her gARggles.

Izzy asked, "What's the plan?"

"To handle this on my own, but it looks like that's out the window. Right now I'm calling an old friend who lives here on the Pendulum—or at least he used to. I need to see about buying some supplies."

Baird placed a call, waited, and a few moments later Tote's face materialized. His beard was slightly grayer and trimmed a bit differently, but otherwise he looked the same.

"Baird, my dear friend, it's been far too long!"

"It has."

"My lord, let me look at you. You haven't aged a day!"

Baird said, "Oh, come on now; I've aged at least three days."

Tote laughed. "I'm so happy to see you! We have so much to discuss!"

"I'd like that, Tote. When my job's done, we'll catch up."

"A job, you say? Will you need supplies?"

"Yes."

"It'll take some time to get you the things you need, I'm sure. You must let me make you dinner. You can give me your list then. We'll eat, we'll talk. Then I can get you what you need."

Baird shook her head. She only had two days left to get into the Toolbox, and that was assuming that she would die around midnight on day seven, which seemed like a less reasonable assumption with each passing hour. Any delay at this point was to assume an unknown amount of risk. But on the other hand, saying no to Tote was a well-known, very large amount of risk. "Okay. If you insist, I'll come to dinner. Where should we meet?"

"Don't you worry about that. I'll send someone to get you. Where are you now?"

"The spaceport transportation center."

"Perfect. Someone will be there to get you soon. I assume you're alone."

Baird turned and looked at the most recent Izzy clone standing beside her. "No. I'm with someone."

"Are they trustworthy?"

"He's as trustworthy as either of us is."

Tote smiled. "So not at all! Excellent! I can't wait to meet him. Stay put. Someone will be there soon."

Baird put away her gARggles. "We're going to dinner."

Izzy nodded. "So I gathered. I assume that was one of your underworld cronies."

"The croniest. He doesn't know about the Toolbox, and we should keep it that way."

"Understood."

"He said he'd send someone to get us, so I guess we stay put until they show up."

Behind her, Baird heard someone clear their throat. She turned around to find two uniformed sheriff's deputies: one a man, the other a woman. The woman said, "Miss Baird, please come with us."

Baird said, "I'm sorry. My name is Heather Woodruff."

The deputy smiled. "Oh. I'm terribly sorry for the mix-up. Miss Woodruff, please come with us."

38

The deputy escorted Baird, keeping an iron grip on her elbow. Behind her she could hear Izzy walking, guided forward by the second deputy.

Baird continued to be surprised and unnerved by the minor changes she saw since her previous visit. She heard no vendors shouting for her attention, saw no obvious pickpockets plying their trade. The overall mood of the people seemed much more relaxed and friendly, until the people saw the sheriff's deputies, at which point the crowd parted, as if nobody wanted to get within grabbing distance.

They passed right by the public tram stop, going instead to the emergency services stop, where they waited for a specially designed tram car that would whisk them at high speed, on specially designated tram tracks, to wherever it was the deputies intended to take them.

Izzy asked, "Why are you arresting us?"

The deputies traded a look and snorted with laughter. The female deputy said, "How dare you level an unfounded accusation at the department. Did we say we were arresting you? No, we did not. We asked you to come with us."

"So, we're free to go?" Izzy asked.

"You have every right to leave," the deputy said, "if that's what you want to do."

"Then will you please let go of my elbow?"

"Nah. You can try to remove my hand yourself, but that sounds like assaulting a deputy, doesn't it?"

The male deputy nodded. "Yup, a clear case of it, I'd say. We'd have to arrest someone who did something like that."

"So, we're *not* free to go," Izzy said.

"You have every right to leave. That doesn't mean that it's easy, or even possible."

The male deputy, who was holding Baird's arm, said, "As officers of the law, we often have to explain some Doug's rights to them. Not just what their rights are, but how rights work in general."

They stood by the track for a minute or so before a police tram pulled up: a long, white, lozenge-shaped object designed to hold up to ten people. Baird could tell from one quick look at the two doors on the car's side, and the metal mesh built into some of the windows, that one half of the car was designed to transport officers. The other was for prisoners.

The vehicle's door opened. Inside Baird could see four deputies, all leering at her like hungry muggers eyeing a delivery guy carrying a sack full of cash and a stack of fresh pizzas. None of them made any move to get out of the car. Instead, a fifth officer leaned forward out of the dark recesses of the car's interior. Baird couldn't really see the officer's face, as her view was blocked by his enormous cowboy hat and mirrored wraparound sunglasses.

Baird said, "Sheriff."

Sheriff Calhoun smiled silently, staring at Baird for what felt like several seconds before he said, "Well, hello, Miss Baird."

"I'm sorry, Sheriff, but I'm afraid you have me confused with someone else," Baird said, making no attempt to look sorry or afraid.

"Of course I do." The sheriff glanced at the deputy holding her. "What's the alias du jour?"

"My name is Heather Woodruff."

"Nice to meet you, Miss Woodruff. If you and your associate would hop in, we'll drive you to where you'll be staying. I like your hat, by the way."

Baird smiled. "It's not as nice as yours."

The second door, the one meant for prisoners, flew open so abruptly that Izzy jumped involuntarily and stepped back away from the car. The deputy gripped his arm tighter, planted her other hand in the center of his back, and shoved him headfirst into the car.

Baird stepped toward the car. The deputy holding her hand guided her through the opening and let go of her as she entered and settled into the hard seat.

Izzy clambered up off the floor and looked at the door just in time to see it slam shut with a loud, final-sounding bang. The two deputies who had escorted them to the tram smiled smugly and waved as they receded into the distance.

The prisoner section and the officer section were separated by a sturdy metal mesh embedded in a thick, transparent barrier. Baird could see Calhoun and the four uniformed deputies sitting on comfortable seats, all facing the prisoner cell, since nobody had to drive.

Izzy said, "It's filthy in here. When was the last time you cleaned this car?"

Calhoun said, "Mister, if we made any attempt to keep that part of the car clean, do you think it would look like that?"

"I suppose not."

Calhoun stared at Izzy, or at Baird. At least, Baird assumed he was staring at one of them. It was hard to tell with the mirrored glasses. It struck her for the first time that the uncertainty was why authority figures probably chose mirrored glasses. They may have been gARggles. If not, they blocked her view of his ridiculous wood-grain Brow. Calhoun could have been checking his messages for all she knew, but as long as she didn't know for sure what he was looking at, she would assume he was staring at her.

Finally, one of the deputies broke the tension. "Sheriff, where should we take the prisoners?"

Calhoun said, "I suppose that depends. Miss Woodruff, who is this guy?"

Baird thought for a moment, trying to puzzle out what the sheriff was really asking her. In the end, she said, "A business associate."

Calhoun nodded. "Yeah. Yeah, that's what I hoped you'd say, because I know what business you're in and what kind of people you associate with." He turned to the deputies and smiled. "Let's take these two to Site B."

The deputies exchanged knowing looks. The car started moving at a much faster rate than the normal civilian trams could manage.

Izzy glanced at Baird, trying to hide his concern. Baird returned the eye contact, *not* trying to hide her lack of concern.

One of the officers looked at Baird and Izzy and shook his head in a cruel, exaggerated mockery of sympathy. "Oh, man, this is bad. You two wouldn't know about Site B."

"What makes you so sure?" Baird asked.

"Because it's a secret."

Baird nodded to Izzy. "His logic holds up."

"It's where the sheriff takes some of his perps. The ambitious ones."

Calhoun motioned toward the deputy who had been talking, and then the one controlling the tram car. "These are deputies Morgan and Hurley. They were nice enough to give us a lift. These two"—he motioned at the other two deputies—"Boro and Abernathy, they're my elite guard. The locals refer to them as the *shovers*. You might say that they know where all the bodies are buried, but if you said it too loudly, and it got back to them, you might end up as one of the bodies, if you know what I'm saying."

Baird nodded. "Yeah, I think I can puzzle it out."

"I bet you can. When we get to Site B, Boro, Abernathy and I will be getting out too. The three of us and the two of you are going to be having a conversation."

Deputies Morgan and Hurley laughed. Then Boro and Abernathy laughed, which made Morgan and Hurley laugh harder.

Izzy looked at Baird. "Why are you smiling?"

Baird stifled a chuckle. "What? Me? Nothing. It's just, you know, it's nice to see people enjoying their work."

Sheriff Calhoun said, "I couldn't agree more. And speaking of people who enjoy their work, gentlemen, this young lady is, allegedly, the infamous Brangelina Baird."

"No, I'm not," Baird lied.

"So you claim, but I am alleging it, so my statement was accurate," Calhoun said. "Though she's never been charged with a crime, Miss Baird is suspected of involvement in hundreds of high-profile thefts across the system, including the Wartzberg Pearl heist."

Deputy Morgan asked, "Wartzberg Pearl? What is that? I've never heard of that."

Calhoun laughed. "You are green, ain't 'cha?"

Deputy Abernathy said, "The Wartzberg Pearl is a famous unsolved theft."

"Famous because unlike most unsolved thefts, pretty much everybody knows who did it." Calhoun pointed at Baird.

Baird said, "Nothing's ever been proved."

"See," Abernathy said, "there was this mid-range trillionaire named Wallace Wartzberg. Made his money in shipping, not too bright. He decided that he wanted to show off his wealth, so he bought the largest naturally-occurring pearl ever found."

Calhoun picked up the story. "But he was nervous. He was rich enough that he could afford to buy the pearl, but he wasn't so rich that he could afford to lose it. So he surrounded it with this amazing security system, the most elaborate ever devised. It cost more than the pearl did in the first place."

"The pearl must have really been something," Deputy Morgan said.

Baird said, "You're picturing a big white ball, but that's not how it looked. It was a disgusting ninety-pound lump shaped like the meat out of a walnut. More gray than white, and it had a greasy kind of shine to it, like it was always wet." Baird shuddered. She looked at Calhoun and smiled. "Of course, I only know that because I saw it in a museum once."

Calhoun nodded. "Of course."

"But you stole it anyway?" Deputy Morgan asked.

"No," Baird said flatly. "I didn't steal it."

Calhoun said, "She didn't steal the pearl. She stole the security system. The whole thing, gone, even the wiring, and she left the pearl right where it was, untouched."

"What? Why?" Morgan asked.

Calhoun said, "The security system was more valuable than the pearl. And it's a lot easier to sell used cameras, sensors, and wiring than it is to sell a famous giant pearl."

"Especially one that looks like a gigantic booger, I'd assume," Baird said.

The tram car rose through several floors of the Pendulum, but not as high as Baird would have liked. It stopped only a few floors up from the spaceport and docking level, which were at the very bottom of the space station.

The people milling about still seemed economically disadvantaged, but the overall mood was fairly relaxed, until the citizens noticed the police tram's presence. All motion and conversation stopped, and every head swiveled, looking to see who would come out of the tram car.

The door of the officers' compartment opened. All four deputies stepped out, hitched up their pants, and graced the locals with their best icy glares. When they'd fully asserted themselves, Calhoun climbed out of the car, and all the citizens averted their eyes.

The door to the prisoner compartment slid open with alarming speed. Baird stepped out of the tram. She took one step, then felt a strong push on her left shoulder that made her stumble forward. Behind her, she heard Izzy's feet shuffle against the floor.

"Hey," Izzy said, "we're going. No need to shove."

The deputies, and several of the bystanders, laughed.

Calhoun walked ahead, leading Baird, Izzy, and the four deputies to a nondescript door directly under a light, opposite the tram stop. Calhoun stood in front of the door long enough for a hidden scanner to confirm his ident chip.

A surprisingly deep click emanated from within the door, as if whatever mechanism creating the sound was very large and powerful. Instead of swinging open or sliding to the side, the door receded straight back, showing the wall to be more than a foot thick. When the door cleared the wall, it slid to the side, revealing a hallway of cold gray walls and a cold gray floor illuminated by ceiling-mounted fixtures that emitted a light that somehow also managed to be cold and gray. At the end of the hall, a pair of unpainted metal doors waited in the least welcoming manner imaginable.

Calhoun entered, exuding the air of a man feeling his stress melt away as he returns home from a hard day's work.

Baird and Izzy both lurched in behind him, rushing not out of a wish to enter, but in an attempt to remain on their feet after another hard shove from Calhoun's elite guards, who followed them in, always remaining within easy shoving range.

The other two deputies, Morgan and Hurley, started to enter, but they stopped when Calhoun and his shovers turned and stared at them.

Calhoun said, "That'll be all."

Deputy Morgan said, "But Sheriff, we'd be happy to stay with you, just as extra help, until you get these two perps processed."

Calhoun shook his head. "No, that won't be necessary. You're free to get on with your regular duties."

Morgan frowned but nodded and stepped back out of the doorway. Hurley stayed put. "But Sheriff, it's just, we've always been curious about Site B, and we've never had the chance to actually go in."

Calhoun stepped toward Deputy Hurley, who seemed to physically shrink, despite the fact that he was several inches taller than the sheriff.

"The reason that you've never entered Site B," Calhoun said, "is that it's not your job to enter Site B. What goes on here is none of your business, literally. Do you understand that, Deputy Hurley?"

"Yes, sir."

Deputy Hurley seemed to have aged at least a decade in the few seconds he'd been talking directly with the sheriff. He was obviously desperate to get out of the sheriff's sight, and the look on Calhoun's face gave the impression that he wanted that too, but the deputy's instinct for self-preservation prevented him from leaving until Calhoun told him to.

Calhoun stared at the deputy through his opaque mirrored sunglasses but said nothing. Instead, he leaned slightly to the side, reached for the doorframe, and pressed a button on a small control screen. Baird heard a loud hiss and saw the door slide back into alignment with the doorframe and push forward into place, hiding Deputy Hurley from view and, presumably, pushing him out of the doorframe and out onto the pedestrian walkway.

39

Sheriff Calhoun stood and watched as the door shut, sealing Baird and Izzy in with him and his two elite deputies. When the door's motion stopped, Calhoun took a deep, satisfied breath and turned around to face Baird.

He broke into a wide grin and tapped his fingers on the side of his mirrored wraparound glasses, which instantly went crystal clear, revealing that they were ground to an aggressive prescription and magnified Calhoun's eyes so much that they seemed to take up nearly a quarter of his face.

"Miss Baird, it's so good to see you again!" He took off his cowboy hat, revealing his exquisitely styled blond pompadour, now a little grayer at the temples than Baird remembered. Calhoun threw his hat Frisbee-style to one of his two deputies. "I wish you'd called ahead and told us you were coming."

"Why?" Baird asked, smiling herself. "So you wouldn't have had to take me into custody?"

Calhoun walked toward Baird, rubbing his hands together. "No, so I could have made a much bigger spectacle out of it. An alleged criminal of your stature deserves a proper welcome. By the way, sorry about the shoving. It's an important part of the image."

"I understand. Sheriff Worthington Calhoun, this is my kid brother, Isaac."

Calhoun extended a hand to Izzy, who took it uncertainly and shook it unconvincingly.

"Call me Izzy." Izzy turned to Baird, "And I'd rather you didn't call me your kid brother."

Calhoun laughed. "Said every kid brother since the beginning of time. I've already introduced deputies Boro and Abernathy, Miss Baird, but I don't think you've quite realized that you already know Deputy Abernathy."

Abernathy was a well-built young man in his late twenties or early thirties. Baird squinted at him. He smiled back at her. Then, he and Calhoun enjoyed a brief chuckle at Baird's expense before Abernathy held up both of his hands to shield his nose and eyes, but at a strange sideways angle. "Do you recognize me now, Earth Woman?"

Baird's eyes widened, and she snapped her fingers a few times while trying to come up with a name. "Trent? You're Trent, aren't you?"

Izzy asked, "You know him?"

"Yeah. Last time I was on the Pendulum, Trent and some friends of his betrayed me." She slapped Trent on the shoulder. "Where are your friends?"

"Prison, where they belong. I flipped on them immediately, then the sheriff offered me a job. Said he liked my initiative."

Baird said, "Well, I'm glad everything worked out, then."

Sheriff Calhoun walked toward the closed doors at the end of the corridor. "Why are we standing here in this nasty hallway? Let's go somewhere a little more pleasant to catch up."

Calhoun opened the doors, revealing an elevator. They all crowded in. Calhoun pressed the single button on the control panel, and the lift began to rise.

Baird asked, "How did you know I was here? When did you find out?"

"When Tote told me," Calhoun said. "He said he was going to send somebody to get you. He sent us."

"Ah," Baird said. "So, you work with Tote."

"You could say that," Calhoun said.

Baird could tell from the sense of acceleration that the lift was rising quickly, but the ride still seemed surprisingly long.

In time, the lift slowed to a stop, and the doors opened to reveal a large, elaborately decorated apartment. All of the furniture looked very expensive and very comfortable. Thick dark-red carpets covered the floors. Thick dark-red drapes covered the windows. The only window left uncovered was a large skylight with a breathtaking view of the Earth far above them and the tether-web stretching down to the station, showing that the apartment was at the top of one of the buildings in the Dome district.

Soft music of the kind that made one feel either classy, randy, or sleepy, depending on what time of the evening it was, wafted through the air, mingling with the aroma of something delicious cooking.

Calhoun stepped out of the elevator and into the room. "Here we are, home sweet home. Abernathy, Boro, that'll be all for the evening."

The deputies thanked the sheriff and stayed in the elevator as Baird and Izzy stepped out. Abernathy said, "It was good to see you again, Miss Baird."

"You too, Trent."

As the elevator doors closed, Baird heard a familiar voice say, "Dear, is that you?"

Tote stepped around a corner, wearing a velvet robe, holding a sizzling frying pan and a pair of tongs. "It is! And you have our guests! Brangelina, welcome!"

Calhoun walked across the room to where Tote stood. "Clive, they were exactly where you said they'd be. Now, you keep our friends company while I go freshen up."

Calhoun gave Tote a peck on the cheek and disappeared down the hall and into one of the rooms.

Baird hugged Tote, taking care not to get burned with the frying pan.

After they'd exchanged friendly greetings, Baird said, "Clive Tote, this is my brother, Izzy. He's a cyber-security and infiltration specialist."

Tote bowed slightly. "It's a pleasure to meet you, Izzy. Any brother of Baird's is welcome here, especially one with such a useful specialty."

Baird said, "Izzy, this is Clive Tote. He's involved with the Pendulum's criminal element."

"These days I *am* the Pendulum's criminal element. If a dangler gets his pocket picked, I get 20 percent of the wallet's contents. Not that we'd allow as base and undignified a crime as pickpocketing to occur on our beloved Pendulum." Tote returned to the kitchen. Baird and Izzy followed.

Tote put the frying pan back on the range and set down the tongs, choosing instead to stir a pot. "Worthington has completely wiped out petty crime."

Baird leaned against the counter. "I knew that was his goal."

"Yes, which is why you sent him to me. Thank you so much for that, by the way."

Baird arched an eyebrow. "It seems to have worked out."

"It's a good partnership. He keeps street crime down so that the poor people are happy. I keep the large-scale crimes nonviolent and interesting enough to keep the rich people from getting either scared or bored enough to leave. And because we're a couple, he gets to enjoy my profits, and I get access to his power."

Calhoun walked into the kitchen wearing silk pajamas in the same color as his uniform, with a silk badge sewn over his heart. "And he can't get enough of me. He loves the whole tough-guy sheriff thing. These pajamas were a gift from him, you know."

"Guilty!" Tote said.

"Yeah you are," Calhoun said. "I might have to take you in for questioning later."

"Please, Worthington, not in front of our guests."

"Oh, right. Sorry." Calhoun busied himself with a bottle of wine and some glasses. "So, Baird, what brings you to town? I know you can't be here to steal the *Ibu* again, because we never replaced it."

Izzy looked at Calhoun, then back to Baird. "You stole the *Ibu*? That made system-wide news."

Baird said. "Allegedly. I figured you'd have a fake one made and claim you found it."

Calhoun handed full glasses to Baird and Izzy. "We considered it, but instead we just made a big deal out of it being gone and used that as an excuse for a station-wide crackdown. We put in a holo-projector that makes it look like the *Ibu* is still there for a minute or so at the top of every hour. We have a recorded speech about how we miss it. We play inspirational music, make a real show of it. More people go to see it now that it's gone than they ever went back when it was actually there."

Tote said, "It was beautiful alleged work, Baird. Your objective disappeared without a trace, you got some violent punks off the streets, and you brought Worthington and me together."

"And you got me my best deputy," Calhoun added.

"Yes, young Abernathy," Tote said. "You really turned his life around. He was a failing street punk, and now he's a very successful corrupt lawman."

Calhoun nodded. "If I have my way, he'll be the crooked sheriff one day."

❬ ◆ ◆ ◆ ❭

Izzy pushed his dessert plate away and leaned back into his chair. "Clive, that was great."

"Yes," Calhoun agreed. "You outdid yourself." He rose to his feet and started collecting everyone's dirty dishes. Baird started to join him, but Calhoun swatted her hands away.

"No! You sit. You're a guest. I'll take care of the dishes. And consider yourself lucky. I'm not known for giving people slaps on the wrist."

Tote watched Calhoun's back as he carried the dirty plates and flatware off to the kitchen. Once the sheriff was out of sight,

Tote turned to Baird. "So, what brings you to the Pendulum? Something interesting, I hope."

Baird said, "I'm afraid not. I'm just stopping in for supplies. My business is on the ground." She pointed straight up through the skylight at the blue sphere of the Earth looming overhead in a sea of black.

"What kind of supplies?"

"Some small electronics. And I need someone with a pharmaceutical-grade micro-printer to make some pills in a specific shape."

"How soon would you need these items?"

"As soon as I can get them. Now, if possible."

"It's not, but I'll have a rush put on it. As usual, I'll be adding my brokerage fee."

Baird said, "I wouldn't have it any other way."

"Neither would I. What else will you need?"

"A space suit and a pair of mag boots."

"But I thought you said your job was on the surface."

"It is."

Tote stared at Baird for a moment. "Fair enough. What else?"

"Access to the Pendulum's shipping manifests."

"A little light reading?"

"What can I say? I've always found inter-colony commerce fascinating."

Izzy touched Baird on the arm. "I can get those for you."

Tote raised an eyebrow but said nothing.

Baird said, "I know you can, but I think it's best if we let Tote handle this."

"But," Izzy said, "he's going to charge you his—what did he call it, his brokerage fee? I can get you the same information, and it won't cost you anything."

"I know that you want to help," Baird said, "but I'm a professional. I know what I'm doing. And in this case, instead of having you break in and steal the information I need, it's best to go ahead and buy the information from Clive. If you're looking for something illicit on the Pendulum, it's safer just to buy it through him. Suppliers who aren't Clive Tote, and their clientele, don't tend to last long."

Izzy looked at Baird, then at Tote, then at Baird again. "You know, why should I go to the trouble to break into the system when he can probably just pay someone to download the information you need?"

Tote said, "Smart lad. Play your cards right and you could be the person I pay to download it."

Calhoun returned from the kitchen. "So, I hope you've all had fun, talking shop while I was in the other room."

"What makes you think we were talking shop?" Tote asked.

"You always save business for when I'm not in the room." Calhoun retook his empty seat at the table and addressed Baird. "He still feels weird about bringing up his work in front of the sheriff. Don't worry. Anything you do planet-side is none of my business. And you know my attitude toward crime here in my jurisdiction."

Baird said, "You're against it, unless it's interesting and nonviolent."

"Which is your alleged specialty. Any chance of you doing something noteworthy before you head up to Earth?"

Baird sucked on her teeth for a moment, trying to decide what to say next while looking at the three men at the table, who were staring at her intently.

"Well," she said, "I did have an idea for how to get to the surface. I need to find a way to get down there fast, without leaving any trail, and if I can do it in a way that has some flair, more's the better, but all of the usual freight and passenger systems are carefully monitored."

"What did you have in mind?" Tote asked.

"The thing is, the Earth's not really above us," she said. "It just looks like it is. If I could put on a space suit and push off from the station with enough thrust, I'd just pick up speed as the Earth's gravity pulls me in. I'd shoot straight down the middle of the tether web. Nobody would hear me pass, because I'd be in a vacuum, and nobody would see me because I'd be too small, moving too fast."

Calhoun shook his head. "That's one hell of an exciting idea, Baird. The speed, the danger. It has a lot of visual interest. You'd be invisible and silent, until you hit the atmosphere and burn up. I'm betting you'll probably be plenty visible then."

Izzy watched Baird closely, waiting for her response to that.

"Yeah, thanks," she said. "I was pretty taken with the idea, but reentry's just one of the reasons it wouldn't work."

Izzy asked, "What?"

"Yeah," Tote said. "Completely unrealistic. You'd have to launch yourself on a perfect trajectory."

"If you could manage that," Calhoun added, "which you couldn't. It'd take as much thrust as taking off from Earth. You could do it from the station on the tether's midpoint, but you'd have to get there, which is as hard as getting to the ground."

"Yup," Baird said. "That's why I figure I'll just steal a ship and fly down to the surface, hypothetically."

Izzy slumped back in his chair. "Well, that's disappointing."

Baird patted him on the knee. "I know. That's why I'd appreciate it if you'd all spread a rumor that I did it the way I just described."

Calhoun asked, "Could you do me a favor? When you steal your hypothetical ship, take the most expensive one you can find."

Baird looked insulted. "Sheriff, I'm in your jurisdiction! I wouldn't dream of doing anything less."

Tote said, "Please, don't take the *most* expensive ship you can find. That would be mine."

40

Baird grunted and cursed her way through the forest's undergrowth, trudging backwards, dragging a sack larger than herself. Her gaze drifted upward to the ship she'd stolen and flown to the surface. Now it hung, impaled on a dozen or so trees, leaking multiple fluids and emitting nasty-looking clouds of vapor.

Finding a place to land a spacecraft is a lot easier when you don't care if it will ever be able to take off again. She had looked for a conveniently located clearing but found none, and at the end of the day, her schedule was more important to her than the ship owner's insurance premiums.

Something tickled the skin just above her upper lip. She brought her free hand up to scratch it. When she pulled her hand away, blood stained the tip of her index finger. Cursing to herself, she paused, reached into one of her cargo pockets, and pulled out two of the emergency stab-wound dressings Rivet Gun had given her. She shoved the small cotton plugs into both nostrils at the same time. They expanded instantly, blocking off the blood flow and distorting the shape of her nose.

"Feek! It's like giving birth to twins through my nose!" Taking a moment to recover, she turned to see where she was actually going. The sunshine filtered between the trees, revealing an open space beyond.

Baird looked past the wreckage and the forest to the tether, the immense cord woven from many much smaller, merely huge cables, which connected the Pendulum to the Earth. Surrounded by the woods as she was, the tether was only visible to her as a glowing image in her gARggles, stretching straight up until it diminished to nothing. Deep underground, near the lowest point of the tether, a second line began. This one extended horizontally out from the base to run directly beneath Baird's feet. The gARggles rendered a red dot moving along that second, subterranean line, tiny at the moment, but getting larger.

Baird resumed dragging the sack. Just beyond the trees, there was a sheer drop of twenty meters. Directly below her, train tracks emerged from a tunnel, and there was a steady stream of cargo from the Pendulum, riding in mag-lev containers. The line in her gARggles that passed below her feet followed the tracks perfectly as they stretched into the distance, curved, and disappeared into the trees. That turn caused the top speed for this section of track to drop to eighty kilometers per hour, slow enough to make what she planned to attempt possible, but fast enough to discourage a saner person from trying it.

Looking back toward the tether, Baird saw that the red dot was now a tiny red rectangle. It represented the specific cargo container she wanted, now only a little over a minute away.

Baird commanded the strand to form itself into a harness, wrapping around her waist and shoulders. Most of the strand remained free and wove itself into a structure that looked like an oversized backpack. A single cord extended behind her, connecting her to the sack she'd dragged through the brush.

Baird opened the sack and pulled out a pair of chunky gray mag-boots that she had rewired to boost their field strength and to work with her neural interface.

Glancing to the ground behind her as she pulled the boots on, she saw that the red rectangle was now a fully rendered box, discernable despite the substantial motion blur. Only seconds remained.

She sat on the top edge of the tunnel opening, her feet dangling down over the track and the rushing cargo containers beneath. The timing would be critical, and as such would be handled automatically by the gARggles. The countdown display was only there to keep her from being surprised when the events she had so carefully planned finally occurred.

Baird watched each of the final five seconds tick by.

"Feek . . . Feek . . . Feek . . . Feek . . . Feek . . . FeeEEEEEEEK!"

The overpowered electromagnets in the boot soles yanked Baird off the tunnel. The strand-harness pulled tight around her torso as the sack followed her over the edge. She heard a deafening clang and felt an impact that jolted every joint in her body. The boots' soles stuck to the top of the container but slid backward several feet, emitting a terrible grinding noise as Baird and her sack accelerated the rest of the way up to the train's speed.

The large mass of strand on her back inflated into an air-filled cushion just in time for Baird to bend back at the knees and slam down on the top of the container. The inflated cushion took most of the impact, leaving her winded but not concussed. She tried to sit up, but she was instantly deafened and pummeled across the entire front of her body by a wind that felt like a million tiny fists.

She lay back down and used the strand to secure the sack, locate and open the hatch built into the container's roof, and pull herself and the sack inside.

She dropped into the dark shipping container.

The strand closed the hatch and recoalesced around her. Baird stood in the pitch darkness, but her gARggles provided a glowing wire-frame view and text callouts so she could see her surroundings. She looked over crates, cartons, and barrels full of processed food and manufactured goods from the off-world colonies.

She found a large tank containing several hundred liters of ferromagnetic lubricant, which she herself had ordered. Baird smiled as she opened the sack and pulled out the components of her space suit.

◄ ◆ ◆ ►

Baird sat in total darkness, simmering in her own anger. She fumed primarily at herself for ever being dumb enough to count on a shipment—any shipment—to arrive on time. Her plan required the tank of lubricant in which she was hiding to make its way from the elevator base to its destination in the fourteen hours the delivery company guaranteed, not the twenty-six hours it actually took.

Thanks to the space suit's systems, she had air, water, nourishment, and a means of dealing with other bodily needs. What she did not have was time. The shipper delivered her to her destination well into day seven of her illness, which could be the last day of her life. Even in trying to take control of her own fate, she found herself subject to other people's decisions and mistakes.

She passed the time by reading her gARggles, trying not to obsess about the time, and hoping that the queasy feeling growing in her gut was just travel sickness.

As she had every time she sensed a prolonged lack of motion, Baird stood up as far as she could, which was sort of a bent-kneed stoop. The top half of her helmet emerged from the fluid in which she had been submerged. She activated her helmet light.

The portion of her face shield that was still in the liquid resembled a glossy black bowl only inches from her face. The slim portion of the glass above the surface oozed with a thick black gunk.

The idea of arriving in a secure location hidden in a tank of ferromagnetic lubricant had come to Baird years before, but she had saved it for a special occasion. She reasoned that nobody would question a large lubricant delivery, because everybody understands the need for lubrication but fears that if they ask what needs so much lubricant, they might end up being the one who gets assigned the dirty job of doing the lubricating.

Total submersion in the magnetic goo blocked her life signs from scanners, but it also cut off all communication with the world outside of her space suit. Now that her helmet's built-in antenna was no longer beneath the surface, she could ping the remote sensor she had procured from Tote and affixed to the exterior of the tank.

Her gARggles displayed a map indicating that she was exactly where she wanted to be: inside the apparently abandoned shopping mall that the Toolbox used as its headquarters, sealed away in the maintenance storage room just off the main entrance hall, near where the underground tram stopped. She'd found this storage room on one of her first visits to the Toolbox, when she had cased the building for vulnerabilities—because it was a building, and she was who she was.

The remote sensor provided a full view of the room. She saw numerous other tanks, drums, shelves, boxes, and a closed extra-large door, but no people.

Baird unlatched the hatch in the top of the tank, pushed it open, and—for the first time in over a day—stood up straight.

Her helmet, shoulders, and arms rose out of the tank. It took several seconds for the black fluid to roll down the front of her face shield enough to allow her to see clearly with her own eyes. Even then, a thin film tinted everything she saw.

She clambered out of the tank and instantly started to slide off of its curved top. She tried to stop, but the entire exterior of her space suit was covered in a thick coating of lubricant. She tumbled to the floor just slowly enough to make her attempts to stop feel more desperate and pathetic, but not so much that her landing caused any less noise or pain.

She lifted one of her gloved hands and watched the thick globs of lubricant roll down her fingers and wrist, marveling that a substance could be both sticky and slippery at the same time.

She wiped her right hand on the side of the tank, hoping to remove some of the gunk. Instead, the force of her hand pressing against the tank's surface caused her to slide away slowly but steadily, carried on a bed of lubricant.

Still drifting sideways, she brought her hand down to the latch at her space suit's waist, but wearing thick gloves covered in slippery goo made operating the mechanism nearly impossible. Of course, the strand could have easily opened the latch, were it not sealed up in the suit with her. The last thing Baird wanted was to get lubricant on the strand. It would probably compromise its functionality and leave a permanent, strangely slippery stain on her sweater.

After some fumbling and muttered epithets, she managed to get two fingers hooked under the lever in such a way that they would not slide off. She gave it a mighty tug. The latch opened. Her right arm flew out to the side with great force, and her elbow struck the floor. She glided across the room, flat on her back, moaning, "Ugh, funny bone."

She finally stopped sliding when she hit the door.

Pressing her hands to the floor to lift herself was useless. Applying pressure to the wall only caused her to slide on a diagonal tangent until she hit a set of shelves, which she hooked her toes beneath and executed a single sit-up.

She lifted her arms straight up, worked the upper half of the suit over her head, and tossed it aside, watching as it slid across the floor.

After she kicked herself free of the bottom half, Baird left the empty suit in the corner, a slimy, oozing heap. Ideally she would have preferred to dispose of this evidence, or at the very least hide it, but to do so would mean touching it, and she was hesitant to risk getting any of that cursed goo on her.

She popped a quick pain reliever for her still-persistent headache and removed two blood-encrusted stab-wound dressings from her nostrils. Then she vomited, forcefully but quietly, aiming strategically at the corner of a box to dampen the splash.

The underworld has no HR department. A professional criminal often has to work while sick. As such, Baird had long ago trained herself to cough, sneeze, hiccup, and vomit almost silently. She achieved this over the course of three extremely unpleasant days. It would have been two, but the hiccups proved stubborn.

As she took several deep breaths to recover from the vomiting, she remembered Screw Jack telling her that nausea meant the end was "too near."

She took great care to step in the few clean spots left on the floor, avoiding the wide smears of lubricant as if they were lava. She opened the door just a centimeter and sent the strand out to see if her way was clear.

The hallway itself appeared empty. In the distance, around a corner, she found a lone guard facing the other way.

She readied her dart gun pin. Tote's suppliers had come through; for the first time since she'd left on the Manhattan mission days earlier (years, really), she had a full arsenal: ten tranq darts and five neural scramblers. She loaded the gun, making sure that the tranquilizers would fire first.

Baird stepped out into the hall.

Seconds later she returned, struggling in her weakened state to drag the unconscious guard. She paused for a moment, looking at the wide streaks of lubricant she'd left on the floor. She shoved the guard through the door onto one of the slime trails, put a foot on his ribcage, gently pushed, and watched him slide across the floor and into the jumbled components of her discarded space suit.

"Huh. Slick," she said. Then she nearly vomited again.

She followed the hallway and peeked around the corner into the Toolbox's arrival hall. The building teemed with people milling about, headed this way and that, sitting around the edges of the large room and talking about the work they were avoiding. Her gARggles told her that her destination was at the far end of the headquarters. Sunlight streamed in through the skylights, making it impossible to sneak through the building past all of these Tools undetected.

Luckily, she never planned to go through the building in the first place.

41

After hoisting herself up over the edge of the roof and fighting back a fresh wave of nausea, Baird took stock of her surroundings. She saw a vast flat monotonous plane of dirty, sunbaked tar, broken up occasionally by rusted metal boxes and pipes. It reminded her of the lava fields on Io. Far below her, another flat plane surrounded the building. Long ago, people had parked their vehicles there. Now trees, shrubs, and wild grass encroached, lines of thicker, older growth suggesting the locations of expansion seams in the long-buried asphalt.

Baird's gARggles pointed the way to the Toolbox's top-secret research and development facilities, where they designed equipment, developed weapons, performed experiments, and maintained the R&D department's secure servers. If there was any place in the solar system where Baird could find out once and for all if she was truly dying, it was there.

She started walking toward the goal marker, hunched over, partly because that's how one walks when sneaking, but mostly because that's how one walks when they feel ill. The overlap had never occurred to her before.

Sickness aside, she tried to enjoy the rare pleasure of getting to walk around outside without any sort of space suit. She knew there were no sensors on the roof, or guards posted who could spot her. The Toolbox was meant to look abandoned, and the irony of security system design was that any system meant to detect people hiding was, invariably, easy to detect and difficult to hide.

If your enemies were well funded and thorough enough, then human guards, active radar, sonar, lidar, and even electrically powered cameras and microphones could be detected, and their presence would be a dead giveaway.

In order for their headquarters to look convincingly abandoned, they essentially had to abandon it. Its chief defense required defenselessness.

Of course, since she was walking on the roof of a building, risking a long fall in full gravity, she experienced a powerful wave of dizziness and nausea. She staggered away from the roof's edge and waited a moment, dry heaving and grasping a rusty old antenna for support until the queasiness passed.

She crouched low and moved slowly, feeling worse with each passing moment. When she reached the spot where the research and development node was connected to the rest of the building, she cautiously approached a skylight. At night the glass turned opaque to prevent light from inside leaking out and providing evidence that the building wasn't abandoned. During the day, however, the glass was perfectly clear, allowing light in.

Baird made her way to a shed-like structure in the middle of the R&D wing's roof, which accommodated a door and a stairwell down into the building. She sat on the roof, legs splayed, leaning back against the door as she used the strand to pick the lock, defeat the intrusion sensors just inside the door, and verify that there were no guards inside. When that was done, she delayed a full thirty seconds before reluctantly standing back up.

Baird snuck down the darkened stairwell in a manner that fell somewhere between staggering and almost falling. She used her gARggles to guide her and the strand to scout ahead. The going was slow, and she had to duck into a doorway or two as people walked by, or as her digestive system demanded her attention, but in time she made it to the medical research lab, which was behind a large ident-secured blast door meant to keep the researchers segregated from the rest of the staff—a move that fostered enhanced concentration, improved security, and a minimized risk of the entire staff being killed by the researchers' mistakes.

She neutralized the ident scanner. According to her intel, on the other side of the door, a hallway led to various secret labs. At this time of day, she expected the hallway to be deserted but the labs to be full, with everyone hard at work on their projects. She hoped that would be the case, and that she could access the Toolbox's data without any human interaction. In her condition, she had doubts about successfully hacking into the file system to find her information—though, given how she felt, the idea that she was going to try to find out if she was dying or not sounded like a cruel joke.

Baird believed she could power through and do what needed to be done as long as she met minimal resistance. If she got spotted, she'd just have to do her best and see what happened, but she feared the worst.

She readied her dart launcher, triggered the door, and hoped to see an empty hallway.

The door moved to the side.

Baird saw at least five scientists milling around at the far end of the hallway, but they did not worry her. She focused instead on the man in a lab coat and scrubs standing just inside the door, facing her. She shot him in the throat with a dart, causing him to instantly lose consciousness and fall to the ground.

"Oh, feek. What are you doing here?" Baird moaned, as she looked down at the fallen form of her brother, Izzy.

Another Izzy, also wearing scrubs and a lab coat, stepped out of one of the labs. "Same thing the rest of us are. Helping you. Cool outfit, by the way."

Baird jumped and nearly put a dart in him as well. When she'd caught her breath, she looked down at her cargo pants and shirt with its integrated hood and gloves, which had all taken on the brilliant white color of the wall behind her. She exhaled sharply, looked at the conscious Izzy, and snarled, "What do you mean, the rest of you?"

He smiled, and in a loud voice said, "Guys, she's here."

All of the scientists milling around further down the hall turned and looked, revealing themselves to be Izzy clones. Baird saw more than a dozen Izzys, all wearing lab coats, scrubs, and Brows with their probes engaged, accessing the lab's databases. They turned and greeted her, some saying hello, others saying hi. Some just waved. Viewing them through her gARggles, she could see multiple display windows hovering in front of each clone.

In the corner, three scientists sat on the floor, tied up and gagged, watching the events in their lab with horror.

Baird leaned against the wall and sank to the floor, glaring up at the closest Izzy, "How the hell?"

The Izzys, all of them, answered, but then they all stopped short when they heard everyone else speak. Then they all laughed. Then a few of the Izzys physically nearest to Baird all volunteered to talk, laughed, and finally, three of them pointed to the Izzy right next to Baird and told him to go ahead.

The nearest Izzy said, "When he found out you were coming here, the clone on the Pendulum manipulated the cloners here to make as many of us as he could. The cloning facility is at the end of the hall."

Most of the Izzys pointed back out the open lab door.

Baird looked back into the hallway and saw two more Izzys carrying the one she had tranquilized away. The one carrying the unconscious clone's feet was only wearing scrubs.

"What?" Baird asked. "Weren't there enough lab coats for everyone?"

The Izzy in scrubs said, "No, there weren't. I'm totally stealing this guy's, though. He doesn't need it."

Baird turned back to the clone nearest her. "Why did Izzy— not you, the other one, the one on the Pendulum—why did he create you all?"

"To help you, Bran. He warned us that you might be mad, but really, we all already knew you would be."

She pressed her head against the wall and closed her eyes. "Yeah, knowing that doing something will make me mad and doing it anyway doesn't make me less mad."

The clone put a gentle hand on her shoulder. "It never does. It's just, he knew that once you got into the building, your first priority would be to get into the medical R&D database. That's what we do, and there's a whole bunch of us. It's going to be a lot faster for us to do it than it would be to do it yourself."

"But I want to do it myself!"

"Feel free. If it means that much to you, we won't stop you."

All of the clones looked at Baird. Even the scientists tied up in the corner watched Baird expectantly.

Baird nodded. "Okay, then."

She remained seated on the floor and tried to ignore the feeling in her stomach and throat as she focused on her gARggles. She could see the clones watching her in the background, and she pulled up an interface screen and accessed the Toolbox Research and Development network. A great many options scrolled down the screen. Just looking at them made her want to take a nap, but she would definitely need to throw up first.

Baird said, "You already know, don't you?"

"Yeah, we know."

Baird took off her gARggles and looked at the clone. "And I assume, since you can see that I'm crazy feeking sick and none of you is rushing to put me in a stasis pod, that I'm not really dying."

"That's right, Bran," the clone said. "You're not dying. You don't have a terminal illness. They infected you with an engineered virus designed to give you some predictable symptoms but that wouldn't interfere with your ability to do . . ."

"Whatever they wanted me to do," Baird said, gritting her teeth.

"I'm afraid they've been lying to you and manipulating you for years."

"Is there anything I can do about the symptoms?"

The nearest Izzy said, "Yes." One of the distant Izzys rushed forward with an injector and knelt next to Baird. She glared up at him. "Then why didn't you stick me with it first thing, instead of letting me sit here and suffer?"

The Izzy who gave her the injection smiled, but also mumbled, "You're mad at us for helping without asking first, then you're mad that we didn't help without asking first."

The spokes-Izzy said, "Bran, the good news is you aren't dying. That's gotta make you happy."

"Yes," Baird said, still forcing her words through her teeth. "I'm delighted. Now I just need to know who to thank. Who did this? Whose idea was it?"

"We don't know for sure. We found files and reports going back several years, but everything before that was deleted."

"And you can't get any of it back?"

"No. Sorry. We've tried. All we've been able to do is find the last person to read them before they were deleted."

"The person who deleted them."

"Maybe. We don't know for sure, but he was definitely the last person to access the files before they were deleted."

"Who?" Baird asked. "Who was it?"

"Your first handler. Screw Jack."

Baird flashed back to her last in-person meeting with Screw Jack. In her mind's eye, she saw him pouring her a drink. "Where is he?"

"In the building."

In the same way that an ice cube can feel as if it's burning your skin, Baird's smile communicated her absolute lack of cheer. "Good. He and I are going to have a talk. Can you tell me where to find him?"

"Yes," the Izzy clone said. "He won't be hard to track down."

42

Baird stood in the dark with her back pressed against the wall, waiting while the strand worked its way around the corner, scanning for guards. It found none. She recalled the strand and reactivated her gARggles' link to the Izzy clones.

"I'm in."

The spokes-clone's face appeared, floating in front of her. "Really? That was fast. You must be feeling better."

"I'm at about 50 percent. I think I'm going to stay here and have a little rest for a second. I want to seem healthy when I confront Screw Jack for making me sick."

"Smart. How'd you make it all the way over to the archive wing without being seen?"

"I have my secret methods."

"I wish you hadn't killed the feed before you did it."

"That is how I keep my methods secret."

"Bran, we're your brother. After all of this, you still don't trust us?"

"The only reason all of you are here to complain about me not trusting you is because one of you did something you knew I didn't want you to do. Besides, I trusted Izzy completely, but you're all clones of him, not him."

"We're all essentially the same person—him. We're copies of him with his memories, so for all intents and purposes we are him, and also, we remember full well that you didn't trust him completely. You never told him anything."

"Didn't want to put him in that position. I have to keep people at arm's length. I got that from Dad. Izzy understood."

"No, he didn't. *You* remember how he acted. *We* remember what he thought. He always hoped that if he proved himself enough, you and Dad would finally fully embrace him."

"Wow. That's kinda sad."

"How so?"

"Well, he was trying to get something that wasn't possible. I mean, I don't really fully embrace anybody, and Dad certainly didn't. Izzy was already the closest person to me and the one I trusted the most. Even more than Mom. I loved him. He was my brother. He spent his whole life trying to get me to give him something, thinking I was withholding it, when he already had it."

"You're right, Bran. That is sad," the spokes-clone sniffed.

"Izzy, are you crying?" Baird asked.

"No, it's one of the others."

"But you said you're all the same person. Why would only one of you cry?"

"Okay, fine! We're all crying! Happy?"

"No."

"It was just so good to hear you say that you love us."

"Him. I loved, past tense, *him*!"

"And we're him, Bran."

"This is why I don't talk about my feelings. Feek like this."

"We love you too, Bran."

"Whatever. Did you guys look up what happened to him, you know, before they started making you?"

"A few of us are poking around in the database to try to find out. He went on some mission, designated at the highest level of secrecy, and disappeared. A year or so later, they started making us. So far that's all we've got."

"I know you'll keep at it. When you find out, let me know."

"Will do. How are you feeling?"

"Less sick, more angry. I'm going to get moving again. How many guards are there between here and there?"

"None. There were four, but I reassigned them. I also closed an emergency bulkhead behind them to keep anyone from returning. You should have the place to yourself for about ten minutes."

Baird followed her map around two bends and past rooms full of servers, supplies, and other things the Toolbox wanted to keep around but didn't want to have to look at. Eventually, she found the entrance marked *Long-Term Bio-Stasis Dormitory*.

"Is it locked?"

The Izzy clone said, "Not anymore."

Inside, Baird found an open space filled with upright spaceline-grade bio-stasis pods—several rows of them arranged on either side, with a clear path to walk down in the middle. All of the light came from the sparse fixtures on the ceiling and the control panels on the sides of the pods. On some level, Baird could sense that she was in the company of a great many people, which made the silence of the room more unnerving.

Baird whistled. "Man, look at all those stiffs."

"Bran, you probably shouldn't call them stiffs. They're people."

"Yeah, I know they're people. Stiff people. I was one of them until recently. I figure I have the right to call them whatever I want."

"Does it feel familiar? They stored you here between missions. You've spent most of the last decade in this room. I could direct you to your empty pod-slot if you'd like."

"No thanks. I don't believe in nostalgia. How many people are in here?"

"A little over a hundred and fifty."

"Do they all think they're dying?"

"Some. Some are injured. Some are just in hiding. They caused some trouble, and this is the Toolbox's version of laying low until the heat is off."

Baird put a hand on the wall of an occupied stasis-pod. "It would be hard to lie lower, or for the heat to be further off."

"Agreed. Some are just people who are too valuable to kill, but they know too much to be turned loose."

"Which is Screw Jack? Hiding, injured, or a troublemaker?"

"I don't know. Haven't been able to track down the information yet. You can ask him yourself. He's in row six, third pod in on your left."

"And I wake him up through the panel on the pod?"

"Usually, but I already started the process remotely."

"Cool. I'll be back in a bit." Baird heard Izzy protesting as she removed her gARggles.

"Calm down," she said. "I'm leaving the audio feed live."

Baird set her clothes to revert to a solid black, and she took off the hood and gloves while the strand knitted itself back into a sweater. She hadn't told Screw Jack her secrets before, and she had no intention of starting now.

She didn't intend to take any chances; she kept the dart launcher assembled and ready, concealed in her hand.

Baird opened the door to Screw Jack's pod. She wanted to watch him wake up.

He stood, motionless, frost clinging to the inside of the pod. Then he exhaled sharply, his breath visible in the chilled air. Baird heard the injectors in his arm clicking and whirring. He still looked handsome and distinguished, even while gritting his teeth, squeezing his eyes shut, and sweating profusely. Baird glared at him for a moment, then cleared her throat.

Screw Jack's eyes popped open and scanned the area frantically, until they landed on Baird. His face broke into an expression of pure delight. The injectors let go of Screw Jack's arm. He staggered out of the pod, grabbing Baird's shoulders.

"Saber Saw! I'm so glad to see you. You're not dying! I found proof. It's all a lie. It's awful. I'll help you fix it."

Baird pulled her gARggles out of her pocket, but instead of putting them on, she held them up to her mouth. "You hear that, Izzy? That's how you tell someone they aren't dying."

"So you know?" Screw Jack asked. He looked at the gARggles, folded up in Baird's hand. "Izzy? Speed Square! Your brother, Isaac Baird! He's helping you?"

"Many of him. We'll get to all of that. First things first."

"Agreed," Screw Jack said. "After your last mission, I went looking for answers."

"That was what? Newtah?"

"Yes. The entire situation didn't sit well with me, so I did some digging. I found out that the agent you took prisoner didn't infect you. We did, when you got your vaccination meds after the mission to Manhattan."

Baird remembered the pills in the paper cup and cursed herself for taking them.

"I considered smuggling you away right then and there," Screw Jack said. "but I still thought you were ill, and I didn't want to tip my hand. I did some more digging. When I found proof that the virus they'd given you was just an engineered bundle of symptoms and nothing that would kill you, I made my move, but it was too late. They were on to me, and they stuck me in stasis. I've been here . . . How long have I been here?"

Baird put on her gARggles. She started to ask Izzy, but before she could get the words out, he said, "Seven years."

Baird relayed the information to Screw Jack, who did not look happy to hear it. "Have you been asleep all that time too?"

"No. They've woken me up a few times to do jobs for them."

"Oh, Saber Saw, I'm so sorry. They sent you on jobs without a handler?"

"They told me you'd gone looking for answers and had gotten infected with the same disease I had. They reassigned me to a new handler. Some chick named Vise Grip."

"Vise Grip! Vise Grip couldn't have been your handler. She's the General Contractor."

"What?"

"Yeah, Vise Grip is the General Contractor. I met with her a couple of times about other operations, and about recruiting you, actually."

Baird said, "So when you were out of the picture, she took a more personal interest. That means that she was in charge when I was first infected, and when you were put on ice. Sounds like she's the one I need to talk to. Izzy, any idea where she is now?"

After a few seconds of searching, the Izzy clone said, "Two rows forward, last stasis pod on the right. She's been there for five years."

Baird relayed this information to Screw Jack, who nodded. "She must have been replaced. Usually a General Contractor at least tries to stick around for life, but if one gets outmaneuvered and loses the job, they can't exactly go live in a retirement community. They know far too much."

"So, you just put them in stasis for the rest of time?"

"No, just until their knowledge is too outdated to do any real damage."

"Okay. Izzy, is Plumb Bob the current General Contractor?"

Screw Jack laughed. "Plumb Bob? No way! I mean, Plumb Bob's a good guy, but he isn't General Contractor material."

Izzy said, "Looks like he's right. Plumb Bob is still a handler. Anyone else you want me to look up?"

"No. It'll be faster if you just look up who the General Contractor is instead of eliminating everyone who isn't."

"We can't," Izzy said. "The identity of the General Contractor doesn't appear anywhere in the records. They remove any reference to the General Contractor for the duration of their tenure. As far as the records are concerned, Vise Grip seemed to disappear one day. She reappeared out of nowhere the moment she retired, and they put her in stasis."

Baird said, "So you can't tell me who the General Contractor is. Can you tell me *where* the General Contractor is?"

"Oh, yeah. In the General Contractor's office. It's over in the administrative wing. There's a full brace of meetings scheduled."

"The admin wing isn't too far. Screw Jack, you've been to the General Contractor's office. What's the security like?"

"Tight! It's a thicket of scanners and sentry turrets. It'd be insane to go in there."

"Sounds like a challenge."

"It sounds completely pointless," Screw Jack said. "Saber Saw, you're out! You're not dying. Your symptoms will go away on their own in a few days. Hiding is your specialty. Why not just take off?"

"My specialty isn't hiding. My specialty is getting away with things. Everyone's sure I'm a thief, but nobody can prove it. I sneak, I evade, and I deceive, but I will not hide. I'd much rather walk out than run away. Besides, if I just disappear, I'll never be free, because I'll always have to worry about being found. No, I need to make it clear that I'm going, that I'll never come back, and that they'd better not try to make me."

"You want them to be afraid of you."

"If they won't respect my wishes, I'll settle for them fearing my wrath. I think showing up in the General Contractor's office will send a pretty clear message that no place is safe from me."

Screw Jack said, "I'm in. Unless they've rearranged the place, there's an armory on the next floor down. I say we get some weapons and fight our way in while we have the element of surprise."

Baird shook her head. "No, sorry. Getting killed isn't really my style." She pulled up the map. "I'm sure I can find a way in. There's a way into every room, just waiting for someone clever enough to find it. I'm going in quietly, and I'm going in alone. Screw Jack, you go meet up with Izzy and his team."

"Who did he bring? Anyone I know?"

"I think you know all of them. Izzy, I'm going to send Screw Jack to your location."

The Izzy clone said, "Great. I'll set him up with all of the clearances he'll need to get through any security."

"You're sure you can do that?"

"Absolutely. If I was able to give you clearance to walk all the way to the General Contractor's office, bump the next person scheduled to meet with him, and give you their appointment slot, getting Screw Jack into the research wing will be no trouble."

"Were you really able to do all of that?" Baird asked.

"Yup. Your appointment is in fifteen minutes."

Baird squeezed her eyes shut and pinched the bridge of her nose. "Izzy, I don't appreciate you foisting your assistance on me without consulting me first."

"I know, but I said I'd help you any way I could. Against your will is the only way I can."

43

Baird walked through the hallways of the Toolbox headquarters, her head held high, at a pace calibrated to be fast enough to suggest that she knew exactly where she was going but was not trying to get there in a rush.

She adjusted her sweater. Screw Jack and the Izzy clones had all complained at not being allowed to accompany her. Wearing gARggles, or for that matter, a Brow, was strictly forbidden in the General Contractor's presence, but she had modified the weave of her sweater to include a hidden pocket where she could hide hers and provide her small army of unsolicited assistants with audio and front-facing video feeds of everything Baird experienced.

As she entered the administrative wing, she walked beneath an obvious ident-chip sensor array.

She saw no display indicator light, or any other sign that she had been scanned, but a guard standing at attention nearby and watching all traffic through a Brow made no effort to stop her, which was all the invitation to pass that anyone ever got.

She walked through a sort of bullpen or cubicle farm, past secure conference rooms, and into an elevator with ident-chip scanners built into its ceiling. After the exact amount of time a scan would take, she felt the elevator rise.

It was a short ride. The building was not tall. Baird suspected that the elevator was more of a security barrier than a conveyance— an excellent opportunity to scan and sort those who wanted to see the General Contractor, then hold the ones that the General

Contractor did not also want to see. Baird cast her eyes downward to look at her gARggles, concealed in the weave of her sweater. "I hope you're still receiving this feed," she muttered. "Because if you aren't, there's nothing I can do about it."

The doors opened onto a large, sparsely decorated room. A few very expensive chairs sat along a wall covered with equally expensive paneling, holding a single painting: a simple portrait in a ridiculously ornate frame. The rear wall was bare, save for a large intimidating door and a large intimidating desk with a small intimidating woman sitting behind it. In front of the desk, a large angry man shouted various protests, utterly failing to intimidate anyone.

"I have a confirmed appointment," the man snarled.

The woman stared blankly up at him, past the probe of her pencil-thin, polished chrome Brow. "I'm not denying that you did at one time, agent Rabbit Plane. But you don't now."

Baird listened to the argument but found herself drifting toward the painting. It was a portrait of the Toolbox's founder, Damon Carlton, standing straight and tall, wearing a beautifully tailored suit and resting his right hand on a globe, because commissioning an oil painting of himself didn't quite send the message that he was a megalomaniac well enough for his liking.

The image was blurry but striking, despite the artist's derivative style, a clear imitation of the "big gobs of paint" style pioneered by the famous portrait artist Geoffrey Krok. He wanted to charge a lot for his paintings, so he painted them in a way that made the act of painting look difficult in order to justify the high price. When his stuff became a hit, people started imitating him, and what followed was a generation of portrait paintings that looked like the surface of the dip bowl at the end of a party.

"But," the man at the desk sputtered, "it was confirmed!"

"Yes," the woman agreed. "It was, but that was in the past. Now it is the present, and your appointment is no longer confirmed."

Baird leaned in, peering at the lower corner of the portrait, and let out an angry little grunt. It was a genuine Krok! This sloppy picture of a smug jackass was priceless, the only genuine Krok in the solar system that wasn't in a museum or a large collection. Baird burned at the thought that they had her stealing things for money when the Toolbox could have sold this one painting and funded their entire operation for years.

Deep inside her, something changed. When she'd stepped off the elevator, she felt she'd been wronged. Now she understood that she had been wronged *for no good reason*. The crime was no less egregious, but it was much more insulting. That insult hardened her resolve, but it also simplified things. She still had to take her adversaries seriously, but she no longer felt any need to respect them.

The angry man at the desk asked, "If it was confirmed and now it isn't, what does the confirmation even mean?"

"It means that you definitely had an appointment then," the woman behind the desk explained. "If you had come back when you had the appointment, there would have been no problem."

"You would have let me in?"

"No, because your appointment was for today."

Baird walked up beside the angry man and cleared her throat. The receptionist turned and looked at her. "Yes?"

The angry man rounded on Baird. "Hey, I was talking to her!"

Baird looked at him sympathetically and put a hand on his shoulder. "I know you were. I'm going to spare you any more confusing banter about the past tense. My business will only take a second, then I'll be out of your way."

The man furrowed his brow at Baird but said nothing.

Baird turned to the receptionist. "I have an appointment with the General Contractor."

The receptionist glanced into the middle distance. Baird knew without needing to be told that she was checking the ident scan from the elevator against the General Contractor's schedule in her Brow. She moved her hand through the air and jabbed it forward to select something. "Sir, your next meeting is here. Yes, I'll send her right in."

The receptionist stood, removed her Brow, placed it on the desk, and motioned toward the door. "Butt Chisel, the General Contractor will see you now."

Baird made a mental note to never again let her younger brother choose her fake code name.

The receptionist started to walk toward the door to show Baird in, but the angry man shouted, "You're letting her in?"

"Yes, sir. She has an appointment."

"*My* appointment!"

The receptionist excused herself and walked Baird to the door, which swung open silently of its own accord as they approached.

Once inside, Baird saw a large, empty space with a raised platform at the far end. Most of the illumination came from specifically aimed lights shining down on the top of the platform, where a semicircular desk partially surrounded a tall-backed chair, turned away from the door.

The back wall held several screens: some showed tactical maps, some columns of figures and blocks of text. At least two showed live feeds from various missions. One was a static shot showing an informant tied to a hospital bed, shouting something, tears streaming down his face. The other screen was the point of view of an agent infiltrating a hostile installation. The agent bolted out from around a corner and aimed a weapon at a very surprised-looking guard. The end of the weapon consisted of two nozzles and a coil, clearly a version of the device Baird had stolen for the Toolbox while she was on Titan. The agent fired. The coil pulsed with light, and the nozzles fired two chemicals that flew with shocking speed. The two streams mixed during their flight, hitting the guard in the face. His entire head burst into a rough, energetic flame, like a burning pile of loose gunpowder, as he fell to the ground.

Baird felt horrified and vindicated at the same time.

The chair in front of the screens rocked back and forth subtly as whoever sat in it fidgeted.

The door swung shut behind Baird, further reducing the amount of light available. The receptionist smiled at Baird and walked ahead, leading her toward the desk.

Baird pulled the pin off her sweater as she walked, dismantling and reassembling it silently.

The receptionist stopped in front of the desk, nodded reassuringly at Baird, and announced, "I have your next appointment, sir. Agent Butt Chisel."

The chair stopped fidgeting for half of a second, then slowly spun around to face the visitor. The instant he saw Baird, the man sitting in the chair leapt to his feet and shouted, "Bran?"

Baird gasped, "Izzy?"

The man behind the desk was undeniably Izzy. The original Izzy. He had a noticeable amount of gray at his temples. The lines in his face, while probably not noticeable when his features were calm and placid, multiplied and became obvious when his expression showed any strong emotion, as it very much was at the moment.

To Baird's surprise, she felt a wave of relief. She thought of her brother as an ally. Even finding him here, working in this office, sitting in the seat of her greatest enemy—the head of an organization that had wronged her severely while pretending to be her friend—couldn't quite break the feeling that Izzy was on her side. For a moment, her indecision kept her from acting.

Izzy asked, "How did you get in here? I ordered all my field agents to apprehend you on sight and put you back in stasis."

Baird shot the receptionist with a tranq dart. As the receptionist fell, Baird swung her arm around and aimed her dart launcher at Izzy, lining up her shot before the receptionist's unconscious body had hit the ground.

Izzy dropped back into his chair and stared at Baird in shock for a moment. He put his hands up. "Sorry," he said. "I shouldn't have said that."

"No," Baird agreed. "You shouldn't have."

"It's good to see you, Bran."

"I don't believe you."

"You haven't aged a day."

"On the contrary, I've aged seven days. I guess I have you to thank for that."

Izzy winced, and in an unconvincing tone, he said, "You're welcome."

Baird advanced quickly, climbing the steps of the platform and standing directly in front of Izzy's desk, her dart launcher aimed directly at his face. "You shouldn't be making jokes, Isaac. Do you have any idea how angry I am?"

"Yes, some, but I have no idea why. Bran, you're acting like I've taken something from you."

"You did! You took ten years of my life!"

"No, I didn't. First of all, I didn't do this to you to begin with. It was done well before I became the General Contractor. As far as I knew, you just disappeared. I spent a couple of years getting good and used to the idea that you, my sister, my only living relative, had blown me off, *again*. It wasn't until I took this job that I learned what had really happened to you."

"And you let it keep happening, which is just as bad!"

Izzy shook his head. "It's not just as bad. It's not even half as bad."

Baird leaned forward, thrusting her dart launcher closer to his face. He recoiled back into the seat. "Okay! Okay. It's almost as bad. Three-quarters as bad!"

Baird's gun hand trembled with anger. Izzy stared up at her tiny bronze gun, and then at her face beyond it, twisted with silent fury. Much lower down, below where Izzy could see, Baird's sweater slowly began to unravel at the bottom hem. The strand worked its way down the back of her right leg.

"Look," Izzy said, holding his hands up and forward, showing surrender and a readiness to shield his face if need be. "I get that you're angry, and I understand why, but what you need to understand is that we didn't steal those years from you. We just delayed them. You're going to be alive years longer than you would have otherwise."

Baird relaxed, but only slightly. "Unless I have an accident or get killed by Toolbox guards for threatening the General Contractor."

"Hey, I didn't tell you to come in here and shoot poor Tack Hammer. That was your decision. But don't worry, I wouldn't let the guards kill you."

"You'd put me back in stasis, wouldn't you?"

"You work for the Toolbox, Saber Saw. A smart mechanic never throws a tool away. You hold on to it, because you might just need it one day. Bran, you're perfectly safe. You've always been perfectly safe. The last thing I or the Toolbox want is for any harm to come to you."

"The Toolbox lied to me. You lied to me!"

"Really, Bran? You're going to complain because someone deceived you and took something from you? That's a bit hypocritical. Or in your case, I guess it's just *allegedly* hypocritical."

"Why?" Baird asked. "Why did this happen to me?"

"You knew too much, Bran."

"About what? I'd just started. I wasn't even a full agent yet."

"Yes, and your final probationary mission was to recover an unknown piece of tech."

"A worthless mind-control device that didn't even work."

"And you got it, and also brought in its inventor."

"Yeah, the worthless scientist who'd wasted years of his life and giga-sollars of . . . no. Don't tell me—"

"I can see how he seemed worthless to you, but if you take the time to listen to his theories—"

"No! Mind control never works!"

"It never has, but that doesn't mean it never can. And the applications—"

"Are horrifying! The applications are horrifying! If any sane person found out what you were up to, they'd do everything they could to stop it."

"The Toolbox had given you a full psych evaluation. They knew you'd feel that way. That's why you had to be neutralized, as a precaution at first, then more permanently when they decided to pursue Dr. Higson's work. If you learned we were working with him, you could've gone to the authorities, offered a deal, destroyed us, and gotten yourself immunity for all your crimes in one shot."

"The idea that you think I'd go to . . . You know, that actually would be a really good way to handle it." Baird took a breath. When she began talking again, she sounded quieter, and more tired. "You're telling me if I hadn't brought him in alive, this wouldn't have happened? I lost nine years of my life because I *didn't* kill someone?"

"Who could have guessed, right?"

"Then why take me out of stasis and make me steal things?"

Izzy hesitated, then shrugged. "Scientific breakthroughs don't come cheap."

"Oh, feek!"

"There are ongoing costs."

"You've made me do things against my will so I could help fund a project that will allow you to make everyone else do things against their will?"

"That's one possible use of the technology."

"It's mind control! Its only use is to make people do things they normally wouldn't want to do!"

"That's not the only use! It could make people do things they're ambivalent about, or that they want to do but are . . . too shy."

Baird stopped herself from shouting again, took a breath, and, in a calm voice, said, "I notice you say *it could*, not *it can*. I take it the device isn't quite working yet."

"Dr. Higson says he's very close. Another year, tops."

"He said it would take another year when I talked to him nine years ago."

"And now, he's nine years closer than he was then. He's gotta be zeroing in on it."

"Does he?" Baird said. "Okay, so now I know why *they* did this to me. They were power-hungry idiots. Now I want to know why you, of all people, kept doing it to me."

"Oh, you mean why I didn't fly into a rage the instant I was briefed about your situation, order you and Screw Jack immediately released from stasis, tell you both the truth, and send you on your way? Look, you've only aged a few days since we spoke last. I spent two years thinking you'd ditched me yet again, just like when I was a kid and you never wanted me around. And when Dad left and you decided to leave with him after you found out I was staying with Mom. And when we grew up, and you disappeared for long stretches, only turning up when you wanted something."

"Hey! That's not fair! I didn't just turn up because I *wanted* something. I only called you when I really *needed* something."

"That's worse!"

"No, it's better. It means I didn't want to bother you unless it was important."

"No, it's worse! It meant you didn't want to *bother with me* unless it was important. I eventually realized that really, it had only been a matter of time before you were going to abandon me again."

"And you never checked our secret mailbox for messages from me?"

"I checked every day for over a year! Wondering if you left word of where you were, how you were, and wondering every time I found nothing if you were hurt, dead, or just ignoring me. I stopped because it became too painful. Then I got promoted to this job, and I didn't need to check on it anymore, because I found out where you were. In stasis."

"Yup, and you left me there."

"You were safe, and this way you weren't going to take off again. We both know if I'd set you free, you would've eventually found some reason to leave. It's what you do."

"You don't know that."

"Don't I? Be honest. I asked all your handlers. You never once asked any of them how I was. You're here now because you want something, but you have no intention of sticking around, do you?"

Baird blinked at him. "No! Of course not! Not now!"

Izzy smiled. "See? Doesn't exactly disprove my point, does it? And maybe letting you think you were dying was a bit heartless—"

"Maybe? A *bit?"*

"Okay. *Probably* pretty heartless. But you need to understand, after you disappeared, I spun out of control for a while. I volunteered for all of the most dangerous missions I could. I saw things, things most people can't even imagine. It changed me. I understand the solar system in a way that most people wouldn't want to. And I came to understand you better, Bran. That's why I can forgive you."

"You? Forgive *me?"*

"Yes, for always leaving me. I came to see that you and Dad had the right idea. Attachments to other people are vulnerabilities to be avoided."

"That's not how I feel! That's not how Dad felt! We didn't avoid getting attached to you! We were attached to you! He loved you, and I loved you very much! We were just both really bad at showing it!"

Izzy said, "Really?"

"Yes!"

"That's so good to hear. Thank you. Still, though, the end result is the same."

"So you got your feelings hurt and decided to turn your back on everyone, then later, you find out the terrible mess I'm in and you use your anger as an excuse to not help me."

"Self-pity doesn't become you, Bran. You're a thief, and now you're angry because we made you steal things?"

"Yes! You *made* me! You convinced me I had no choice, and you sent me in unprepared under bad conditions. Meanwhile, you just sat here in your office, deciding who would risk their lives for you and how they'd do it. It's probably really easy for you, since you don't make attachments."

"Being the General Contractor is more of a sacrifice than you know. It's a lot of responsibility, a 24/7 job. And I haven't asked anybody to do anything I wouldn't be willing to do myself if I could. Hell, when R&D came up with an experimental short-duration cloning technology they wanted to try, I let them use my DNA and memories! I may be here in this office, but I'm also out in the field! I've died dozens of times in the name of the cause!"

"No, you haven't. Other people have. Some of them were copies of you, but they weren't you. You viewed them as disposable, pawns, cannon fodder, all of the things people at the rear making decisions have always thought of the people at the front doing the actual work."

Before Izzy could reply, Baird heard the door behind her start to open. She turned to look, but her attention was diverted again by a grunt of exertion from Izzy's chair.

She turned back and saw Izzy pressing down into the arm rests with both of his hands, propelling himself out of the chair and over the desk toward Baird. He came to his feet, put his hands out in front, reaching for Baird's throat, and leapt. He did not get as much thrust as he'd have liked, because his feet were tied together by a section of the strand.

Izzy tripped forward onto his desk. Baird spun the barrel of her dart launcher around, pressed it into his neck, and shot him with a scrambler dart. She figured that a clearly alive and distressed General Contractor would be much more useful to her as a distraction or a hostage than an unconscious and possibly dead one.

She vaulted over the desk, past Izzy's flailing form, and hid behind his chair, where she listened to the sound of many footsteps running in. Baird closed her eyes, concentrating on the strand. The view from the strand's tip was a blur, thanks to Izzy's uncoordinated attempts to move.

The strand let go of Izzy's legs, fell to the floor, and turned, giving Baird a look at the many armed men who had entered the room.

Baird recalled the strand, and as it knit itself into the back of her sweater, she formed the dart launcher into a pin, stuck it to her chest, and stood to face the invaders.

"Hey, guys," she said, stepping out from behind the chair.

Several of the clones said, "Hey, Bran," in unison. They all stood in their lab coats and scrubs, holding deadly-looking combat zappers.

"By the way, *Butt Chisel*?"

Screw Jack kept his weapon pointed in the direction of the desk. "I suggested 'Drain Snake.' You have everything under control?"

The original Izzy tried to get up, but instead threw himself off the front of the desk and rolled painfully down the steps.

"Yeah," Baird said. "I think so. I certainly don't remember calling for backup."

All of the Izzy clones spoke at the same time, making it impossible to make out what any one of them were saying. Then they all stopped, realizing that they weren't effectively communicating anything.

Screw Jack said, "When they saw who the General Contractor was, they insisted on coming and dealing with him themselves. I could see I wasn't going to stop them, so I came along and showed them the armory on the way."

Baird looked at the clones. None of them looked back at her. Instead, they all stared at the original Izzy, who was writhing on the floor. Screw Jack smiled. "Lots of us feel disgusted with what we've become. Not many get to have that experience before they actually become what they're disgusted with."

Baird asked, "When you say *deal with him themselves*, what exactly do you mean?"

The clones looked at each other, then all turned to one clone—the one Baird surmised had done the talking back in the lab. The spokes-clone said, "He said himself that he had died dozens of times for the cause. Maybe one more time wouldn't hurt."

The original Izzy tried with renewed energy to get to his feet, but he only flopped around on the floor a bit more violently.

Baird shook her head. "No. I'm not going to be a party to murder."

The clones laughed. The spokes-clone said, "Technically, it would be suicide, but we were just messing with him. I'm thinking we'll probably just keep him in stasis until we need him. That's right, Isaac. Don't like being called Isaac, do you? Yeah, see, we know that, because we're you. And we're not going to kill you, because we might just need to thaw you out every now and then to ask you a question. See, it occurs to us that if you're the General Contractor, and we're you, that means *we're* the General Contractor. All we have to do is generate a new clone every two weeks and pass ourselves off as you. Of course, you've aged a bit. If only we had experience making ourselves look older than we are. Oh, wait, we do! We might even be able to direct R&D to work on extending a clone's lifespan. None of us in this room will live to see it come to fruition, but it feels nice to be part of something bigger than yourself sometimes. And since there's so many of us for it to be bigger than, that means it's pretty all-caps big."

The spokes-clone laughed. Most of the other clones followed suit. Two of them high-fived.

"Yeah," the spokes-clone said. "This is a pretty sweet setup you've left for us, Isaac. And of course, while we're running things, we'll be in a pretty good position to make life easier for our favorite agent. Isn't that right, Bran?"

The spokes-clone waited for an answer, but none came. "Bran? Bran?" He turned around, scanning the room. He saw the other clones, all of whom looked confused; the original Izzy, lying squirming on the ground; and Screw Jack, standing at the back of the room next to the open door to the vestibule.

"She's gone," Screw Jack said. "She snuck out while you were making your little speech. And if I'm not mistaken, she took the portrait of Damon Carlton with her."

EPiLOGUE

Baird leaned back into the bed with a deep, satisfied sigh. She lay motionless for nearly a minute before she realized that, while it felt great to not be doing anything, she was already bored. A commuter trip on a spaceliner meant staying in a stasis pod. This flight was more of a pleasure cruise for tourists and stasis-phobes. Baird had an entire stateroom in which to stay, wide awake and doing nothing for two weeks.

The in-room entertainment system was filling the ceiling with all sorts of information the Martian Tourism Board wanted to make sure Baird knew about her destination. Currently, the narrative was bogged down in descriptions of the various junkets a traveler could take, for a modest fee, to see historic probes, rovers, and crash sites. Baird feared it would be a while before they got to the particular attraction she had come to visit.

She tilted her head to the side and saw her gARggles sitting on the desk across the room, where she had dropped them as she stepped into the hotel room. Baird remained perfectly still as the strand worked its way to the desk, grasped her gARggles, dragged them back to her, and slid them onto her face.

A quick check showed seven messages waiting for her. Six of the messages were from Izzy, or multiple Izzys. Three of the messages were marked *Urgent*. None was labeled *Briefing*.

One message was from Tote. Baird smiled and closed the message page. She would continue to ignore Izzy, all of him, for the time being. She needed some time to figure out how to handle having dozens of brothers, most of whom would die soon and one of which was now her sworn enemy.

Tote, she would call now. Baird felt no need to listen to the message first. Any message from Tote was essentially an invitation to call him back, as he had an understandable aversion to saying anything pertaining to his business into any device that recorded his voice.

Baird put in the call. Tote answered almost instantly, his face appearing in her gARggles.

"Baird, my dear! Thank you for calling back so quickly!"

"I never put off calling you, Clive. It's the highlight of my day."

Tote smiled as if he was equally embarrassed by, and grateful for, Baird's flattery. "It's sweet of you to say so, and in this case, I suspect it'll be true. That original Krok you found sold for five giga-sollars."

"That's almost full retail."

"Believe me, I noticed. The broker said that the buyer was motivated. Usually I'd assume it was some collector, but I half suspect they're a fan of your work. The broker asked about you, specifically."

"Asked what?" Baird asked.

"How you were. If you were on the Pendulum. I didn't tell her anything, of course."

"Thanks for that. Who was the broker?"

"A local woman. She skirts around the outer edge of the underworld without getting her hands dirty, so, you know, my kind of people. Worthington says he thinks you worked with her once. Her name's Brousseau. Ring any bells?"

Baird smiled. It was good to know that Pry Bar was still alive. She almost certainly still worked for the Toolbox. That meant that the Izzys probably used her to buy their painting back. Since she'd left them and Screw Jack in charge, and they knew who stole the painting to begin with, they must have meant for her to get this payday. It was a nice gesture. It almost made her want to listen to the Izzys' messages.

Almost.

Baird said, "Yeah, she sounds familiar. If you bump into her again, feel free to tell her that you have reason to believe that I'm doing fine."

"Will do. Your brother has also called more than once, asking about you."

"I hope he's not bothering you." As she spoke, Baird noted that the video feed to her ceiling had moved on from early artifacts of manned space exploration to beauty shots of Mars's renowned underground wine country.

Tote's eyes narrowed. "If he had been bothering me, he would have stopped by now, one way or the other. Are you avoiding him?"

"Yeah, right now. But not forever."

"I understand. I won't give him any information about you, but I won't hurt him, unless he forces me to."

Baird said, "I appreciate that." Her attention drifted to the tourist information feed playing across her ceiling. She saw what she'd been waiting for: Beautifully composed images of Cooke's Auction House. It looked exactly as it had during her last visit.

Baird said, "Hey, Clive. Say, hypothetically, that I was planning a job."

Tote laughed. "Okay. Hypothetically, you're planning a job."

"If I were to do said job, I might end up with a fairly unique piece of merchandise to move when I was done. I'd suspect that it might behoove the person I turned to for help in moving this piece of merchandise to start putting out feelers now."

"That sounds like a prudent hypothetical course of action. What exactly would this piece of speculative merchandise be?"

"It could, possibly, be a weapons-grade, continuous-fire, high-intensity laser I came across during a job that gave me several painful burns and a powerful urge for revenge."

"Allegedly," Tote added.

"The job and the burns are alleged. My urge for revenge is a solid fact."

ACKNOWLEDGEMENTS

As is often the case, I'd like to thank my wife, Missy Meyer; Rodney Sherwood; Matt Sugarman; Steve Feldberg; and the team at Audible.

I would also like to thank Theodore W. Hall, the creator of SpinCalc, which made it possible for someone with my poor math skills to get the details of the Newtah Space Station at least somewhat close to right.

And of course, I'd like to thank anyone who chose to either read or listen to this book. I am tremendously lucky to get to make up stuff like this for a living, and that wouldn't be possible without all of you.

ALSO BY SCOTT MEYER

ABOUT THE AUTHOR

After an unsuccessful career as a radio DJ, and a so-so career as a stand-up comic, Scott Meyer found himself middle-aged, working as a ride operator at Walt Disney World, and in his spare time producing the web comic *Basic Instructions*. He slowly built a following, which allowed him to self-publish his first novel, *Off to Be the Wizard*. The book's indie success brought him a publishing deal, and the rest is history.

Scott lives in Arizona with his wife, their cats, and his most important possession: a functioning air conditioner.

Made in the USA
Columbia, SC
01 October 2022

68333943R00202